JUSTICE LIES BLEEDING

This is a work of fiction. Names, characters, organisations, places, events and incidents are either products of the author's imagination or are used fictitiously. Any resemblance to actual persons, living or dead, or actual events is purely coincidental.

Copyright © 2024 James Harper

All rights reserved

No part of this publication may be reproduced, or stored in a retrieval system, or transmitted, in any form or by any means, electronic, mechanical, photocopying, recording, or otherwise, without express written permission of the publisher.

www.jamesharperbooks.com

ISBN: 9798302095596

PROLOGUE

1990

AMOS CHURCH WAS COLD, WET AND HUNGRY. THE ONE THING HE wasn't was drunk—the only thing he wanted to be. Sweet oblivion courtesy of cheap booze. Something strong to silence the voices in his head, blur the images behind his eyes, and who cares if he never woke up again.

All day long he'd sat with his arse going numb on the cold, wet pavement, his pride a memory as distant as the faces of his former comrades. Red beret on the ground in front of his crossed legs ignored by the passers-by as if it were a steaming dog turd, the selfish ungrateful bastards unaware of the hardships he'd suffered in the name of *their* country, *their* freedom. And their faces—when not averted, that is. Pity in a woman's eyes here, contempt on a man's curled lip there. Don't ask which is worse.

And for what?

Two pounds sixty-seven pence in change, an ancient one-franc piece, two smouldering dog ends, a half-eaten chocolate bar . . . he'd known worse days, even if he couldn't remember when.

He'd knocked it on the head at five-thirty as if begging were a job with regular hours like any other, then got himself something to eat at the Booth Centre Salvation Army hostel on Oxford Street, warming the stiffness out of his legs at the same time. Then he went in search of somewhere to sleep as the rain started coming down in earnest. A higher power he never questioned or attempted to understand led him inexorably towards Southampton Old Cemetery—as it always did when his spirits were at a low ebb.

He liked it amongst the old gravestones, the untamed wilderness of its dark corners in the midst of the bustling city. It suited the blackness of his mood. If by chance he didn't wake in the morning, where better to be found stiff and cold and unremembered than in this old, holy place amongst the lichen-stained headstones with their faded words of remembrance and sorrow.

He entered by the Hill Lane entrance and immediately sat down under the protection of a big old oak tree. Back against the ancient, ivy-clad wall, staring up through the leaves and branches of the tree above his head as it dripped coldly onto his face, the nearest graves only feet away.

A car drove past on Hill Lane as he sat there, tyres noisy on the wet asphalt, music from the radio audible even through the closed windows. Something cheerful that grated on his frayed nerves, made him scramble to his feet, go in search of silence.

Head down against the rain, he made his way along the path into the depths of the cemetery. Some sixth sense, a throwback to his Army days alerting him to danger nearby, made him look up, his pulse quickening.

Immediately ahead, three dark figures hurried down the

path towards him, features obscured by black hoodies pulled low over their faces, moving with the easy grace of youth.

Fear tightened Amos' gut. He wasn't half the man he used to be. Booze and the deprivations of life on the streets had seen to that, his speed and strength fading along with his will to face each new day.

Except he was wrong.

They weren't yobs out for a bit of fun rousting bums and winos, making themselves feel big as the three of them picked on the weak and downtrodden. They parted as they approached, two on one side, one on the other. Amos got the impression of two boys and a girl, although her presence didn't ease the thumping of his heart. Spiteful young bitches liked nothing better than to egg on the pimply, cocky youths, feel something warm between their legs as their adolescent menfolk kicked and punched, consumed by a watered-down bloodlust.

They passed with nothing more than a shoulder barge when the nearest boy failed to move far enough out of the way. The youth bounced off, his bulk far less than Amos', a curse muttered under his breath as he stumbled off the path onto the wet grass.

Amos turned as they hurried towards the gate. Not to curse them back. A hard-wired survival instinct honed by military training that made him wary of anyone or anything unseen behind his back. The youths paid him no attention, hell-bent on getting away.

And it struck Amos that they had the air of running away from something.

Or someone.

He whipped around quickly to face into the depths of the dark cemetery again, worried his instincts had let him down. That he'd got things arse about face, the youths the prey, not the hunters, fleeing for their own safety.

There was nobody there, the path ahead deserted.

Amos cursed himself for the jitteriness of his nerves, ashamed to think about what he'd become. He started down the path again, more vigilant now the cemetery wasn't his exclusive domain. Fifty yards further on, a path had been beaten through the long grass on the left. A mental image flashed through his mind. Watching the retreating youths, the wetness of their jeans-clad lower legs. They'd been the ones to beat this path into the overgrown, more secluded areas of the graveyard.

Amos set off into the deeper gloom himself. Hackles rising as if back on patrol in some godforsaken, inhospitable corner of the globe, every sense heightened, alert for the first sign of danger.

Except, already he knew the threat was past. Fate had not singled him out on this particular day.

He saw it half-hidden behind one of the older headstones tilting backwards.

The body of a man face-down in the long grass, the back of his head glistening wet—and not from the rain.

Amos had seen enough death in his life, had been the cause of some of it, to know the man was beyond helping. He was already in the presence of his maker. Amos hunkered down beside him, felt his neck for a pulse all the same. His fingers came away bloody when he found none, the body still warm if not physically twitching.

Once more, a mental image of the three youths hurrying out of the cemetery, their faces hidden, flashed behind his eyes. And in his mind, the bitter questions that plagued him from dawn to dusk.

What had he done for his country?
What had his country done for him?
Who owed who?

More pragmatically, *who would the police believe if he reported it?* Three young people with their whole lives ahead of them or one ex-serviceman with PTSD, a drink problem and a history of violence living rough on the streets?

The relentless unfairness of life hit him hard in that moment of uncompromising clarity, the familiar resentment surging inside him.

He owed the dead man nothing.

And he needed a drink like he'd never needed one before—

A sudden sound made him freeze. Off to the right, behind one of the larger gravestones. He narrowed his eyes, squinting into the deepening gloom through the rain. Adrenaline surged in his veins, the impression of being watched overwhelming him. Barely breathing, he listened hard, filtering out the sounds that belonged—leaves moving in the breeze, the soft hiss of the rain coming down.

Weaker-willed men might have fled at the imagined prospect of some undead creature dressed in filthy rags climbing out of a nearby grave. Not Amos. It was the living who wished you harm, not the dead.

An undernourished fox trotted into sight as he stared intently into the darker corners under the trees, the rain soaking its fur making it look scrawnier still. It stopped dead, ears pricked and nose in the air as it studied Amos, then continued on its way.

Amos didn't waste another second.

He ran his hands quickly over the corpse, felt a bulge in the inside jacket pocket. The fat, leather wallet in his hand a second later felt like approval from on high. Validation of the decision to behave exactly as every other person on the planet did. Look after number one.

He pulled out the cash—more than fifty pounds—and stuffed it into his coat pocket, then wiped his fingers and the wallet clean as best he could on the dead man's jacket before slipping it back where he'd found it.

Amos wasn't a career criminal, nor did he watch cop dramas like *Inspector Morse* on the TV. But even he should have noticed the dead man's blood he transferred from his fingers to the banknotes before he stuffed them into his pocket.

Unfortunately for him, the owner of the late-night off-licence where Amos bought himself a bottle of Johnnie Walker Red Label to celebrate his unexpected windfall noticed the stain immediately. He was on the phone to the police the minute Amos was out the door—and Amos didn't shuffle very fast these days.

1

PRESENT DAY

'DON'T SAY IT,' DI MAX ANGEL WARNED, KNOWING HE WAS wasting his breath.

Beside him, DS Catalina Kincade bit back a smile as he drove them through the imposing stone-built, mock-Tudor arch of Southampton Old Cemetery's main gate at the end of Cemetery Road. He made a right turn towards the Non-Conformist Chapel where the crime scene technicians' vehicles were parked haphazardly in the narrow lane, along with the first responder's liveried patrol car and the forensic pathologist's ageing Saab. She looked left and right at the ranks of orderly and not-so-orderly gravestones on all sides.

'Which one do you think Doctor Death . . . I mean Durand lives in?'

One day, should a miracle occur and his case load evaporated overnight, he was going to get to the bottom of the animosity between her and the pathologist, Isabel Durand. Today, that situation felt a very long way off.

He parked beside Durand's Saab, raised an eyebrow at Kincade.

'Got it all out of your system?'

She rocked her hand, scrunched her face.

'For the time being.'

'Heaven forbid the two of you should behave like a pair of professionals.'

Kincade took a moment to look around before they headed off to where the crime scene arc lights back-lit the gravestones amongst the trees like a set from a low-budget horror movie.

'I never knew this place was here. Is it still in use?'

'Not sure. I doubt it.'

'It reminds me of Highgate.'

The remark would have meant nothing to most of his team, beyond a passing reference to the fact that all old cemeteries looked alike. Lots of old weathered stone and faded flowers left by the recently bereaved or the forever guilt-ridden, the smell of damp earth and decay, and an all-pervading reminder of one's own mortality and insignificance. Here today, gone tomorrow. Some cemeteries were better known than others on account of their famous residents—Karl Marx in the case of Highgate in North London or Eva Perón in Cementerio de la Recoleta, Buenos Aires—but essentially, they were all the same.

Except Angel knew that wasn't what she'd meant. In her mind, *Highgate* was still synonymous with *home*. The joking as they drove into the cemetery was suddenly a thing of the past. She'd been unprepared for the way in which her memories ambushed her, as he always was when his did him, the unexpected reminder of how much had been lost amplified in this place dedicated to death.

The way she set off without another word towards the hum of the mobile generators in the trees only confirmed it.

He followed behind, knowing the dip in her spirits wouldn't

last long. The sight of Durand crouching over the morning's main attraction like a giant white-suited bird of prey protecting its kill was all it took. He felt Kincade's smile from six feet behind her as she addressed the pathologist.

'You didn't have far to come, Doctor.'

Angel groaned to himself at the double-edged barb. Durand's autopsy suite located in the bowels of University Hospital Southampton's main campus was only a mile away as the Angel of Death flies. The look Durand gave Kincade from behind her mask made it clear she'd understood the sub-text, as if she'd been privy to Kincade's earlier remark in the car.

'I understand you used to live equally close to the famous Highgate Cemetery, Sergeant.'

Angel winced at the way Durand inadvertently poked her finger into the open wound of Kincade's melancholy. He stepped past Kincade before the situation deteriorated further.

'What have we got, Isabel?'

Durand was not known for her sense of humour. Despite that, the location brought what little there was to the fore.

'Strange as it may seem in a cemetery, Padre, a dead body. Although I suspect the circumstances are unlike most of your experience in that field.'

Angel smiled with her at the reference to his past life. Kincade kept her thoughts to herself, convinced the relationship between Angel and the pathologist was more than professional. At times she wondered what provided the glue to bind that relationship, the common ground a failed Catholic priest and a woman who cut up dead bodies all day long might share. She pushed the distracting thoughts aside, concentrated on the scene before them.

Durand had stood up and moved to the side so that they could get a better view of what they were dealing with.

A woman sat on the ground, propped against one of the

older headstones. Legs parted and extended in front of her, skirt hitched up to reveal the pale flesh of her inner thighs and a flash of white panties. Her hands were held together at chest height as if praying, head bowed so that her lips rested on her fingertips. Her coat was unbuttoned, blouse ripped open so that her hands sat between the swell of her breasts. A pair of black tights had been wrapped around her wrists to hold her hands in position before rigor mortis took over, then looped around her body and tied at the back to stop them from falling into her lap.

'She's been posed,' Angel said to nobody in particular, as Durand concentrated on the victim's injuries.

'There is evidence of blunt force trauma to the back of the head.' Indicating the affected area as she said it, immediately raising a finger to stop them from jumping to conclusions. 'But that's not the cause of death.'

Angel hunkered down, his knees complaining as he did so. He rested a blue-gloved finger lightly on the victim's hair hanging down from her face.

'Can I?'

'You may,' Durand replied, correcting his grammar at the same time.

Angel pushed the victim's hair out of the way to reveal a livid raised welt circling her neck.

'Strangled.' He allowed the hair to fall back again. 'With the tights used to secure her hands, perhaps.'

'Asphyxiation due to ligature strangulation,' Durand agreed, as he straightened up again.

'Was the victim wearing the tights?'

Durand, never keen to commit herself in advance of the autopsy, pulled a face as if he'd asked her which leg the victim pulled on first when putting them on in the morning. She answered nonetheless, her tone hedging her bets.

'Probably not, Padre.' She took hold of the foot of one of the tights' legs. 'This doesn't look as if it's been worn.'

'It's brand new, straight out of the packet,' Kincade said, without any of Durand's hesitation in her voice.

A spasm of irritation passed over Durand's face at the interruption. She extended her hand towards the body as she replied.

'Would you care to take a closer look, Sergeant?' Sounding like, *if you're so bloody clever...*

Angel knew Durand well enough to know there was more to be deduced from the cursory, scene-of-crime examination— something she was hoping Kincade would miss. He'd noticed it himself, said nothing as Kincade took up the challenge.

She crouched down a lot more easily than he had, moved the deceased's hair out of the way without asking permission. She released it again almost immediately, as if to emphasise how easily she'd passed Durand's test.

'No gouging around the ligature mark. That implies she was strangled whilst unconscious after the blow to the back of the head.' She curled her fingers into a claw, held them at her neck. 'Any conscious person would try to get their fingers under the ligature. You won't'—putting a lot of emphasis on the word as if laying down the law to her children—'find excoriated tissue under the deceased's nails, Doctor. Unless she had an itchy neck immediately before being attacked, of course.'

Durand nodded her grudging approval.

'Very good, Sergeant. I *will* check under the fingernails just in case. If that's okay with you?'

Angel stepped in and stated the obvious before he witnessed his first actual fistfight in a graveyard.

'It's not a mugging gone wrong. Was her purse still on her?'

Durand pointed to where an evidence marker sat on the grass two feet to the side of the victim's right leg.

'That's where her bag was found. Her purse was still in it.'

'Any ID?'

'Driving licence. Her name's Lois Sheppard.'

'I sense a *but*. No phone?'

Durand shook her head.

'No.'

The implications were clear. Whoever killed Lois Sheppard didn't care how quickly she was identified. It suggested a pragmatic killer. One who knew the victim would be identified easily enough and didn't waste time trying to conceal that fact for the sake of a very limited head start. Taking the deceased's phone implied something else. The killer knew the police would request the victim's phone logs from the service provider, find out who the deceased had been in contact with. The only reason to take the phone was to find out for themselves. It made the chances of it being a random killing almost zero. That was a big plus point. Stranger killings were everybody's worst nightmare.

For now, he went back to the basics.

'Time of death?'

'From the combination of rigor and livor mortis, body and ambient temperatures, I'd say twelve to sixteen hours.'

'Early yesterday evening,' Angel confirmed without needing to check his watch. 'She was out here all night.'

Leaving Durand to it, they went in search of the first responder. They didn't follow any marked path, picking their way between the old gravestones back towards the Non-Conformist Chapel. The circuitous route through the long grass interspersed with clumps of wildflowers prompted the question Angel threw Kincade's way.

'She's obviously been posed, but is the grave she was propped up against significant? It's not exactly next to the main path.'

'No, but it's secluded. Secluded is always good if you're going to kill someone and take the time to dress the scene.'

'If that's where she was killed.'

'True. Doctor Death should be able to tell us whether the victim was moved after she's done the post mortem.'

'I didn't think you had that much confidence in her abilities.'

'I don't like the woman, but that doesn't mean I think she's crap at her job.'

He didn't have the time or the inclination to go down that road, concentrated on Lois Sheppard.

'What do you think about the pose?'

'Marks out of ten, you mean?'

He refused to laugh, stuck to the point.

'*No*. Its significance. The gravestone she was propped against and all the rest of it.'

'You're not thinking Satanic rites and all that bollocks, are you?'

The forcefulness of the reply coupled with her dismissive tone surprised him momentarily.

'Not exactly a sacrifice, no, but some significance.'

'Could be. You're better placed to say what it might be.' She pointed down at the ground, the sly smile he was getting to know on her lips. 'Don't you have to learn about the opposition when you're in priest school?'

'It's called a seminary.'

'Or do they refuse to teach it in case the new priest recruits are tempted to change sides? The devil used to be an angel, didn't he?'

He ignored the continued attempt to bait him, voicing his own thoughts on the way Lois Sheppard had been presented to the world.

'There's definitely a sexual element to the pose. Legs parted and skirt pulled up, the ripped blouse. I'm surprised there wasn't a message written in red lipstick on her breasts. *Whore,* or *sinner*, something like that.'

'That generally says more about the killer than it does about the victim. Suppressed sexual urges causing him to view sex as a sin and all women as whores.'

He felt the discussion hovering on the periphery of his own past. In particular, the element that fascinates the public the most—celibacy, with its tabloid-headline repercussions.

'That's a bit deep for this early in the morning, Sergeant.'

She clamped her hand over her mouth, her voice muffled from underneath it.

'Did you know you only ever call me *sergeant* when you want me to shut up?'

'I hadn't noticed. Rest assured, I'll be putting that insight to good use going forward. *Sergeant*.'

They'd arrived back at the Non-Conformist Chapel, effectively putting an end to the random collection of thoughts that had passed for conversation. The first responder, PC Vaughn Dunlap, was waiting for them.

'Who found her?' Angel said. 'A dog walker?'

Dunlap smiled—*it wasn't one of the residents*—and pointed at his patrol car.

'Mrs Violet Herring. She walks her dog here every day. The dog found the body when she let it off the lead.' He dipped his head to see into the back of the car, dropped his voice. 'I think she's asleep. It won't be long before she's a permanent resident here.'

An indignant voice came from inside the car before either Angel or Kincade could respond.

'I heard that, Constable.' A sprightly old woman with silver hair cut in a no-nonsense style close to her head clambered out of the back seat, waved a telescopic hiker's walking stick she clearly didn't need at him. 'For your information, young man, there are no new burials here apart from half a dozen or so each year to existing family plots. I wish it were possible for me to be buried in this beautiful place, but, alas, it will not be so.' She glared at Dunlap a moment longer until he'd shrivelled to her satisfaction, before turning her beady eye on Angel and Kincade. There was no more kindness in her tone or gaze than when she'd dressed down the hapless PC Dunlap. 'One of you look as if you ought to be in charge.' She pointed her stick accusingly at Kincade. 'If any of the TV programmes have an ounce of truth in them, it's you.'

Kincade's voice had far too much relief in it for Angel's liking when she replied.

'It's him, actually.'

Angel stuck out his hand, dwarfing Mrs Herring's as she took it. He felt as if he'd reached into one of the older graves to help pull out its occupant.

'Detective Inspector Angel, Mrs Herring.'

A grin cracked the old lady's furrowed face, surprisingly good teeth on show as she laughed.

'You're in the right place then.' She flicked her stick in the vague direction of the crime scene. 'If that was me, I'd like an Angel working to find out who killed me.'

Angel wasn't quite sure how to respond as Kincade and Dunlap suppressed the smiles on their faces.

'Maybe we could start by you talking me through what happened.'

Mrs Herring gave a firm, business-like nod. The sort of short, sharp, efficient gesture his father favoured.

'There isn't much to tell.' She put two fingers between her lips, gave a shrill whistle. A small brown dog of indeterminate parentage jumped out of the patrol car and came to stand by her leg, tail wagging, as if it had been summoned to explain its part in the story.

'I was taking Jasper for his early-morning walk.' She indicated the dog with her walking stick as if they thought Jasper might be her husband. 'We entered by the Hill Lane gate at a few minutes after seven. In case you're wondering, all the gates are open twenty-four hours a day.'

I didn't think you'd climbed over the wall, Angel thought, although on the evidence so far, he wouldn't put it past her to have vaulted it.

'I let Jasper off the lead after fifty yards or so,' Mrs Herring went on. 'He ran off as usual, but didn't come back when I whistled for him as he usually does.'

Angel looked down at Jasper sitting at Mrs Herring's feet, mentally wagged his finger at him.

Bad dog. No treats for you tonight.

'Then Jasper started barking,' Mrs Herring continued. 'I thought he was chasing a squirrel. When he still didn't come back, I was forced to go to him.'

Angel gave the dog a disapproving look.

Or tomorrow.

Mrs Herring glanced in the direction of the activity in the trees, sadness replacing the no-nonsense efficiency of her account so far.

'That's when I came across that poor woman's body.' The melancholy was short-lived, the matter-of-fact tone soon back. 'Don't worry, I didn't touch anything, although my first instinct was to cover her up. I do pay some attention to those stupid TV shows where the boss is always a lesbian with too many personal issues to do her job properly.' She glanced at Kincade as if she were proof of the pudding, got a polite smile back. 'I immediately called you. That's it.'

From the evidence so far, Angel was confident Mrs Herring would have volunteered a detailed description of anyone she'd seen in the vicinity, had there been anyone. Procedure dictated that he ask, nonetheless.

'Nobody,' the old lady confirmed. 'Not on Hill Lane between my house—I live on Hill Lane—and the cemetery entrance. And certainly, nobody in the cemetery at that time in the morning. That's why I go at that time.'

'What about in the evenings? Does . . .' He struggled for the dog's name as it looked expectantly up at him, then gave up. 'Do you take your dog for a walk in the evenings?'

'I take *Jasper* for a walk at five-thirty every day, yes, as well as in the mornings. I don't want him getting fat.' She glanced at Kincade as if she thought a twice-daily walk would do her good, too.

'What about last night?'

'Of course.'

Angel almost asked at what time. Except he knew the answer. Five thirty on the dot.

'I didn't see anything unusual then, either,' Mrs Herring confirmed before he could ask. 'I'd have said so if I had. There were more people around, of course, but nobody acting suspiciously.'

And I bet there isn't much gets past you on this street, he thought, as he thanked her for her help and sent her on her way.

'God help any mugger who picks on her,' Kincade said, when the old lady was safely out of earshot.

Angel couldn't disagree.

'Remind you of anybody you know?'

She didn't need to answer, the knowing smile sufficient.

His father. Ex-Warrant Officer Class 1, Carl Angel.

It's a shame you didn't move in with her and not him, he thought sourly, as they watched the old lady march purposefully away, her dog struggling to keep pace, forget about a chance to cock its leg.

2

The most direct route for Amos Church to walk to work was to enter Southampton Common via the entrance on Hill Lane opposite the Bellemoor Tavern, cut directly across the common in a south-easterly direction, exiting by The Cowherds pub. From there, it was a straight hack down The Avenue into the city centre.

Thirty-four years ago, it would have ticked Amos' only box—somewhere to get a drink at both ends of the pleasant walk across the common.

Except these days Amos didn't drink.

A near-death experience from swilling too much illegal hooch in HMP Isle of Wight had kicked his drink problem into touch permanently. Put paid to any ideas about an early release, too. But he had no doubt it had saved his life, given him a second chance.

He kept a single bottle of Johnny Walker Red Label on a display shelf at home. A daily reminder of what it had cost him. It was full, too. A test of his resolve only the twist of a cap away. When he first got out, he'd been tempted to buy eighteen bottles —one for each year of his sentence—and make a display of them. A minute's consideration of his woodworking abilities had put an end to that stupid idea.

He didn't fully understand why he chose to remind himself of the loss of almost a third of his life, but whatever it was also dictated the route he actually walked to work every day.

Ignoring the entrance opposite the Bellemoor Tavern, he would continue down Hill Lane as far as the entrance to Southampton Old Cemetery. The same entrance he'd used thirty-four years ago on the fateful night he stole fifty pounds from Eric Impey's wallet, and the nightmare of the next eighteen years began. As he had on that night, he would make his way through the cemetery passing the Non-Conformist Chapel on his left, then follow the curve around and out the main entrance, Cemetery Road directly ahead. It meant walking two sides of a triangle instead of one, but he'd done it for so long he couldn't imagine going any other way.

Just not today.

Shit, he thought, when he saw a uniformed police officer standing in front of the cemetery entrance. Thumbs hooked in his stab vest, the attitude he projected and the yellow crime-scene tape behind him making questions redundant.

Amos briefly considered carrying on as if he'd had no intention of using the entrance. He stopped anyway, his pulse quickening. Not only at the presence of the police officer—a knee-jerk reaction to anything related to the criminal justice system he doubted he would ever leave completely behind—but also the location.

Amos didn't believe in coincidence.

He pointed past the officer, wasted his breath.

'Is it okay if I cut through there?'

'I'm afraid not, sir. You'll have to use an alternative route.'

It was pointless, but Amos couldn't stop himself from glancing at his watch.

'I'll be late for work.'

The officer made an attempt at looking sorry, didn't quite pull it off.

'I'm afraid it's unavoidable, sir. I'm sure your boss will understand when you explain.'

Amos looked past him, saw the arc lights illuminating the trees. He had a feeling he knew exactly which grave the police presence was centred on.

'What's going on?'

'It's a crime scene, sir.' The cop indicated the tape behind him, hooked his thumb back inside his stab vest. 'I can't say any more than that. The cemetery is likely to be closed all day.'

Amos was tempted to push for more details. Except he didn't want the officer to look at him in a different light, maybe remember something he'd been told on a training course about killers returning to the scene of the crime.

Because Amos had no doubt history was repeating itself. That the white-suited men and women moving around between the trees in the distance were involved in the early stages of a murder investigation.

He felt like saying to the cop on the gate, *the officer in charge would be interested in what I've got to say.*

Except, once bitten, twice shy.

They hadn't believed him thirty-four years ago. Why should they believe him now?

He didn't have another eighteen years of his life left to lose, not if the way he felt when he climbed out of bed each morning was anything to go by. He gave the officer a nod and a smile as he headed off like any other law-abiding citizen would, his mind racing.

Was it connected to the woman who'd called him the day before yesterday asking to meet? Then called again last night, a call he'd ignored. The same icy chill gripped him now as it had when she'd said it was a personal matter she wanted to discuss. Only one personal matter in Amos' troubled life was worthy of the word *discussion*.

He'd agreed to meet if only to get her off the line. Telling himself he would decide nearer the time whether to make a last-minute excuse in the hope she gave up and went away.

Now, if he was right—and in his heart he knew that he was—there would be no decision to make. Trouble was, the police wouldn't be so easy to fob off. Not when they found his name and number in her phone or call logs.

It seemed to him the sky darkened in that moment, his world tilting. As if waking from the familiar nightmare. Sitting bolt upright in his bed, sweat-soaked sheets twisted around his shaking legs, the echo of a silent scream on his lips. And in his mind, three dark figures approaching out of the gloom, faces obscured as they hurried past him, their night's work done.

So many different faces had filled those dark hoods over the long years the nightmare had plagued him. An ever-changing merry-go-round of the people who had moved through his life, scant few of them improving it. His father. His mother. The crusty old judge who sent him down. The lazy cop too idle to look beyond the end of his nose and the easy result Amos presented him.

Amos knew as he hurried down the street that when, finally, the carousel of faces stopped its relentless spinning, crystallising into a single face that did not fade with the coming of the morning light, it would be the last face Amos saw before that of his maker.

Today, he was very glad the Johnny Walker Red Label was a lot further than the twist of a cap away.

3

DCI Olivia Finch caught Angel and Kincade in the corridor as they were on their way to the Major Incident Room to give the first, preliminary team briefing. She smiled broadly at the sight of them—at him in particular—alarm bells going off in his head as a result. Nothing work-related would've put a smile like that on her face.

She proved him right when she took hold of his jacket lapels, pulled them apart as if opening the curtains first thing in the morning. Nodded approvingly, the smile growing wider as she dragged Kincade into the conversation, just as she'd been about to carry on and leave them to it.

'Doesn't he look smart, Cat? His mother must be ironing his shirts for him.' She let go of his lapels, dropped her eyes to his feet, the smile slipping. 'She's not making such a good job of polishing his shoes, though.'

Angel wished he'd never confided in her, told her that his mother—separated from his father for the past fifteen years—was back in the country for the first time since she went back to Belfast. The visit was his sister, Grace's, fault, but she had no room to accommodate their mother. Angel, on the other hand, had plenty of room to spare, rattling around in his house on his own.

'I'm glad my family circumstances provide so much amusement, ma'am.'

'At least you're getting your shirts ironed, Padre. I bet she irons your underwear, too.' She leaned away to get a better view of him. 'Are you putting on weight as well, now that you're not living on beer, sausages and cheese on toast? It must be like being a kid again.'

'It is, ma'am. She takes her Pirelli slipper to my backside every time I use a bad word or blaspheme, as well.'

'It must be worn out by now if she does,' Kincade muttered under her breath.

Finch's brow furrowed, genuine curiosity in her voice now.

'Did she really used to do that, Padre?'

'*Does*. Not *did*.'

'No wonder you turned out the way you have.'

'Will there be anything else, ma'am?'

Finch gave him a final once-over look up and down as if he'd meant any more personal remarks.

'No, you'll do,' she said, moving away. 'But have a word with her about the shoes. Your father would be horrified.'

'Did she really hit you with a slipper?' Kincade asked, as soon as Finch was out of earshot.

'Why? Do you want to ask her for tips on technique?' He raised his arm, brought it sharply down. '*Whack!* Keep your girls in line.'

She sucked the air in through her teeth, a sharp hiss as if he'd actually slapped her.

'You'd get charged with assault for that these days.'

'Didn't do me any harm.'

That's a matter of opinion, she thought, as they continued on their way.

. . .

ANGEL WAS GREETED BY A SEA OF BARELY-SUPPRESSED SMILES AS HE took his place at the front of the incident room. His former vocation, coupled with the crime scene locus in Southampton Old Cemetery, provided almost limitless scope for the sort of irreverent gallows humour that acted as a pressure relief valve for the unrelenting stresses of the job.

He got out ahead of it.

'I'm looking for volunteers to process every grave within a hundred yards of the one the victim was propped against. Clean them, identify the occupants, trace any living next of kin, try to identify a possible connection.' He stared out over the room at all the men and women inspecting their shoes. Looked at Kincade, standing off to his right. 'Where did all those stupid grins go, Cat?'

'Beats me, sir.'

He cleared his throat ready to launch into it for real when the first bars of David Bowie's *Ashes to Ashes* sounded from the back. He bit down to stop himself from smiling, scanning the room to see where DC Craig Gulliver was standing.

'That's a bit before your time, isn't it, Craig?'

'Wasn't me, sir.'

Gulliver didn't need to look at Lisa Jardine standing beside him, her grin giving her away.

'Can't beat the eighties,' she said, the music stopping abruptly when she pocketed her phone.

Your dress sense looks like you believe it, came from somewhere and warranted a raised middle finger in response.

Angel got started before things deteriorated. Behind him on the incident board a photograph of Lois Sheppard posed against the gravestone that was her temporary final resting place occupied centre stage, supported by more detailed shots of the ligature mark around her neck, the way her hands had been posed and the tights used to bind them. An aerial view of the cemetery and surrounding common showed the crime scene location, as well as graphically demonstrating how many potential entry and exit points to the scene existed.

He took them through what little they had at this early stage —not much more than the victim's identity and the time and probable cause and method of death. The paucity of information was in stark contrast to the number of questions that came back at him from the floor.

Gulliver started it off, or at least attempted to.

'Is the location—'

Dead centre of town, came from off to the side.

A chorus of groans went up at the cheesy joke, a second one called out as they died down.

People are dying to get in there.

Gulliver looked around to see if there were more, tried again.

'Is there any significance to the location or the gravestone she was left leaning against?'

'The gravestone is unlikely,' Angel said. 'It's one of the older graves. The SOCOs cleaned it up sufficiently to read the inscription . . .' He looked at Kincade after he tried and failed to recall the details.

'Walter Bidwell. Died in eighteen sixty-seven. If there's a link, it's been passed down through a lot of generations. It's too early to say whether the cemetery itself is significant.'

'What about the pose, Padre?' Olivia Finch called out from the side of the room, the smell of real coffee in her cup from her private supply wafting the question past the assembled throng's twitching noses.

Angel didn't miss how the question was addressed to him personally, rather than to either of them presiding at the front. Everyone always came to him when they wanted to understand the motivations behind the worst crimes people committed, the unspeakable things they did to one another. He wasn't sure what they thought he'd been told in the confessional. They'd have been disappointed to hear the mundane truth of it.

'Sexual connotations, obviously, although without any movie-style accusations or justification. *Whore* or *sinner* or something along those lines.' He extended his hand towards Kincade. 'As Cat pointed out, that often says more about the killer than the victim. We'll obviously be looking at known sex offenders to see if there's anyone with a predilection for graveyards or an interest in the occult. We also have to be aware of the possibility that it's an attempt to point us in the wrong direction.'

'Any sexual interference?' Jardine called out.

'We won't know for sure until after the post mortem, but early indicators suggest not.' He tapped the photograph of Lois Sheppard on the incident board with his index finger to illustrate what he said next. 'Her blouse has been ripped open and her skirt pulled up over her thighs, but her underwear doesn't look as if it's been touched. There's no visible staining, either.'

'What was she doing in the cemetery?' This from Gulliver.

'Good question. She either arranged to meet somebody there who killed her, or she went there for some other reason and was followed. An initial visual inspection of the tights used to strangle her suggests they were brand new and unworn. That could imply she'd arranged to meet the killer who brought them along specifically. That seems more likely than being followed by a person who happened to have an unworn pair in their pocket or bag.'

A uniformed PC at the front put her hand in the air, rather than call out as the detectives were in the habit of doing. Angel told her to go ahead.

'You said pocket or *bag*, sir. Does that mean we could be looking at a female killer?'

'It's possible. The victim would be more likely to agree to meet with another woman in such a secluded location at night. Or it could be a couple working together.'

A ripple of murmured agreement went around the room. The last major case they'd worked had involved a Romanian brother and sister working—and killing—together.

'There's also a chance she was killed elsewhere and taken to the cemetery to be posed,' Angel went on, 'although it doesn't seem likely. It's risky to transport the body. And if you're going to pose a body in a cemetery, it sort of makes sense to kill them there.'

'Is that your own graveyard experience providing that insight, sir?' Gulliver said, his face deadpan while his colleagues all smiled to themselves.

Angel beamed at him.

'Looks like I've got my volunteer to clean and research all the neighbouring graves...'

PATRICK QUINN OPENED HIS EYES WHEN HE HEARD THE BEDROOM door open, the afternoon sunshine slanting through the big sash window making him squint. He might as well have kept them shut for all the good it did him. Pumped full of morphine sulphate for the pain and anxiolytics for anxiety, what remained of his life was a confused daze, drifting in and out of consciousness, his vision blurred in the ever-decreasing moments of lucidity. He knew the end was near—the pain never allowed him to forget—but he couldn't have said what day of the week it was.

He turned his head towards the person approaching the bed, felt the warm breeze from the partially open window cold on his clammy skin, his mouth dry as he croaked out a few words.

'Is that you, Lois?'

Knowing in his heart that it wasn't. That what he'd inadvertently set in motion in his drug-addled selfish quest for peace meant the next time he saw her would not be on this side of the grave.

'No, it's me.'

The voice came to him through the hazy fug of his confusion, its familiarity provoking memories rooted in the past, the most distant now the clearest—too clear by half in all honesty. A woman's face above him looking down, even if he couldn't have said whether she was smiling as Lois smiled at him or not.

She hadn't been smiling the last time he saw her, that was for sure.

'Hello, you,' he said, trying for a smile himself. Something brave to reassure this woman who'd been the closest thing to his own flesh and blood he'd ever had, the only family he'd ever known.

Or wanted—at least, that's what he used to think, back when she felt the same about him.

'How are you feeling?' she said, sounding as if she cared and giving the withered, bony claw that used to be his hand a squeeze.

'Ready to go now.'

Another hand squeeze before letting go altogether, the deathly cold of his touch unsettling her.

'I'm sure. It makes me want to weep seeing you like this.'

Then pick up the pillow and do what needs to be done. You were desperate to do it the last time you were here.

'Ask Lois to come in, will you? I need to use the bed pan.'

Even through the shifting haze that passed for wakefulness

these days he saw her stiffen, then turn away, go to stand at the window looking out at where he would never venture again.

'Lois isn't on duty, today.' Her voice colder now, an edge to it he hadn't heard for thirty years or more, not outside of his nightmares. 'I'll ask the other girl on my way out.'

He tried to raise his hand, couldn't find the strength to lift it more than an inch or two off the covers. Not to wave goodbye. Nor even to touch the crucifix on the wall above his head, a vain attempt to ward off the evil he felt here in this room with him. But to push her away, stop her from planting a perfunctory kiss on his brow.

He was the one dying, but hers was the cold touch of death itself. The lips that once promised everything he'd wanted from life held no attraction for him now, no comfort or joy in their chaste sisterly caress.

I hear you praying I'm dead the next time you call, he whispered inside the echoing loneliness of his head as she pulled the door quietly and respectfully shut behind her.

4

'Finch was right,' Kincade said, glancing sideways at Angel as he made a left out of the car park onto Southern Road. 'Your mother's doing a great job of ironing your shirts. You look so smart, you should take the lead.' She leaned towards him, peered into the driver's side footwell, but it was too dark to see whether he'd given his shoes a much-needed shine.

Cross-checking the address on Lois Sheppard's driving licence with the Electoral Register had identified sixty-eight-year-old Mrs Eileen Sheppard as also resident at the address—her mother, presumably. They were on the way to the house now, to bring the unsuspecting old lady's world crashing down around her ears.

It seemed to Angel that Kincade always found a reason why it should be him who did the deed—although standing around like a spare prick at a wedding, not knowing where to put your eyes while your colleague said the actual words, wasn't a lot better.

He could've challenged her on it, or even pulled rank, but the lighter they kept the mood, the better, on the short journey to Bassett Heath Avenue, two miles directly north of where Mrs Eileen Sheppard's daughter had been found.

'Is that why you deliberately don't iron yours?' he said with a quick glance at her.

'I don't know what you're talking about.' Her voice indignant as she smoothed her blouse with her hand. 'But I can do it if you like.'

He gave her another quick look, couldn't have read her face if his life depended on it.

'No, I'll do it.'

Now, she studied him. She didn't think he enjoyed the unenviable task, but he had strange ideas about duty and responsibility. As if by having the seniority to push unpalatable tasks onto junior officers made it his duty to do them himself.

Nobody could deny he was good at it.

It might have been the ten years he'd spent as a priest, except back then he would've fallen back on the old lies that a better life awaited on the other side. That wasn't something the next-of-kin in a murder enquiry expected to hear from the police—they wanted to know if they'd caught the murdering bastard yet.

'What's it like having your mother living with you,' she said, to get her mind off the task ahead.

'It means you don't need to ask whether I'm available for a beer after work.'

'That bad, huh?' A sudden mischievous gleam lit up her eyes. 'Sounds like Durand's liver is about to take a bashing. I don't envy her doing autopsies first thing in the morning with a hangover.'

He ignored the attempt to bait him, made a left onto Bassett Heath Avenue. What they saw put an immediate end to the joking.

'That's the victim's car,' Kincade said, as Angel parked behind it.

Entering Lois Sheppard's driving licence number into the PNC had identified her as the registered keeper of the yellow Renault Clio they were sitting behind. Uniformed officers were currently trying to locate it in the vicinity of Southampton Old Cemetery.

'She might have walked,' Angel said. 'A mile down Bassett Avenue and then another mile across the common. It was a pleasant evening.'

Kincade was aware that after his wife had died he'd taken a six-week leave of absence, using the time to walk the *Camino Frances*, a four-hundred-and-ninety-two-mile pilgrimage from St Jean Pied de Port in France to Santiago de Compostela in Spain. It meant they had very different ideas about walking.

'That's a four-mile round trip. I'm assuming she wasn't expecting it to be a one-way trip when she set off.'

'Not in the way you're suggesting, no. She might have been planning on going for a drink, getting a cab home.'

It was possible, maybe even probable—in normal circumstances. Except these were far from normal circumstances. It opened up a third possibility. That Lois Sheppard had been taken to the cemetery in the killer's vehicle.

EILEEN SHEPPARD SAGGED VISIBLY AS SOON AS SHE OPENED THE door.

If an uninvited man and woman standing on your doorstep aren't Jehovah's Witnesses, they're police. And Angel and Kincade didn't have the air of Jehovah's Witnesses, the stapled-on smiles proclaiming they were here to bring the joy of salvation into your life.

Their faces said they brought a different message. One more grounded in the nitty-gritty of the real world and the people who populate it.

'Is it about Lois?' Eileen said through the hand already at her mouth, her voice making it clear she knew the question was redundant.

'I'm afraid so, Mrs Sheppard,' Angel said in the way that always made Kincade determined to practice in the mirror. 'May we come in?'

Eileen led them down the hall and into a bright, airy sitting room at the front of the house, its light soon to be extinguished by the darkness to come. A large watercolour took pride of place on the chimney breast above the fireplace. Angel glanced at the bottom right corner, saw the name *Lois Sheppard* and wondered if fate ever grew tired of its spiteful tricks. Familiarity would have caused the painting to blend into the background along with the other furnishings and knick-knacks in the room. Now, it would be a constant reminder for Eileen Sheppard of what she had lost, the many talents her dead daughter had possessed.

The icing on the cake of grief.

'She's dead, isn't she?' Eileen said, a statement more than a question.

Angel dropped his eyes briefly.

'I'm afraid so.'

'How?'

The worst question, the one requiring the hardest answer.

'She was murdered.'

Eileen bit down hard on her knuckle. A strangled sob leaked out from behind it as her legs gave way beneath her. She dropped heavily onto the sofa, the tabby cat that had been asleep on it waking with a start. It glared malevolently at them all, leapt off and ran from the room.

'How?' Eileen said again. It sounded a lot like, *I don't want to know*.

'She was knocked unconscious.' Putting a lot of emphasis on the word, before dropping his voice. 'Then strangled.'

Eileen's face told him his attempt to soften the blow, to stress the lack of suffering, hadn't registered. The shock was too great for her to identify nuances in language. It would be a comfort in the days ahead, but for now he came out and stated it bluntly, the words a lie for all he knew but needing to be said just the same.

'She was unconscious. She wouldn't have suffered.'

Not for the first time, his brother's face was in his mind as the solicitous words slipped softly through his lips on their mission of mercy.

Had Cormac suffered when he put the barrel of his SA80 rifle in his mouth and blew the top of his head halfway back home?

Would he, Angel, have believed anybody who told him that he hadn't?

Sometimes wanting to believe something isn't enough.

Eileen was looking at him as if the same doubts were tormenting her own mind, before she dropped her eyes to the safety of her lap, continuing to gnaw at her knuckle as she did so. The tick of an antique wall clock marked time as they sat in silence for what felt like a lifetime. Angel breathed deeply, concentrated on his pulse to slow it, knowing the same simple exercises could do nothing to ease the torment raging inside the hollow shell of a mother slumped on the sofa opposite them. After what seemed an age, he spoke again, volunteering information rather than simply responding to Eileen's questions.

'We don't know the significance at the moment, but she was found in Southampton Old Cemetery.'

Eileen's head came up as if he'd said they found her at the bottom of an open grave.

'The cemetery? What was she doing there?'

Angel and Kincade watched Eileen's own mind go to work on her. Images spawned by a lifetime of TV and Hollywood flashing past behind her eyes, none of them making any sense, nor connected to the daughter she'd raised and loved.

'We're hoping you might be able to shed some light on that,' Kincade said, 'but we'd like to ask you about Lois first.'

Eileen sighed, the gesture filled with stoic resignation. As if they'd told her she would be required to attend the autopsy, perhaps even assist. A different cat to the tabby that had just left the room walked in and made a bee-line for Eileen's lap, jumping up a moment later.

'What do you want to know?' Eileen said, stroking the cat absentmindedly.

'Has she always lived here with you?'

'No. She used to be married. She moved in with me after the divorce. They didn't have any children.'

'What caused the marriage to break up?'

Eileen's initial shock was fading fast, the questions giving her a focus. Something to keep the full force of her grief at bay, if only for a short while.

'If you're thinking the break-up was acrimonious and her ex is somehow connected to her death, you're way off. He lives in America now, anyway. He always said the reason it fell apart was because she put so much emotional energy into her job, she had nothing left for him. If you ask me, he was right.'

She said it as if they should've known what Lois Sheppard did for a living. Kincade was forced to ask.

'She was a palliative care nurse,' Eileen replied, sounding as if it was only one step down—or perhaps up—from the Prime Minister.

Angel groaned inwardly as fate continued with its campaign. *The bigger they are, the harder they fall.* He wouldn't be surprised if Eileen told them her daughter worked with the homeless in her spare time and took old people out for a ride in her bright yellow car on a Sunday afternoon. He didn't want to think about what it would do to Eileen if she found out how her daughter had been posed, the implications, untrue or not.

'Did she work in a hospice?' Kincade asked.

Eileen was getting into her stride now. As if by talking about her daughter in enough detail, the sad final act of her life might be put off indefinitely.

'Let me give you some background.' She smiled at them, a fleeting gesture that was gone almost before it started, the reason for it apparent from what she said next. 'Growing up, she always wanted to be a police officer. Then my husband got sick with cancer. Lois saw how the nurses were with him, how they made his life more comfortable at the end. After he died, I never heard another word about the police. She qualified as a nurse, specialised in palliative care. She worked in a number of hospices over the years, but then she moved to a private company providing palliative care at home. The pay was better, and . . .' She paused and blew her nose, but it was more embarrassment at what she wanted to say than grief causing the interruption. 'I don't know how she did it, working in an environment where there's only ever going to be one outcome. At least working with people in their own homes means you're only dealing with one dying person at a time. Not a whole hospice full of them where they're falling like flies only to be replaced by another one. Lois never said it like that, but I think that's what she felt.'

Angel might have pointed out the flip side—by caring for a single patient, she would have necessarily become more emotionally attached. He understood now why she might have welcomed the prospect of a four-mile round-trip walk after work. The catharsis of physical exertion. Right up there with the catharsis of mindless violence.

'I was so happy when she decided not to join the police,' Eileen went on. 'I thought to myself, now I don't have to worry about her. I know it's not like America, but still. Now, it's like she made the dangerous choice after all. All that death she surrounded herself with rubbed off on her.'

It wasn't a theory Angel planned on writing on the incident board. In the circumstances, he could forgive Eileen for any temporary blips in rational thought.

'Who did she work for?' he said.

'Cura Palliative Homecare. She's worked for them for about five years. She was very happy there.'

'Do you know any of the details? Where she was working, who she was caring for?'

Eileen shook her head, looking as if he'd accused her of being the worst mother he'd ever come across.

'As I said, I don't know how she did it. I didn't really want to hear about it, either. What was she going to say? Old Mr So-and-so died today. Or Mrs What's-her-name is having a really bad time with the pain and screams all day long. Does that make me shallow and uncaring? I don't know. But Lois was happy to leave it behind at work when she clocked off.' She pushed herself to her feet suddenly, the cat in her lap tumbling off. Angel and Kincade both rose with her. 'I need a cup of tea.'

'I'll make it,' Kincade offered.

'No, I'll do it myself. I need to be doing something. Not sitting here with your colleague in an embarrassed silence while we wait for you to come back.'

They dropped back into their seats as Eileen bustled from the room. The displaced cat watched her go, decided it wasn't dinner time. It sidled up to Angel instead and rubbed itself against his legs as he scratched it behind the ears.

Kincade waited until they heard the kettle being filled before whispering.

'Sounds like we're looking for the man who killed Saint Lois.'

'I was thinking the same thing,' he said, brushing cat hairs from his trouser leg. 'Let's hope we don't find out she was soliciting in the cemetery. You've definitely got the job of breaking that news if we do.' He stood up, almost tripped over the cat, went to take a closer look at the watercolour on the chimney breast. 'She painted this, too.'

'Do you recognise it?'

'It looks like the marina at Buckler's Hard on the Beaulieu River. It's not far from where Durand lives in Beaulieu itself.'

'Where you'll be spending a lot of time until your mother goes home.'

He turned away from the painting, caught the grin on her face. Thinking, *if only you knew*.

He'd recently had lunch with Vanessa Corrigan, the deputy governor of HMP Isle of Wight. Without doubt, the relationship would progress, the chemistry between them impossible to ignore. Despite that, they were taking it slowly. He hadn't told her about Claire and her death yet, but he got the impression she sensed on a deeper level a reason other than the demands of both their jobs holding him back.

Whatever happened going forward, one thing was certain. He wouldn't be saying anything about her to Kincade. And certainly not to the gossip-monger masquerading as a police officer called Lisa Jardine.

Eileen came back in with a tray containing three mugs of tea and an unopened packet of biscuits. She placed it on the coffee table in front of the fireplace, adjusted it until it was just right, before sitting down without picking up a mug. A few minutes to herself is what she'd needed, more than a hot, sugary drink. The heaving sobs they'd heard—and studiously ignored—over the sound of the kettle boiling supported that view. He was thankful he hadn't still been inspecting her daughter's painting when Eileen returned.

He took a mug of tea he didn't want, sipped it, so as to make the whole exercise seem less pointless.

'If we can talk about last night now. I'm assuming you weren't expecting her to come home.'

Seeing him take another sip of tea, Eileen took one of the remaining mugs for herself. She cradled it in her hands as if its warmth would help get her through to when they got out and left her alone.

'She's got a boyfriend. That sounds so stupid at her age.' Her voice caught at the reminder that Lois would be forever stuck at an age that was too old for her partner to be called a boy, but far too young to die. 'Partner, lover, whatever you want to call him. His name's Jason Maddox. He's a nice man. They see each other two or three times a week, but Lois always stays at Jason's place. I know she's a grown woman and what she gets up to, but I didn't want to have to listen to it from the bedroom next door. They didn't have fixed days when they saw each other. I didn't think anything of it when she didn't come home. I don't need her to ring me to tell me what she's doing. I didn't want her to feel as if she was fourteen again.'

'Do you know what plans she had for last night?'

Eileen shook her head, self-accusation behind the gesture.

If only I'd taken more notice...

'She said she was meeting someone, but she didn't say who or where.'

'We saw her car outside. Were they picking her up?'

'She didn't say. She always leaves the car at home if she's going to have a drink.' Sounding as if she thought they might prosecute Lois posthumously for drink drive.

'I don't suppose you've got one of those doorbells with built-in CCTV?'

Eileen looked horrified at the suggestion.

'Lois said they spy on you and send everything back to Amazon. Same as that thing you talk to. Albert?'

'Alexa?' Kincade suggested, managing not to laugh.

'That's the one. I wouldn't have it in the house.'

'Did she have an interest in cemeteries?' Angel said. 'There's a Friends of Southampton Old Cemetery society.'

Eileen looked at him as if he'd told her they held a disinterment every Tuesday night if she was interested.

'No, nothing like that.'

'What interests did she have outside of work?'

'She read a lot. Crime novels, mainly. And she liked to go to the gym.' Eileen took hold of a large handful of flesh around her midriff, gave a self-deprecating smile. 'She didn't want to end up like me. I used to tell her she was wasting her time. If God decides you're going to have big hips and a large backside, the quicker you learn to live with it, the happier you'll be.'

Kincade smiled politely back at her as Eileen ran her eyes up and down her figure.

'How did Lois seem recently?' she said. 'Was she her usual self? Anything on her mind?'

'It's so hard for me to tell. She might not have talked about work, but that doesn't mean I couldn't tell when she'd had a bad day and was feeling down. I am her mother, after all. Do you have children?'

The unexpected question took Kincade by surprise momentarily.

'I do, actually. Two girls.'

'Then you'll understand.' She leaned forward, put her hand on Kincade's knee. 'I hope for your sake nothing ever happens to them. We're not supposed to bury our children.'

Kincade was aware of a stillness coming over Angel, her thoughts along the same lines. His parents had not expected to bury their youngest son, Cormac. And Angel blamed himself for them having to do so.

In the midst of the shared reflections on the unfairness of life, Eileen came alert as if there was still hope for her own daughter if she acted quickly enough.

'Something strange happened last week. Maybe strange is too strong a word, but I found some papers in Lois' room when I was cleaning. Like I said, she normally left work at work, never brought anything home.'

'Did you see what they were?' Kincade said.

The excitement went out of Eileen in a heartbeat.

'No. I didn't look at them. I was afraid of what I might see. But they weren't there the next time I cleaned her room.'

'Do you mind if we send somebody to take a look?'

'If you think it'll do any good.'

'We won't know until we try. We'll also need a list of your daughter's close friends. People she might have confided in.' She ignored the hurt look that appeared on Eileen's face that her daughter might have been closer to a friend than her own mother, and carried on. 'Not now, but if you could give it some thought and let the officers who search her room know.'

They wrapped it up after that. Eileen trailed behind them towards the front door, her voice filled with regret, the words themselves condemning her.

'I feel like I haven't been any help at all. All I've told you is how selfish I am, how much I didn't want to hear about what Lois dedicated her life to.' Her voice cracked, but she fought her way through it, determined to give them a lump in their throats to take away with them. 'Now, I'd give my right arm to listen to all the dreadful things she had to deal with, just to hear her voice again.'

5

Angel stopped off at The Jolly Sailor in Bursledon on the way home. It wasn't strictly on the direct route from the station to the village of Hamble-le-Rice where he lived, but it wasn't much of a detour.

Despite what he'd said to Kincade about being available for after-work drinks at all times, he was alone. After a long day at work he needed a little time to himself to unwind—and he sure as hell didn't get that at home with his mother fussing over him. Interrogating him about his day, her harsh Belfast accent grating on his nerves, as she served him dinners twice as large as he was accustomed to eating, until he felt like a goose fattened by *gavage*—force feeding—to produce foie gras.

He found a table outside, sat with his back against the weathered brick of the pub wall. The Hamble River was directly ahead of him, a pint of Badger Best Bitter in his hand. The tide was out, rowing boats lying haphazardly on the glistening exposed mud, the sound of halyards slapping against masts on the yachts moored in the marina on the other side of the river competing with the raucous calls of the gulls.

The gulls' cries brought his sister, Grace, to mind. Kincade had assigned a ringtone on her mobile to her mother that sounded like gulls fighting over fish heads. The first time he heard it go off, he immediately thought of Grace. He assigned the same ringtone to her, safe in the knowledge she was unlikely ever to call him while they were in each other's company.

He was tempted to turn his mobile off in case she called him now, shattered his small oasis of calm before doing battle with their mother. He didn't, of course. *I wanted a bit of peace and quiet* wasn't an excuse Detective Superintendent Marcus Horwood wanted to hear if Angel missed an important development in the critical first twenty-four hours of the investigation.

He was halfway through his first pint when his phone did ring, but not the ringtone he'd assigned to Grace. Nor was it Kincade or another member of the team calling.

The number was still in his contact list, through inertia and laziness more than anything else. It wasn't a number he'd ever thought he'd see appear on the screen.

'I didn't expect to hear from you again, Inspector,' Angel said by way of greeting as his mind went spinning away.

A good-natured chuckle he remembered well came down the line.

'I shan't ask whether the fact that you are is a good or a bad thing.'

I wouldn't be able to tell you if you did, Angel thought, his pulse picking up at the prospect of his peace of mind being more comprehensively shattered than his mother or sister ever could.

He'd met Inspector Virgil Balan of the Poliția Română when investigating the murder of a people trafficker called Ray Constantin. Balan was Constantin's Romanian half-brother and had come to the UK to offer unofficial assistance. The problem was, Angel hadn't known whose side Balan was on—the Romanian police who paid his salary or the people-trafficking gang his half-brother worked for. He still wasn't sure, even after he received a package from an anonymous sender containing the severed fingers of two of the gang's thugs, the remainder of their bodies never recovered.

'Calling for an update on the case against your brother's murderers?' he said, knowing that wasn't why Balan had called, but needing something to fill the echoing void that was currently his mind.

Balan then demonstrated, as he had when Angel met him, how good his research was, how thorough and professional he was in everything he did.

'I'm not worried about that, Inspector. I'm aware of the jokes about your Crown Prosecution Service. How CPS actually stands for *Can't Prosecute Service*. But I have no doubt they will make a case, that justice will prevail.'

Not for the first time, Angel was tempted to ask Balan to define the word *justice*. Despite Balan's perfect English, it was possible they held very different views on the meaning of the word.

A sudden thought blindsided Angel, his head snapping from side to side in his panic.

'Where are you?'

Again, the good-natured chuckle Angel guessed hid so much.

'Don't worry, Inspector, I'm still in Bucharest. Nor do I have any immediate plans to return to the UK.'

I bet you don't.

Angel relaxed, took a swallow of beer as Balan continued.

'I'm calling on a personal matter. Personal to you, not me.'

Angel couldn't help the snort of laughter that slipped out. On the occasion they'd met, Balan had hijacked the conversation. He'd asked Angel a lot of detailed personal questions, some of which Angel had answered, others not. It meant Balan knew a damn sight more about him than he did Balan.

'That sounds ominous.'

'Bogdan Florescu.'

Angel felt as if a tidal wave had swept up the Hamble River and hit him full-on, left him breathless, his heart racing, as it receded.

Kincade's predecessor, the much-liked and sorely-missed DS Stuart Beckford, had been driving when a Romanian lorry driver fell asleep at the wheel and ploughed into their car when they were out in a foursome with their wives for the evening. Angel's wife Claire was in the front seat and was killed in the head-on collision. Both men blamed themselves. Angel for playing the fool in the back seat, threatening to play his harmonica to the point where Claire unclipped her seat belt to reach around and confiscate the irritating instrument. And Stuart Beckford for ignoring or forgetting about—it made no difference now—the airbag warning light he'd seen a couple of days previously.

Stuart Beckford had been signed off on long-term sick leave with stress ever since. The two men hadn't spoken since the funeral, an ever-widening gap as time drove a wedge between them until at some point time itself would be sufficient to leave them forever unreconciled.

And the name of the Romanian lorry driver who absconded back to Romania to evade British justice was Bogdan Florescu.

Angel downed the last of his pint in an attempt to alleviate the dryness of his mouth, waved a girl collecting empty glasses over. He put his hand over the phone's microphone, asked her to get him another drink. He was going to need it.

She gave him a tired smile, like she'd heard it all before.

'There's no table service. You'll have to go to the bar.'

Angel stayed put.

It wasn't only that he didn't want to join the ranks of ignorant patrons who talk loudly on their mobile phones in pubs and restaurants. The upcoming conversation promised to be something he wouldn't want to share with other drinkers happy to eavesdrop on conversations a lot more interesting than football or the pig's ear politicians were making of running the country.

'I wouldn't have thought you had time to look into my past after you were called back to Bucharest so urgently, Inspector,' he said.

'You know how it is, Padre. Do you mind if I call you Padre? It's ridiculous both of us calling each other inspector. Please call me Virgil.'

Angel could've gone the pompous route, said he'd rather keep it formal, stick with inspector. Except that wasn't him. And it was a uniquely personal matter, after all.

'Padre's fine, Virgil. You were saying I know how it is...?'

'Junior officers panicking when there's nobody around to hold their hand. Even if it had been something that warranted calling me back so abruptly, your background is sufficiently interesting that I would have made the time to learn more about you. I'm very grateful for all the hard work you put in catching my brother's killers. I suppose I was looking for a way to repay you.'

Angel didn't believe a word of it, even if he couldn't think why Balan had decided to take an interest in him.

Something in the silence coming from Angel's end told Balan what Angel was thinking. He laid it on even more heavily as a result, becoming more personal at the same time.

'You helped me with the death of my brother. Obviously, it is far too late for me to do anything for you concerning your own brother's death, but I thought there might be something else. Perhaps I'm justifying my thinking after the event, but you struck me as a man who has known tragedy in his life. It didn't take very long on the internet to find the circumstances of your wife's death. I have to tell you I am ashamed it was one of my countrymen who was responsible. Worse, that he fled the scene and did not accept the consequences of his actions.'

As when they'd met, Angel was struck by Balan's slickness. He said all the right things. All his actions were explained and made perfect sense. Despite that, the overriding impression was of a hidden agenda behind everything he said.

Angel got a sudden vivid mental image of Bogdan Florescu shirtless and tied to a wooden chair in a filthy, dimly-lit basement. The smell of human excrement in his nose after the petrified Florescu soiled himself, his face streaked with blood and dirt and sweat. Virgil Balan standing to one side, his hand outstretched towards the helpless man. *He's all yours.* Angel hoped he was never put in the position of finding out how he would react.

In the same way that he'd been unable to decide which side of the law enforcement line Balan was on, he couldn't say whether Balan was offering to do something about Bogdan Florescu officially or unofficially.

'I'm listening, Virgil.'

Balan laughed out loud, genuine amusement as if enjoying sparring with a worthy opponent.

'A leopard does not change its spots, eh, Padre? You were wary of me when we met, suspicious about my allegiances. Now, you are unsure what I am offering to do for you. Does that say more about you, or me?'

'Perhaps both of us.'

'Because we are so similar?'

'You think so?'

'I do not *think* it, Padre, I *know* it. I believe you do, too, even if you'd rather not admit it.'

What Angel would happily admit was that he needed another drink. Pretty soon, he was either going to have to tell Balan he'd call him back, or break his rule about being a rude prick on his phone standing at the bar.

On the other end of the line Balan cleared his throat.

Here it comes, Angel thought.

'I haven't made any enquiries so far,' Balan said. 'A lot of my countrymen work in your country. I'm sure they commit a lot of crimes there. I'm too busy with our own crime here to be worrying about helping the British police with theirs, unless my superiors ask me to do so. This is not for me. It is for you, Padre. If you tell me you're not interested, that will be the end of it. I understand that your position as a police officer complicates the issue. As a man, you may feel you have put it behind you, that your life will not be improved by seeing Florescu punished. It will not bring your wife back. Any satisfaction you feel will only be temporary. You might enjoy longer-term peace of mind knowing you rose above small-minded ideas of retribution.'

'You're in the wrong job, Virgil. You should be a psychiatrist.'

'We need to be to do our jobs properly. You know that as well as I do. Without understanding why people do what they do we are lost.'

I wish I knew about you, Angel thought, getting to his feet as he felt the conversation drawing to a close.

Except Balan had one last surprise for him.

'I saw that your colleague Stuart Beckford was driving at the time of the accident. The fact that the four of you were all in the car together suggests you were also friends. I am sure he is consumed by guilt, whether it is justified or not. It's what people do. You should discuss my offer with him. Then get back to me, let me know whether you want me to find Florescu for you. We will speak soon, Padre.'

In his haste to get inside and to the bar, Angel almost

collided with a man coming out of the pub carrying two pints of beer. By the time he came back out again, the table he'd been sitting at was occupied by a couple of young women whose raucous laughter suggested the bottle of Prosecco in an ice bucket on the table wasn't the first one.

Ahead and below him, the private jetty provided for the pub's waterborne clientele was empty. He made his way down the ramp, stood looking down the river, trying to make sense of the conversation with Balan.

Faced with no obvious motivations for Balan's offer beyond the one given—that Balan wanted to repay him for doing nothing more than his job—his mind wandered into esoteric realms more suited to movies than his own life.

Was Balan trying to trap him? Offer him Florescu unofficially so that Angel might take personal revenge against him with his fists or an iron bar, secretly recording it to use against him? If Balan was dirty with ties to the people-trafficking gang, a senior officer in his pocket would be invaluable.

He gave up trying to second-guess Balan's motivations, one thing settled in his mind for sure. He would get in touch with Stuart Beckford. Together they would decide what to do. It would give them a shared purpose. Get them past that awkward stage of why neither of them had made contact so far.

He could thank Balan for that already.

Time would tell what else they might have cause to be grateful for.

Or forever damned.

6

'Nice offices,' Lisa Jardine said, as Craig Gulliver pulled into one of the spaces reserved for visitors in Cura Palliative Homecare's car park. 'There must be lots of money in death.' Her lip curled as she craned her head forward to look up through the windscreen at the modern glass-fronted building towering above them. 'I bet the nurses don't see much of it.'

'I don't suppose they do,' Gulliver agreed, as they climbed out. 'That's not why they go into it.'

'A bit like us, you mean? Doing something worthwhile. Making a difference and all that bollocks.' She pointed at a black 7-series BMW parked in the nearest non-visitor space. 'I bet that doesn't belong to one of the nurses.'

'Do you drive the same car as the Chief Constable?'

'Maybe. I don't know what he drives.'

Gulliver gave up. Jardine was known for the sharpness of her tongue, her habit of telling it how it is. He put it down to coming from the frozen wastes of the North East. Straight-talking Northerners and all those clichéd stereotypes. Except, today, she seemed more prickly than normal. It didn't bode well for the upcoming meeting with Cura Palliative Homecare's HR director,

Natasha Rivers, if Ms Rivers wasn't as forthcoming as Jardine might like.

Walking into the corporate atmosphere of Cura's domain, Gulliver got the feeling she wouldn't be.

A young woman with a smile that suggested Cura had a dental care division for people with their life ahead of them, as well as the palliative care division for those with not long left, met them as they got out of the lift on the top floor. She led them across the thickly-carpeted reception area with its tasteful prints on the wall to Natasha Rivers' spacious corner office.

Gulliver groaned when the receptionist opened the door and Natasha got up from behind her desk. He'd been hoping for a matronly middle-aged woman who looked as if she'd done her time at the nursing coal face before moving reluctantly behind a desk. Natasha Rivers was the polar opposite. A thirty-five-year-old business professional who knew more about budgets and forecasts than catheters and bed pans. She was dressed in a tailored dark-blue business suit with a subtle pinstripe over a crisp white blouse, glasses she probably didn't need perched on her nose and her prematurely-greying hair that she made no attempt to colour pulled back off her face. He felt Jardine bristling beside him before Natasha even opened her mouth.

Natasha came around from behind her desk, shook their hands in turn. Gulliver first, then Jardine. Things went downhill from there. She extended her hand towards a man who looked like an undertaker getting up from one of a pair of cream leather sofas facing each other across a low coffee table positioned in front of the floor-to-ceiling window.

'And this is Harold Horne,' Natasha said. 'He's a partner in Horne Smith Brickhouse, our solicitors.'

And they were off.

'We weren't planning on interviewing you under caution, Ms

Rivers,' Jardine said, as they took their seats like the opposing teams they were on opposite sides of the coffee table.

The smile Natasha gave Jardine demonstrated she was on a higher level of the staff dental healthcare plan than the receptionist.

'It's not every day we're asked for a meeting by the police. I wasn't told what it was about other than it concerned Lois Sheppard. It might be a complaint that she helped one of our patients on their way, for all I know.'

Jardine smiled back, not so much showcasing the brightness of her smile as demonstrating a desire to sink her teeth into Natasha's slim neck.

'I'm afraid it's something equally as serious. Lois Sheppard was found dead in Southampton Old Cemetery early yesterday morning. She'd been strangled.'

Surprise, then horror chased each other across Natasha's face before she got it under control and the business demeanour was back.

'I'm so sorry to hear that. It's awful. I shall write to her mother as soon as we're finished here. She was one of our best palliative care nurses. I was aware that she missed her shift without explanation yesterday.'

Four out of five ain't bad, Jardine thought to herself. The first four sentences had been appropriate, if a little by rote. The final sentence sounded as if she'd have appreciated being given earlier notice so she had a chance to arrange alternative cover—they were running a business here, after all.

'I didn't know Lois personally,' Horne said, sounding like the undertaker he resembled, 'but I know she'll be sorely missed by everyone here at Cura.'

Gulliver couldn't help wondering if he was spending too much time with Jardine, her cynicism rubbing off on him.

What a complete and utter waste of insincere breath, he thought.

He didn't know what was worse—the right words spoken without an ounce of sincerity or the wrong words spoken from the heart. At times he was glad he'd disappointed his parents by not following his father into the corporate world—after all the money they spent on his education, too. He didn't think he'd have lasted five minutes, although even that would've been four and a half more than Jardine.

The corporate side of the table shared a look, an unspoken agreement passing between them. They'd discharged their responsibilities in an adequate and professional manner, the meeting now at an end. They started to rise together before Gulliver stopped them.

'We've got a few questions.'

Two pinstriped backsides hit the opposite sofa with a soft *whumpf.*

'Of course,' Natasha said, making it sound like, *I'll give you two minutes.*

At least you didn't look at your watch, Gulliver thought as he launched into it.

'We'd like the details of who Lois was caring for recently.'

Natasha and Horne looked at each other again.

I'll put a screen between the two of you if you do that again, Gulliver thought, as he waited for an answer.

'I don't see how that's relevant,' Natasha said. 'Lois' patients are hardly in a position to kill her even if they'd wanted to, which they wouldn't. She was very highly thought of wherever she went.'

'I realise that. But it's standard procedure to interview a victim's employer and co-workers, establish exactly what they were doing and who they came in contact with in the period leading up to their death. I'm sure you have standard procedures yourselves. Or do your nurses make it up as they go along?'

Natasha didn't have a chance to respond before Jardine jumped in.

'Or as you would say, adopt a pro-active approach to whatever challenges they are faced with on an ongoing and real-time, dynamically-assessed basis.'

Natasha glared at her momentarily, before replying to Gulliver.

'Naturally we have standard procedures. What we also have is a commitment to patient confidentiality.'

Jardine jumped back in before Gulliver could respond.

'I'm guessing your nurses work long hours?'

What everyone heard: *you work them like dogs*.

'Longer than the administrative staff,' Natasha admitted, 'but probably no longer than you and your colleague work.'

Good answer, Gulliver thought, as Jardine pushed her point.

'We wouldn't be doing our jobs if we ignored who she spent the majority of her waking hours with, whether they were on death's doorstep or not.'

Gulliver mirrored Jardine's pose, staring directly at Natasha, challenging her to disagree.

Horne leaned sideways towards Natasha, the voice of reasonableness personified.

'I don't think there's a problem divulging those details, Natasha.'

She gave him a curt nod, got up and went to sit at her desk.

'Patrick Quinn,' she said after a minute's typing and clicking with the mouse.

'We'd like the names of the other nurses who worked shifts with her,' Gulliver said.

'Of course.' Sounding like, *you would*. 'I'll print everything out for you.'

A minute later, Natasha came back with a single sheet of paper folded in half, handed it to Gulliver. She didn't sit down.

Gulliver smiled at her. *Not so fast.*

'Just a few more questions.'

Natasha sighed as if it was already feeling like a very long day.

'Would anyone like coffee, seeing as we're going to be here for a while?'

Jardine and Gulliver both declined. Natasha shrugged, *suit yourselves*, went to a small espresso machine sitting on top of a modern pale-wood bookcase behind her desk.

'Like being in DCI Finch's office,' Jardine whispered to Gulliver while everybody waited for the machine to dispense the coffee, the aroma filling the room, making Gulliver wish he'd said *yes* to a cup.

'Fire away,' Natasha said, carrying the drink back with her and taking her seat, knees pressed primly together, the espresso cup held resting on them. Everything about her body language from her elbows held close into her body to her feet placed side-by-side was tight and closed up, at odds with her invitation to ask whatever they wanted.

'Was Lois particularly friendly with any of her colleagues?' Gulliver said. 'Somebody she might confide in.'

Natasha shook her head, not a denial, but in frustration.

'I can give you a list of her colleagues' names, but what you're asking is very subjective. I don't work with the nursing staff on a day-to-day basis. I'm not privy to their relationships between one another.'

No, you meet them once a year in your luxury office, tell them times are hard, you're not getting a pay rise, Jardine thought.

'As HR director, don't you take an interest in your staff?' she said, putting all the emphasis on the word, *interest*.

'Professionally, yes, of course. But like in your job, some of my duties are unpleasant. Disciplinary matters, terminating someone's employment, and so on. It's necessary to keep a distance.'

The line of questioning was going nowhere as far as Gulliver could see, beyond Jardine trying to get Natasha to admit she was a cold-hearted bitch who liked nothing more than sacking people a week before Christmas. He took it in a different direction.

'You're a private business, aren't you? Your patients have to pay for the care you provide.'

Natasha stiffened. It was better than dealing with Jardine, but not by much, the scope for criticism huge.

'That's right. It's possible to get palliative care at home on the National Health, but it's not always easy. That's why people come to us. A lot of them have insurance, but others pay themselves.'

'I assume it's expensive.' Congratulating himself on not looking around the plush office they were sitting in as he said it.

'It isn't cheap,' Natasha admitted. 'The best never is.'

'I bet it racks up if the patient . . .' He paused, rejected *doesn't die quickly enough* and came up with a softer alternative. 'Needs care for a long time.'

'May I ask where this line of questioning is going?' Horne cut in.

'Money is a major motive behind a lot of crime,' Gulliver told him. 'I'm establishing that a lot of money might be involved here. At the moment, I have no idea whether or how that impacts on this particular situation, but we need to ask. Who paid for Patrick Quinn's care?'

Horne gave him a sad smile. As if he was indeed the undertaker he resembled and a customer had asked if the coffin not be cremated along with their dearly departed, and could they get a rebate on it?

'I'm afraid that isn't something we can divulge. Not without a court order.'

'Not a problem,' Jardine said before Gulliver could respond. 'We'll get a warrant organised asap.' She looked at Gulliver. 'I think we're done here.'

Everybody got up together. Nobody made a move to shake hands. Not there and then, or at the door after Natasha had seen them out, leaving the receptionist to escort them to the lifts.

'YOU DIDN'T LIKE HER, DID YOU?' GULLIVER SAID, AS THEY RODE the lift down.

'You must be a detective.'

'What was it about her?'

'How long have you got? The snooty cow doesn't give a shit. I bet she doesn't even meet people face-to-face when she sacks them. Sends them a text. Or a Zoom meeting. If she ever gets murdered—'

'By you?'

'—we'll have a massive pool of suspects to work through.'

'Starting with you?'

'I wish, Craig, I wish.'

As he'd identified before the meeting, she was more prickly than normal. He didn't ask what the problem was, invite her to re-direct her ire towards him. He had a good idea, anyway. Her younger brother, Frankie. A young man who saw it as his duty as a red-blooded male from the North East to ensure the Jardine family achieved a net zero law-enforcement target after his big sister became a cop.

Now wasn't the time or the place to poke that particular bear. Instead, he concentrated on the meeting.

'They didn't like being asked about the money, did they?'

'I'm not surprised. If you're in the business of profiting from people's bad health and death, the less said, the better.'

They were both quiet as they left the building, mulling over the question of whether money might have played a part in Lois Sheppard's murder.

Gulliver made a point of putting himself between Jardine and the shiny 7-series BMW as they passed it, a ploy Jardine didn't notice, her attention on what she said next.

'Maybe Quinn's been hanging on for ages and the costs for whoever's paying the bill have got out of control. They offered Lois money to put a pillow over his face, and she refused, threatened to report it? Then they killed her before she did. Posed her in the cemetery as a red herring.'

'Did you think that up yourself, or was it in a book or a film?'

'No, it's all me. At times I think I've got a direct connection to the worst side of people.'

At times he agreed with her.

7

'You seem very . . . I can't think what the best word is,' Kincade said. 'Serious?'

How about tired? Angel thought.

He hadn't been able to shake off the effects of Virgil Balan's call all night, his mind too bloated with unwelcome memories to allow him the luxury of sleep. As Balan had shrewdly identified, in his role as a man and a husband rather than a policeman, Angel had reached an understanding with himself. He didn't hate Bogdan Florescu, or think he was necessarily a bad person. He hadn't set out to cause the harm he'd brought about. He'd committed a crime by driving for too many hours without a break, falling asleep at the wheel as a result.

Angel didn't know his circumstances, but guessed he was driven by the same factors that motivate everybody. Above all else, a desire to provide for his family. Working long hours away from home to buy a house, pay for a sick parent's care or his children's education, or perhaps simply put food on the table. It was also understandable that he absconded back to Romania. Spending up to fourteen years in a British jail for causing death by dangerous driving, leaving the family he was trying to provide for in a worse position than before, would've ticked all of fate's malicious and destructive boxes. A lose-lose situation all round. As Balan said, it wouldn't bring Claire back. Would it have lessened his loss knowing Florescu's life—and that of his family—was equally blighted? That Florescu would spend a decade or more regretting a momentary lapse?

The last thing he needed was for the same old questions to hijack his mind once again, but with a difference this time. To have the final say over whether Florescu was brought to justice —of whatever kind—or not.

The same image that had gone through his mind as he talked to Balan—Florescu tied to a chair in a basement and at Angel's mercy—had haunted him all night. His own past hadn't made things any easier. As a priest he'd taught others that it was better to forgive than to seek retribution. Had he ever believed a word of it? Did he now?

A disturbed, sleepless night had been guaranteed until he finally rolled out of bed at 5 a.m. and started the new day feeling like one of the walking dead.

'I've got a lot on my mind.'

She gave him a sceptical look.

'And you don't normally?' She smiled, the mischief running high. 'It's your mother, isn't it? Thinking of ways to get rid of her. I'd be the same. Worse. I wouldn't have let her come in the first place.'

'I didn't. She turned up unannounced and uninvited. Anyway, you're particularly cheerful. That can't be anything to do with living with my father.'

When she'd first moved down from London, she'd lived in a penthouse apartment in the up-market Ocean Village marina owned by one of her estranged husband's friends who was on secondment in New York. When that arrangement came to an abrupt and unscheduled end, an off-the-cuff facetious remark by Angel resulted in her moving in with his father while she looked for more permanent accommodation. It was a situation both Angel and his sister viewed with horror.

'Actually, I think it is,' she said, turning wistful. 'After living with Elliot and the girls for so long, I found it hard being down here on my own, coming home to an empty apartment every night. Harder than I expected.' She smiled again, a wry, self-deprecating one this time. 'Harder than anyone here would've expected of me. It's good to get back to living with someone else.'

'I hope the two of you aren't about to call a family gathering. All dewy-eyed and holding hands. *We've got something to tell you.*'

'I shan't dignify that with a response. Sir. Now I've told you my dirty secret, what's on your mind?'

He raised a hand, took hold of his little finger ready to count the points off.

'We've got the murder of Lois Sheppard for a start . . .'

'Liar, liar, pants on fire.'

'I beg your pardon, Sergeant.'

'And don't go pulling rank. *Sir.*'

He looked at her looking right back at him for a long moment. When Virgil Balan turned up out of the blue, Angel hadn't told Kincade until after he'd met with him. She'd been offended, hard as she tried to not let it show. Later, she told him it made her feel he didn't trust her. Bridges had been mended subsequently, but they both knew something had been lost. Confiding in her about Balan's call and offer—something he didn't plan on telling anyone else—would help patch things up further.

'I stopped off at the Jolly Sailor in Bursledon on the way home last night—'

'Anything to put off going home.'

'—and took a phone call I wasn't expecting.'

Kincade knew the circumstances regarding his wife's death.

She was also acutely aware of her predecessor, DS Stuart Beckford. She felt his sadly-missed presence in everything she did, worrying that she was constantly being compared to him, by senior and junior colleagues alike.

'Not Stuart Beckford?'

You have no idea how close you are.

'No. But he comes into it.'

He sat back in his chair, crossed his arms over his chest and watched her mind go to work. In the end, she was forced to admit defeat.

'I give up.'

'Inspector...'

Her brow creased at the unexpected title, the answer erupting out of her mouth a moment later.

'Not Balan?'

He patted the air, *keep it down* as she stared open-mouthed at him.

'Yep. He's been doing background research on me. He offered to find Bogdan Florescu for me.'

It struck him that he'd used the same phrasing as Balan had. Balan hadn't simply said, *find him*. He'd said, *find him for you*. The addition of those two words—*for you*—felt as if they made a big difference. Allowing for the possibility it would be for him personally, and not for the benefit of the British justice system.

'What did you say?' she asked.

'He wasn't looking for an answer straight away. He suggested I discuss it with Stuart Beckford. That's what I'm going to do.'

'What's your gut feel?'

Angel honestly didn't know.

He believed Beckford felt worse about the situation than he did. They both felt responsible, but Beckford hadn't paid such a high price for his mistake. Stress prevented him from working, but at least he hadn't lost his wife. And in the arse-about-face way life works, his guilt was greater as a result. Did that make him more likely to give Balan the green light? With the stipulation that it was to stay between them should Balan find Florescu, before booking a flight to Bucharest.

'I don't know. What would you do in my position?'

She wagged her finger at him, a gesture her girls would recognise.

'Uh-uh. This isn't about me.'

'It's not the time or the place for it, either. Over a drink after work would be more appropriate.'

She couldn't help laughing out loud.

'You *really* don't want to go home at night, do you?'

He shrugged rather than confirm the blindingly obvious.

'Don't say anything to my father about it. He'll tell Grace and she'll tell my mother. She'll probably call Stu Beckford herself—'

She patted the air, *don't worry*.

'I do have an interfering mother, myself. I know how it is.'

He got to his feet, the thought of the complications his meddlesome mother and sister would cause making him feel like he needed some fresh air—something that was going to be in very short supply in the next couple of hours.

'C'mon. Let's go and watch Doctor—'

'Death?'

'—Durand carve up Lois Sheppard.'

She smiled at him as she stood up and pulled on her coat.

'Don't ever let me catch anyone saying you don't know how to show a girl a good time.'

8

'I've never noticed that before,' Kincade said, as they approached Southampton General Hospital's visitor car park, the entrance to Hollybrook Cemetery on their right, with its winged angels flanking the gothic stone arch. She looked to the left, the main hospital building immediately opposite on the far side of the car park. 'Let's hope they don't have any wards on this side of the building. I wouldn't want to look out of the window from my sick bed and see where I'm going to end up if the surgeon's got a hangover.'

He smiled with her at the unfortunate proximity of the two closely-related facilities, before changing the subject.

'I think we'll stay for the whole show, today.'

'Really?'

'Yeah, why not?'

Generally, he chose to leave after the external examination. Before the Y-incision was made and the pathologist started unpacking the deceased's innards. It wasn't squeamishness. He'd seen more than enough blood and gore in his time as an Army chaplain in Afghanistan and Iraq, fought with the slimy writhing mess of a dying soldier's glistening intestines as they tried to spill out of the screaming man's stomach cavity, for the clinical dissection of an already-dead body to bother him.

He chose to leave because nothing much was gained by watching Durand remove and weigh the internal organs, passing comment on their general condition or any abnormalities that were immediately apparent, then slicing off samples for testing and storage. Anything of use to the investigation was more likely to be revealed by the results of the toxicology and histology tests. They could read those in the autopsy report at their leisure, or ask for an early heads-up from the pathologist if they were looking for anything in particular.

'Including the head dissection?' she said.

The order in which the pathologist deconstructed the body was not set in stone. It was perfectly acceptable to perform the head dissection in order to gain access to the brain before making the Y-incision, but at every autopsy Angel or Kincade had attended, the head had been saved to last.

'Maybe not the head,' he agreed.

'Good. The bone dust aggravates my sinuses.'

'It's the stomach contents I'm interested in.'

'I'm with you,' she said, his thought process falling into place. 'Besides, you can't beat walking around for the rest of the day with the smell of semi-digested food in your hair and on your clothes.'

Their arrival at the autopsy suite saved him from having to reply. The sight of Lois Sheppard on the autopsy table gave rise to his opening remark as they joined Durand in her antiseptic domain.

'She reminds me of the tomb of a medieval Knight in an old church.'

'I know exactly what you mean, Padre,' Durand agreed.

Lois Sheppard was lying fully-clothed on her back, hands still bound together above her chest as if praying, the tights that secured them in situ. The fact that she was laid out flat compared to how they'd last seen her sitting leaning against a tombstone in the cemetery prompted his next question.

'Did you have to break the rigor mortis?'

Kincade smiled to herself as a bizarre image popped into her mind. Of the crime scene technicians picking the victim up fixed in a rigid *L* shape. Having to manhandle her into the body bag, then fit the awkwardly-shaped package into their vehicle—easier perhaps for one of them to throw it over his shoulder and carry it from the cemetery to the morgue, a short journey in the opposite direction a corpse would normally travel.

'We did,' Durand confirmed.

'That makes it less likely the body was moved post-mortem.'

'We'll have a better idea once I undress her and we take a look at the degree and positioning of livor mortis.'

Everybody in the room understood the implications. Rigor mortis had set while the body was in a sitting position. Had the victim been killed elsewhere—and left in a different position for a length of time sufficient for rigor mortis to set—the killer would have needed to break the rigor mortis in order to sit the body against the gravestone. It would then not have been necessary for the pathologist to break it again. Rigor mortis does not reset once broken.

Durand cut the tights binding the deceased's wrists and took a moment to inspect both of the tights' feet using a hand-held lens.

'As I said at the scene, it looks as if they are unworn. Either brought to the scene by the killer for that express purpose or, less likely, the murderer happened to have a spare pair with them. In this modern age, I would not presume to say whether that implies a woman was involved.'

She held Angel's eye as she said it, a faint smile on both their faces. Two dinosaurs together, enjoying the meeting of their minds, a small oasis of sanity in a world turned on its head.

'Nor me, Isabel. Were the tights also used to strangle the victim?'

The smile slipped from Durand's face at being asked to commit without the benefit of a detailed examination. She inspected the tights closely, nonetheless, paying particular attention to where they appeared creased and stretched.

'I can see traces of what is most likely skin tissue here and here.' Indicating two distinct areas, then pointing at one of them. 'This is the area that was used to bind her hands.' She took hold of the other tights leg, held a section towards Angel that looked as if it had got caught up in the washing machine. 'It's possible this area here was used to strangle her. I'll be able to tell you for sure after I've examined it more closely.'

After passing the tights to the waiting exhibits officer, she took hold of the body's left hand as if helping her off the table.

'I will now take fingernail scrapings.'

She looked directly at Kincade—*if that's okay with you, Sergeant*—an unspoken reference to their discussion at the scene. The lack of gouging around the ligature mark had caused Kincade to assert that there would be none of the victim's own excoriated skin tissue under her fingernails due to already being unconscious from the blow to the back of the head. Other possibilities existed. An accomplice might have held the victim's hands while she was strangled.

After bagging the samples, Durand removed the victim's outer clothes. She spent a long time examining Lois Sheppard's blouse where it had been ripped open, a number of the buttons missing as a result. She paid similar attention to her skirt that had been hitched up over her thighs. Both areas of clothing had been subjected to considerable force. They were the areas most likely to contain trace evidence transferred from the killer.

'No evidence of antemortem torture or post-mortem mutilation of the breasts,' she said after removing Lois' bra, with as much emotion as if she'd remarked on the lack of tan lines.

'Be thankful for small mercies,' Angel whispered under his breath, the likelihood of a deranged psychopath on the loose receding.

Durand didn't respond, busy concentrating on the victim's panties.

'As I pointed out at the scene, they don't appear to have been touched. The blouse and skirt were handled roughly. Not exactly in a frenzy, but it's unlikely the killer calmed himself sufficiently to carefully move her panties out of the way at the height of his excitement, putting them back equally carefully after he'd finished. I would be surprised if vaginal and anal swabs identify anything.'

With the body naked, Angel remarked on something he'd noticed at the scene, now more apparent.

'No cuts or grazes or even dirt or grass stains on her knees or hands.'

Durand made a visual inspection even though it was obvious from where Angel and Kincade stood.

'Very true, Padre.'

'If she was hit over the head from behind, you'd expect her to pitch forward, land on her knees or hands. It suggests somebody caught her as she fell. We're looking at a minimum of two people.'

Durand didn't pass comment on the implications, concentrated on the neck injury, confirming her initial assessment at the scene.

'Subject to the results of the toxicology tests, the cause of death is asphyxiation due to ligature strangulation.'

After completing her examination of the front of the body,

she stood back to allow her assistants to turn the body onto its front. Angel immediately stepped closer to get a better look.

'Livor mortis is consistent with the position she was posed in.'

'I agree,' Durand said.

The purple discolouration was clearly visible on the buttocks, the backs of the legs, the heels and on the elbows. Exactly where the blood of a seated corpse with its hands held as if praying would pool according to the laws of gravity. It was further evidence the body had not been moved post-mortem. Lois Sheppard had been posed shortly after death, livor mortis developing while she was in that position.

Determining whether a body has been moved is crucial in all investigations. Separate disposal and killing grounds provide double the opportunity for forensic evidence and potential witnesses. An additional consideration existed in Lois Sheppard's case. If she'd been killed in the cemetery where she was found, what was she doing there? People are killed in all sorts of places as they go about their daily lives—but not normally in a graveyard at night. It increased the chances that the location was significant and not simply a convenient, secluded dumping ground.

'What about the head wound?' Angel asked.

Durand gave him a look—*give me a chance*—before inspecting it.

'I'll be able to say more once I have access to the skull and the brain, but the damage is consistent with a blow sufficient to render the victim unconscious, but not kill them.'

With the external examination completed, the autopsy assistants flipped the body onto its back once more, ready for Durand to begin the final indignity of turning Lois Sheppard from a person into a collection of organs.

She selected a scalpel ready to start the Y-incision, looked their way.

'Staying to the bitter end, Padre? That's not like you.'

'Variety is the spice of life, Isabel.'

'As you wish.' She glanced at Kincade. 'Don't mess my floor up, Sergeant.'

'If I could put my fingers down my throat without her noticing I'd make myself sick deliberately,' Kincade whispered as Durand started sawing away.

Despite the sharpness of its edge, even a scalpel cannot cut through skin and fat and muscle all the way down to the bone in a single cut. It's necessary to saw through the different layers. It's that manual effort that gives the procedure an added visceral dimension, as if cutting into a particularly tough steak. They watched as Durand worked her way down from Lois Sheppard's right shoulder, around and under her breast to the sternum, repeating the procedure on the left side before continuing the cut down to her groin, making a small detour around her navel on the way.

The body was fresh and had been refrigerated overnight. It didn't smell too badly. Autolysis and putrefaction had barely got started. It would be a different story once Durand cut into the stomach.

Angel had never made the mistake of applying a vapour rub under his nose. Given five minutes to adjust, the body acclimatises to any smell to the point where it is no longer noticeable. All applying a menthol rub beneath the nostrils achieves is to continually stimulate the olfactory system, reminding yourself to smell. You'll never get used to the decomposition odours, but they will have a pleasant menthol overlay.

The procedure progressively took on the semblance of a butcher's shop back room. Durand cut back each of the three fleshy flaps created by the Y-incision using a PM40 heavy-duty blade, pulling the top, triangular flap up and over the face before using a pair of rib shears to snip each rib at the sides of the chest cavity. She went back to the PM40 and used it to separate the ribs from the muscles holding them in place, freeing the breastbone and attached ribs for removal and allowing access to the internal organs.

'We're in,' Angel muttered to himself as Durand lifted the body's protective cage out of the way.

'We are indeed, Padre,' she replied, surprising him as always with how acute her hearing was.

'Any chance of starting with the stomach, Isabel?'

Durand paused and gave him a look.

'What would your response be, Padre, if I popped into your office and asked you to interview all of the witnesses and suspects first, then brief the media, leaving the next-of-kin notification to last?'

'I'd politely point out that's not how it's done.'

'My point exactly, Padre. However, if you'd stuck around for the internal examination more often, you'd know that I always begin by removing the intestines and stomach first.'

She snipped the small intestine where it joined the stomach, lifted it up and cut away the fat and attachment tissue holding it in place with a sawing motion akin to playing a violin. After removing it completely along with the large intestine, she removed the stomach and placed it on the organ-dissecting table at the side. Using a scalpel, she cut the stomach open following the line of the longest curvature.

Angel was glad he wasn't closer, although it wasn't so much the smell of partly-digested food and gastric acid, as the appearance of the contents of the stomach which are sufficient to put any observer off stews or chunky soup for a while to come.

'She ate a meal within a period of two to three hours before being killed,' Durand said, picking through the contents with a pair of forceps. 'That's how long the human body takes to digest a meal and move it to the small intestine. Fatty and protein-rich foods take longer.' She peered at something Angel and Kincade couldn't see from their side of the room. 'Looks like the deceased didn't chew her food thoroughly.' She twisted her head towards them. 'Would either of you care to take a closer look?'

Angel extended his hand towards Kincade.

'I'll pass, thank you, sir.'

'We'll take your word for it, Isabel,' he said. 'The tox tests will identify whether she drank any alcohol with—'

'Her last supper,' Durand finished for him. 'They will, Padre. We will of course test for date rape and other drugs, as we normally would. I assume that's what you're interested in?'

It was, indeed. If the toxicology tests identified the presence of Ketamine, GHB or Rohypnol, it would go some way to explaining how Lois Sheppard had been persuaded into the cemetery if she hadn't chosen to go herself.

'We'll be on our way now, Isabel,' he said, already heading for the door. 'Have fun with the other organs.'

'More than you can imagine, Padre.'

Nothing would surprise me, Kincade thought, and said something different.

'That's her dinner taken care of for tonight. Stew again.' Then, more constructively, 'There's a pub on the edge of the common about half a mile from the cemetery, isn't there?'

'Two. The Cowherds on the east side, the Bellemoor Tavern on the west.'

'You're thinking she met her killer for a drink and a bite to eat, they slipped something into her drink and then they took a little walk together...'

'My thoughts exactly. I'll get Gulliver and Jardine to check with her mother whether she ate at home before going out when they search her room.'

'Just one question. Why did we have to stay for all of that, instead of you asking Doctor Death to give you a call and let you know if the victim had eaten anything immediately before being killed?'

'Good question, Sergeant. Why didn't you suggest it earlier?'

9

Sheila Doherty was worried about Patrick Quinn. He wasn't long for this earth. Already maxed-out on anxiolytics and morphine sulphate, he was confused and delirious. It gave Sheila the creeps when he grasped her hand, his touch as cold as if he were already dead, and called her Lois. It was bad enough that a friend and colleague had been murdered. To be mistaken for her made Sheila want to cross herself every time she heard the name on his spittle-flecked lips.

She called her supervisor, a palpable aura of long-suffering patience oozing out of the phone as Bridget Tate answered.

'What is it, Sheila? I'm very busy.'

'I'm worried about Patrick. He's delirious and becoming increasingly agitated.' She bit her tongue, caught herself before she said something she might regret. *Ever since that stuck-up bitch left.* 'I think we should call a priest for him.'

'A priest?' Making it sound as if Sheila had asked for the Pope himself to attend. 'Is he asking for one?'

'No.'

'So, what's he saying?'

Sheila felt a bit silly, now that Bridget was asking her to

repeat Patrick's ramblings verbatim, the accusation coming through loud and clear. She was making a mountain out of a molehill.

'He keeps repeating, *I'm sorry, please forgive me.*'

A heavy sigh came down the line that could've been Bridget's own last breath going out of her.

'You mean he wants a priest to hear his confession?'

That wasn't what Sheila meant at all. She just couldn't find the right words, if any existed.

'No, it's not that. It feels like there's something more.'

'You're being melodramatic, Sheila. You've seen enough people die to know how the doubts creep in at the end. Is there a God, after all? Will I be judged for my sins and found wanting? I assume you've read Mr Quinn's notes.'

'Of course.'

It had taken a while, there'd been so much to wade through. A history of drug and alcohol abuse had dogged him his whole, relatively short life—he was only forty-nine, after all. He'd suffered from depression and had tried to kill himself on more than one occasion, the first time when he was still a teenager. He'd been diagnosed as a paranoid schizophrenic and had spent time in prison, as well as being sectioned under the Mental Health Act at one point. A troubled life if Sheila had ever seen one. Nobody expected Patrick Quinn to make old bones. Then he'd gone and proved them right by getting pancreatic cancer.

The silence coming down the line from Bridget's end suggested that given some of the symptoms of Quinn's mental disorders—delusions, hallucinations, disorganized speech and thought processes—Sheila shouldn't be surprised about a bit of babbling as he prepared to meet his maker.

'I think we should notify the next-of-kin,' Sheila said.

'There isn't any.'

An image of the blonde woman who'd visited, the one who'd

let herself in with her own key, was immediately in Sheila's mind —as were a number of very unprofessional thoughts. How the woman looked as if the quicker Quinn died, the sooner the spiralling costs stopped, the better. Sheila had seen it before many times. Greedy relatives desperate to get their hands on an aged relative's money, stop the funds haemorrhaging into the carers' coffers. Except the woman didn't look as if she needed any, what with her designer clothes and the white convertible Mercedes with the red roof she turned up in like Lady Muck herself.

'What about the woman who visits? The blonde one. I can't remember her name.'

'Ingrid Fischer, you mean?'

The name sounded about right to Sheila. German sounding. She didn't have a problem picturing the woman as a mercilessly efficient nurse assisting a Nazi doctor with his inhuman experiments.

'That's probably her.'

'She isn't family. She's a friend. I'll let her know, anyway.' Bridget hesitated, not one hundred per cent sure about bringing up what she wanted to say at this point, given Sheila's already-troubled state of mind. 'Natasha Rivers asked me to put together a list of all of Lois' colleagues for the police. You should expect to get a call from them, especially seeing as you've taken over from Lois.'

Sheila's breath caught, her mind filled with TV-inspired images of sitting across a table from a pair of stony-faced detectives twisting her every word.

'What would they want from me?'

'How am I supposed to know?'

Immediately, Bridget regretted snapping. It was the whole Quinn situation getting to her. And not only Lois being murdered. It had started before that. All the secrecy about who was paying for his care. As if he was the Prime Minister's criminal half-brother, and the PM was trying to distance himself from him. The most likely candidate was Quinn's regular lady visitor—although Bridget guessed she was more of a well-dressed, highly-paid gofer in a nice car rather than the person holding the purse strings.

The fact was, she *had* snapped. And now Sheila was sulking on the other end of the line. Just when Bridget needed to broach the most delicate topic.

'I'm sorry I snapped, Sheila. Lois' death has really thrown me out of kilter.' Again, she hesitated, the memory of Natasha storming into her office in her mind. Her face like sin, demanding Bridget put together a *list of Lois' fucking colleagues*, to use Natasha's own words. 'It's best if you don't say anything about what Patrick has been saying to anyone else. It's only the confused rambling of a dying man, after all. I shouldn't really tell you this, but the company has over-extended itself moving into the new offices. Things are tight, and we don't need any scandal—'

'What do you mean, scandal?'

'Perhaps that's too strong a word. But you know what the police are like—'

'I don't, actually.'

'If you tell them Patrick has been saying strange things and they think it's connected to Lois' death—'

'What if it is?'

'—there'll be a lot of unwelcome publicity for us. People asking questions. *What are Cura's nurses getting up to when they're supposed to be providing palliative care for the huge fees they charge?* You don't have to be guilty of anything to be tainted by association. As I said, things are tight. If the company goes under because clients are scared off, we all lose our jobs. I don't know about you, Sheila, but I can't afford for that to happen. But it's your choice.'

Yeah, right, Sheila thought, as Bridget put the phone down on her. *Go ahead and blab and lose all of us our jobs.* Some choice. Emotional blackmail was the term she'd use.

The call saddened her, as well as angering her. The lasting impression was that nobody was interested. Nobody cared about Patrick, or even Lois. All that mattered was that everyone kept their jobs in the fancy new offices Sheila never got to go in.

She went into Patrick's room and sat with him, held his cold and prematurely-withered claw of a hand in the plump warmth of her own. She was glad she hadn't said more than she had, relayed what he kept repeating word for word, and not the truncated version she'd passed on.

I'm sorry, please forgive me, Amos.

Lloyd Impey came out of his office at 5:29 p.m. in time to catch Sharon Oldfield before she headed home. He didn't miss the surreptitious glance at her watch as she saw him approaching.

'Has Amos been in today?'

Sharon relaxed visibly when she saw his empty hands. At least he wasn't about to dump something supposedly urgent on her desk at knocking-off time, an irritating habit that infuriated her.

'No. He wasn't in all day yesterday, either.'

'Did he call in sick? Or call at all?'

Sharon shook her head as she got to her feet, started pulling on her coat.

'Not a word. I tried calling him, but his phone was switched off.'

They stood looking at each other for a long moment, a shared thought in their minds.

Poor old Amos had fallen off the wagon. After all these years, too.

Impey's next question proved it.

'How's he been recently?'

Sharon took a minute to think about it, picturing Amos as she knew him. A man comfortable in his own skin. At peace with himself having somehow found a way to put the horrors of his past behind him. At times, she wanted to ask him how he did it. Whether it was necessary to suffer the hardship to find the peace. But try as she might, she couldn't think of anything that might have caused him to throw away what he'd made of his life for the sake of a drink.

'Same as ever.'

'There's nothing bothering him?' Lloyd tried a wry smile, wasn't sure he pulled it off. 'Apart from me working you all like dogs, of course.'

Sharon smiled back as she shook her head, the insincerity matching his, masking the sourness of her thoughts.

Damn right he worked them like dogs. His cow of a mother waltzed in once a week and ordered him around like he was still twelve years old, so he made sure the shit rolled downhill. She wanted to ask him, *does it make you feel better? Help you forget that you're a middle-aged man working for mummy?*

Sharon pushed the bitterness aside, thought about Amos.

'I can call in at his house on the way home.' Picturing Amos comatose on the floor as she said it, vomit in his salt-and-pepper beard and a puddle of it on the floor beside him.

'No, I'll do it.'

She slipped her bag off her shoulder, all thoughts of leaving on time forgotten—not that she resented it in the circumstances.

'I'll ring round the local hospitals. He might've had an accident.'

'Good idea.'

'And I'll call the police. Report him as missing.'

Impey's face said that wasn't such a good idea, even before he opened his mouth.

'They wouldn't be interested. He's a grown man. There's no suspicion of foul play. All you'd get is a patronising lecture on how busy they are. How they can't be chasing after every supposed missing person who woke up one day and decided they were sick of their life or their wife or whatever.'

'I suppose.'

She sat down at her desk, logged into her computer and did a search for all the local hospitals. Impey went back into his office and closed the door behind him.

He sat for a long while thinking, before pulling out his mobile to make a call.

'I hope you're not calling about money,' the man on the other end said, none of the good humour that had previously characterised their relationship in his voice. 'I already told Ruth things are tight.'

You don't know the meaning of the word, Impey thought, and softened it.

'I very much doubt that. It's not why I'm calling. Amos Church has gone AWOL.'

'Okay.' The voice wary now, no hint of the earlier rebuke in it.

'Do you know anything about that?'

10

'I WANT TO IDENTIFY AS A SARDINE,' ANGEL ANNOUNCED, AFTER Gulliver and Jardine piled into his and Kincade's shared broom cupboard.

Kincade nodded her approval at the correctness of his terminology. Not so long ago, he'd have said that he *felt like* a sardine. Now, under her expert guidance, he was getting his head around all things woke. She joined in, looking pointedly at DCI Finch, who'd dropped in five minutes earlier for an update.

'I want to identify as a drinker of decent coffee.'

Me too, came from everyone in the room.

Finch ignored Kincade's pointed remark and the accusing glares from her team, looked at Jardine.

'What is it, Lisa?'

'Do you want the good or the bad news first, ma'am?'

Beside her, Gulliver rolled his eyes.

'The fact that you've mentioned good news is good in itself, so you've already started with the good news, making the question redundant.'

It took Jardine a moment to process what he'd said, responding in her usual manner when she did.

'If that's what Oxford Bloody University does for you, I'm glad I didn't go.'

Everybody currently in the room was privy to Gulliver's privileged background, even if it wasn't widely known amongst his colleagues, the majority of whom thought he'd attended a local school before completing his education at the University of Portsmouth. In reality, he'd boarded at the renowned independent school, Winchester College, before going up to Oxford. Despite that, he'd chosen not to join the fast-track graduate scheme. It was a decision that endeared him to his peers, but did nothing to enhance his career prospects.

'Let's start with the bad, Lisa,' the sardine said, before Gulliver responded with a jibe about Jardine's heritage—the lack of electricity and running water in the North East, or something similar.

'We didn't find anything useful in Lois Sheppard's room. She didn't leave her phone there by mistake, and she doesn't have a laptop or personal computer.'

'Any sign of the papers her mother mentioned seeing?'

Jardine shook her head.

'No. We gave the room a really good going over. There's nothing.'

'I think we're ready for the good news, now, Lisa,' Finch said.

'You might want to get a fresh cup of coffee, ma'am. There's lots of it. Good news I mean.'

Get me a cup while you're at it, came from Kincade's direction.

Finch peered into her cup, shook her head.

'No, I'll make this last.'

'Savour it,' the sardine said.

'Exactly, Padre. Let's hear it, Lisa.'

Jardine took hold of her little finger, ready to count the points off, an encouraging sign that implied she needed more than one finger.

'Her mother confirmed she didn't have anything to eat at home before going out.'

The implication was clear. The remains of the meal Durand had identified in the victim's stomach had been eaten whilst she was out. It increased the likelihood she'd met her killer beforehand, thereby giving them an opportunity to spike any drink she might have eaten with her meal.

'She also gave us the details of a couple of Lois' friends who she was most likely to confide in.'

'And finally...' Gulliver cut in.

Jardine pointed her finger at him.

'*Hey!*'

The barked exclamation was sufficient for Gulliver to hold up his hands in surrender, as if she'd stuck a gun in his face, not a finger.

'Her mother also told us,' Jardine continued, 'that a neighbour saw Lois getting into a car.'

'We had a word with him,' Gulliver added.

Jardine ignored the interruption, comfortable that it hadn't stolen her thunder. She picked it up from there.

'His name's Neville Prescott. He was washing his car in his drive when Lois walked past. They had a joke together and he threatened to soak her with the hose. Typical bloody man. Little boys in men's bodies. Anyway, he came out onto the pavement as if he was going to spray her as she was walking away. He saw a white convertible Mercedes with a red roof waiting at the corner. It was parked side-on, so he couldn't see the registration. Lois got into it and they drove off. He reckons it was a blonde woman driving, but he couldn't swear to it. The roof was up.'

She paused as everybody let the information sink in.

Angel was the first to break the silence, the three women in the room groaning at what he said.

'Thank God for grown men acting like little boys, eh, Craig?'

'Absolutely, sir.'

'The exception that proves the rule,' Kincade countered, and got a couple of solid nods from Finch and Jardine. 'It sounds like the driver didn't want to be seen picking Lois up outside her house.'

There was a momentary lull as the further implications sank in. Again, Angel was the first to break it.

'Either it was a bloody good guess that the car had arrived, or the driver called Lois, *I'm here.*'

'Or they had a pre-arranged time,' Finch pointed out.

'True.'

'Maybe not,' Gulliver said. 'Prescott said it was twenty past six. If you're making arrangements, you normally make them on the hour or quarter or half past.'

'If you're OCD, you do,' Jardine muttered under her breath.

'It's a valid point, Craig,' Angel said. 'We'll find out as soon as we get the victim's call logs from the service provider.' He looked at everybody in the room, 'I think that's about it—'

The raucous sound of squabbling seagulls interrupted him. Kincade immediately looked at her mobile on her desk, even though the sound was coming from his. Gulliver and Jardine headed out as if being chased by a flock of gulls, Finch following behind them.

'I didn't know you'd used that ringtone,' Kincade said, smiling at him as the phone continued to ring. 'Aren't you going to answer it?' Then, when it became obvious he wasn't, 'Who've you assigned it to? Obviously not me.' She thought for a moment, the grin on her face telling him when she'd worked it out. 'Grace.'

'Yep.'

'She doesn't normally ring you at work.'

She was still smiling at him, enjoying the small bond created between them. That he'd chosen the ringtone she'd assigned to her pain-in-the-arse mother for his own, pain-in-the-arse sister.

Exactly, he thought, her innocent pleasure making him feel worse about the suspicion growing in his mind. *Normally* wasn't the right word, either. *Ever* was more appropriate. That was why Kincade had never heard it go off before.

'It might be important,' she said, a sudden thought occurring to her. 'She hasn't had a blood test, has she?'

'Not to my knowledge.'

According to Angel's sister—a hypochondriac who actively looked for symptoms of insidious diseases in everyone she met—their father was suffering from late onset Huntington's disease. Carl the old warhorse refused to take her seriously. After he obstinately refused to take a blood test, Angel had taken one himself. Huntington's is one of nature's great gambles. There's a fifty-fifty chance of the faulty gene being passed down from parent to child. Angel had tested negative, a huge relief to him, but proving nothing in relation to their father. Despite being the one to badger Angel and their father, Grace was scared to take a test herself.

The unwelcome suspicion continued to grow in his mind, the longer he sat talking to Kincade. He was deliberately playing down just how unusual it was for Grace to call him at work, what that implied about the topic she wanted to talk about. It meant he ought to call her back immediately. And it definitely meant he shouldn't do it in front of Kincade.

He got to his feet, picked the phone up off his desk.

'Maybe I should call her back, after all.'

Kincade narrowed her eyes at him as he headed for the door.

'Should I be worried? You think she's persuaded your dad to throw me out?'

It was a possibility. Grace had been horrified when she heard Kincade was about to move in with their father. As a criminal defence lawyer, police officers were the enemy, every last one of them a fascist oppressor prosecuting innocent citizens on the basis of their own prejudices and personal agendas. Angel wouldn't put it past Grace to try to persuade their father to throw Kincade out.

Except the tightness in his gut told him it was worse than that.

Much worse.

Grace started with a lie.

'I only want what's best for Dad.'

There were so many things Angel could've said, all of which would end the call then and there. They'd had conversations go that way in the past, would do so again in the future. Today, he bit his tongue.

'Uh-huh.'

'Don't say it like that, Max.'

'Like what?'

'Like I'm a suspect—'

'I thought they were all victims.'

'—who's given you a perfect alibi and you don't believe it.'

It would've been so easy to carry on in the same vein, sooner or later—depending on her mood—reaching the point where she accused him of being a Nazi and slammed the phone down. Instead, he stated the obvious in order to deflect her.

'You never call me at work. You've got me worried.'

'You should be.' She hesitated, and he pictured her face as she worked up the courage to come out with something she knew was going to cause a problem. 'You know I'm not happy about your sergeant—'

'Her name's Cat.'

'—living with Dad.'

'You made that very clear, yes. Although you weren't so clear about why.'

He wasn't sure what he felt, now his suspicions about the reason for the call had been proved right. The first time he'd talked—not really the right word—to Grace after she heard Kincade was moving in with their father, she'd threatened to use her London contacts to look into Kincade's past. Today's out-of-character call suggested she'd done exactly that. And what she'd discovered had warranted an immediate phone call.

He'd always harboured his own suspicions about the explanation Kincade gave for her demotion from inspector down to sergeant. That she'd used excessive force when arresting a protester at a rally—a protester whose mother happened to be a leading civil-rights lawyer. The officer making the arrest along with Kincade had been kicked out of the force altogether. It was rumoured that it was only nepotism that prevented the same happening to Kincade—her uncle being a big noise in SO15, the Met's anti-terrorist division. Nor had Angel been able to find details of Kincade's misconduct hearing.

'I asked some people I know to look into her,' Grace said.

Again, he bit back his immediate response.

People with an axe to grind against the police, you mean?

'You told me you were going to.'

'And they've found some disturbing information.'

Angel's heart was racing in his chest, his pulse throbbing in his temple. Despite the pounding, his mind was as clear as he'd ever known it.

He didn't want to hear about it like this.

He already felt guilty at the way he'd rushed out of the office to make the call so that Kincade didn't overhear. The thought of listening to Grace talk with a told-you-so smugness in her voice about how her contacts had dug around in Kincade's life made him feel sick. To have to endure Grace listing the disturbing, as she called them, reasons why the woman he worked closely with every day was not fit to live in his father's house would be a backstabbing step too far. He did his best to be honest with people in everything he did. He couldn't think of a way to be more dishonest and underhand if his life depended on it.

'I don't want to hear it, Sis.'

Grace snorted, her voice filled with contempt.

'Head in the sand. Way to go, Max.'

'And I hope you're not thinking of filling Dad's head with whatever *disturbing* information your contacts might have found.'

'Not might. *Have* found. But you go ahead, stick your head in the sand. Pretend it'll all go away. I would've thought you'd want to know the truth about your second-in-command.'

'I do. But from her.'

Grace laughed out loud, even if it sounded put on.

'Don't hold your breath, Max.'

A sudden wave of sadness washed through him at what his sister had already done. It didn't matter that he'd told her he didn't want to hear it. That he would hang up if she tried to tell him anyway. He didn't doubt Grace's contacts had found something. And now he would look at Kincade differently.

With the sadness came anger. Ten years as a priest and the horrors of Iraq and Afghanistan hadn't elevated him above human weakness, made a saint of him.

And Grace had always been able to push his buttons like no-one else.

'Talking of head in the sand, Sis, have you booked a blood test for Huntington's yet?'

'Piss off, Max.'

And the final result—everybody loses, he thought to himself as the phone went dead in his ear.

. . .

Angel had walked as he talked—or argued. By the time Grace hung up on him, he was outside in the car park. He slipped the evil messenger of doom that was his phone into his pocket, looked up at his office window. Either it was a trick of the light, or Kincade was standing at it, looking out.

He couldn't go back in there now. Couldn't risk the conversation currently running through his mind turning real.

That was about me, wasn't it?

Even with the accusation only in his imagination, he felt himself squirm, his inability to lie damning him.

Yeah.

She's been digging, hasn't she?

Standing in the car park, he nodded his agreement, the words not coming.

And suddenly a wet sheen to her eyes, because he knew she wasn't as hard as she liked to make out, even if nobody else did. Then her voice, barely more than a whisper.

Just give me a bit of time.

And he'd nod like an idiot, come out with some crap about *whenever you're ready* as she left the room, standing a little less tall or straight than when the stupid seagulls ringtone went off and his sister started to slowly poison his mind.

He checked his watch, decided to call it a day.

I hope you have a shitty night, too, Sis, he thought as he got in his car and headed home.

11

KINCADE'S CAR WAS IN THE CAR PARK BY THE TIME ANGEL GOT back from interviewing Jason Maddox on his own the following morning. He wondered if she would come out with an excuse about why she hadn't been on time as he rode the lift up. Unusually heavy traffic or an accident. Living with his father in the village of Middle Woodford, a few miles north of Salisbury, meant a thirty-mile commute, the furthest any of his team lived from the station. She would then have to compound the lie by claiming her phone battery was dead. And that she didn't have a charging lead in the car...

As it turned out, she threw it back at him the minute he walked into their office.

'You ran off very abruptly after the call from Grace. Is everything okay?'

He held her open gaze, unable to decide what was going on. Had she guessed why Grace called and was pushing him to challenge her? Get it all out in the open, because she couldn't bring herself to do it?

Or was it all in his head?

He avoided the issue by being truthful.

'I don't want to talk about it right now.'

'No problem. If Grace has found a way to persuade your dad to kick me out, I'll find out soon enough.'

He felt like turning around, taking the lift to the ground floor and back up, starting again. He needed to change the subject—even if it meant adding her unexplained absence to the small herd of elephants assembling in the room.

'I just got back from interviewing Jason Maddox.'

She nodded as if it had never been the plan for them to go together in the first place.

'And? You don't look very excited.'

'I'm not. He's actually her *ex*-boyfriend.' He caught sight of a grin forming on her lips, headed it off. 'That's not because she's dead. She obviously hadn't got around to telling her mother.'

'He dumped her?'

'She dumped him.'

'*Uh-oh*. I hope you checked his bin for packaging from a pair of tights.'

He scrunched his face as if he'd known there was something he'd been meaning to do.

'It slipped my mind.'

'Sloppy work, sir. Seriously, do we need to look at him? Jilted boyfriend and all that crap?'

'He's a lot younger than her, too. At least ten years.'

She sucked the air in through her teeth, her worst suspicions confirmed.

'Dented male pride. Best get down there and arrest him on the spot.'

'They've re-written that saying, have they? *Hell hath no fury* . . '

'Everything else gets turned on its head these days, so why not? Did he tell you why they broke up? He didn't catch her screwing his best friend in the cemetery, did he?'

The conversation was growing increasingly bizarre. Not only her last remark, but her mood. He was now convinced she'd guessed why Grace called him, and took herself off somewhere quiet to think. She ought to be in a foul mood as a result, not joking and flippant.

Unless she'd decided to come clean, and a load had been lifted. It's tiring living a lie. He'd seen that fact demonstrated over and over in the interview room. There comes a point with most people—the real crazies excepted—where they'd rather admit to their crimes and suffer the consequences, rather than struggle against their own conscience as it slowly and inexorably grinds them down.

'No. Same reason her mother gave for the split with her husband. Too much invested in the job, nothing left for him. He mentioned it, she accused him of being clingy and dumped him.'

'A wasted journey, then.'

He rocked his hand, not ready to completely write it off.

'Maddox told me she'd got worse after she started caring for Patrick Quinn. He accused her of being obsessed with him.'

'That won't have helped.'

'No.' He smiled at the memory of how embarrassed Maddox had become. 'It gets worse. He admitted that in the heat of the argument he accused her of providing Quinn with extra comfort not covered under the terms of her employment contract.'

He expected her to laugh out loud, especially after her previous facetious remarks. She didn't even smile with him, the light going out of her eyes. She looked as ill at ease as Jason Maddox had. With the question of her past never far below the surface, he wondered if he'd touched a raw nerve. Whether her marriage failed because she overstepped a similar line.

'That's the kiss of death for a relationship,' she said, sounding as if she was talking from bitter experience. 'It also gives him a reason to hate her. His pride's going to take a serious bashing if he thinks a dying man's getting what he isn't.' She held her hands together as if praying in front of her chest. 'It fits with the way she was posed. Begging for forgiveness. Giving a dying man extracurricular relief has got to be a sin.' Lifting an eyebrow at him as she said it.

'I'd call it unprofessional, more than a sin.'

'Did you ask him where he was on the night she was killed?'

'Strangely enough, I remembered to do that, yes. He was at home watching TV. Alone. How did he put it? *Because my ex-bloody-girlfriend is too busy running around looking into the life of a man who'll be dead by the end of the week.*'

'We better get a move on and interview him, in case he is,' she said, tapping away at her keyboard. 'Although it might cause a problem if we need to call him as a witness.'

'What are you doing? Looking up Patrick Quinn?'

'I wasn't, as it happens. I'm looking for places to live in case Grace persuades your dad to kick me out.'

You can stay at my place if he does, he thought. *I'm checking myself into a lunatic asylum if you keep messing with my head like this.*

12

Gulliver and Jardine were tasked with identifying the eatery where Lois Sheppard consumed the meal Isabel Durand had found semi-digested in her stomach. The Bellemoor Tavern and The Cowherds were the two pubs closest to the scene of the crime, both of them a little over half a mile from where Lois' body was found.

To get from The Bellemoor to the scene involved a walk straight down Hill Lane. Anyone planning on killing Lois would not choose to walk down the street with her as she staggered along beside them under the influence of a date rape drug, if that's what had happened. A quick call to The Bellemoor also identified that, due to a problem in the kitchen, they hadn't been serving food on the night Lois was killed.

That left The Cowherds, widening the net from there if it didn't pan out.

Like Angel, Gulliver was struggling to understand the woman he spent all day working with as they drove there now. The previous day, when interviewing Natasha Rivers at Cura Palliative Homecare, Jardine had been at her most acerbic. Again, like Angel, Gulliver had been reluctant to push too hard, wary of opening up a can of worms he might not be able to get the lid back on. Today, she was in a different mood altogether, the subject she raised surprising him.

'What did you do at university? I can't remember.'

'Drank a lot of beer...'

'I meant in between that, you twat.'

'The correct terminology is I *read*—'

'You're saying you didn't write any essays?'

'Of course, I did.'

'Then you didn't only *read* it, you *did* it. Sounds to me like you should've taken a course in common sense while you were there.'

Gulliver didn't bother getting into an argument he couldn't ever win, went for the easy option.

'I did Politics, Philosophy and Economics. PPE.'

'I thought that was something you use to stop plumbing joints from leaking.'

'I think you'll find that's PTFE.'

She waved it off, a minor detail.

'Whatever. Anyway, you should've become a politician, not a cop.'

'If you say so.'

'It's obvious. Politicians decide what they want to do based on their personal agendas. They think about the philosophy of what they should be doing, and decide bollocks to that. Then they work out how much it's going to cost the taxpayer to pay for it.'

'Maybe you should've become a lecturer instead of a cop seeing as you've got such a good grasp of it.'

'Maybe I will. It's probably better paid than this job.'

The uncharacteristic melancholy in her voice told him what was wrong—and that he'd been right. It was her brother's situation weighing on her mind. Driving around with him all day long only served to highlight the contrast between them. Him with his privileged background and Oxford University education, and Frankie in trouble with their own Northumbria Police colleagues the whole time. He guessed she was wondering how Frankie might have turned out if he'd enjoyed the same leg-up in life Gulliver had.

Being less than five minutes away from The Cowherds meant it wasn't an appropriate time to get into a conversation that was unlikely to be a quick, two-minute affair.

Instead, he left her to gaze absentmindedly out of the window as he concentrated on driving and the upcoming interview with an assistant manager at The Cowherds. With a photograph of the victim and a description of the distinctive car she arrived in, as well as the time of arrival to within a few minutes of six-thirty, they were confident Lois would be remembered if she'd been there at all and they weren't barking up the wrong tree. In a perfect world, she'd be caught on CCTV, along with the blonde woman who'd accompanied her and a nice clear shot of the white Mercedes' registration plate.

The world remained in its less-than-perfect state when they parked in one of the dozen or so parking spaces at the front of the pub and Jardine glanced around after getting out of the car.

'No CCTV.'

A young man wearing chef's black and white check trousers who didn't look old enough to be trusted with a sharp knife was sitting at one of the picnic tables arranged between the pub and the parking spaces, texting on his phone and smoking. He'd looked up from his phone as they got out of the car, recognised them for what they were and overheard Jardine's comment about the lack of CCTV.

'That's because the pub doesn't own those parking spaces. Anyone can park there. Dog walkers, joggers, whatever.'

Murderers, Gulliver thought, and said something more constructive.

'Do you have your own car park?'

'Round the back.' Hooking his thumb over his shoulder as he said it. 'We've got CCTV there.' Whatever he'd been doing on his phone was now forgotten, their interest in CCTV causing him to jump to the obvious conclusion. 'Is it about the woman who was murdered in the cemetery?'

'That's right,' Gulliver confirmed. 'Were you working that night? About six-thirty?'

'Yeah, I was here.'

Gulliver took out a photograph of Lois Sheppard her mother had provided them with, handed it to him.

'Do you recognise her?'

The young man took a long drag on his cigarette while he studied the image, as if the nicotine might stimulate his memory. It didn't.

'Nah. Never seen her before. But I'm stuck in the kitchen except when I'm on a break.' Holding up his cigarette in case they thought smoking was his job.

Behind them on The Avenue, the main north-south route into the city centre, something powerful and throaty went past with a roar of exhaust. The chef's head snapped to the side to follow its progress as if his nose was tied to its bumper with a piece of string.

'*Nice car*. Aston Martin Vanquish.'

'Are you into cars?' Jardine said.

'Like to be. But on my wages . . .'

She smiled with him like she knew how it was.

'We're actually interested in the car the woman arrived in. A white Mercedes convertible—'

'With a dark red roof?' the chef finished for her.

'You saw it?'

'Yeah.' He pointed at a parking space two away from where Gulliver's more modest A-Class Mercedes was parked. 'It was parked right there.' A smile broke out on his face. He immediately killed it. 'Sorry. It's not funny. It was in one of the spaces not covered by the CCTV. People always park in front if there's a space free.'

And if they don't want to be caught on CCTV, Jardine thought sourly.

'I didn't see the registration, either,' the chef added. He pointed behind him to the entrance to the rear car park. 'I don't sit out here and smoke when there are customers around. I was standing over there. I could see the car, but the tables were blocking my view of the registration. And I wouldn't have been looking at the number plate anyway. Not unless it was a personalised plate.'

It wasn't a problem. With confirmation that the distinctive car had been in the vicinity and with a very narrow time frame, it would be an easy job to identify it from ANPR or other highway cameras positioned on the main route into town.

'Did you see the driver?' Gulliver said, going for broke.

The chef shook his head apologetically.

'Nah.'

'So you didn't see it drive away?'

'Sorry.' He glanced at his watch. 'I better be getting back.'

'He reminds me of Frankie,' Jardine said, as they watched him head back towards the kitchen, confirming Gulliver's earlier suspicions. 'He worked as a trainee chef for a while. Bought the check trousers and clogs. He only lasted a week. Didn't like the way the chef ordered everybody around.'

'Sounds like somebody I know.'

They'd started towards the pub entrance. She immediately stopped mid-stride.

'Are you saying I have a problem with authority?'

'It doesn't come naturally to you, that's all.'

'Better than being an arse-licker.'

Last time I try to cheer you up when you're down in the dumps, he thought, as Jardine set off towards the pub entrance again.

Getting confirmation that the white Mercedes had been parked outside the pub had been an unexpected bonus before they'd even stepped through the door. Things continued in the same vein once they got inside. The assistant manager, Tony Gallo, hadn't been on duty on the night in question, but he showed Lois' photograph to the kitchen and serving staff, one of whom remembered Lois and her companion-cum-potential killer.

Anna Kaminski was dressed all in black as ninety-nine per cent of all female pub staff are. Black T-shirt, tight-fitting short black skirt over black leggings and black Doctor Martens shoes, the distinctive yellow stitching the only colour in her whole outfit. She led them back outside after Gallo brought her trailing behind him from the kitchen, took them to one of the picnic tables.

'They were sitting here.'

Gulliver looked left and right. The table was the furthest from where the chef had been standing when he noticed the Mercedes. More importantly, it was the closest to the footpath that led into the common, and from there, to the cemetery.

'She was definitely with someone else?' he said.

'That's right. Another woman. She was blonde.'

'Did you get a good look at her?'

'Not really.' She dropped her eyes momentarily, as if worried she'd brought the whole investigation to a grinding halt. A slight tremor entered her voice when she spoke again, an understandable trait in someone not accustomed to being interviewed by the police. 'Her back was to me when I came out. The woman who was murdered was sitting facing me.'

Jardine cut in, her words not only to reassure Anna that she was doing fine, but also to try to jog anything that might be in her subconscious.

'I'm guessing you were really busy?'

'Yeah. It was crazy.'

'You're doing well to remember them at all. Was there anything about them that sticks in your mind? Were they rude or impatient?'

Anna shook her head, glanced at her boss still hovering on the periphery, as if worried her continued employment rested on giving satisfactory answers.

'Nothing like that. But they seemed like a really odd couple.'

'In what way?'

'How they were dressed.' She laughed, a quick nervous stutter. 'It's like they had a mix-up about where they were going. The woman who was killed was dressed normally, but the blonde woman looked like she was going to a movie premier or something. I don't mean she was wearing a long black evening dress, but she was much better dressed than her friend. She was wearing a really nice designer suit and shoes. You could tell they were expensive.' She glanced down at her own attire, smiled. 'I dress like this for work, but I like nice clothes.'

Gulliver and Jardine shared a look.

Not exactly the outfit of choice for somebody planning on killing someone.

'How did they seem together?' Gulliver said. 'Laughing and joking? A serious discussion? Arguing? Sitting in silence?'

Anna thought about it for a long moment. She glanced at Gallo again before answering.

'It was a bit awkward. Like the woman who was killed was being taken out by her boss, and they didn't really know each other. But it wasn't nasty, like I'd interrupted an argument.'

They were interesting and perceptive observations that

immediately made Gulliver think of Natasha Rivers. It was easy to imagine her behind the wheel of a convertible Mercedes in her smart, pin-striped suit. She'd make any member of staff she took out feel uncomfortable, too. But much as he knew Jardine would've liked Ms Rivers to be implicated in Lois Sheppard's murder, Natasha's hair was dark and prematurely greying, not blonde.

Gulliver had a couple more questions as they drifted back towards the pub, the interview drawing to a natural close.

'Did you see who bought the drinks?'

Anna shook her head, her face making it clear she understood what was being asked, aware of the problem date rape drugs posed.

'No. I only serve the food.'

'And did you happen to see them leave?'

'No. Sorry.'

They called it a day at that point. Gallo told Anna she could take a break if she needed one. She declined, clearly desperate to get back in the kitchen and tell anyone who stood still long enough about her role in solving the crime.

'What do you think?' Gulliver said to Jardine after they thanked Gallo for his help and headed back to the car.

'Apart from who kills somebody while they're dressed up to the nines, you mean?'

'Apart from that, yeah.'

'This is too easy.'

It wasn't necessary for either of them to voice the alternative way of phrasing it.

We're missing something.

13

Even before Gulliver and Jardine got back and reported their findings, the list of identifiers pointing towards the blonde driver of the white convertible Mercedes was growing longer.

Kincade was working her way through Lois Sheppard's mobile phone call log and cell-site data report that had been waiting for her when she got in that morning. She ran a neon-yellow highlighter pen through an entry in the call log, in preparation for requesting details of the number's owner from the service provider.

'Looks like you were right and Finch was wrong.'

Angel dipped his head at her, happy to accept praise wherever he found it.

'It happens so often, you'll have to be more specific.'

Her mouth became a perfect O.

'Brave words when she's not in the room.'

He gave her a look. *Are you going to tell me or not?*

'Lois Sheppard took a call at seventeen minutes past six on the evening she was killed,' she said. 'It lasted five seconds. Long enough for, *I'm here. Okay, see you in a minute.*'

'The driver of the Merc.'

'Gotta be.'

'Any other calls to or from the number?'

'Nope.' She waved the report at him. 'At least not within this time frame. You'd expect to see a call a few days or a week beforehand to make arrangements.'

'Unless the arrangements were made face-to-face. Somebody she works with, perhaps?'

'I don't suppose many nurses drive a convertible Mercedes.'

'And Elliot never allowed you to drive his Maserati?' Then, under his breath, 'Sensible man.'

The mention of her estranged, rich banker husband put a scowl on her face as much as the annoyance at herself for the hasty conclusion she'd jumped to.

'True. And forget him *allowing* me. Like it was a special treat if I was a good girl. I'm a much better driver than he is, anyway. That's not all.'

He'd gone back to what he'd been doing before she identified the call from the driver of the Mercedes, only half-listening to her as she boasted about her driving abilities. Something in the way she said *that's not all* made him look up again, knowing she wasn't about to simply mention something else she was better at than her husband.

She got up from her desk, carried the call log over, a palpable air of excitement coming with her. She laid the report on top of the papers in front of him, tapped the last entry on the report.

'Look at that.'

He did as she instructed, saw the entry she was indicating, her finger rigid as it hovered under the details of the call. It was outgoing. At ten seconds' duration, it was almost as short as the previous one. But it was the time that was significant. He looked up sharply at her.

'Twenty to eight. An hour after the Merc picked her up.'

She assumed what he called *Kincade position #1*—left arm crossed over her body, right elbow resting on it, forefinger pushed into her top lip—and summed her thoughts up in four words.

'It could be anything.'

'Maybe leaving a voicemail?'

They both went back to the report, ran their eyes up the page. Kincade was faster at it than he was, excitement in her voice when she pointed at another entry.

'There it is again. Two days before she was killed.'

'Two and a half minutes this time.'

'Long enough for a proper conversation.'

He raised a cautionary finger, as if warning her against jumping to another hasty conclusion.

'Only if she called a man.'

He expected her to come back with, *ha, bloody, ha*. Maybe append *sir* to it, if he was lucky. Except he was wrong. She crossed both arms over her chest this time, a challenge in her voice to accompany the aggressive pose.

'You reckon? You clearly haven't been out for a beer with your dad recently. I've never known a man talk so much.'

'Are we talking about the same person here?' He put his hand level with his eyebrows as if saluting. 'About so tall.' Then laid his index finger along his top lip. 'Silver moustache like a stiff scrubbing brush.'

'That's him.'

Angel wasn't actually surprised. Difficult relationships between fathers and sons were hardly uncommon. The lyrics to Mike & The Mechanics' *The Living Years* were suddenly running through his mind, poignant words that always made him determined to try harder with his old man.

Joining the priesthood instead of the Army like any dutiful son would hadn't helped. Nor had his father's eleven-year stint at Her Majesty's pleasure in HMP Whitemoor. It was encouraging that Kincade's company was bringing him out of his shell. And with that thought came the sickening reminder of what Grace was about to do.

Kincade couldn't help but notice the effect her words had on him.

'Are you okay?'

'Yeah. Just trying to get my head around this stranger claiming to be my old man.'

She smiled with him, but they both knew what he'd been thinking.

'Better get back to this call log,' she said a little too brightly, sounding as if one of her girls had skinned her knee and she was trying to head off the tears.

Five minutes later, Gulliver and Jardine turned up while she was still working her way through it.

'*Jesus!* Did somebody's dog die?' Jardine said, walking into the almost chewable atmosphere in the room. 'A bit of good news is what you two need.'

Angel came alert, worked some enthusiasm he didn't feel into his response.

'What have you got, Lisa?'

They listened without interrupting while Jardine took them through the conversations with the staff at The Cowherds pub. The mood in the room improved progressively as Jardine's account corroborated the line of thinking they'd been developing. But it was the waitress' observations about how Lois Sheppard's companion had dressed that prompted what Kincade said after Jardine had finished.

'Fancy car, expensive clothes. Sounds like Lois Sheppard was out with somebody she didn't normally socialise with. You've gotta ask yourself why.' She waved the call log at Gulliver and

Jardine. 'We'll ask her companion when we interview her. We've got her number.'

Jardine was already halfway to the door, natural competitiveness spurring her on.

'We'll have her registration from the ANPR footage and a name from the PNC before you get anything from the service provider.'

Kincade hooked her thumb somewhat insubordinately at Angel in acceptance of the challenge.

'Beers are on him if you do.'

'Why me?' Angel complained when Gulliver and Jardine had left the room like they'd been sucked out by a giant vacuum cleaner.

'Because you're the one who's so desperate to not go home, that's why.'

He didn't waste his breath arguing, knowing it wouldn't be long before he owed Gulliver and Jardine a beer. Despite the letters *N* and *P* in its name, the ANPR system records more than number plates. Searches by vehicle make and colour are also possible. With a distance of under two miles down a straight road in a ten-minute time frame, it wasn't going to take long to identify the car.

Nor did it.

Gulliver and Jardine were back in under an hour, almost tumbling into the room as they tripped over one another.

'*Got her!*' Jardine announced, as if the woman was already in custody. 'Ingrid Fischer. She lives in a penthouse apartment in South Western House.'

The up-market address confirmed what had already been said about Ingrid Fischer. South Western House had started life as Southampton's most prestigious hotel, famous for housing the Titanic's passengers before they embarked on their ill-fated voyage.

'Beers are on you, sir,' Gulliver reminded Angel, in case he'd forgotten about the wager.

He held up his hands in defeat, not that the outcome had ever been in doubt. Besides, it wasn't the price of a few rounds in the pub that was troubling him. If that's all each major step forward in an investigation cost him, he'd be a happy man.

As Gulliver and Jardine had said when they came away from The Cowherds—it had been too easy.

Too easy by half.

INGRID FISCHER STOOD AT THE BEDROOM WINDOW LOOKING DOWN on her car parked at the kerb. She *loved* that car. The rich burgundy-red of the roof contrasting with the gleaming white of the paintwork gave it a certain cachet. Not the brash, in-your-face look that screamed *I've got more money than you have*, but classy and elegant in an understated way.

That didn't change the fact that if she could turn back the clock, she wouldn't have driven it when she met Lois Sheppard. It had been stupid. But Lois had been so excited to be seen climbing out of it, she'd have become wary if Ingrid had turned up in anything else.

Ingrid was no more vain than the next person, but she couldn't deny she enjoyed the way heads turned when she got out of it herself, unfolding one long leg, then the other. Now, the wrong heads would turn. Heads with pointy police helmets on them, if they still wore them these days.

Behind her in the bed he would never leave, Patrick Quinn shifted position and moaned softly in his sleep.

Ingrid left the window to sit beside him, took his hand in hers and tried to ignore the shudder that went through her. A spike of anger pierced her as she caught sight of the crucifix on the wall above the bed, the carved figure on it accusing her with his gaze. She wanted to rip it off the wall, flush it down the toilet.

Damn you and your stupid religion. You think God will forgive you because you say sorry at the last minute? Do you really think it's that easy?

She turned her head away, refused to look at it, lest it cast its evil spell over her, too.

She looked at Patrick, instead. He was at peace—relatively speaking. His breathing shallow although sometimes difficult, skin cold and clammy to the touch. He'd gone downhill so fast in the last few days. As if he was able to let go now, allow nature to run its course. Was that what unburdening yourself did for you?

She closed her eyes, but all that did was bring the memory of the argument back. She could still feel the chill in her stomach as he looked up at her, eyes clearer than she'd seen them in a long while, a smile on his lips as he damned them all.

I told Lois what we did.

And her response. Words to be ashamed of.

It's alright for you. You'll be dead in a week. What about us?

Not her finest hour.

Except that hadn't been the end or the worst of it, Patrick's words flowing out of him as if they carried every evil thing inside him away with them.

I asked Lois to find Amos. Tell him I'm sorry.

Ingrid shook the unsettling memories away, pulled out her phone. Then startled as the door opened and the replacement nurse, Sheila, walked in.

The woman glared at her with undisguised hostility, as if the phone in Ingrid's hand was actually a pillow she planned to smother Patrick with—*or was that nothing more than her own guilt?*

'How is he?' Sheila said, her voice not betraying any emotions Ingrid might have imagined.

Ingrid controlled the urge to snap at the woman, *how the hell am I supposed to know*, found an easier answer in the truth.

'He's been asleep the whole time I've been here.'

'That's good. He's been very agitated recently.'

Here we go again, Ingrid thought and kept the sentiment off her face. *Will it never end?*

'Really?'

'I'm afraid so. Crying out. Becoming really distressed.'

'Isn't that normal? I'd be distressed if I knew I only had days left.'

'Only if you're not prepared to go.' Looking up at the crucifix as she said it.

Not another one, Ingrid thought, as Sheila came to stand beside her looking down on Quinn.

'Have you known him long?'

Ingrid studied the shadow of a man lying on his death bed, searching for any sign of the Patrick Quinn who lived in her memory.

'Most of my life. We grew up together.'

'But you're not family?'

'Not in the blood sense, no.'

Sheila was quiet a moment, and Ingrid hoped she was about to leave, allow her to make the call she wanted to make. Except Sheila wasn't ready to go just yet.

'He hasn't had an easy life, has he?'

Ingrid almost laughed out loud at the understatement.

'No, he hasn't.'

Which of us have?

'Can I ask you something?'

This time, Ingrid did laugh out loud. A faint flush climbed up Sheila's neck as she realised the stupidity of the question.

'Sorry, I've already asked lots of questions. I shouldn't be so nosy.'

'Don't worry about it. Go ahead and ask.'

'Do you know someone called Amos?'

Ingrid's breath caught in her chest. She dropped her eyes as if thinking, chiding herself to do exactly that before opening her mouth in future.

'I think he was a friend of Patrick's a long time ago. Why?'

'He keeps asking him to forgive him.'

Ingrid shook her head as if it was as much a mystery to her as it was to the nosy interfering Lois substitute.

'You know he spent time in prison? It might have been something to do with that. He never talked about it much.'

Sheila smiled and nodded along like it made sense. But Ingrid knew she didn't believe a word of it as she left the room.

Ingrid went back to her phone as soon as the door was shut behind her, hit speed dial #1.

'Where are you?' the only voice she'd known longer than Quinn's asked.

'With Patrick.'

'I thought you might be. How is he?'

'Still hanging on in there. You should see him one last time before it's too late.'

'You know I can't do that. It's too upsetting for me.'

'You'll regret it when it's too late.'

She knew what he'd say, even before the words were out, echoing her own thoughts as she watched Quinn asleep in his bed.

'Add it to the list.'

14

Amos Church was dozing on the sofa when the front door opened. Instantly awake, he came off it faster than he'd moved in more years than he cared to remember, the once-familiar rush of adrenaline coursing through his veins. Head snapping from side to side, looking for a weapon as his mind tried to assimilate the unfamiliar surroundings, the threat of sudden danger the unexpected intruder represented.

'Jesus, you're jumpy,' Jesse Hamilton said, coming into the living room. 'Lucky I didn't catch you in the kitchen, or I'd have a carving knife buried in my guts.'

Amos dropped back onto the sofa feeling old and stupid.

'Only if I remembered which end to hold. And if I had the strength to use it.'

Jesse batted the comment away.

'Don't be so hard on yourself.' He dropped a folded newspaper onto the coffee table in front of Amos, loosened his tie and undid his top shirt button before lowering himself into the armchair opposite. He sat perched on the edge, gym-toned and tattooed forearms resting on his thighs, his eyes on the paper between them as if they were engrossed in the final moves of a tense game of chess. 'Look at that.'

All Amos knew was that he didn't want to, his pulse still racing, and not from being startled by Jesse. The headline jumped off the page at him when he forced himself to look.

Nurse brutally murdered in Southampton Old Cemetery.

He skimmed the article without picking the paper up, as if worried that by touching it he would be more deeply implicated. Like a twisted version of musical chairs—the man left holding the newspaper when the music stops gets convicted of the crime. He felt sick when he saw the name *Lois Sheppard*. Threw himself backwards on the sofa, head on the cushion top, staring up at the ceiling.

Jesse was well aware of Amos' background.

Like Amos, he'd spent time in the Army. Like Amos, he hadn't known what to do with his life when he came out, unable to function in society without the discipline and regimented predictability of military life. *Unlike* Amos, he hadn't embraced the oblivion found in alcohol. Instead, he'd made his way to the charity for ex-servicemen where Amos worked. With Amos' help, he'd landed a job as a chauffeur-cum-bodyguard for a rich man with an over-inflated opinion of his own importance. As Jesse liked to say, he was in the business of massaging egos. And being an ex-Para massaged needy egos far better than a cook from the Logistics Corps.

There'd been an instant bond between them, Amos having also served with the Parachute Regiment. They'd become friends. Over the course of that friendship, Amos had confided in Jesse to the point where they were bound to one another as strongly as any camaraderie forged in the hardship of combat. And, as in the Army, there were rules set in stone that never needed to be spoken. Assistance would always be provided. Questions would never be asked.

'It's the same cemetery,' Jesse said.

Amos worked himself upright again, looking as if all that remained for him to do was to push over his king to admit defeat in the game of chess they'd been playing—one that felt like a metaphor for life itself.

'I know. There was a cop on the gate. I saw all the excitement going on through the trees.'

He didn't say that he would put everything he owned—admittedly not much—on it being not only the same cemetery, but the same grave.

'That's why you called me?'

'Yeah. I didn't go into work. And I didn't want to go home.'

Jesse shook his head at his friend's obvious distress.

'You really don't trust them, do you?' He held up his hands before Amos could reply. 'I'm not blaming you. It's understandable.'

What it is, is worse, Amos thought, *not understandable*.

Jesse pushed himself to his feet as if it was his own past coming back to bite, headed towards the kitchen.

'I need a beer.'

Amos trailed after him bringing the newspaper with him, leaned against the counter as Jesse went to the fridge. Jesse opened the door, caught himself and closed it again.

'*Shit*. I forgot.'

'Have a beer for Christ's sake.'

'No. Let's have a cup of tea instead.'

'Have a bloody beer.'

'No. I really fancy a nice cup of tea. Honest.'

Amos went to the fridge, opened the door.

'If you don't have one, I'm going to. Then you really will be responsible for me falling off the wagon. You think I can't watch somebody have a drink without snatching it out of their hands?' He took a can of Brewdog Punk IPA off the shelf as if he was proving he could even touch one without throwing away sixteen years' sobriety, handed it to Jesse. 'You open it. That's a step too far.'

Jesse grinned with him as he took the can.

'I'll make you a cup of tea, anyway, if you like.'

Amos gave him a pained look.

'Do I look like a man who wants a cup of tea?'

'No, you look like a man who wants a beer.'

'Exactly. So drink yours and stop bloody talking about it.'

Jesse took a long swallow. By the time his Adam's apple had stopped bobbing, the light-hearted mood was a thing of the past.

'I know you, Amos. There's something else.'

Amos sighed unhappily, ran his hand through his hair.

'She called me.'

'Who?'

'The woman who was murdered. Lois Sheppard.'

The words didn't register immediately. If Jesse had taken another mouthful of beer, Amos would've been wearing it a split-second later.

'*You're shittin' me!*'

'I wish. She called a couple of days before she was killed. Said she wanted to meet.'

'What for?'

'She was very vague. Said she wanted to discuss a personal matter.' Making quotes in the air as he said it. 'Like she thought I'd refuse if she came out and said it.'

They both knew it could only be one thing.

Jesse pulled out a chair, sat down at the table. He pushed the beer can away, his thirst deserting him as he said the name that had blighted Amos' life.

'Eric Impey?'

'What else can it be?'

'Did you meet her?'

'No. We'd arranged to meet on the day after she was killed. I hadn't decided if I'd go.'

Amos had drifted towards the sink as they talked. He filled a glass with water from the tap, drank it down and placed the glass upside-down on the draining board. He guessed that even if he'd given in and thrown away sixteen years, the beer, or even a glass of whisky, would've tasted no different than the water had. He felt the weight of the crushing inevitability of it all, history repeating itself—except this time he didn't even have himself and alcohol to blame, just fate's maliciousness, pure and simple.

'Things are different these days,' Jesse said, trying and failing to sound as if he believed it. 'Tell them the truth. What you've just told me.'

Amos shook his head, a soft smile on his lips at his friend's attempt to play down the impending shitstorm.

'It gets worse. She called me on the night she was killed. I let it go to voicemail, so I don't know what she wanted. I'm one of the last people she contacted, if not the very last one.' He threw his hands in the air, an edge of panic entering his usually-calm voice. 'I haven't got an alibi. I was at home watching TV. How do I prove we didn't agree to meet the first time she contacted me, then she called me on the night, said, *I'm here*. Then I went out and murdered her because I'm a crazy sick fuck who already did eighteen years for murder to get the price of a bottle of whisky.'

'You can say you were here with me.'

Amos laid a hand on his friend's shoulder, squeezed, the physical contact expressing his thanks better than words ever could.

'I don't want to drag you into it.'
'I'm already harbouring a fugitive.'
'*See!* You're doing it. I'm already a fugitive.'
'I'm only trying to help.'

An uncomfortable silence stretched out. Jesse leaned across the table to retrieve his beer, took a noisy slurp. When Amos still didn't say anything, he picked up the paper, read the article again.

'She was a palliative care nurse,' he said in an attempt to kickstart the conversation.

It did, but not in the way he was hoping.

'Great. I murdered a woman who looks after dying people. I must be some special kind of monster.'

Jesse shook his head in despair, went back to the article.

'What's so funny?' Amos said when Jesse coughed out a laugh a moment later.

'The cop in charge that you're meant to ring is called Angel.'

'So? You think that's funny because she was killed in a graveyard?'

Jesse ignored Amos' continued determination to be bad tempered, explained.

'There was a WO1 in the regiment called Angel.'

'I don't remember.'

'He probably wasn't a warrant officer when you were in. Anyway, he went to prison for murdering a squaddie who called his son a pussy after he topped himself in Iraq, or something like that.'

The unusual circumstances pushed aside some of Amos' melancholic bad temper, a spark of interest taking its place.

'You think they're related?'

'Could be. Why? Would you talk to him if they are?'

Amos gave it a moment's thought, shook his head.

'Probably not.'

Jesse left him to himself after that. But he'd have a word with some of the guys from the regiment. See if any of them knew any more about the Angels. It was the least he could do for Amos, miserable grumpy old bastard at the moment, or not.

15

ANGEL WAS UP AT THE BAR OF THE WELLINGTON ARMS, THE nearest pub to Southampton Central police station, buying a second round of drinks for Gulliver and Jardine, when Kincade slipped away unnoticed. He'd pointed at her almost-empty glass with a question on his face as he got up from their table, but she'd shaken her head and turned an imaginary steering wheel in her hands, mouthed, *I've got a long drive, remember?* at him.

In the morning he'd want to know why she snuck away. Except by then he'd already know.

She drove more slowly than normal. Not so much a subconscious command from brain to right foot delaying what she'd decided to do, as needing to get the timing spot on. She wanted Angel's father to already be in the pub by the time she got back. Give her some time alone in the house she was already thinking of as home.

And she had a lot on her mind. Everybody knows serious thinking, a heavy right foot and country roads do not play well together.

Angel's revelation about Inspector Virgil Balan's surprise call had rocked her back on her heels. It had also been an unwelcome reminder that she was as human as everybody else, with all the same failings. After the initial surprise, the implications for herself had overshadowed what Angel might decide to do.

It wasn't that she didn't want to see him reconciled with Stuart Beckford. Just not at the expense of her job. She had no doubt Angel would now make contact. They'd patch things up. And who knows, DS Beckford's stress might fade away as a result, leaving him fit and raring to go, eager to get back into his old job. Where did that leave her? Maybe she deserved to be kicked out of Carl Angel's house, selfish bitch that she was.

She saw him as she drove down the street. Striding out purposefully ahead of her towards the pub, his back ramrod straight, head up. The familiar refrain ran through her head, made her smile.

Quick march, left, right, left, right...

No sign of the gait or balance problems associated with Huntington's disease, that was for sure. The thought immediately made her think of Grace, the one to first suggest her and Angel's father might be suffering from the insidious disease.

She'd never met Grace, but she might soon have good cause to hate her. She wasn't so stupid that she didn't know why Grace had called her brother at work. The fact that he'd driven off rather than come back into their office and face her only proved it.

That morning, she'd set the alarm early and left the house before Carl was up. She'd driven aimlessly, crossed the River Avon via the bridge in the middle of the village, made a left down a single-track lane with no name. After half a mile, she parked in the entrance to a field and made her way across it to the river. There, she'd sat at the water's edge watching the water swirl and eddy, bulrushes swaying in the breeze and insects dimpling the surface of the water, the silence interrupted only by the occasional slurp as a hungry dace or chub gulped down a quick meal.

It had been a pleasant and restful way to pass an hour, but it hadn't been necessary. In her heart, she'd known there was no decision to make. She had to get out ahead of it. The way Angel hadn't even asked her where she'd been proved he'd guessed what was coming.

Now, she went directly up to her room. The care Carl Angel had taken in preparing it for her could still bring a lump to her throat if it caught her in an unguarded moment.

She looked around, took it all in, as if it was already decided that tonight would be the last time she saw it. The blue and white striped duvet cover on the white-painted brass bed; the distressed chest of drawers and matching wardrobe she now knew were a deliberate attempt at shabby chic, rather than because he'd bought them from a junk shop; the thick Oriental rug he'd brought back from Iraq on the stripped and polished pine floor; and the battered leather armchair in the corner, her current destination.

She dropped into it and pulled out her phone to call her girls. Listening to their excited chatter as they told her about their days would calm her—admittedly at the cost of making her wonder if they'd ever get a chance to visit, whether the bunk beds Carl had bought specifically would ever be slept in.

At least that was the plan.

She should've known better. Fate never sleeps, never misses an opportunity to stick its finger in your eye. And this evening, its weapon of choice to slice little pieces off her sanity was her youngest, Daisy.

'When can we come to stay?' Daisy demanded without even saying, *hello*.

'Soon.'

Two sentences in, and already a whiny edge had made inroads into Daisy's voice.

'You *always* say that. Daddy says you never tell the truth.'

Kincade closed her eyes. Pictured a tender part of her estranged husband's anatomy pinned to a workbench, herself with one of Isabel Durand's sharpest scalpels in her hand...

She was still trying to think how to respond to Daisy's accusation, when her daughter made things worse.

'I want to meet Angel's dad.'

Kincade groaned, slumped deeper into the chair.

'He wants to meet you, too, Daisy.'

'Isla says he's a general.'

At least that put a smile on her face.

'I'll be having a word with your sister about telling lies, don't you worry.'

A sudden serious note entered her daughter's voice.

'Will she have to go to confession?'

'Very probably.'

Daisy brightened immediately.

'Can I go, too?'

Kincade was relieved Angel wasn't privy to the conversation. He would've told Daisy that it was necessary to commit a sin first, adding that it needed to be a serious one, her daughter enthusiastically taking up the challenge.

They spent a while longer chatting before Daisy handed over to Isla who denied all knowledge of promoting Carl Angel, but mercifully said nothing in the following five minutes to increase her mother's angst and sense of impending doom.

Kincade finished the call feeling like a prisoner on death row who'd just eaten her last meal. She left the house as soon as she'd freshened up, no detour via the fridge, her appetite having deserted her. Following in Carl's footsteps, the same *quick march, left, right, left, right* refrain played in her head as it always did.

And always would when she walked to a country pub—whether tonight was the last night she stayed in Carl's house or not.

He was sitting holding court at the big table in the window as he usually did, a couple of his similarly-aged drinking buddies hanging on his every word. An even-older—in dog years—border collie was asleep under the table.

'You've been promoted,' she said when he looked up and smiled at her.

'Really? To what? And by whom?'

'According to Daisy, you're now General Angel.'

'Is that so?' He drained the last inch of beer in his glass, sucked the foam out of his moustache and started to slide along the bench in order to get out from behind the table. 'That calls for a celebration. What are you drinking?'

'No, I'll get them. It was my daughter who promoted you, after all.'

She took his empty glass from him and those of the other two old boys who'd quickly downed theirs at the mention of a celebration, went to the bar. Telling herself that if Declan behind the bar said, *good to see you, Cat* or anything else to make her feel welcome and part of the local community, she'd punch him full in the face.

Lucky for him, he didn't, but Carl made up for it when she handed him his pint by raising it in a toast.

'Here's to your girls. I'm looking forward to meeting them.' He tried to work a disapproving look onto his face, failed miserably. 'I didn't buy those bunk beds for nothing.'

She felt like pulling her hair out.

Jesus Christ, will you all just stop! Don't you think it's hard enough as it is?

'Aren't you going to sit down?' Carl said. He caught his friends' eyes to make sure they were paying attention when it became obvious she wasn't. 'We don't drink that fast, do we, lads? You've got time to rest your feet before you have to go to the bar again.'

She counted silently to ten, her face impassive as a wax doll, as the three old farts howled with laughter. The dog under the table stirred at the disturbance above its head and yawned loudly, made Kincade want to run screaming from the room and never look back.

'Do you mind if we sit outside?'

Carl twisted around to look out of the window, craning his neck to look up at the sky.

'It looks as if it might rain.'

'Surely ex-warrant officers are waterproof.'

'I think it's started already,' one of the other old farts said, made Kincade want to throttle him.

Carl looked again, squinting through the glass.

'I think you're right.'

She was tempted to grab him by the ears or the moustache or whatever she could get hold of, drag him out.

Do you want me to stand on the bloody bar and shout so everyone can hear?

'There's something I need to tell you.'

All of the good cheer disappeared in the blink of an eye as he caught her tone, the choice of the word *need* rather than *want* or the even-milder *would like* alerting him.

'That sounds ominous. I feel like I'm back in uniform and you're about to tell me the Royal Artillery Johnnies shelled a nursery school or a hospital by mistake because you fed them duff information.'

If only, she thought, leading the way outside to where the ghosts of her past misdeeds waited to condemn her.

16

'You're very cheerful this morning,' Angel said.

I feel it, Kincade thought, thinking back to his father's reaction after she'd finished telling him the real reason for her demotion from inspector down to sergeant. It was an exchange that would stick in her mind for years to come, like a scene from a favourite movie.

Green doesn't suit you.

What?

That's the colour your face has turned. Either you ate something out of date you found in the fridge, or you thought I was going to throw you out on your ear.

It crossed my mind.

He'd sat up straight on the bench outside the pub as a gentle rain they barely noticed settled on them, barked an order that was more appropriate for the parade ground.

All the people who've never made a mistake in their life they bitterly regret stand up now.

Head pivoting from side to side like a meercat on the lookout for predators.

See anyone on their feet, Cat?

And that had been it, her limbs suddenly weak as the adrenaline flooded out of her, a hot pricking at the backs of her eyes.

Almost.

He'd taken a larger-than-normal mouthful of beer, then put his hand on her arm—the first physical contact between them apart from shaking hands when they first met.

I can't guarantee Max will be so understanding. I'm not sure he ever believed all that forgiveness crap he used to peddle.

His final remark had stayed with her long into the night as she lay awake in the bed she'd be sleeping in for a while to come yet. All she had to show for it by the time she finally fell asleep was confirmation that she didn't know Angel at all. She was getting a good feel for him workwise, but as far as personal issues were concerned, he was a mystery—one that deepened with every piece of his history he did reveal.

She would need to pick her moment carefully for when she told him what she'd told his father. Her secret was safe with Carl, of that she had no doubt. And even if she wasn't sure when the right time might be, it certainly wasn't now—in the car on the way to interview Lois Sheppard's close friend, Moira Woodward, whose details Lois' mother had supplied.

'Last I heard, being cheerful wasn't a crime.' She looked out of the window at the faces of people on the street going about their daily lives. 'If it was, it wouldn't take up much of our time from the look of it.'

He smiled with her. Kept his eyes on the road so that she couldn't see how far it extended. Didn't push her. That in itself, coupled with him not saying a word about the way she'd slipped away from the pub without saying goodbye, told her he was well aware of what was going on.

She might not understand him, but he didn't have a problem reading her.

Ten minutes later, she couldn't help smiling to herself when Moira Woodward opened the door to them.

There's no chance of you getting arrested for being cheerful, she thought, following Moira through the house and out onto a small patio at the back.

'Do you mind if we sit out here?' Moira said.

A quick glance into the sitting room as they walked through the house had been sufficient to tell Angel what was wrong.

'No problem.'

Moira immediately confirmed his suspicions.

'I've got one of Lois' paintings on the wall in the living room. Every time I see it, it reminds me of her. My husband never liked it, but I felt obliged to put it up. Now, I'd feel guilty if I took it down. Like the first thing I thought when I heard she was dead was, *thank God, I can take it down and stop Steve complaining.*'

Not for the first time, Angel was struck by the strange and different ways sudden death and grief affect people, the random things they choose to say. He lowered himself into one of the uncomfortable-looking cast iron chairs, the metal cold through the thin fabric of his suit trousers.

'Have you known Lois long?'

'Since school. Then we went into nursing together. I packed it in when my son was born and never went back. But we've always been like the sisters we never had.'

It was a cruel twist of fate that the closer the interviewee was to the victim, the greater their pain and sense of loss, the better it was for them. They could almost gauge the chance of getting something useful from an interview by the length of the face of the person opening the door or the redness of their eyes.

'Do you know her other friends?'

'Most of them.'

'What about Ingrid Fischer?'

Moira made a show of thinking about it, her brow furrowing,

worried that an immediate negative response would be indicative of not taking her friend's death seriously enough.

'I don't think so.'

'She drives a white convertible Mercedes with a red roof,' Kincade prompted.

Moira shook her head.

'That doesn't sound like anyone Lois knows. Why are you asking about her?'

The horror creeping across Moira's face told them what she'd really wanted to say, but didn't dare.

Is that who killed her?

'Lois went to The Cowherds pub with her on the evening she was killed,' Angel said. 'We were hoping you might know why.'

'I just told you, I've never heard of the woman.'

Angel ignored the defensive note in Moira's voice—as if they were accusing her of deliberately making their jobs harder—and re-phrased the question.

'Did she tell you she was meeting anyone at all?'

An immediate change came over Moira. The mild indignation gave way to the dismay of earlier, aimed squarely at herself this time—had she held the key to Lois' murder and could've prevented it if she'd acted sooner?

'She told me she was meeting someone, but not on the night she was killed. She wasn't meant to be meeting him until the following day.'

Angel and Kincade shared a look.

It was possible the last call Lois ever made, the one she'd made over an hour after Ingrid Fischer picked her up, had been to bring forward a meeting scheduled for the following day. In effect bringing her death forward by one day.

'It was definitely a man, was it?' Kincade said.

'Definitely.'

'Do you know his name?'

Moira drew in a deep breath, as if to increase the oxygen flow to her brain, her face compacting.

'She told me, but I can't remember.'

Angel watched her as she raced headlong down the road to the land where the *if-onlys* live. A land where rational thought is unheard of and a person can happily crucify themselves for their failure to achieve the impossible or see into the future. Everybody goes there at some point in their lives. He was a regular enough visitor himself to show people around. Cormac's last words to him—*I don't know what to do, Max*—were like a fanfare from hell welcoming him home every time he returned.

'It was an unusual name,' Moira said, more to herself than them, staring intently at Angel. 'It was a bit like yours. Not Angel, but something like it.'

Lucifer? Kincade thought, and suggested something more constructive.

'Priest?'

'No, that wasn't it.'

'Stop trying too hard to remember and it might come to you. Can we step backwards—'

'*Church!* That was it. Amos Church.'

The name meant nothing to them. It was the sort of name that would stick in the mind, had they encountered it before. They both worked up a smile to match Moira's, before Kincade carried on.

'That's extremely helpful. If we could step backwards now, identify why she arranged to meet him. We talked to Jason Maddox. He told us he broke up with Lois—'

'I never liked him.'

The depth of feeling in Moira's voice stopped Kincade dead, made her change tack.

'Why not?'

'He's one of those men who look at you like they're

imagining you without your clothes on. Lois only saw him a couple of times a week. I think he was seeing other women as well.'

Like being cheerful, it's not a crime, Kincade thought, flicking the bullshit and spiteful gossip detector into overdrive as she studied Moira.

'That's something we might re-visit. Mr Maddox told us they broke up because Lois became obsessed with her latest patient. Do you know anything about that?' She stopped Moira before she had a chance to reply as another question occurred to her. 'Did Lois give you any papers or documents to hold onto for her?'

'No, nothing like that. Will you excuse me a sec. I need to go to the loo.'

Angel was out of his chair almost before Moira was, like a perfect gentleman who always rises when a lady leaves the room. The way he massaged his rump suggested otherwise, scowling at the chair.

'I've never sat in such an uncomfortable bloody chair. I nearly asked her for a cup of tea just to give me an excuse to stand up. It's a pity her friend Lois didn't make seat cushions instead of paint.'

'You shouldn't have such a bony arse. Sir.'

'I didn't realise you paid so much attention to it.' He pulled out his mobile to move them on, pecked out a text. 'I'll get Gulliver to run the name *Amos Church* through the PNC, see if anything pops out.'

'A dodgy priest?'

He stopped tapping away, gave her a look.

'I'm not sure if that's a very bad joke, or a dig at me. Suggesting I'm a dodgy priest.'

'*Never!*' Then, after a deliberate pause, 'You'd be a dodgy *ex*-priest. Sir.'

Moira came back out of the house before he could respond. He took his uncomfortable seat again, the short, unprofessional exchange having served to confirm his earlier observation. Kincade was in an unusually cheerful mood.

'Going back to Lois being obsessed with her patient,' he said. 'Did she say anything to you about that?'

Moira's face fell, the satisfaction at being able to provide useful information outweighed by the dismay that she really did have information that might have made the difference between life and death.

'His name's Patrick Quinn. Lois told me he confessed to her about killing someone years ago . . .' Her hand flew to her mouth, connections that didn't exist when Lois confided in her becoming all too clear. 'It was in the same cemetery where Lois was killed.'

Angel sat forward in his chair, as much to ease the pressure on his bony backside as to demonstrate his interest.

'Did she go there as a result of what Mr Quinn said?'

'Not specifically. He was very confused. Drugged up to the eyeballs and drifting in and out of consciousness.' She dropped her eyes momentarily as if what she was about to say had been her idea. 'Lois even thought about reducing his medication in the hope that he became more lucid. She didn't, of course. So, it was all very vague. Sometimes he said *I* killed somebody, other times it was *we*. And he chopped and changed between saying he buried the body and just left it lying there in the cemetery.'

'Did he say who he allegedly killed?'

'No. That's why Lois became so obsessed. He teased her with a few details which only made her more interested in what he wasn't saying. She wanted to join the police before she became a nurse. Maybe it was the inner cop in her coming out.'

Angel smiled with her as if it was a phenomenon they encountered all the time, moved swiftly on.

'Did she think about telling anybody? Her boss? Us?'

Moira gave him a look. It suggested Lois could have found plenty of better ways to waste her time.

'She wouldn't have told her boss. Not unless she wanted a patronising lecture on the side effects of the drugs Quinn was on. And would you have believed her?'

'If it was the unsubstantiated ramblings of a man pumped full of drugs, perhaps not,' he admitted.

'There, you've just said it. *Unsubstantiated* ramblings. It's obvious she was trying to get some facts so people didn't think she was as delusional as Patrick Quinn.'

'Did she tell anyone else about this?'

'Not as far as I know.'

And that's the crux of it, Angel thought. *As far as you know.* Because he was convinced she'd told someone. And that's what got her killed.

'How did Amos Church fit into what Quinn was saying about killing someone?'

Moira dropped her eyes, clearly embarrassed to repeat what her friend had confided in her.

'It sounds so melodramatic, but Quinn kept asking Amos to forgive him.'

17

PATRICK QUINN LIVED—AND WAS DYING—IN A VICTORIAN SEMI-detached house close to the city centre. An ageing Ford Mondeo with a flat nearside front tyre and a giant dollop of crusted-on seagull shit on the windscreen was parked in the drive, a Nissan Micra at the kerb immediately outside the house.

Arrangements had been made for Angel and Kincade to interview Lois' replacement, Sheila Doherty, at the house. Quinn spent most of the time asleep, allowing her plenty of free time in the house, the location less formal and intimidating than an interview room.

That didn't stop Sheila from looking as if she'd been kept stewing in a holding cell for three hours when she opened the door. Either that, or she'd mistaken their knock for the Grim Reaper.

Angel was convinced she mentally added *of death* to his name when he introduced himself.

He didn't normally inspire nervousness in witnesses. They seemed to identify the ex-priest in him and view him as an avuncular figure. The unease he saw in Sheila was not down to him. He suspected she was about to lie—whether to get the interview over as quickly as possible by giving uniformly negative answers or for an ulterior motive was unclear. He decided to let Kincade off the leash. She often clashed with female interviewees for reasons he couldn't identify. That antagonism was needed to shake something loose today.

Sheila led them into an overly-warm but cheerless sitting room that looked as if it had last seen a lick of paint in the 1970s. It and the furniture in it felt tired and worn out and on its last legs. As if the cancer killing its owner in his bed above their heads had spread to the fabric of the house itself. Already Angel couldn't wait to get out.

He nodded to Kincade, *over to you*. She cut straight to the chase.

'We understand Mr Quinn said some strange things to Lois.'

'Like what?'

'That he murdered somebody.'

Sheila pursed her lips. It wasn't the reaction either of them expected.

'I don't want to speak ill of the dead, but I'm very disappointed in Lois. Telling whoever you've spoken to about the ramblings of a dying man, and then that person telling you. It's like Chinese whispers. It sounds to me like you're taking it seriously, too.'

'We have to, Mrs Doherty. Has he said anything like that to you?'

'Of course not.' Sounding as if Kincade had asked whether Quinn put his hand up her skirt.

Kincade was right on it.

'Why *of course* not? If he told Lois, why shouldn't he tell you?'

The faultless logic of the question threw Sheila momentarily. She used both hands to smooth away imaginary creases in the skirt Patrick Quinn hadn't put his hand up.

'Let me re-phrase that. No, he hasn't said anything about

killing somebody to me. I have to say, you see detectives twisting people's words on TV, but I never dreamed it was true.'

'I'm sorry if that's how it feels,' Kincade said, sounding about as sorry as a mosquito feels for sucking your blood. 'Let me rephrase it. Has he said anything unusual?'

'All patients say unusual things when they're full of morphine. He thinks I'm Lois. It's very unsettling.'

But not as unsettling as our questions, Angel thought, and kept silent while Kincade maintained the pressure.

'Give me an example of what he says to you when he thinks you're Lois.'

You're going to rub a hole in your skirt pretty soon, Angel thought, as Sheila grew ever-more flustered.

'My mind's a blank.'

Kincade paused as if thinking of a random suggestion to pull out of the air.

'Has he ever asked somebody called Amos to forgive him?'

Sheila hesitated. It was fast but not fast enough.

'I don't think so.'

'Has someone asked you not to tell us, Mrs Doherty?'

'Of course not.' She gave Kincade a tight smile. 'I suppose you're going to pick me up for saying that again.'

Kincade pulled her head back, held up her hands.

'Not at all. That would be an extremely serious matter. Any sensible, intelligent, law-abiding citizen would be affronted by the suggestion that they'd lied to the police in a murder investigation.'

They both stared hard at her. Sheila dropped her eyes. Kincade addressed her next question to the top of Sheila's head.

'Does he mention the name Ingrid Fischer?'

Sheila's head came up, suspicion in her eyes that it was a trick question.

'Of course.'

The immediate response, spoken with the same conviction she'd used to say the opposite, caught them both out.

'Why of course?' Kincade said.

Sheila's expression was easy to read—*I can't win*.

'Because she visits most days.' She saw the confusion that had shifted onto their faces. 'I don't understand. Ingrid Fischer is the closest thing Patrick has got to family. I thought that's why you asked about her.'

Kincade shook her head.

'No.' Trying to make that one, small word sound like, *of course we knew*. 'The reason I asked is because Lois went out for a meal with her on the night she was killed.'

The suspicion returned to Sheila's face, as if they were back to twisting her words.

'What for?'

'I was about to ask you that. Did Lois get particularly friendly with Ingrid?'

'I doubt it.'

'That sounds very definite.'

'Obviously, if you're spending a lot of time in a patient's house you get to know the family, if there is any. But not someone like Ingrid. She's a very cold fish.'

The observation was consistent with the remark made by the waitress at The Cowherds. The suggestion that it felt like a person being taken out by their boss now made sense.

'Could Ingrid have taken her out to say thank you for what she was doing for Patrick?'

'It's possible.' Sheila leaned forward, lowered her voice. 'Without being too mercenary, we'd prefer cash or a bottle of wine. You've got nothing in common apart from the dying patient. It's not much fun for either of you to go out and talk about that all evening. If someone asked me, I'd make excuses.

And with Ingrid Fischer, it would feel like a punishment, not a reward.'

'Do you know anything about her?' Kincade asked.

'Not really. I've only had one proper conversation with her.'

'What did you talk about?'

'She told me they've known each other all their lives, but they're not family. She talked about Patrick mainly, not herself.'

'What about him?'

'That he'd spent time in prison, but she didn't say what for. He's got a history of drug and alcohol abuse. Maybe it was to do with that. You should be able to check.'

Kincade managed to keep a straight face as she thanked Sheila for the advice.

'We'll do that, Mrs Doherty. As soon as we get back.'

Sheila relaxed visibly at Kincade's enthusiastic acceptance of her suggestion, her guard slipping.

'And when I asked her about Amos, she said he was somebody Patrick knew in prison, but I didn't believe...'

She trailed off as she realised what she'd said, her hand going to her mouth.

Kincade made sure all of the previous antagonistic edge had gone from her voice.

'You *have* heard of Amos?'

Sheila nodded unhappily, embarrassment and shame stealing her voice.

'Was Mr Quinn asking for forgiveness?' Kincade prompted.

Another nod.

'Did somebody ask you not to mention it?'

And another.

'Ingrid Fischer?'

This time, Sheila shook her head, the change taking a moment to register.

'No?' Kincade said.

'No. It was my supervisor. She said she didn't want any scandal. Apparently, the company is in trouble financially. If Lois' death is connected to things Patrick said, it wouldn't look good.'

Deliberately withholding evidence in a murder investigation to save your own financial skin doesn't look great either, Angel thought, but chose not to increase Sheila's distress.

Instead, he leveraged his avuncular *you can trust me* persona, worked a reassuring note into his voice as if writing off a parishioner's sins in the confessional.

'We understand why you tried to keep out of this, Sheila. And we're prepared to overlook it. But you must be completely honest with us from now on.'

Sheila nodded like they wouldn't be able to torture a lie out of her.

'Why did you say you didn't believe her about Amos being someone Mr Quinn knew in prison? Has Mr Quinn said anything to make you think that?'

Sheila scrunched her face, clearly unhappy struggling to find a way to put her misgivings into a coherent form.

'It's just a feeling. She didn't let it show, but she was annoyed I asked her. If it had been something to do with when Patrick was in prison, that would all be in the past. Water under the bridge. This feels like it's a problem now. Something that's going to cause trouble in the future.'

'When Mr Quinn is dead and gone.'

'Exactly. When I went into his room yesterday, she was there. I hope nobody ever looks at me the way she was looking at him. Like she wanted to smother him with a pillow.'

Before he goes and says something else,' Angel thought, getting to his feet to bring the interview to a close.

. . .

'Why don't you ask me?' Kincade said, once they were back in the car, a slightly aggrieved edge to her voice.

'Ask you what?'

'What I think. If we interview a witness and come away feeling like we're going backwards, the first thing you do is ask me what I think. Now, when it's blindingly obvious, you don't bother.'

'Maybe because it's so obvious.'

'Do you want to know what I think or not?'

'I get the feeling you're going to tell me anyway.'

She gave a firm nod, *you got that right*.

'I think after Quinn confessed to Lois about killing somebody, he told Ingrid what he'd done. She wasn't sure if he was telling the truth or it was the medication talking, so she took Lois out to find out what she knows. On the face of it, to say thank you. It's easy enough. She says, Patrick just told me something really weird. Has he said anything to you? If Lois says yes . . .' She yanked her hands violently apart as if tightening a ligature around somebody's neck.

He rocked his head from side to side, the assessment in line with his own thinking. And with the same problem.

'Choosing to pick her up in a distinctive white Mercedes with a red roof? As if she wants to be caught.'

'Unless she's working with somebody else? Somebody else who's got a lot to lose by Quinn blabbing just before the man upstairs'—pointing an irreverent finger upwards—'puts him out of our reach forever.'

Angel had put his phone onto silent before they set off that morning to interview Moira Woodward. Given what he suspected had happened between Kincade and his father the previous evening, he didn't want to risk Grace calling him again while he was with Kincade.

He'd felt it vibrate while they were interviewing Sheila Doherty, but didn't get a chance to check it until they got back to the station. He stopped to have a quick word with Jack Bevan on the front desk while Kincade went straight up to see what Gulliver had found, if anything, by running the name Amos Church through the PNC.

Bevan waited until the lift doors had closed on Kincade before speaking.

'She seems very cheerful, Padre.'

'So would you be, Jack, if you spent all day with me.'

Bevan gave him a look that implied he'd heard some strange stories from nutters walking in off the street over the years, but Angel's remark had them beat hands down.

'Isn't vanity a sin, Padre?'

'Not one you have to worry about, Jack, that's for sure. Anyway, let me run a name past you. Amos Church.'

Bevan pretended to think about it, but the barely-suppressed grin told Angel he was too busy concentrating on what he was about to say.

'It rings a bell.'

Angel refused to laugh or even smile.

'Get it, Padre? Rings a bell. Church bells.' He waved his hand in disgust. 'Forget it.'

'You should do the same with jokes. So? Does the name mean anything?'

'How long ago?'

'Does it matter?'

'Not really.'

'I'll take that as a no, then.'

It does ring a bell followed him all the way into the ground-floor toilets.

Once there, he checked his phone, thankful for his foresight when he saw Grace's name.

'It's Inspector Ostrich,' Grace said, instead of *hello*. 'Stuck your head in any good sand recently, Max?'

It would've been so easy to go the childish route.

Been for any good blood tests lately, Sis?

As it happened, Grace carried on talking without giving him a chance to say anything at all.

'I thought I'd let you know I'm going to pop in to see Dad tonight.'

Angel did the translation from spiteful sister to English.

I'm going to tell him what my contacts found out about your detective sergeant.

'You might get to meet Cat while you're there.'

'I was calling to suggest you take her for a drink so that I don't.'

Angel was suddenly sick of all the pussy-footing around.

'I think she told Dad herself last night.'

'Yeah, right.'

'You don't have to believe me—'

'I don't. You're just trying to stop me from—'

'Telling tales?'

'—saying anything. Besides, some tales need to be told. Has she told you?'

'Not yet.'

'Always the last to know, eh, Max?'

He took a deep breath, let it out. He was no less irritated at his sister afterwards as before.

'I just want to say that you won't do yourself any favours by telling him something he already knows.'

A stunned silence came down the line at him, followed by an incredulous squeak.

'I don't believe it. *You*, trying to tell *me* how to keep in Dad's good books. Have you got delayed PTSD or something? Has your memory suddenly and conveniently erased itself? *Jesus Christ*, Max, you're something else.'

'You took the words right out of my mouth, Sis. But you go ahead and do it if you want. Just remember, you'll have to listen to me telling you, *told you so*. You know, I'm actually looking forward to it.'

He was ready to end the call, disgusted with himself at his slide into petty, snide remarks. But something in his tone had wormed its way into her subconscious, started the doubts in her mind.

'Why do you think she's already told him?'

He told her about the marked change in Kincade's mood from one day to the next, the way she'd snuck away the day before without telling him.

'It's like a load has been lifted.'

'Don't give me any of your religious bullshit, Max. You're saying she told Dad and he hasn't thrown her out?'

'I didn't see any suitcases in her car.'

'He's going senile. It's the—'

It was as if somebody clapped loudly right beside his ear, her mouth banged shut so fast. They both knew what she'd been about to say.

It's the Huntington's.

And that was something she didn't want to get into.

Seemed she didn't have the stomach for any more conversation, either, the phone going dead in his ear with barely a goodbye.

He felt better for speaking his mind. He didn't want to see Grace hurt or have her make a fool of herself. But he still hated her for the way she summed up how he felt.

Always the last to know, eh, Max?

18

CRAIG GULLIVER WAS SITTING IN ANGEL'S CHAIR WHEN HE GOT upstairs, swivelling back and forth as he took Kincade through what he'd found on the PNC. He started to get up as soon as Angel entered the room. Angel waved him back down again.

'Don't worry. Stay there.'

Gulliver continued to stand up and come out from behind the desk.

'That's alright, sir. I was warned that I shouldn't sit there too long, anyway. Apparently, I'll either come over all religious or I might even turn celibate.'

'Is that so?' Giving Kincade the evil eye as he said it.

'Best not to take any chances,' Gulliver said, moving out of the way to let Angel sit down.

Kincade smiled at Angel as if butter wouldn't melt. He felt like saying to her, *look what happened to the last person who sat in your chair*. He went back to Gulliver.

'If it wasn't the warmth of the good Lord's love you felt sitting in my chair that put the smile on your face, Craig, I'm guessing you found something on Amos Church?'

'Absolutely, sir . . .'

'I've already heard it,' Kincade said, getting to her feet and heading for the door as Gulliver repeated himself for Angel's benefit.

In 1990, Amos Church, a twenty-seven-year-old ex-serviceman living rough on the streets had been convicted of the murder of Eric Impey, a thirty-eight-year-old married man and father of two. Impey had been bludgeoned to death with what the pathologist guessed was a hammer or something similar in Southampton Old Cemetery—the same cemetery where Lois Sheppard was killed thirty-four years later. The murder weapon was never found, but the motive was straightforward enough—robbery. Amos Church had a drink problem and had stolen fifty pounds from Impey's wallet which he'd used to buy a bottle of Scotch. The shopkeeper who sold it to him knew Amos and occasionally sold him cheap booze if Amos had enjoyed a successful day of begging on the city's streets. On this occasion, he'd become suspicious when he saw the wad of notes Amos was carrying. He'd sold Amos the whisky, not wanting to antagonise him—Amos had a reputation for becoming aggressive when drunk—and had subsequently seen what looked like blood on the notes Amos used to pay for the whisky. That suspicion turned out to be correct, the blood subsequently matched to Eric Impey and also to bloodstains found on Amos' clothes. He was convicted of the murder and served eighteen years of a life sentence, during which time he kicked his drink habit and was released on licence in 2008.

'He maintained he was innocent throughout,' Gulliver said. 'Claimed he went to the cemetery looking for somewhere to sleep—'

'Same as Doctor Durand,' Kincade added happily, coming back into the room with three cups of coffee squashed together in her hands.

'And stumbled across the body,' Gulliver finished. 'He

claimed Impey was already dead. He also said he saw three people hurrying away from the scene. He thought one of them was a woman.'

'Have you told him the best part?' Kincade said, trying to hide her smile behind her coffee cup.

Angel looked at her, then at Gulliver, also working hard at not smiling too broadly.

'Spit it out, Craig.'

'He's ex-Army, sir. Want to guess what regiment?'

Angel was aware of Kincade off to the side, holding her forefinger along her top lip as he'd done the previous day when impersonating his father.

'Really?' he said.

'Yep. The Paras.'

'I'll ask your dad if . . .' Kincade started, then coughed—very unrealistically, Angel thought—as if she'd choked on a mouthful of coffee. 'I'd ask your dad if he knows him next time you speak to him, sir.'

Angel hadn't missed the slip, the way she'd said, *I'll* ask him. Gulliver didn't appear to have noticed.

'I might do that,' Angel said, and meant it. For now, he moved on and away from his father and any potentially disastrous revelations. 'Have you spoken to the probation service yet?'

Having been convicted of murder, Amos Church would spend the rest of his life on licence. The conditions of that licence meant keeping the probation service updated with his home address and place of work, amongst other things. It made their lives a lot easier—assuming Church played by the rules and supplied correct details.

'I have . . .' Gulliver confirmed.

Something in the way he said it made Angel sit up and take notice.

'What?'

'A couple of things. The first is more of an interesting aside. He works for a charity who help ex-servicemen. Walking With Heroes.'

'Makes sense,' Angel said. 'Help prevent others from making the same mistakes he made. What's the other thing?'

'His home address.' Gulliver glanced at Kincade to see if she was paying attention, but she was busy rooting through the papers on her desk. 'He lives in Upper Shirley.'

He didn't need to spell it out for Angel, who put it into words anyway.

'Half a mile from Southampton Old Cemetery.'

'Exactly, sir.'

Kincade interrupted as the implications hung in the air.

'Got a phone number for him, Craig?'

'Uh-huh.'

She read a mobile number out from the papers in her hand.

'Is that it?'

Gulliver checked the notes he'd made of his discussion with Amos Church's probation officer.

'Yep. Was that a good guess—'

'Or the last number Lois Sheppard called on the night she was killed?' Angel said.

Kincade waved the call log she was holding at him.

'You got it. Church is the person Lois Sheppard called to arrange the meeting that never took place on the day after she was killed. It was also him she called on the night, an hour after Ingrid Fischer picked her up. The question is, was that second call the reason she didn't make it to the arranged meeting? She called her killer. *I know my appointment's tomorrow, but can you fit me in now?*'

Gulliver snorted with laughter while Angel allowed himself a more restrained smile.

'An interesting way of putting it. A bit like rescheduling a dentist's appointment. Except Amos killing her doesn't fit with what we've been told about Patrick Quinn asking Amos to forgive him.'

Identifying the murder of Eric Impey in 1990 had changed everything. Until that point, Quinn's confession to Lois Sheppard that he'd murdered someone, along with the associated implication that Amos Church had been wrongly convicted of that murder, could still have been attributed to confusion and delirium caused by his medication. With the identification of an actual murder—and one that Amos had been convicted of—Quinn's story suddenly rang true.

'There's no reason for Amos to kill Lois because she was trying to uncover the truth,' Kincade agreed, picking up on Angel's thinking.

'We need to speak to Amos Church asap.'

'I think you're right, sir. And before somebody else gets to him.'

'FOR CHRIST'S SAKE, AMOS, YOU CAN'T JUST HIDE HERE WITH YOUR phone switched off and hope it's all going to go away,' Jesse Hamilton said, the exasperation he felt causing him to be sharper than he'd intended.

Amos gave Jesse a dirty look, fear and aggression coming together in his voice.

'Are you saying you want me to leave?'

'I didn't say that.'

'What, then?' He rolled his eyes heavenwards, a here-we-go-again note entering his voice. 'We're back to going to the police, are we? Trust that they'll do the right thing second time around. Except last I heard, it was *third* time lucky.'

'I didn't say that, either.'

'No, but you're thinking it.'

What I'm thinking is that it's like dealing with a petulant teenager, Jesse thought, and didn't say. The way Amos was going, it would only take one wrong word for it to come to blows between them. Because Christ knows, something had to release the tension building in the house—and they both knew the best release valve looked a lot like mindless violence.

He swallowed his anger, tried to reason with him.

'You might think you're on your way back to prison—'

'I am if I call the police.'

'—but I don't. And unless you want to be unemployed and begging on the streets again when this all blows over, at least call work. Say you've got a family emergency to deal with, whatever. But call them.' He fixed Amos with an uncompromising stare, one that said he wasn't afraid to tell it how it was. 'Because you know what they'll be thinking if they don't hear from you.'

'I'm not stupid.'

'No, you're just acting it.' For a split second, he thought he'd gone too far, Amos shifting position on the sofa as if thinking about lunging at him. Jesse pressed on regardless, said what needed to be said. 'They're going to think you're back on the booze. In hospital or crashed out in some filthy alley. You remember those days, Amos? Waking up in a shitty alley stinking of piss. Yours, or some wankers who thought it was a laugh to piss on a sleeping wino.' He cleared his throat, uncomfortable with what he wanted to say next. Strong emotion always did that to him. 'You saved me from ending up in that life. I'm not going to sit here and watch you slip back into it.'

Amos pushed himself to his feet, an abrupt sudden movement. Not to lunge at Jesse to shut him up, so that he didn't have to listen to the same shit outside his head that was going around and around inside it. But to get away.

'Okay, okay. I'll call them. Happy now?'

Jesse shook his head. *Not even close.*

'Uh-uh. You can't prove you haven't got booze on your breath over the phone. Pop into the office. Two minutes to say you've got personal issues to deal with and breathe alcohol-free breath all over them. They'll understand.'

Like fuck they will, Amos thought, knowing Jesse was right. He pulled out his phone, made a big fuss of turning it on.

'There. Now they can track me, find me here. You'll get done for harbouring a criminal, perverting the course of justice, but that's what you wanted.'

Jesse took a deep breath, let it out in a rush. Thinking, *give me hormonal teenagers any day.*

'Well done, Amos. Now make the bloody call.'

'Are you going to sit and watch me?'

'You bet your arse I am.'

Amos made the call, held the phone towards Jesse so that he could hear when it was picked up, prove he hadn't called the talking clock.

'Hi, Sharon, it's me,' he said when it was answered, immediately holding the phone away from his ear. 'I know, you've been worried. I'm sorry. I've got a lot of shit going on I need to deal with. But I'm going to call in to have a quick word with the boss so he doesn't sack me.'

He gave Jesse a thin smile after he ended the call, the question he'd asked out loud a minute ago hanging in the air.

Happy now?

Jesse gave him a solid thumbs-up, hoping to hell he hadn't just made a big mistake with somebody else's life.

19

Angel had definitely made a mistake by dropping into DCI Finch's office to update her after he'd tasked Gulliver with running Patrick Quinn's name through the PNC. She started by tapping the newspaper on her desk with her fingernail.

'Superintendent Horwood is getting a little nervous about that.'

Angel didn't need to look to know what she was talking about, the headline easily coming to mind.

Nurse brutally murdered in Southampton Old Cemetery.

'And we don't want that, do we, ma'am? It could have a disastrous effect on his golf swing.'

'Heaven forbid, Padre.' She picked up the paper, skimmed the article quickly, then tossed it in the waste paper basket. 'It doesn't help, the way they make such a song and dance about her being a palliative care nurse.'

'You mean it elevates it to a higher level of seriousness compared to the murder of a police officer, for example? Or an abortionist.'

Finch gave him the look that never required words. He was not to be an arse his whole life.

'You know what I mean, Padre.'

'I do indeed, ma'am. Which is why I choose to be so flippant about any suggestion of a murder victim hierarchy. The implication that the Super's golf swing might be more adversely affected by the worthiness of her profession.' He raised a finger to stop her from interrupting. 'However, I feel your pain, having to keep the Super satisfied...'

'I think I'd prefer the word *appraised*, Padre.'

'Less scope for smutty innuendo?'

'Exactly. You were telling me about how you feel my pain...'

'Indeed. And I'm pleased to report that I've got enough to enable you to keep the Super more than satisfied. I'm not sure what word you'd like to describe that situation—'

'*Don't!*'

The bark actually made him jump.

'I wasn't going to suggest anything.'

'Just spit it out, Padre.'

He took her through the latest developments, her mood improving progressively as he did so. That didn't stop her immediate response from being true to form, highlighting what they hadn't achieved.

'Have you interviewed Fischer or Church yet?'

Give me a chance was on the tip of his tongue and stayed there.

'Not yet, no.'

'It sounds as if we need to take a good look at the Eric Impey case, too.'

'It's right up at the top of the list. Immediately under interviewing Fischer and Church, ma'am.'

She narrowed her eyes at him, alert for any hint of insubordination—beyond the normal, that is.

'Who was the SIO on the case?'

'Gulliver didn't say, and I haven't seen the file myself.'

'Let me know who it was, since we appear to be looking at a possible miscarriage of justice.'

'Anybody in particular you've got in mind?'

She looked disapprovingly over the top of her glasses at him, then told a lie.

'I don't know what you're implying, Padre.'

'Somebody who had a reputation for cutting corners in the interests of a quick result, perhaps?' He flicked his eyes at the ceiling, the realm of the top brass above, didn't say any more. He didn't need to.

Finch's glasses came off altogether. Pointing at him with them.

'If you're suggesting progress up the greasy pole is dependent on the number of results, as opposed to the quality of them, and if you had any particular names in mind, the Super was still walking the beat thirty-four years ago.' She extended her hand towards him. 'But feel free to pop upstairs and discuss the case and any shortcomings it might have with him.'

'I think I might pursue other avenues first, ma'am.'

'A wise choice, Padre.' She suddenly smiled—not a very friendly one—telegraphing where the conversation was headed. 'It's interesting Church was in the same regiment as your father. You could start by asking him if he knew him.'

'I plan to,' he said, heading for the door.

Except it was already too late. The remark about his father had concentrated her mind on his family.

'How's it going with your mother? What does she do all day long?'

It was clear Finch wasn't going to let him get away with a quick, *don't ask me* as he escaped. He diverted away from the door to her private coffee machine, the rules of engagement clear in his mind. If they were talking shop, he had to make do with the brown sludge from the machine by the lifts. But if she wanted to grill him personally...

'Help yourself,' she said, after he already had.

'She's been catching up with old friends. Spent a lot of time with Grace. She's been to Cormac's grave...'

'On her own, or with your father?'

'On her own.'

'A step too far?'

'At the moment.'

'Has she seen him at all?'

'Not yet.'

'Would you be able to keep those answers any shorter? Ever heard of volunteering information because a person shows an interest?'

He nodded, the reprimand noted and immediately acted upon.

'And she's been busy ironing my shirts and underpants, of course. As you yourself pointed out the other day. She also gives me a hard time over the continuing rift with Stuart Beckford at every opportunity.'

The words were out before he could bite them back. Finch was on it, on him, immediately.

'So she bloody should, Padre. I would, too.'

It wasn't a conversation he wanted to get into. Not at any time, but particularly not with the memory of Virgil Balan's offer in his mind. He would feel duty bound to mention it if they continued with the conversation. He headed it off with something provocative.

'Why can't women leave men's personal lives alone? Why do you always have to interfere?'

'That's simple, Padre. We get sick of having to pick up the pieces every time you make such a godawful mess of it.'

I recommend you don't stick your nose into Kincade's, he thought, finally making it to the door.

GULLIVER WAS IN ANGEL AND KINCADE'S OFFICE ONCE AGAIN when Angel got back from updating Olivia Finch. This time he was lounging against the wall, not sitting in Angel's chair.

'Still worried about catching a dose of celibacy from my chair, Craig?'

'Can't be too careful, sir.'

'So, what have you got?'

Gulliver's face immediately fell, as if it was already too late.

'An unfortunate case of cuckooing...'

The phrase referred to the exploitation of property owners by criminals who use their homes for illegal activities such as drug dealing or prostitution. Before the increased awareness and subsequent crackdown on County Lines drug dealing by the National Crime Agency and nationwide police forces, those property owners were as likely as the criminals themselves to be prosecuted, rather than treated as victims.

Patrick Quinn was one such victim. As an addict, a homeowner, and with a history of mental health issues, he ticked all the boxes of the drug dealers supplying him as the perfect target for cuckooing.

They followed a tried and tested pattern, initially befriending him and asking for his help. It's a particularly cynical, cruel and effective strategy used to target isolated individuals or those with mental health issues or learning disabilities. At first, that help consisted of storing drugs at his property. In return, he was supplied with the drugs he craved for free—in effect rent for the use of his property. The dealers also played on his fears, telling him that if he didn't help them, they would be forced out of business and his supply would dry up. In time, things moved up a gear. The dealers set up shop in Quinn's house, cutting the drugs and dealing from it, a much safer environment than dealing out on the streets where they risked arrest and the constant threat of being robbed or beaten by users and rival dealers. They continued to ply him with drugs to keep him compliant, but increasingly used the threat of violence against him and other negative tactics—the withdrawal of his supply, for example, akin to limiting a naughty child's TV time.

When the house was eventually raided in 2012 as a result of increased complaints from neighbours, Quinn was arrested and charged along with the dealers too slow to get away.

'He got eighteen months,' Gulliver finished. 'Did his time in HMP Isle of Wight.'

It was a sad indictment on the judiciary system, and one that was much less likely to occur in the current environment—scant consolation for Patrick Quinn. And not much use to them, either.

'I can't see how it might be relevant to the Lois Sheppard case,' Angel said. Except Gulliver looked as if he disagreed. 'What is it, Craig?'

'It might be nothing, but Quinn's defence called a character witness to speak on his behalf in court...'

He looked from Angel to Kincade and back again, made them work for it. Kincade beat Angel to it by a heartbeat.

'Ingrid Fischer. Quinn's nurse said she's the nearest thing he's got to family.'

Gulliver shook his head.

'Nope.'

Kincade did a small double take after congratulating herself too early.

'No?'

'Afraid not. That was a bit unfair. It's not a name we've come across. Not all of it, anyway. Conrad Fischer.'

Kincade rolled her eyes like she'd meant to say Conrad but Ingrid slipped out.

'Gotta be related.'

'Hell of a coincidence if not, Sarge.'

'Her brother?'

Angel tuned them out. Thinking back to the last time Gulliver had been in the room, talking them through the Eric Impey case. How Amos Church had maintained he was innocent the whole time, claiming he'd seen three people leaving the cemetery, one of whom was a woman . . .

20

Kincade stalked into their office the next morning, looking as if the first person to open their mouth in her presence would find her fist in it.

Shit, Angel thought, putting down the forensics report that had been waiting for him when he got in that morning.

'Everything okay?'

It struck him how bizarre the rules of human engagement often are as he said it. The question is always posed from a positive viewpoint—*is everything okay?*—when all the evidence suggests it isn't. A more logical *what's wrong?* often causes more problems, as any man who's said it to a woman knows to his cost.

Kincade turned a look on him that could've lifted the paint off the woodwork.

'You don't want to talk about it?' he suggested.

'Don't ever let anyone tell you you're not in the right job. Sir.'

He let her sit down and pretend to look through the papers on her desk. The forensics report was on his desk waiting to be discussed. Except she needed to get whatever was bothering her off her chest if she was going to be able to think straight.

Something drastic to kickstart the process was required. He pulled his harmonica out of his pocket, played a quick riff from Neil Young's *Heart of Gold*.

She came alive as if he'd set off the fire alarm.

'Okay, okay. No more grumpy cow.'

'Grumpy?'

'You choose a better word.' She made a half-hearted attempt at a smile. 'I almost got to meet Grace last night.'

The name *Grace* registered before the word *almost*, caused an overall delay in the sentence making sense—which it still didn't when he got the words the right way around.

'What do you mean, almost?'

'Exactly what it sounds like. It didn't quite happen.'

He put her deliberately obtuse attitude down to residual grumpy cow effect, tried again.

'How did it nearly happen?'

'We were in the kitchen having a spot of fridge tapas...'

'Fridge tapas?'

'Uh-huh. All the little leftovers. Anyway, we heard a car pull up outside. Carl was out of his chair so fast, he must have been expecting it. I followed to see what was going on, but he'd already gone outside and shut the door behind him. I went into the front room and looked out the window, saw him talking to Grace.'

'How did you know it was her?'

She gave him an incredulous look.

'Apart from the fact that I've got eyes in my head, you mean? She looks just like you. Anyway, talking isn't the right word. They were arguing.'

He watched her closely as she talked. To anyone unaware of the history, she looked as if she had no idea what the argument had been about.

'Carl was shaking his head like he didn't want to hear

whatever Grace was saying,' Kincade went on. 'Grace was waving her arms around as if she was directing a plane in to land. They kept at it, until suddenly they both ran out of steam. Stood there staring at each other for a minute. Next thing, Grace gave him a quick peck on the cheek, got in her car and drove off. So, as I said, I nearly met her.'

Anyone without his inside knowledge would ask what happened next. He played along.

'Did he say what the argument was about?'

'The usual. Huntington's. Giving him a hard time about going for a blood test.'

His father had lied. Angel knew it. He knew Kincade knew it. And that she knew he knew. That only left one thing he didn't know.

'I refuse to believe anyone would be as pissed off as you are this morning at *not* meeting my sister.'

That brought the grumpy cow straight back out of the byre or wherever it had been hiding.

'I'm not.'

'You want to talk about it?'

'Not really.' She caught sight of the harmonica still in his hand. 'But if I must.'

He couldn't ever remember hearing such resignation in her voice. It could only mean one thing. He gave her time, not wanting to be the one to bring it up.

'Carl caught somebody snooping around the house.'

One sentence and he knew his suspicions were on the right track. He didn't waste his breath asking whether it had been a burglar.

'Carl reckons he was a private investigator. He asked about me living there. It's not a secret, but it was like he wanted to confirm it first. Then he asked Carl a lot of questions about him, not me.'

Angel leaned back in his chair, hands behind his head. One thought in his mind as he stared up at the ceiling.

It never rains but it pours.

'Elliot hired a PI to dig the dirt?'

'Yep. Your dad told him to piss off, but if the prick's persistent, he'll get to the bottom of it eventually.'

It wasn't necessary to spell it out.

If her estranged husband's investigator uncovered the fact that Carl Angel had served eleven years in HMP Whitemoor for killing a man, it would not stand Kincade in good stead as far as any custody battle for her girls was concerned.

Elliot had already threatened her. Told her that if she didn't roll over and allow him and what Kincade called his gold-digging bunny-boiler Hannah Who-Gives-A-Shit-What-Her-Last-Name-Is custody, he would be forced to tell the court the truth behind her fall from grace.

Taken together, those two issues were like a bullet in the head of her custody hopes.

'Did you speak to Elliot about it?' he said.

'That wouldn't have been a good idea. I think he records all our conversations.' She dropped her eyes momentarily, a small smile creeping across her face. 'I had the phone in my hand when your dad persuaded me not to.'

'Persuaded?'

She grinned, *you got me.*

'Grabbed the phone out of my hand. Wouldn't give it back until this morning.'

'I know the feeling. He used to do that with our toys.'

'That explains a lot.'

Her mood was very different to when she'd first arrived, sufficiently so for him to wave the forensics report at her.

'Forensics on the tights used to strangle Lois Sheppard are back from the lab.'

A spasm of irritation flashed across her face that he'd let her waste ten minutes complaining about her personal life.

'You should've said.'

'I'm saying now.'

'Anything?'

'Uh-huh. Traces of saliva. Unfortunately, no match to anything in the national database.'

The holy grail was a match to an identified DNA sample. A living, breathing person. After that came a match to an unidentified sample recovered from a previous crime scene. What had been recovered from the tights was a massive step forward, but would only be of any use when they had a suspect to compare it to.

'Anything else?'

'Yep. Cat hairs.'

She nodded to herself as she thought back to notifying Eileen Sheppard.

'Lois Sheppard's mother has got a house full of cats.'

'Exactly. The lab will no doubt find them all over Lois' clothes. Could be we're looking for somebody allergic to cats.' He clenched his fists, drew his crossed wrists towards him as if pulling Lois Sheppard into his body as he strangled her. 'Cat hairs got up his nose and he sneezed.'

'Maybe we should send kitty some cat treats as a thank you.'

He dipped his head, *maybe we should*.

'I'll leave that with you. By the way, did you get a chance to ask my father about Amos Church?'

'I did . . .'

He groaned, answered his own question.

'He said it rings a bell.'

'Yep. You obviously take after him and think alike.'

'No. Jack Bevan said the same thing yesterday.'

'On a serious note, he said he didn't remember him, but he'll ask around.'

Angel wasn't hopeful.

After obtaining Amos' contact details from the probation service, they'd tried and failed to get in touch. His phone was permanently switched off and there'd been no answer when uniformed officers visited his address. They had details of where he worked, but Angel was wary of contacting his employer until it was absolutely necessary. Giving a job to a man with a criminal record for murder was an act of faith on the employer's behalf. A call or a visit from the police might make them question the wisdom of that generous act, and jeopardise Amos' position.

Given the newspaper coverage of Lois Sheppard's murder in the same cemetery where Amos allegedly killed Eric Impey, Angel guessed Amos had gone to ground. Other ex-Army buddies were the obvious choice, leveraging the bond forged in the military. Hence the barrel-scraping ploy of asking his father, in the hope that he might identify a mutual ex-Army contact— one who was prepared to betray that trust.

Angel wasn't holding his breath.

21

'Ve haf vays of making you talk,' Jardine said.

Gulliver took his eyes off the road to glance at his partner, her cryptic remarks having reached a new high—or was that low?

'What?'

'I'm practising for the interview. Ingrid Fischer sounds like a German name.'

'And you thought you'd do your bit for Anglo-German relations by talking like a caricature Nazi?'

'Might as well live up to the reputation we've got with some people.'

'The *might as well be hung for a sheep as a lamb* approach to policing, you mean?'

She nodded like she couldn't have put it better herself.

'Better than all the politically correct, woke bullshit they come out with these days.'

Gulliver might have wasted his breath, suggested there was a middle ground in there somewhere, had he not just turned into Patrick Quinn's road. Jardine pointed at the white Mercedes parked in front of Quinn's house.

'There it is. The vehicle of choice for stupid people who want to get caught and make our job easy.'

The remark was a little too close to the bone for Gulliver's liking, given they were looking at the possibility of a miscarriage of justice in the Eric Impey case caused by sloppy police work. He took the conversation in a less contentious direction.

'Nice car, though.'

Jardine grinned at him, pointed at the Ford Mondeo parked in the drive with a flat nearside front tyre and a giant dollop of crusted-on seagull shit on the windscreen.

'I'm afraid that's more your style, Craig.'

Ordinarily, he would've come right back at her. *At least we've got cars down in the South.* Make a disparaging remark about transport in the North East, how it was of the four-legged variety. Except he was still wary of saying anything that reminded her about home and the family problems he knew she was bottling up inside, lest she let loose all that pent-up anger and frustration in his direction.

Instead, he made a remark guaranteed to get her agreeing with him.

'On our salaries, I think you're right.'

They walked up the path to the front door in silence after that.

Angel had made the decision to interview Ingrid Fischer at Quinn's house. Despite being the last identified person to be seen with Lois Sheppard, she'd picked her up in a very conspicuous car and taken her to a busy pub. She was either stupid, had a very complicated plan Angel couldn't work out, or she had nothing to do with the murder. Hence the choice of neutral ground, rather than bring her in for more of a grilling in an interview room.

The same nurse Angel and Kincade had interviewed, Sheila

Doherty, opened the door to them. She looked every bit as nervous as Angel had told them she'd been on that occasion. She showed them into the same overly-warm sitting room where Ingrid Fischer was sitting on one of the sofas texting. Sheila left the room without closing the door after her, forcing Gulliver to do it himself. He suspected that if he waited five minutes, then opened it quickly, Sheila would come tumbling ear-first into the room.

Ingrid Fischer's shoulder-length ash-blonde hair and blue eyes fitted Jardine's pre-conceived prejudices perfectly. She was taller than Jardine by a good two inches when she got up from the sofa, her hand on the masculine side, nails short and veins prominent, when she extended it to shake hands.

Gulliver refused to look at Jardine, knowing what was running through her head.

Ve haf vays...

He jumped in first, before she actually came out and said it.

'That's a nice car you've got.'

Ingrid dipped her head appreciatively.

'Thank you.'

'We understand you picked Lois Sheppard up in it on the night she was killed and took her to The Cowherds pub.' He paused to give her time to nod her confirmation. 'Can you tell us the purpose of that outing?'

Ingrid's gaze immediately lifted towards the ceiling.

'I wanted to thank her for everything she was doing for Patrick.'

'Our colleagues spoke to the replacement nurse. She told them that was unusual. Without being too mercenary, they'd prefer cash every time.'

Ingrid's face said people like her always do. Her words reinforced it.

'I'm fortunate enough to not have to worry about money. I didn't want to come across as the sort of person who throws it around because it means so little to them. I prefer to give up some of my time.' The pleasant half-smile that had been fixed on her face now slipped, the sadness that replaced it something Gulliver guessed she practised in the mirror. 'I bitterly regret it now, of course. The proximity of the pub to where poor Lois' body was found suggests she might still be alive if I'd simply given her money.'

Jardine jumped in at that point, thankfully not in an exaggerated Germanic accent.

'The waitress at the pub said she thought the atmosphere was awkward between you.'

'Maybe a little bit at first.'

'It wasn't that she was mistaken? She thought awkward, but it was more acrimonious?'

Ingrid shook her head as if to say she couldn't be held responsible for a lowly serving girl's opinion.

'Definitely not. If I was dissatisfied with Lois' performance, I would have spoken to her superiors, not her.'

I'll bet, Jardine thought, as Ingrid gave her a look that suggested Jardine would know exactly what it felt like to be hauled over the coals by her superiors.

'What did you talk about?'

'Does it matter?'

'I won't know until you tell me.'

Ingrid picked her bag up from the floor at the side of the sofa before answering. Jardine couldn't see any visible branding. That fact, coupled with the obvious quality of the leather, screamed that if you had to ask the price, you couldn't afford it. Ingrid dug around inside and came out with an e-cigarette.

Menthol or something bitter, Jardine thought, immediately

proved wrong when Ingrid took a long drag and blew a cloud of fruity smoke directly up into the air above their heads.

'She talked about herself, mainly,' Ingrid said. 'She told me how she got into nursing because of her father dying early from cancer. She was very passionate about it. She had no problem talking once she got started.'

'You didn't talk about you?' Gulliver asked.

Ingrid shook her head and took another drag.

'No. I got the impression she didn't feel comfortable asking me personal questions.'

'Did you talk about Patrick?'

'Briefly. There isn't much to say. We both know he hasn't got long left. I'm surprised he's hung on for as long as he has. It will be a mercy when the time comes.'

A faint beading of sweat had appeared on Ingrid's top lip above the perfectly-applied lipstick. Both Gulliver and Jardine were aware of the stifling heat in the room, a trickle of sweat running down the centre of Jardine's back. She got up and went to the radiator in the bay window, turned the thermostat off and opened a window.

'Thank you,' Ingrid said.

Her relief was short-lived when Jardine stayed beside the radiator, putting herself out of Ingrid's line of sight. Although they thought it unlikely Ingrid had any direct involvement in the murder, neither of them had missed the indefinable air of evasiveness coming off her. They were about to move onto the difficult questions. Keeping her unsettled while they did so could only work in their favour.

'We were told Patrick's been saying strange things,' Jardine said.

Ingrid twisted around to look at her.

'I don't suppose that's unusual. It's probably the medication he's on.'

Everybody wants to blame the bloody medication, Jardine thought. For once, what she actually said was more provocative than what she was thinking.

'Not everyone admits to killing someone when they're delirious.'

Ingrid looked at her as if she hadn't heard properly.

'Is that what he said?'

'It is,' Gulliver confirmed, forcing her to turn back towards him again. 'Have you ever heard him say that?'

'Definitely not.'

'Did Lois ask you about it?'

'I'd have told you if she had.'

'Can you think why he might have said it?' Jardine said, forcing another twist—and probably a visit to the osteopath after the interview was over. She didn't give Ingrid a chance to respond, expanding on the theme. 'Seems to me it's a bit like dreams. However odd they are, they're generally based on something that's happened to you recently.'

'No smoke without fire,' Gulliver added, always happy to contribute a cliché.

Ingrid looked back and forth between the two of them, choosing to address Gulliver when she replied. It sounded as if she was reading from a prepared statement.

'I'm not aware of anything in Patrick's past that might be coming out now.'

'And you'd know,' Gulliver said. 'You've known him all your life.'

'That's right.'

'Did you visit him in prison?'

The question took Ingrid by surprise. She quickly used it to her advantage when she replied, made Gulliver wish he'd never asked.

'I did, actually. I have to say, it's disgraceful how he was treated. Like a criminal and not the victim he was. He's not the only person to suffer as a result of lazy policemen looking to cut corners in the interests of a quick result . . .'

While giving their own careers a boost at the same time, yadda, yadda, yadda, Gulliver thought, cutting her off mid-rant.

'So you'd know if anything happened in prison?'

Ingrid looked mildly indignant at being interrupted so abruptly, adding rudeness to laziness on the list of policemen's shortcomings.

'I think he'd still be in prison if he'd killed anyone in there, if that's what you're suggesting.'

'It wasn't, actually. Does the name Amos mean anything to you?'

The sudden change in direction threw Ingrid momentarily, as it was meant to, keeping her mind off-balance as well as her body twisting.

'No, should it?'

'Maybe,' Jardine said from behind her. 'We've been told Patrick keeps asking Amos to forgive him. If a dying man has something preying on his mind to the extent that he's begging for forgiveness, it seems reasonable that the person who knows him best, a life-long friend who even visited him in prison, might know something about it.'

Ingrid had finally got fed up with all the twisting back and forth. She stood up, went to stand in front of the faux-log gas fire so that she could see them both at the same time. Now Gulliver was the only one still seated. If he got up as well, it would feel very confrontational. They'd wanted to unsettle Ingrid, not antagonise her. He stayed where he was as Ingrid responded to Jardine.

'As you rightly say, Constable, it seems reasonable. That doesn't make it true.'

'Would you like to take a moment to search your memory?'

Gulliver heard something different as Jardine offered Ingrid the opportunity to lie.

Here's a shovel. Get digging.

'I don't need to,' Ingrid said. 'But if you're determined to waste everybody's time while I go through the motions and tell you the same answer at the end...'

Gulliver stopped her before she did so just to prove a point.

'That won't be necessary. How do you know Patrick?'

Ingrid's expression turned wistful, as if overcome by memories of better days.

'Our parents were friends. We spent a lot of time together as children.'

'Are any of them still alive?'

'Sadly not.'

It seemed to Gulliver there was a challenge in there somewhere—*now try and prove I'm lying.*

'Tell me about Patrick's life.'

The wistfulness morphed into something altogether more sad, recalling memories that weren't so rose-tinted.

'It hasn't been a happy one. He's spent his whole life fighting against problems with alcohol and drugs—'

'No need to re-visit the way the justice system failed him,' Jardine muttered under her breath.

'He's also had mental health issues. He's a paranoid schizophrenic. He was even sectioned under the Mental Health Act at one point. If you're looking for something to explain his incoherent death-bed ramblings, the answer will be in there somewhere.' She paused briefly for effect. 'If you can be bothered to look for it.'

'It doesn't sound as if he had much time for a steady job.'

'No, he was always in and out of work.'

Gulliver waved his arm in the air, took in the room with a wide sweep of his hand.

'How did he afford to buy this house?'

The answer was bouncing off the walls. Despite that, Ingrid hesitated before putting it into words.

'He didn't. I bought it.'

'That's very generous.'

'Isn't it? But I don't want to mislead you. I didn't buy it specifically for Patrick. I already owned it. I allow him to live here rent free. I don't want him living in a cardboard box on the street.'

'Nice to be able to do that for your friends,' Jardine cut in.

Ingrid turned her cold eyes on her. The look on her face said that even if she was the richest woman in the world and Jardine the poorest, she wouldn't give her the steam off her piss.

'I hope you get to the point where you find out for yourself whether you've got it in you to be so generous, Constable.'

Gulliver winced as if the barbed comment had been directed at him. Jardine didn't bat an eyelid, continuing with the attack.

'Are you paying for his care?'

'I am. Not that it's any business of yours.'

'Is it expensive?'

'Very. And I'm happy to pay it, knowing he's getting the best care possible.'

Jardine moved away from the radiator by the window, came to sit beside Gulliver on the sofa. Now Ingrid was the only one left standing. She hesitated a moment, then took the seat she'd been sitting in earlier rather than look like a pupil in class standing up to answer the teacher's questions. She sucked hard on her e-cigarette, the smoke hanging in the air between them after she exhaled.

Jardine leaned forward and waved it away, before coming out with an obvious lie.

'I don't want to be judgemental . . .'

'And yet I sense you're about to be.'

'But you're rich and he's a . . .' She paused, searching for the right word. Gulliver prayed she didn't use the one he knew was on the tip of her tongue—*fuck-up*—then relaxed when she found one that wasn't overly pejorative. 'A lost cause. How did your parents get to be friends?'

'Are all of your friends in the same financial situation as you are?'

'More or less.'

'Then I suggest you broaden your horizons, Constable. To answer your question, ignoring for now whether it deserves an answer or not, I have absolutely no idea. It's not the sort of thing children ask their parents. Maybe it's different where you're from.'

You bet, Gulliver thought, *they eat their young up there.*

Ingrid let out a weary sigh when Jardine didn't reply, glanced at her watch.

'Are we almost done? I was hoping for some time with Patrick, but it doesn't look as if that's going to happen.'

'Not long now,' Jardine said, 'but we're happy to wait if you want to pop upstairs for ten minutes.'

Ingrid waved the offer away, the gesture easy to interpret.

The quicker this is over, the better.

'Can you account for your movements on the night Lois was killed?'

'Absolutely. After leaving Lois—'

'What time was that?'

'Seven-thirty-ish.'

'Did you leave together?'

'No. I left her finishing her drink. She'd told me she'd recently broken up with her partner. She was thinking of calling him, trying to patch things up. I had to leave because I had another engagement. A charity cocktail party.'

Jardine nodded like it made sense.

'The waitress said you were all tarted up.'

'That's a different way of putting it, but yes.'

'Was it in aid of Walking with Heroes?'

'No.'

The response struck Jardine as being off. Incomplete. Most people in Ingrid's position would've said, *no, why do you ask?* Or, *no, who are they?* The implication was that not only was the name known to Ingrid, it wasn't unreasonable to ask if she'd attended their cocktail party.

'Did you go alone? With your husband?' She glanced at Ingrid's ring finger. 'Are you married?'

'Not any more, I'm not.'

The forcefulness of the reply was hard to ignore. Jardine didn't.

'That sounds like it was a mistake. Was the break-up acrimonious?'

Ingrid pursed her lips, the sourness of the look on her face something her ex-husband wouldn't miss.

'What it was, was none of your business. To get back to something that is, I went with my brother.'

'Who? Conrad?'

'That's right.'

She looked at Jardine in a different light now. Not just an antagonistic cop with a good line in sarcasm and very likely a problem with rich people, but someone who does their homework, too. Someone to be wary of.

'We saw that he was a character witness at Patrick's trial,' Jardine explained. 'We were wondering if you were related.'

'Well, now you know.'

'Was it a good bash?'

'Is that a roundabout way of asking if I left early in order to go back and murder Lois Sheppard?'

'Not at all. Just wondering. I've never been to one myself.'

Ingrid came as close to a smile as she'd got all interview. It wasn't necessary for her to put her thoughts into words.

And you won't be getting an invite from me.

'You don't look as if you're having trouble holding back the tears because you're not getting a cocktail-party invite,' Gulliver said, once they were back in the car.

'I'd have more trouble holding down my lunch.'

'You haven't had any yet.'

'That's lucky, then. No wonder the waitress at The Cowherds said the atmosphere was uncomfortable. Lois Sheppard would've died from terminal indigestion if she hadn't been strangled first.'

He waited to see if she'd finished, steering the conversation in a sensible direction when it looked as if she had. Or at least tried to.

'What's the verdict?'

She held her right elbow into her body, pivoted her forearm violently outwards.

'*Boing!* That's the combined bullshit and lie detector hitting the stops, if you were wondering.'

'I'd worked that out for myself. What in particular?'

She glanced briefly at her hands, palms up and fingers splayed.

'If I had more fingers, I'd count off all the lies—'

'Don't even think about taking your shoes off to use your toes.'

'—but basically, she knows damn well what Quinn's ramblings are about and who Amos is. And she definitely took Lois out to pump her to find out how much she knew.'

'But she didn't kill her.'

'Not personally, no.'

'Nor did her brother, who might have known Quinn as long.'

She shifted in her seat to face him at an angle, pulling her seat belt away from her body to facilitate doing so.

'That's another thing—'

'How they met, you mean?'

'Yeah. It doesn't feel right.'

He couldn't stop the laugh from slipping out as he thought back to Jardine questioning Ingrid about it.

'I thought you were going to call Quinn a fuck-up.'

She gave him a big, shit-eating grin back.

'I nearly did. It's a real pain in the arse when you can't use the best words or phrases.'

'I thought you recovered very well.'

'Thank you. And I didn't even go to Oxford Bloody University.' She turned to sit properly in the seat and face front, immediately twisting towards him again when something else occurred to her. 'She also knows who Walking With Heroes are, the charity Amos works for.'

'I agree. But it doesn't matter how many lies she told, she couldn't have killed Lois Sheppard. If her alibi checks out, which I'm sure it will.'

'True. But she's got plenty of money. She could've paid somebody to do it.'

He took his eyes off the road to look at her, see if she was being serious. The frown of concentration on her brow suggested she was.

'A five-grand hit ordered through the dark web, you mean?'

'Why not?' She dipped her index finger as if clicking a computer mouse. 'Add to basket. *Click!* Enter a discount code if you've got one. *Click!* You think that's how it works?'

'I'm sure it is.'

'Do you think you can pay using PayPal?'

'They're missing a trick if you can't. High-value items like that.'

'Do you think—'

He held up a hand to stop her.

'Enough now. Try using the random brain synapses that pass for thinking in your mind to figure out who else benefits from Lois Sheppard's death, if it isn't the Fischers.'

22

Richard Terrell's wife, Lucy, was hysterical when he got home from the gym.

Hand clamped over her mouth, she pointed at where their nine-month-old Pomeranian Husky mix, Jake, was lying on its side in its basket, looking for all the world as if it were dead. Terrell went to it, crouched down beside it, felt something break inside him when it whimpered pathetically. He placed his hand on its side, felt the heartbeat faint beneath his hand, saw the smears of blood matted in the fur on the backs of its hind legs.

Lucy heaved in stuttering gasps of air, words fighting their way out against it.

'He's been poisoned. He ... he ... he ...'

Terrell stood up as the dog whimpered again, went to her.

'Slow down.'

He tried to take her hands in his. She slapped them away. Held both of hers over her mouth as if the dog had eaten something foul that spewed out of her.

'Tell me what happened.'

She heaved in air again, sniffed, swallowed.

'He was eating something in the garden. I couldn't see what

it was. I didn't think anything about it. A little while later he was sick. I saw blood in it.'

She went past him into the utility room, came back with a plastic bag filled with vomit. Thrust it accusingly at him.

'See.'

He almost snapped at her. *I believe you. You didn't need to keep it.* Then realised the vet would want to analyse it, an accusation slipping out before he could stop it.

'You should've taken him to the vet.'

He regretted it as soon as the words were out of his mouth.

There was no place for the word *should* in this house, not today.

The criticism put a jolt of life back into Lucy, her voice rising, anger behind it more than hysteria.

'You had the bloody car! Too busy posing in the gym. Drooling over all the pretty young women in their skimpy leotards.' She shook the bag of vomit in his face. 'This isn't all. He crapped on your precious lawn. That had blood in it, too. Some sick bastard threw poisoned meat over the fence. And it's all your fault.'

Already, he was worried that it was.

He'd seen the newspaper, read about the murder in Southampton Old Cemetery. But that couldn't be what she meant. The panic rising up inside him reacted badly to the accusation.

'What do you mean, *my* fault. If you kept a closer eye on him when he's in the garden, didn't spend your whole bloody life watching stupid game shows on the TV, you might have stopped him.'

'Don't you try to blame me.' She threw out her arm, pointing towards the front door. 'If you hadn't had an argument with that idiot across the road because he left his car parked in *your* space for a week—'

'You're being ridiculous. Nobody's going to poison a dog over an argument about a parking space—'

'I *told* you not to go over there. And now Jake's going to die . . .'

He wanted to shout in her face, *you're being hysterical!* He bit his tongue instead. Took the bag of sick from her and put it on the table. Then fought against her until she finally let him hold her hands in his as he worked confidence and reassurance he didn't feel into his voice.

'He's *not* going to die. He's going to be okay. Let's stop arguing and get him to the vet right now.'

'TWO HUNDRED POUNDS A NIGHT,' LUCY SAID FOR THE HUNDREDTH time as they drove home, Jake left in the vet's exorbitantly-priced care. 'It doesn't cost that much for a person to stay in hospital.'

Terrell bit his tongue, said nothing as he threw a sidelong look at his never-satisfied wife.

The minute the vet had assured them they were hopeful Jake would make a full recovery, she'd started on about the cost.

'Two hundred pounds,' she said again, as if he hadn't heard her the first hundred times.

'It's only money.'

'Money we don't have.' Then, when he refused to be drawn into the pointless circular argument, 'We need to go to the police.'

After seeing the newspaper, he knew it wouldn't be long before they came to him.

'There's no point. Do you want to tell them you think it was that prick in the house opposite? I sure as hell don't. You think they'll allocate a dozen officers to canvass all the houses—*have you seen this heartless dog poisoner?* Get real. They'll play the game and take down all the details, which, by the way, are none at all, and tell you they'll get right on it. By the time you're out the door, it'll be in the toilets as emergency bog paper.'

The way she stared out of the side window in sullen silence told him he'd made his point.

God knows what he'd tell her when they turned up at the door anyway.

She wailed when they got in the house and she saw the empty dog basket, blood stains visible on the fleece blanket with its paw-print pattern crumpled in the bottom of it.

'I'm going to bed.'

Thank God for that,' he thought, and poured himself a scotch while she found comfort in her night-time routines.

He waited until he heard the familiar sounds come to an end before he went into the small home office—in reality, the space under the stairs—and fired up the computer.

He would've felt like a man surreptitiously looking at porn if it hadn't been for the tight knot in his stomach, the dryness in his mouth.

He saw the email immediately amongst all the junk and spam, the sender's email address jumping out at him.

Jerusalem_House1990@gmail.com

He suddenly felt sick, as if he'd been the one to eat the meat poisoned with what was most likely rat poison according to the vet.

The subject line let him know what was coming, as if he hadn't already worked it out.

Keep it zipped.

With an emoji of a pair of lips that looked more like a lipstick kiss than a threat.

He opened the email, anger mixing with the fear at the mocking words that preceded the threat.

How's the pooch?

Keep your mouth shut or it'll be your wife next time.

23

'I MIGHT HAVE FOUND SOMETHING INTERESTING?' LISA JARDINE said from the doorway of Angel and Kincade's office.

They both looked up from what they'd been doing as she came in, her excitement forging ahead of her. After she and Gulliver reported back on the interview with Ingrid Fischer, they'd all kicked it around for a while. Everybody had been agreed that the Fischer siblings warranted a closer look.

Their names had been run through the PNC, but without success. Their friend Patrick Quinn might have a chequered past, but they'd kept their noses clean—more accurately, they hadn't been caught, which wasn't the same thing at all.

'I did a search on Google for Ingrid and Conrad Fischer,' Jardine said. 'She barely comes up at all. When she does, it's always in relation to him. Conrad Fischer's sister, Ingrid, sat around all day counting her money, sort of thing.'

'So she's as rich as she was making out?' Angel said.

'Looks like it, sir. He certainly is. He's made a ton of money as a property developer. The company's called Congrid Developments. A combination of their names, so it makes sense that she's involved. But he's definitely the driving force.'

Angel didn't want to piss on her parade, but he felt obliged to say what he did next.

'That doesn't sound terribly interesting, Lisa. It explains how she can afford to pay for the house Quinn lives in and his medical costs, but other than that . . .' He shrugged, threw out a less-than-serious remark. 'Unless you're thinking there's no such thing as an honest property developer.'

'Certainly not the ones Elliot dealt with,' Kincade butted in, the reference to her estranged banker husband putting a scowl on her face as it always did.

'That wasn't what I meant,' Jardine went on. 'Conrad Fischer does a lot of charity work. Most of the pictures of him are at charity events . . .'

'Like the one on the night of Lois Sheppard's murder,' Angel said.

'Exactly, sir. I've looked at dozens and dozens of them, and ninety-nine percent of the time, he's with the same woman.'

Angel made an easy guess based on the rising excitement in Jardine's voice.

'Something tells me it's not his sister.'

She shook her head, glanced at a scrap of paper in her hand.

'Nope. Some woman called Evelyn Crane.' She grinned suddenly. 'Sounds like a useful person to know if you're in the construction business.'

'Better than taking someone called *shovel* or *hod* to an upmarket cocktail party, you mean?' Kincade laughed.

'You got it, Sarge.'

The three of them all shared a look as their thoughts converged. Angel extended his hand towards the two women.

'Ladies first,' he said, like the perfect gentleman he always tried to be.

Kincade jumped in.

'We don't believe in coincidence.'

'No, we don't.'

'So, what should we think about the fact that out of all the charity events Lisa has looked at, the only one he took his sister to was on the night Lois Sheppard was murdered.'

He pretended to think about it, but not for long.

'A cynical person—'

'Like yourself, sir?'

'You, too, Sergeant, you too. That cynical person might say that one or both of them was keen to have a very public alibi to shove down our throats, should we have the audacity to question such important people.' He pointed at the ceiling. 'It wouldn't surprise me if Superintendent Horwood was there, too.'

A told-you-so smugness lit up Jardine's face.

'See what I mean about interesting now, sir?'

'I do, indeed, Lisa. Keep digging. I get the feeling we're only scratching the surface of this.'

ANGEL SPENT THE AFTERNOON IN A PLACE WHERE HE FELT HE WAS spending the majority of his time—the distant past—reviewing the investigation into the murder of Eric Impey.

Impey had been forty-three when he was killed. His wife, Ruth, had been ten years younger than him. She was in Portsmouth staying with her sick mother on the night of her husband's murder. They had two children—Lloyd, aged fourteen, and Helen, a year younger.

Angel performed a quick mental calculation as he read. Ruth Impey would now be sixty-seven, her son and daughter forty-eight and forty-seven, respectively.

The family had lived in Upper Shirley—the same

neighbourhood where Amos Church currently lived—only half a mile from Southampton Old Cemetery where the head of the household was murdered.

Impey worked as an assistant manager in a High Street bank, back in days when banks actually had branches on the high street, and you could walk into one and have a real person turn you down for a loan. Outside of work, he'd been an active member of the local amateur dramatic society.

Angel wasn't surprised to see that a search of the PNC had drawn a blank. By the time he'd finished reading about Eric Impey's life, he wouldn't have been surprised to read that he'd been a victim of an escapee from a lunatic asylum on a mission to rid the world of dull people.

He found a picture of Impey as he'd been in the prime of his ordinariness, studied it for a minute or two. He got the feeling that if he was to close his eyes, he wouldn't be able to describe him at all, he was that forgettable. Impey reminded him vaguely of one of his teachers at school whose name he couldn't remember, an irritation that would bug him for days.

So much for Eric Impey's life.

The question that had vexed the team about his death was the same one that crossed Angel's mind now. What had he been doing in the cemetery that night?

He didn't own a dog, and the lack of any obvious reasons spawned a number of less obvious, aka more fanciful, ones.

The suggestion was floated that he was a closet homosexual taking advantage of his wife's temporary absence to arrange an illicit liaison. The theory was highly dependent on the prejudiced views of Impey's next door neighbour. Angel smiled at the situation the investigating officers had found themselves in when faced with the neighbour's assertion that *the theatre is full of queers*, a reference to Impey's involvement in the local amateur dramatic society. The neighbour's argument was given further weight when he revealed that Impey had no interest in talking about football or cricket—*the sort of things normal blokes are interested in*—over the garden fence. In the absence of any other, less prejudiced and more objective evidence, the closet homosexual theory died a more peaceful death than Impey himself did.

Feeling his eyes droop, Angel took a break to go down to the front desk in order to pick Jack Bevan's brains. Thirty-four years was pushing it. He didn't actually know how old Bevan was or how long he'd been a police officer, but it couldn't hurt asking.

He took the stairs down in order to stretch his legs, prepared himself for some good-natured abuse as he entered the reception area.

Bevan didn't disappoint, using a line Angel sometimes felt his colleagues came out with more than *hello* when they saw him.

'Bless me, Father, for I have sinned . . .'

Angel stopped him immediately.

'I've told you before, Jack, there is no penance I can give you for the sin of being Welsh. Even if I gave you a thousand Hail Marys, two thousand, you'd still be Welsh at the end of it.'

'Couldn't you have a word with the Pope on my behalf?'

Angel shook his head.

'He's stopped taking my calls.' He jabbed his finger at the floor. 'I'm afraid it's an eternity of burning in the fires of hell for you, Jack—'

'At least I'll see you down there, Padre.'

'—although I suppose even that is better than going back to Wales, if you ever retire. On that note, when did you start here?'

Now it was Bevan's turn to shake his head sadly.

'That information is above your pay grade, Padre.'

Angel shrugged, rolled with the disappointment.

'Assuming it was sometime in the mid-sixties, you would've been here in nineteen ninety. Do you remember a DI called Malcolm Arrowsmith? He was the SIO on the Eric Impey investigation.'

Bevan shook his head for real this time.

'I don't think so. I wouldn't forget a name like Arrowsmith. For his sake, let's hope he's dead. Then he won't have to suffer the indignity of you overturning his result with the benefit of hindsight.'

I get the feeling there was more to it than that, Angel thought, as he left Bevan to deal with a woman who'd just walked in.

He bumped into Olivia Finch on his way back to his office, stopped to update her.

'You were asking about the SIO on the Impey murder,' he said, after he'd run through it all. 'It was a DI called Malcolm Arrowsmith.'

She put her hand on his upper arm, a note of sympathy entering her voice.

'Not Superintendent Horwood? I know how badly you wanted it to be him, Padre.'

Angel refused to bite, as Finch smiled at her own joke.

'I didn't catch whether you know the name, ma'am.'

She stuck out her bottom lip, shook her head.

'Sorry.' The light-hearted tone of a moment ago evaporated at the implications of DI Arrowsmith getting it wrong, either through genuine error or laziness. 'Let me know the minute you come across anything that might come back to bite us.' She flicked her head upwards. 'I'm the one who has to manage the Super, remember.'

'I thought the word you used last time was *satisfy* . . .'

The look on her face suggested the most satisfying thing she could imagine at the moment was putting her foot up his backside. He left her before she put it to the test.

Back at his desk, he got stuck into the forensic report.

The pathologist had remarked that it was a particularly brutal attack, the level of violence far in excess of what was needed to incapacitate a person sufficient to rob them. That fact gave rise to a number of theories being put forward.

It was suggested that Impey and Amos Church might have known each other. That seemed unlikely, given the different spheres they moved in. More plausible was that Impey had seen Amos begging on the streets, and Amos was scared of being recognised. Against that, all of the blows were to the back of Impey's head suggesting Impey didn't see his attacker's face. The lack of defensive injuries to the hands or arms supported that view. He'd been hit over the head from behind and beaten to a pulp as he lay face-down in the dirt, basically.

It was also suggested that Amos was sufficiently drunk that he wasn't aware of how hard or how many times he hit his victim. As a highly-trained ex-soldier that seemed unlikely, even under the influence of drink. The idea was further discredited when the shopkeeper who sold him the bottle of Scotch he bought with Impey's money said Amos didn't strike him as being intoxicated when he entered the off-licence.

Another theory was that Amos, suffering from PTSD, mistook Impey's tan-coloured trench coat with the ankle-length garment called a *thawb* or *thobe* worn by Muslim men, provoking a frenzied attack as he relived the horrors of his military service inside his head. That theory fell apart when somebody pointed out that Amos had been out of the military for two years by the time the Gulf War started on 2 August 1990.

At the end of the day, everybody was happy to agree that he was a common or garden vicious bastard with a drink problem and a chip on his shoulder about how unfairly life had treated him.

Unlike his victim, Amos Church's name had been found on the PNC. A year earlier, he'd been arrested for anti-social behaviour after becoming abusive and threatening towards pedestrians who ignored his begging beret on the pavement. The incident coincided with a particularly cold snap, the temperature falling to below zero at night and barely rising above it during the day. The view was that Amos was deliberately trying to get himself arrested in order to spend a night, or hopefully longer, in the warmth and relative comfort of a police cell, three meals a day thrown in, courtesy of the same taxpayers who refused to drop their loose change into his beret.

Unfortunately for him, it was easy for an over-enthusiastic prosecution counsellor to turn the incident into the all-important first small step that escalated into the brutal murder of Eric Impey—conveniently glossing over the fact that there didn't appear to be any intermediate stages in that alleged escalation.

Amos never once wavered from his assertion that he was innocent, claiming he'd stumbled across Impey's already-dead body after seeing three people fleeing the cemetery. He'd been unable to provide descriptions, all three wearing black hoodies, but volunteered that he'd gained the impression—based on nothing he could justify—that they were teenagers, one of whom was female.

In legal terms, the prosecution laughed in his face. The jury took no time at all to find him guilty, the judge sentencing him to a lifetime's free accommodation and meals at the taxpayers' expense.

Angel worked his way through the witness statements, all of which had the feel of going through the motions in an investigation that had been solved the minute Amos was found passed out in an alley, the bottle of Scotch Eric Impey had paid for empty on the ground beside him.

Angel found himself losing the will to live as he worked his way through the file.

Until he got to the statement given by a fourteen-year-old boy called Richard Terrell, that is. Terrell had come forward and volunteered the information after he learned of Impey's murder. DI Arrowsmith promptly did nothing about it, an irrelevant distraction that would only muddy the waters in an already-solved murder investigation—one that was giving Arrowsmith a bruised back, so many people wanted to slap it as they plied him with drink after congratulatory drink.

Angel waved the witness statement in Kincade's direction.

'Now *this* is what I call interesting.'

THE MOMENTARY LACK OF COMPREHENSION IN HER EYES WHEN SHE looked up at him was all it took. The relentless heat of the sun was hot on his skin, the endless dust of the Iraqi desert in his mouth. Acrid black smoke drifting on the wind thick with the stench of burning rubber and flesh, choking him as he fought his way through it to where a soldier with half his face missing and sightless eyes as black as night staggered drunkenly towards him. Behind him, a blazing funeral pyre of twisted metal and dismembered bodies, all that remained of the Foxhound armoured patrol vehicle and its crew before an IED ripped it apart.

The visceral mental snapshot was gone as quickly as it came. Kincade sat up straighter in her chair, made a visible effort to look interested.

'Sorry. I was miles away. What is it?'

'A witness statement in the Impey investigation.'

'You sound as if it's a game changer.'

'It could be. And it was never followed up.'

He felt like clapping his hands, *chop, chop, Sergeant, try to look excited*, when she barely reacted.

Instead, she glanced at her watch, even though he got the impression she knew what time it was to the minute.

'Trust you to find something important now. Just when I was going to ask if you wanted to go for a beer.'

He suddenly realised what was wrong with her. She wasn't distracted or uninterested.

She was nervous.

And he knew why.

She'd decided to tell him what she'd told his father.

Suddenly Terrell's statement was forgotten. It was thirty-four years old. It would still be there in the morning.

Except the timing couldn't have been worse. He'd booked a table for eight p.m. at The Briny, a seafood restaurant in Southsea, with Vanessa Corrigan.

Kincade picked up on his hesitation. Ordinarily, she'd have thrown her eyes, her voice incredulous.

I don't believe it! Dinner with Durand. Again!

The fact that she didn't only reinforced how nervous she was.

They could just about squeeze a quick one in at The Wellington Arms. Except if he was right, it would take a lot longer than one drink to do it justice. Nor would she feel comfortable unburdening herself in the nearest watering hole to the station with the potential for interruptions or eavesdropping. He felt obliged to offer, all the same.

'I've got time for a quick one.'

She waved the offer away, relief washing out of her.

'Doesn't matter.' She paused, let the smile come. 'Besides, you need to get ready for Isabel.'

He didn't correct her, his suspicions confirmed. With the

prospect of telling him postponed, she was back to her normal impudent self.

He dropped Richard Terrell's statement on her desk on the way out.

'Read it for yourself, see what you think.'

Say hi to Doctor Death, chased him down the corridor as he left her to it.

24

Ingrid and Conrad Fischer stood side by side on the flybridge of his Sunseeker 95 yacht, the luminous white ball of the sinking sun obscured behind the Harbour Hotel and the other luxury apartment blocks surrounding Ocean Village marina, the diffused pinkish-orange glow of the sky all that was visible of the sunset.

The large gin and tonic in his hand was almost gone, her Campari & soda virtually untouched on the table behind them. Any other day, she'd make the most of the fact that for once he wasn't moaning about the high-rise buildings spoiling his enjoyment of the sun's daily swan song. Tonight, they had more pressing matters on their minds.

'You've got nothing to worry about,' he said.

'It's okay for you. You didn't pick the bloody nurse up and take her out. You haven't just been interrogated by a rottweiler from the North East with a chip on her shoulder about rich people.'

She sucked hard on her cigarette, blew the smoke straight up in the air.

'I thought you'd given up,' he said, criticism edging into his voice. 'Or at least switched to e-cigarettes.'

She looked at the cigarette in her hand, imagined sticking the glowing end in the female detective's eye.

'After the day I've had, I'm done with toy cigarettes. But don't worry, I won't grind the butt out on your precious deck.'

'What's the problem? You did tell them you were at a charity cocktail party with two hundred other people, didn't you? Two hundred *witnesses*.'

The question irritated the hell out of her. The fact that he'd even asked it. The emphasis he put on *witnesses*, as if it hadn't crossed her mind. For almost fifty years he'd been treating her like an idiot. She didn't care how much annoyance came through in the sharpness of her tone.

'Of course.' Then took another drag, didn't blow the smoke up and away this time. Let it hang in his face, which he hated. 'Except I'm not as vain as you, Con. I don't expect them all to remember me.' She flicked her fingers dismissively. '*Oh, her*. Conrad's little sister. The woman who doesn't exist in her own right.'

He ignored the bitterness and sarcasm, stuck to the point.

'So what are you worrying about?'

'They asked about Amos Church.'

'What do you expect? They're not complete idiots.'

She took a long final drag on her cigarette, flicked the butt out over the water—another habit that pissed him off, worried the other berth holders would complain. He said nothing about it as she went to the table, took a sip of her drink. Then held the glass up with a look on her face as if she'd accidentally drunk dirty bath water.

'You put too much soda in it.'

'What? Not bitter enough? I wouldn't have thought you needed any added bitterness.'

She gave him a tight smile, got back on track.

'They asked how I knew Patrick.'

'*Ah.*'

'Exactly. *Ah.*'

'What did you say?'

'That our parents were friends.' She let her face fall, her voice filled with mock sorrow. 'But sadly, they're all dead.'

He took a step to close the gap between them, put his arm around her shoulder and squeezed, the confidence back in his voice.

'You've got nothing to worry about.'

Easy for you to say, she thought, sliding out from under his arm, the physical contact repelling her. There was none of his confidence in her voice.

'They're putting it together. Next thing we know, they'll be talking to Richard Bloody Terrell. Then try telling me I'm worrying about nothing.'

Her unremittingly negative attitude brought out the worst in him. He threw the last of his drink down his throat, said something spiteful she knew he didn't mean.

'You should've put a pillow over Patrick's face when you had the chance.'

She raised her glass in a silent toast when he turned his back on her, went to stand at the railing staring at the last dregs of the sunset.

Amen to that.

KINCADE HAD JUST PASSED THROUGH ALDERBURY, EIGHT MILES still to go to Carl Angel's house, when he called her.

'The man I caught snooping around is sitting in his car watching the house. You want me to deal with him?'

She wasn't exactly sure what he meant by *deal with*, but it didn't suit her purpose to have Carl simply scare him off in whatever way he saw fit.

'No. Here's what we're going to do ...'

The familiar buzz of adrenaline that had been her constant companion when she worked undercover made a welcome return to her life as she drove the rest of the way. After priming herself to bare her soul to Angel and then have him turn her down, she needed a release. A few drinks in Carl's local would've done the trick, but the prospect of what she'd set in motion was a lot more exhilarating. If it proved to be informative, too, that would be a bonus.

She parked half a mile from Carl's house, made her way on foot to a side street from where she could see the car he'd described—a silver Toyota Prius—parked a few houses down from his cottage.

The excitement in his voice made him sound ten years younger when she called him, the heady rush of adrenaline as familiar to him as it was to her. And more sorely missed.

'I'm in position,' she whispered, despite there being nobody around. 'Don't forget, turn left, not right. You've got to earn your beers tonight.'

He snorted, his voice indignant.

'If I was that senile, you wouldn't have to worry about the man in the car quizzing me, would you?'

A moment later, he came out of the house, headed towards her. The investigator gave him a thirty-yard head start, climbed out of his car, checked behind him and set off in pursuit.

Kincade stepped backwards, her heart racing, hiding herself behind the corner of the house, its side wall directly on the road.

'Take the next right,' she hissed when Carl strode past as if demonstrating to new recruits how to march properly.

The man following upped his pace as soon as Carl

disappeared around the corner, caution abandoned once his quarry disappeared from sight.

Kincade stepped out behind him as he hurried past.

'*Hey!*'

The investigator spun around at the unexpected shout.

Too slow.

Kincade had hold of his left wrist before he knew it. Twisting violently up and behind his back as she turned him, slammed him face-first into the rough stone wall of the cottage. He struggled against her, tried to break free, the harder he fought, the worse the pain. She leaned all her weight into him, breathing hard through gritted teeth, forced his arm higher up his back, muscle and ligament protesting as she levered his shoulder out of its socket. Then a final vicious wrench, his breath catching as the pain stopped him dead, his body suddenly limp in her hands.

She put her lips close behind his ear, the sour smell of his sweat sharp in her nose.

'We can have the whole conversation like this. I can cuff you. Or we can talk like a couple of normal people. Your choice.'

'*Let go of my fucking arm.*'

She ground his face harder into the rough stone of the wall, the stress of the past days combining with her anger at what the man in her hands was here to do.

'Swear at me again and you'll regret it.'

He was desperate to not give in to her. To save face. Except it was hard to do when she was pushing it through a wall.

'Can't we just talk?'

She gave his arm a punitive jerk upwards, an unnecessary reminder to watch his mouth, then let go and stepped away. He spun around to face her, anger and shame at being bettered by a woman on his face.

There was only contempt on Kincade's.

'Who are you?'

He shook his head, said nothing, bolder now his arm wasn't halfway out of its socket.

'I know my husband is tight, but he was really scraping the barrel when he employed you.' She leaned sideways to stick her head around the corner. 'I can read your registration from here. Do you want me to make a phone call, have a colleague run it through the PNC? I'll have your details in thirty seconds.' She saw the initials *PNC* register in his eyes, grinned at him. 'Don't tell me he didn't mention what I do for a living?' Then, when he didn't answer, 'Cheap *and* a liar. No wonder I'm not with him anymore.'

'Your husband is not my client.'

The statement had the clear ring of truth about it. It threw her momentarily—until the horror of realisation hit her.

'I don't believe it. Hannah the bunny boiler hired you?'

'I don't have to answer that.'

She waved it away with a dismissive flick of her fingers.

'Doesn't matter. You should wear dark glasses if you don't want people to read every thought that goes through your stunted mind in your eyes. Give me a business card.'

He gave her a thin smile instead.

'I've run out.'

She was tempted to put him on his arse without a word of warning.

'Don't make me take one.' She cocked her head at him, her voice mocking. 'Funny, I don't hear you saying how you'd like to see me try. In case you were wondering, I've had a really shitty day.' She rolled her shoulders, flexed her fingers. 'Knocking a few of your teeth out on that wall is exactly what I need to work it all out of my system.'

He stared at her a long moment as if it was still his choice.

Pulled out his wallet when he felt he'd made his point, extracted a card and handed it over.

She took it as if her dog had crapped on the pavement and she'd forgotten to bring any baggies with her.

'Filip Nowak.'

Nowak scowled sullenly at her.

She clamped her hand over her mouth, stifled a snigger when she read what was written under his name.

'*Discreet* investigations? Are you serious? I suggest you look the word up on the internet. I hope you didn't buy too many cards.' She immediately waved the comment away. 'Doesn't matter. The sort of person who hires you won't even notice if you cross out *discreet* and write *incompetent* above it.'

She studied the card a moment longer, as if it was something she'd found pinned to the wall in a telephone kiosk in Bangkok. It had no more credibility. Since the law changed in 2022, private investigators in the UK are not required to be licenced. Anyone can operate as a PI without formal training, skills or experience. Professional bodies exist, such as the Association of British Investigators—as the letters *ABI* on Nowak's card proved—but, as with all self-regulating industry bodies, they exist for the benefit of their fee-paying members, not dissatisfied customers.

She turned at the sound of footsteps behind her. Angel's father was coming down the street towards them, as agreed. She winked at him, a gesture Nowak didn't see, assumed an official tone to address him.

'Is this the man who's been stalking and harassing you, sir?'

Carl scowled as if he'd been asked to identify a war criminal.

'It is. I'm not a well man, you know. This man is making me feel very distressed and threatened. I'm scared to leave the house.'

Attaboy, Kincade thought as he crammed in the emotive

words *distressed, threatened* and *scared*, although she hadn't told him to mention his health.

'I'm an old age pensioner,' he went on, getting into his stride. 'I fought for my country. It's not right that I'm harassed like this.' He rested his hand on his chest, heaved air into his lungs with a sound like a cow in distress. 'I don't feel very good.'

Kincade took hold of his upper arm, held him steady, waited for him to relax.

'Do you want to make a formal complaint against Mr Nowak, sir?' she asked, when he nodded breathlessly to let her know he was feeling a little better.

Carl fixed Nowak with a glare that said he'd rather run him through with a bayonet.

'Not this time. But if I see him snooping around again, I will.'

Kincade put her hand on Nowak's elbow, turned him towards his car.

'Let's go, Nowak. I don't know if you're even aware that I used to live in London. I still know a lot of people there. I can make your life very difficult, even if a formal complaint isn't made to the police. Keep out of my life, and I'll keep out of yours.' She let him get in the car, made a circular motion for him to buzz the window down. 'By the way, I wouldn't bother wasting your time asking Hannah the bunny boiler for your fee.'

Kincade and Carl watched Nowak drive away, neither of them convinced it was the last time they would see him.

'That was fun,' Carl said, sounding like he meant it.

'Yep.' She grinned, rolled out the solicitous tone of voice again. 'I hope you're feeling better now, Mr Angel.'

He put his hand on his chest, wheezed noisily.

'I think it's happening again.'

She bit down to stop herself from laughing out loud.

'Can I ask you a question?'

'Fire away.'

'How exactly does three pints of beer help with heart palpitations and shortness of breath?'

He gave her the sort of look she'd been expecting when she told him the truth a couple of nights ago.

'What did you say your name was? Grace?'

Needless to say, they were in the pub shortly after.

25

Angel was the first to arrive at The Briny, a seafood restaurant on the beach at Southsea. Ordinarily, it boasted an amazing view over the water. Currently, it provided its patrons with an uninterrupted view of the Southsea Coastal Scheme, a massive sea defence project that stretched from Old Portsmouth to Eastney. Angel wasn't overly concerned. He knew what the sea looked like, and Vanessa lived in Southsea. She could look at it any time she liked.

He took a seat up at the bar and ordered a margarita, passed the time watching the staff prepare drinks while he waited.

Ten minutes later, Vanessa sashayed in. He suspected the flowy floral dress she wore cost an awful lot of money in order to look carefree. Like something she'd found lying around and threw on at the last minute. She looked as if she'd cycled through the country lanes to the restaurant on an old-fashioned bicycle, a wicker basket on the front filled with wildflowers she'd picked from the roadside hedges. A deliberate attempt to dress as differently as possible to the tailored and sober business suits she favoured for work.

Her long dark hair was arranged in a single French plait that explained her lateness. She wore very little makeup. When she caught sight of him sitting at the bar and smiled, it was obvious why she didn't need it.

Heads turned—both male and female—as she crossed the room towards him. More than one man received a sharp kick under the table from his plain wife. Angel almost glanced at the seat beside him to see who she might be coming to join.

He breathed the smell of her deep into his lungs as she pecked him on the cheek, then followed behind her as they were led to a table in front of a pair of French doors—one of the many that ran the length of the building and led onto the terrace and the sea beyond, had it not been for the building work. The doors were open, a cool breeze carrying the salty smell of the sea to them, even if they couldn't see it.

After they'd ordered a bottle of Pinot Gris, she kicked the conversation off with a timely reminder to him about how good her memory was.

'How's it going with your sergeant living with your dad?'

He couldn't help laughing at how one question could lead to so much.

'Never a dull moment.'

'Really? I'm all ears.'

The remark was patently untrue. But the first proper date other than the quick lunch they'd grabbed together wasn't the time to point out the non-ears parts of her anatomy that he couldn't fail to be aware of as she leaned across the table towards him.

'Did I tell you I don't believe the reason she gave for her demotion?'

'I don't think so, although it doesn't surprise me. You strike me as someone who doesn't believe much of what anyone tells you.'

We'll put that to the test if we ever talk about you, he thought, then took her through it all, starting with Kincade's sanitised version of events, and finishing with his suspicion that she'd told Carl before she was outed by Grace.

Vanessa couldn't stop herself from smiling at his predicament, even if there was no malice it.

'You think she's told your dad, but you still don't know?'

'Uh-huh.'

She studied him for a long moment, sipping thoughtfully at her wine as she did so. The intensity of her gaze made him wonder how many of her charges broke some rule or other in the hope of being hauled before the Deputy Governor, the lack of privileges that might result more than compensated for by the time spent squirming under her disapproving glare.

'There's something you're not saying,' she said.

He let the mischief in his eyes answer for him. *Oh yes.*

'Spit it out.'

'I don't want to over-inflate your ego.'

She spent a moment trying to work out how she could possibly fit into the story. In the end, she was forced to admit defeat.

'I give in.'

'She asked if I wanted to go for a drink as I was about to leave ...'

It took a second, Vanessa's eyes widening when she caught on.

'She was going to tell you tonight?'

'I think so.'

She stretched out her hand, laid it on his.

'I'm flattered that you chose me over a juicy secret.'

'Maybe I don't really want to know.'

She pulled her hand away, studied him even more intently.

'I think there's a chance that's true.'

The waitress turned up at the table to take their orders at

that point—octopus carpaccio followed by sirloin steak for him, Brixham crab and then butterflied mackerel for her. The timing was perfect. It meant he didn't have to think about how right she might be.

'That's not all,' he said, after the waitress had left the table.

'Why do I get the feeling that's business as usual?'

He patted his jacket pocket where his phone sat.

'She texted me while I was on the train. She and my father chased off a private investigator her estranged husband's latest bunny boiler—'

She pointed a finger at him.

'*Careful*. I've been called that before.'

'Should I be worried?'

'Depends. Men use it for women they can't handle. *She's nuts, a bunny boiler*. It's not their own inadequacy.'

He sensed something behind her words that could go the wrong way on date #2. Despite that, he couldn't stop himself from asking the obvious question.

'Is this insight based on someone you might have been married to?'

She gave a firm nod, *you bet your arse*.

'Him. And most of the men I lock up at night.'

'Only most of them?'

'Not the ones who're even crazier, obviously.'

It was definitely time to get back on track.

'Anyway, they chased off the PI that Hannah the gold-digger—'

'At least I haven't been accused of that.'

'—hired to dig the dirt. She's hoping to find something to use against her in the custody battle for her children, which my dad's stint as your guest at HMP Whitemoor won't help.'

She let out a long breath as if it had been her who'd done all the talking.

'I almost feel like it's my fault.' A mischievous glint appeared in her eye. 'Why don't you send your dad a selfie of us?'

He picked up his wine glass, tilted it at her.

'Maybe after a few of these.'

She shook her head, the mischief subtly changing.

'Absolutely not. If you're going to do it, do it now. Before you've had too much to drink. Anyone would think you're ashamed of me.'

'Why would I be ashamed of you?'

The waitress arrived with their starters as he said it. She overheard the tail end of the question out of context—*ashamed of you*—glanced at Vanessa and gave him a dirty look before leaving again.

Vanessa grinned at him.

'I bet she spits on your steak now.'

'You spend too much time in the prison canteen.'

'You have no idea. Anyway, ashamed is the wrong word. You're *worried* he'll show it to your sergeant. I bet you're still hiding behind the pretence of seeing the pathologist.' She wagged her finger at him, enjoyment on her face at his surprise. 'You're going to come very unstuck if you keep forgetting how good my memory is.'

'To answer the question, I allow her to labour under her own misapprehensions.'

She stopped picking the white meat out of the crab shell, pointed her fork at him.

'You've been a priest, an Army chaplain, a police detective, and now you sound like a weaselly lawyer.'

'I must spend too much time with my sister.'

'The one who's caused all the trouble.'

Don't I know it, he thought, as they both went back to their food, eating in a relaxed silence for a short while.

Despite her admitting it might have been the wrong word,

the accusation of being ashamed of her stuck in his mind. It had been a deliberately provocative remark, delivered in a somewhat light-hearted way. But did it hide a deeper insecurity? Something he'd seen in other outwardly-strong women like Kincade? The doubts made him want to justify himself.

'With all the ammunition my past provides my team to use against me, I want to keep part of me private. I don't need jokes about being locked up at night.'

'Fair enough. Is that why you're here in Southsea, rather than me coming to Southampton? Less chance of you being—'

'Caught?'

'Your word, not mine.'

They fell silent as the waitress turned up to clear their plates away, each of them taking a sip of wine. After topping their glasses up, he worked the bottle right down into the ice bucket.

'You like it cold?' she said.

'The colder the better.'

'Like your women?'

The remark felt very different to the things that had been said only a minute before. It was very much tongue-in-cheek, a self-criticism her next words proved before he had a chance to answer.

'Do you think I'm giving you a hard time?'

He rocked his hand.

'For a second date, maybe.'

'It's just that I sense this reticence. Other men I've dated are looking to jump my bones after one drink. You don't even call from one week to the next.'

'I'm guessing those men don't last long.'

'You guess right. And the correct description is, those *disappointed* men.'

'So I'm like a breath of fresh air?'

She threw back her head and laughed out loud, a sudden bark that drew curious looks from nearby diners.

'You are indeed. Although I doubt anybody has ever accused you of it before.'

Not to his knowledge, no, he was forced to admit.

She leaned across the table, put her hand over his.

'I know it's difficult for you. You're the detective. You ask the questions—'

'I'm not doing very well with you.'

Her smile said that was the way she liked it.

'But you're going to have to provide the answers tonight.'

'I might be a detective, but you're a deputy governor in a prison. And I feel like you're gathering evidence to decide which wing to put me in.'

She dipped her head, touché.

'Are you going to tell me or not?'

For reasons he couldn't identify, he took his harmonica from his pocket, placed it on the table.

She glanced at it, smiled at him.

'I'm not sure I've ever been serenaded by a man with a mouth organ.'

'*Harmonica*, please.'

She dipped her head, *harmonica it is*, and already he regretted the light-hearted way he'd chosen into the sad story he now told her.

'I was married until not so long ago . . .'

She listened without interrupting as he spoke, turning the stem of her wine glass in her fingers and taking the occasional sip, their eyes meeting briefly then looking away again as the story sucked some of the joie de vivre out of the evening, as it was always going to.

'Ever wished you could turn back the clock and start the evening again?' she said, when he'd finished. She immediately realised how it had come across. 'I don't mean the evening your wife died. I meant me, tonight. Accusing you of being ashamed of me.'

'Maybe I am.'

She narrowed her eyes at him, put her hand on the ice bucket.

'If I didn't know you were being provocative to change the subject, I'd empty this over your head.'

'Justifying the bunny boiler accusation.'

She shrugged, *you got me*.

'I can understand the reticence now.'

He shook his head, *no you can't*.

'It's not as simple as that. A week ago, things would've been different. Then I took a call out of the blue from an inspector in the Romanian police called Virgil Balan...'

He took her through Balan's offer, but didn't mention the doubts he harboured about what Balan was actually offering him. Whether it was through official channels or whether Balan was offering him the chance to take personal revenge on the lorry driver Bogdan Florescu with his fists or an iron bar.

'It means it's been on my mind more than it would've been before the call. I'm determined to get in touch with Stuart Beckford—'

'And we all know how men can't concentrate on more than one thing at once. I'm happy to wait until you've got your head straight.'

'Some people would say you've got a very long wait ahead.'

'Straight*er*. Just one question.'

The way her eyes dropped to the harmonica still on the table between them gave it away. He picked it up, slipped it back in his pocket.

'Why do I carry it around?'

'Uh-huh.' She pointed through the open French doors at the

darkness outside and the sea beyond the construction work. 'I'd throw it as far away as I could.'

'You don't believe in confronting your demons?'

'Is that what you're doing? Proving to yourself that you've moved on? Until some Romanian cop reminds you all over again.'

'No, it's the opposite. A reminder of how your life can change in the blink of an eye.'

She lifted her glass, extended it towards him for a toast.

'If that's not the best reason to live life for today, I don't know what is.'

26

'You look as if you're full of the joys of spring this morning,' Kincade said, when Angel got into the office the next morning.

He couldn't deny it, even if he was dog-tired, his head still fuzzy. After the *live life for today* toast, they'd ordered a second bottle of Pinot Gris, and he'd ended up missing the last train home. Whether it had been on the cards or not before they discussed Claire's death, there'd been no question of him spending the night at Vanessa's afterwards, an unspoken decision by mutual consent. He'd got an Uber all the way home. His only regret was that he'd come away knowing no more about her than he did when he arrived—a situation he suspected she worked hard to achieve.

'Did Durand open a vintage bottle of children's blood last night?' Kincade asked, when he didn't offer any explanation for his good mood.

He gave her a mildly-disapproving look—it was a little too close to the knuckle given the implications of Richard Terrell's statement that they still had to discuss—then moved the conversation away from him.

'I didn't have as eventful an evening as you did, from the sound of it.'

'True—'

She was cut short by a tentative knock on the door.

'Not interrupting anything, am I?' Isabel Durand said, coming into the room.

Angel didn't need to look at Kincade to read her mind.

You're walking on air, and here's Durand in the building first thing. Did you happen to come in together by any chance?

He was happy to let her think it.

'I had to come in for a word with Olivia Finch,' Durand explained.

Again, Kincade's thoughts forced their way into Angel's mind.

You expect me to believe that?

'So I thought I'd pop in. Lois Sheppard's toxicology report is back from the lab.' She looked directly at Kincade. 'Care to guess what it says, Sergeant?'

Kincade made a lightning-fast assessment of her opponent's expression, went for the most inconvenient result.

'No evidence of date rape drugs?'

Durand gave a grudging dip of her head.

'That's correct. Alcohol levels consistent with a couple of glasses of wine with her meal, but no evidence of drugs of any kind.'

'Not even helping herself to her patient's morphine?'

Angel knew it was a mistake, even if Kincade didn't. The pathologist immediately proved him right.

'You shouldn't judge everybody by your own standards, Sergeant.' Then, to Angel, 'I'll let you work out the implications, Padre. I know it wasn't what you were hoping for.'

It wasn't. They now had to come up with a reason why Lois Sheppard went into the cemetery if she hadn't been led there like a lamb to the slaughter while under the influence of a date rape drug.

He stopped Durand as she headed for the door, held out the Impey autopsy report towards her.

'Can you take a look at that for me, Isabel.'

She took it from him, read the details on the front. He noticed how she didn't read them out loud, the date in particular. She wasn't about to give Kincade the opportunity to ask if she'd performed it herself thirty-four years previously.

'What am I looking for in particular?'

'I just want your take on it. The pathologist remarked that it was a particularly brutal attack, inconsistent with a mugging.'

She opened the report, found a close-up image of the back of what had previously been Eric Impey's head, now resembling a red mush.

'I can't disagree with that.' She studied it a while longer, then broke one of her cardinal rules, volunteering an opinion based on human nature rather than a scientific assessment of the wounds themselves. 'There's some pretty strong emotion behind that level of violence.' She found another photograph, this time of Impey's face, injury free but smeared with dirt. Her assessment was more to herself than them. 'Beaten to a pulp while face-down on the ground. I'll take a look, Padre, let you know what I think.'

He didn't give Kincade the chance to give him a hard time over Durand's early-morning visit, went back to what they'd been discussing before her arrival.

'You were about to tell me how you chased off the investigator. Is *chased off* a watered-down euphemism for kicking the shit out of him?'

'That doesn't deserve an answer. Even I can see that would only strengthen Elliot's case.'

He listened without interrupting as she gave him a blow-by-blow account, as if it had been a pan-European military operation co-ordinated by Field Marshall Carl Angel.

'And you think Hannah the bunny boiler hired him?' he said when she'd finished.

'His face pretty much confirmed it when I mentioned her name.'

'Did you call Elliot about it?'

She shook her head slowly.

'Not yet. I'm going to choose my moment. He won't be happy about her going behind his back. It'll make him wonder what else she might be up to on the sly. When you've got lots of money like he has, you worry about things like that. If I can drive a wedge between them, he might roll over regarding custody. I know what he's like. He loves having the girls around, but he wouldn't want to look after them on his own.'

'He's got your mother.'

'My what?'

'My mistake. Your *interfering* mother to help out.'

She scrunched her face, a lifetime of knowing her mother in her voice.

'There's a world of difference between having her on his side to grind me down, and having to deal with her day-in, day-out as well as looking after the girls.'

'So Hannah the bunny boiler is your new line of attack?'

'For now, yeah.'

'She has no idea what she's got herself into, does she?'

Kincade gave him a quick flash of her eye teeth.

'No idea what-so-fucking-ever.'

He let her enjoy the thought while he searched for Richard Terrell's witness statement on the paper explosion that passed for his desk. Except she wasn't finished.

'Don't you want to hear about the rest of my evening?'

He groaned inwardly, *what now?*

'Grace turned up and the two of you had a fight in the street? In my dad's local?'

She gave him a look her girls would recognise, her voice weary.

'You are so negative.'

I've learned from experience, he thought and didn't say.

'Okay. What else? Surprise me.'

'Your dad might have identified where Amos Church is hiding out.'

She stared at him without saying anything more until he raised his hand.

'I admit you've surprised me. In fact, surprise doesn't come close.'

'He talked to some people from his Army days. Nobody knew Church personally, but one of them said somebody called Jesse Hamilton had been asking about your dad. We were kicking it around in the pub—'

'A congratulatory, mission-accomplished beer after seeing off the PI?'

Mission accomplished for now, she thought and kept to herself.

'Exactly. Your dad mentioned that it was your name in the newspaper as the person to call with information about the Lois Sheppard murder.' She smiled suddenly, the light of proud parenthood reflected in her eyes. 'You know he keeps cuttings every time you're in the paper.'

'He needs to get a hobby,' he said to hide his even-greater surprise.

'Anyway, we were thinking this guy Jesse Hamilton saw your name, remembered your dad from the regiment, and wondered if you were related. So he phones people he knows to try to find out. It could be pure curiosity. One of those completely unimportant details that's going to bug you until you find out. Or it could be more.'

He thought about it, how long a stretch it was.

'More, as in he knows Amos, and he thinks he's involved.'

'Exactly. It's worth talking to him. Because . . .' She rolled her hand in a circular motion.

'We don't believe in coincidence.'

'No, we don't, sir. Apparently, he works as a chauffeur-cum-bodyguard for some big-shot VIP who likes having an ex-Para drive him around.'

'Not Mr Cocktail Party, himself, Conrad Fischer?'

'Carl's contact didn't have that information, I'm afraid.'

They shared a look for a long while, contemplating whether fate was up to pulling off such a coincidence.

They didn't know it then, but bigger coincidences awaited them, only a short phone call away.

KINCADE WAITED FOR ANGEL TO ROOT THROUGH THE PAPERS ON his desk for a while longer before she waved Richard Terrell's witness statement at him.

'I've still got it, if that's what you're looking for.'

'You could have said—'

'Before you messed up the meticulous order of your desk?'

There wasn't anything he could say to deny it, so he didn't try. He leaned across to take the statement from her outstretched hand, quickly read it a second time, even though the details were still fresh in his mind. Like cancer, they weren't about to simply go away overnight.

'What do you think?'

'That maybe Eric Impey didn't lead such a boring life, after all. Although it hardly seems possible.'

'I know it wasn't the seventies, but you tend to forget how much things have changed since nineteen ninety.'

In that year, Richard Terrell, then aged fourteen, had come

forward after Eric Impey's murder. At the time, he'd been a resident of the Jerusalem House children's home in Highfield for two years. He told the officer interviewing him that Impey was what was known as a *social uncle*—a part-time volunteer who worked with the children, often taking them out for the day. Unlike the full-time staff, social uncles and aunts were not properly vetted. It made the vulnerable children in their care easy prey for paedophiles and other abusers who sniff out such opportunities faster than flies find a corpse.

To use Terrell's own words, Impey had tried to *touch him up* after he took him swimming. Terrell had been big for his age, and strong, and had easily fended off Impey's advances. Terrell hadn't reported the incident to anyone at the home, the reasons he gave easily summarised in one word. Pride. It was all about keeping face. Especially for teenage boys. One of the factors that made it easy for the perverts to get away with it.

Terrell claimed he didn't know the names of any children who'd suffered actual abuse, but thought it was his duty to report it, regardless, painting the victim Impey in a very different light, as it did.

The senior investigating officer, DI Malcolm Arrowsmith, had homed in on two facts in Terrell's statement.

He had not actually been abused himself.

He didn't know, or wouldn't give, the names of anyone who had been.

In addition, the manager of the home who accompanied Terrell had been adamant they operated a zero-tolerance policy towards any kind of inappropriate behaviour. He was aware of the scandals in Islington and Lambeth, after all, and it wasn't going to happen in any home run by him.

A verdict of damaged children making up wicked stories about people who were generous with their time was the result, let's get back to railroading Amos Church.

'You think Richard Terrell's memory for the other children's names might have improved with age?' Kincade said.

'There's only one way to find out.'

God was smiling on the righteous that day. A search of the PNC quickly identified Terrell. He'd trodden a well-worn path from disadvantaged childhood to petty crime, amassing a string of offences to his name until the age of twenty-five. He'd turned his life around after that, but had slipped back into his old ways two years previously when he'd been cautioned for vandalising a neighbour's car after the neighbour repeatedly parked outside Terrell's house.

'You should send Jardine to talk to him,' Kincade said, when he got up from his desk and pulled on his jacket.

'I hope you're not suggesting she's from a similar background.'

'Not the disadvantaged part, no. But I'm sure she'll see something of her brother in Terrell. He might pick up on that, open up to her more.'

'And bollocks to whether it's an uncomfortable reminder about her own family problems?'

'She needs to be able to separate work—'

He held up a hand to stop her.

'Time to dismount from your high horse, Sergeant. I was only kidding. I agree with you. That's not where I was going anyway.' He went to the window, looked out and up at the blue sky outside, the occasional fluffy white cloud scudding across it. 'I'm off to sit on a boat in the sun.'

'I'll hold the fort here, shall I, sir?' she said to his retreating back.

27

'I don't bloody believe it,' Paul de la Haye said, as Angel came down the pontoon towards de la Haye's yacht, *Carpe Diem*. 'I didn't work that many cases.'

'What I can't believe is that you're still renovating'—making quotes in the air as he said it—'this old tub. You really don't like spending time with your wife, do you?'

'Not pushing a trolley around Sainsburys or humping bags of compost at the garden centre, no, I don't. So, which of my many failures is it this time?'

Until fifteen years previously, de la Haye had been known as Detective Chief Inspector de la Haye. Now in his sixties, he'd retired on the dot of thirty years, the name of his boat, *Carpe Diem*—seize the day—summing up his attitude to how life should be lived. It wasn't a view of life shared by a lot of his ex-colleagues, most coppers managing to screw up their personal lives through their addiction to the job. At times, Angel worried that he was falling into the same trap.

The boat was moored at the Shamrock Quay marina on the west bank of the River Itchen. The marina took its name from the famous J-class yacht, Shamrock V, built by Camper and

Nicholson on the site in 1931. She was the first British yacht to be built to the new J-class rule, commissioned by Sir Thomas Lipton for his fifth America's Cup challenge, a lifelong ambition he never fulfilled. Angel often thought de la Haye considered the renovation of his yacht to be a similarly lifelong endeavour.

On the previous two occasions Angel had met with him, it had been in relation to old unsolved cases worked by de la Haye —cases which Angel had subsequently solved, admittedly with the benefit of hindsight and fresh evidence. Hence de la Haye's remark about his failures.

Angel beamed at him as he climbed onboard in his uncharacteristic role as the bearer of glad tidings.

'Unbelievable as it seems, it's not one of yours this time.'

De la Haye leaned his head sideways, stuck his finger in his ear and worked it around as if he'd been swimming and couldn't clear the water from it.

'Sorry, I think I mis-heard you.'

'Nope. I searched high and low, eventually found a potential cock-up that didn't have your name all over it.'

De la Haye dipped his head in admiration.

'You must be one hell of a detective.'

'So they tell me.'

De la Haye glanced at his watch, his face falling.

'I would say it calls for a celebration, but it's a bit early. Even for you. By the way, are you still addicted to altar wine?'

'I'm on the non-alcoholic stuff now.'

'Do they do that?'

'Probably not. Gotta allow the clergy a few pleasures in life.'

'If you believe what you read in the papers, they've got plenty of others.'

Angel had known it was a mistake before the words were out of his mouth, de la Haye not missing an opportunity to take a dig at Angel's previous calling. But it was a useful way into the conversation ahead.

'You want to prove to me that your brain hasn't atrophied since you retired?'

De la Haye let his jaw drop, his tongue lolling out.

'Give it a go.'

'Okay. The year's nineteen ninety. We've got a murder that's looking like the wrong man was convicted. Does the name of any particular DI come to mind as the SCUO?'

The grin that cracked de la Haye's face told Angel when he finally caught on.

'The Senior Cock Up Officer.'

'That's the one.'

'It ought to be an actual role. As for a name, I want to say Marcus Horwood.'

Angel grinned right back at him.

'And I'd love to hear you say it. But sadly not.'

De la Haye only needed to give it a moment's serious thought before he groaned out loud.

'Not Malcolm Bent-Arrow?'

'I think it was spelled differently in the file, but yeah.'

De la Haye shook his head, scowled at Angel.

'Couldn't you have waited until the sun was over the yardarm before coming here? Then I could have a beer to wash away the taste of that name. I suppose I could try coffee. You want one?'

'I thought you'd never ask.'

Angel stayed at the top of the companionway steps while de la Haye went into the galley below, carried on the conversation from there. He ran through the Impey murder, not mentioning Richard Terrell's statement for now, concentrating on Amos Church.

'Was Arrowsmith the sort of copper to go for the easy option, ignore anything that didn't fit with what he'd already decided?'

'Definitely,' wafted up from the galley. 'He had a reputation for cutting corners.' De la Haye suddenly appeared at the bottom of the stairs, as if it was important for him to look Angel in the eye when he said what he wanted to say next. It told Angel what was coming. 'Nobody wanted to work with him. You'd work your butt off to find something, and then he'd dismiss it. Your team must feel the same. The only difference is that you don't dismiss it, you forgive them.'

Angel let him have his fun. He stepped out of the way when de la Haye came up the steps a minute later with two mugs of coffee.

'Let me smell yours,' he said.

De la Haye held out a mug with *Skipper* written on it.

'If I want a drink, I have a drink. I don't hide it.'

Angel sniffed anyway, couldn't detect anything. Then took it from de la Haye's hand before he could stop him.

'*Hey!* This one's yours,' de la Haye said, thrusting a mug at him with the letter *W* next to an anchor on it.

Angel took a quick slurp to clinch ownership, pulled a face.

'Forget booze, that'll get rid of the taste of Arrowsmith's name in your mouth. Dissolve the enamel on your teeth at the same time.'

De la Haye sipped at his own coffee.

'Don't know what you're talking about.'

'You should go to Sainsburys with your wife, after all. Then you could choose some decent coffee.'

What de la Haye chose to do was ignore the remark, get back on track.

'What are you thinking, if it wasn't Amos Church?'

Angel took a copy of Richard Terrell's statement out of his pocket, offered it to de la Haye.

'You want to read it to me?' de la Haye said.

Angel shook his head, raised his mug.

'I can't do two things at once.'

Reluctantly, de la Haye went down into the galley again, came back up with a pair of reading glasses perched on his nose. He raised his own mug at Angel.

'Lucky I can multi-task, eh?'

Angel hopped up onto the starboard side deck as de la Haye started reading and walked towards the bow. He spent a minute watching the gulls wheeling overhead, thinking how uncomplicated their lives were, then came back down the port side. De la Haye had finished reading by the time he got back to the cockpit.

'And this was in the file, was it?'

'Yep. Right there for anyone to see.'

De la Haye shrugged, looking like he was responsible for every piece of bad policing to have happened since Robert Peel started the first organised English police force in 1829.

'I don't know what to say, other than I'm not surprised, given it was Bent-Arrow. Thank God it wasn't me, this time.'

Angel clinked mugs with him.

'Amen to that.'

'I assume you'll be talking to Terrell as a matter of urgency.'

'It's happening as we speak. Going back to Arrowsmith, was he just lazy, or was he actually bent? The way you call him Bent-Arrow suggests he was.'

De la Haye waved it away.

'Nothing like that as far as I know. But *lazy arrow* doesn't have the same ring to it.'

'I suppose not. And finding a good nickname is the priority, after all.'

'Exactly. But it also fitted pretty well.' He shot his arm out towards Angel, his hand curving off to the side at the last minute. 'He had a knack of swerving away from the difficult options and decisions.' He paused, and Angel would never be able to decide whether what he said next was a serious observation or yet more light-hearted ribbing. 'I get the impression those are the ones you aim for.'

'BETTER NOT PARK THERE,' JARDINE SAID, POINTING AT THE EMPTY space immediately outside Richard Terrell's house. 'Don't want him to vandalise your car.'

'He'll get a lot more than a caution if he does.'

She leaned away to look at him, seeing him in a new light when he parked in the space anyway.

'Fighting talk, Craig. I like it.'

'You would.'

'That's why we make such a great team.'

'I thought team members were meant to complement each other, not clash.'

'Uh-huh.'

Not for the first time, he gave up, the conversation already too far adrift from any normal definition of reality.

The reason for the available parking space became apparent when a woman answered the door, looking as if her dog had just died.

'Mrs Terrell?' Jardine said.

'That's right.'

'I'm DC Jardine and this is DC Gulliver. We were hoping to have a word with your husband. Is he in?'

'He said he wasn't going to call you.'

Jardine had been expecting one of two possible answers. Yes or no. Possibly a fuller answer of the sort people often feel obliged to give—*he's in the loo*.

Her actual response put a brief dent in the conversation

before she recovered.

'Why did he say he wasn't going to call us?'

Beside her, Gulliver thought it was a pretty stupid question. Millions of people don't call the police every day of the week.

'He said it was pointless. You wouldn't be interested. Too busy with real crimes.'

Gulliver hoped Jardine didn't respond by asking if an unreal crime had been committed.

'What wouldn't we be interested in?' she said, instead, her voice suggesting she was growing tired with the conversation.

'Jake. Somebody poisoned him.'

'Who is Jake, Mrs Terrell?'

Uh-oh, Gulliver thought. *She only turns polite when her patience is wearing really thin.*

'Our dog. Who did you think I meant?'

'Jake was a person's name before it was a dog's.'

'Well, Jake is our dog. And somebody poisoned him.' She thrust her arm out, forefinger pointing accusingly at Gulliver's car. 'It was the man who parks there.'

'That's my car,' Gulliver said, not wanting to miss out on the unreal conversation, forget about an unreal crime.

'The man who *normally* parks in Richard's space,' Mrs Terrell said, her voice suggesting she knew policemen were getting younger but she hadn't realised they were also getting stupider.

'This would be the man whose car your husband vandalised for parking in what he believes is his personal space on a public road,' Gulliver came back at her.

'That's right. I think he's waited until now so that it won't be obvious it's him who poisoned Jake. And we've only had him for nine months.'

Gulliver nodded like now it all made sense.

'He was waiting for you to buy a dog so that he could poison it.'

'That's right.'

He'd have been disappointed if you'd bought a hamster, instead, Gulliver thought, and was professional enough to not say.

'Does your husband agree with you that your neighbour was responsible?'

'No. He said nobody would poison a dog over an argument about a parking space.'

'Did he say who he thought did poison your dog?'

Mrs Terrell shook her head, *he never tells me anything.*

'No. But he was doing something on his computer after I went to bed last night. And when I got up to go to the loo in the middle of the night, he was still awake. He was pretending to be asleep, but I can tell.'

She looked conspiratorially at Jardine, her thoughts easy to read. *We know our men, whatever they like to think.*

'Ask him to give us a call, please,' Gulliver said, handing her a card. 'It's important that he calls us as soon as possible. It could be a lot more important than your dog being poisoned, however upsetting that is.'

'IT SHOULD BE LAW THAT DOGS HAVE TO HAVE DOG NAMES, NOT people's names,' Jardine complained when they were back in the car, still parked in Richard's space.

'Like Rover or Scout, you mean?'

'Exactly.'

'What about Lassie?'

'I don't think you're taking me seriously, here.'

Sometimes it's difficult to, he thought, and moved them on.

'What did you make of that?'

'Apart from the fact that a neighbour with any sense would poison her, not the dog, you mean?'

'Apart from that, yes.'

She thought about it as Gulliver pulled away from the kerb, the contents of Richard Terrell's statement from thirty-four years ago fresh in her mind.

'He's being warned to keep his mouth shut. He came forward back then and was ignored. Now somebody is worried he'll be listened to.'

28

Angel was acutely aware of short periods of downtime in Kincade's presence. Intervals that were long enough to feel awkward if there was no conversation, but too short to talk about the one thing that needed to be discussed.

This was one of those times.

His father's Army contact had supplied them with a phone number for Jesse Hamilton. Jesse hadn't sounded at all surprised when Kincade called him, the opposite in fact, as if expecting it. The overriding impression had been one of relief, as if a burden had been lifted.

The nature of his job meant Jesse was left with time on his hands for long periods of the day while he waited to transport his VIP employer from business meeting to lunch, or from golf course to hotel and wherever else he passed his very important time, on business or otherwise.

Kincade had agreed to meet Jesse in a car park close to the National Oceanography Centre—not far from where she used to live in Ocean Village Marina—while his employer was attending a meeting in one of the NOC's conference suites. The biggest disappointment had been when she asked him his employer's name. He'd told her a name which she now couldn't remember, but which hadn't been the one she wanted to hear. Conrad Fischer.

Hers and Angel's belief in coincidence had not been put to the test.

Yet.

They arrived ten minutes early. It was during this period that Angel wanted to yell at her, *just bloody tell me!* He didn't, of course. They didn't have time for it, nor was it the way to approach what promised to be the biggest test of their relationship. After he'd said goodnight to Vanessa the previous night, he'd spent a long time thinking about what she'd said when he joked that perhaps he didn't want to know.

I think there's a chance that's true.

By the time he fell asleep, he was convinced he *did* want to know, not live his life as Grace had accused him with his head in the sand.

And once that decision had been made, he wanted to know *right now*.

So, time had to be passed in another way.

'My mother wants to meet you,' he said.

She looked at him like she hadn't heard him properly. Or she hoped she hadn't.

'What for?'

'You've moved in—'

'I'm a lodger.'

'—with the man she's still married to. Don't you think she's interested to see what you're like? Or are you happy for her to base her opinions solely on what I say about you?'

It took her a moment to formulate an answer, trying to read his expression.

'There's so much going on in that question I can't get my head around it. Am I supposed to care what she thinks about me? Am I meant to be worried about the things you might be saying about me? Do you care what she thinks about me? Do you care if I care what she thinks? You want me to go on?'

'What I wanted was a simple yes or no about whether you agree to meet her.'

'I'll think about it.'

'If I was to ask one of your girls, I bet they'd say that's your way of saying, *no*.'

'We'll see.'

'That one translates as, *don't hold your breath*.'

'That must be him there,' she said, the words riding out on a tide of relief as she pointed at a lilac-coloured Bentley Flying Spur with a personalised number plate that had just purred in. 'Obviously his boss wants to make sure people notice him.'

Angel stepped out of the car to wave the Bentley over, the big car pulling up on Kincade's side a minute later, facing the opposite direction. Kincade was out of the car before the Bentley had come to a complete stop, bending to look through its already-open passenger-side window.

'Feel free to jump in the back,' Jesse said.

She looked at Angel, immediately wished she hadn't. She felt exactly like one of her girls asking if it was okay to pet the animals at the zoo. He was already coming around the front of his car making a verbal answer unnecessary. Except he opened the Bentley's front door, not the back. With both of them in the back it would be far too easy for Jesse to avoid eye contact or make it indirectly in the rear-view mirror. Jesse took his carefully folded jacket from the passenger seat so that Angel could sit down. Kincade leaned between the front seats to take it from him, laid it equally carefully on the seat beside her.

Jesse's Army background was immediately apparent in his appearance. He wore an immaculately ironed short sleeve white shirt, the sleeves snug around his biceps, and a perfectly-knotted dark blue tie with a repeated 2PARA cap badge pattern. The crease in his black suit trousers was sharp enough to cut the unwary, and Angel could see the shine on his shoes even in the darkness of the footwell.

Jesse stuck out his hand.

'You must be Carl Angel's son.'

'I am,' Angel said, shaking Jesse's hand, opting for a simple confirmation rather than his usual reply—*for my sins*.

'A great man,' Jesse went on, still pumping Angel's hand. 'A terrible thing, what happened to him afterwards.'

Kincade stuck her hand between the seats so that Angel could get his own hand back and didn't get dragged into a discussion about his father's time in prison.

'I'm DS Kincade. I actually live with Carl at the moment.'

Angel knew what she was doing, even if he might not have done it himself. Amos Church had sought Jesse out because he didn't want to be found. They were about to try to make Jesse betray his friend's trust. Any bonding they could achieve in the impromptu luxury interview room would help.

Jesse was looking at her as if she'd told him Field Marshal Montgomery had been her granddad.

'It's only temporary,' she added, with a flick of her head towards Angel. 'You can have too much of a good thing. We understand you were making enquiries about Carl. Was that in relation to Amos Church?'

Closed questions, those allowing the interviewee the option of a simple yes or no, were generally avoided. Today, the direct question would hopefully cut through Jesse's crisis of conscience, torn between loyalty to his friend and doing the right thing.

Jesse leaned his head against the rest, looked up at the roof lining as if inspecting it for rogue specks of dust he'd missed when giving the roof its daily vacuum.

'Amos has been staying with me.'

'We get the feeling hiding out is more accurate,' Angel said, taking over.

'Yeah. I told him he should talk to you, but he wouldn't listen.'

Angel didn't miss how Jesse had said *wouldn't* listen, rather than *won't* listen, putting it in the past. He would return to it later.

'Why is he hiding in the first place?'

Jesse gave an incredulous snort. In that moment, Angel turned from the son of a man to be admired into one of the enemy.

'Because he doesn't trust you lot. You know what happened to him?'

'We've read the file, yes.' The bonding they'd sought to create would've been greatly enhanced by telling Jesse that it looked as if there had been a miscarriage of justice in convicting Amos. It wasn't something they could share with him at this point. Angel watered it down. 'We've identified something that requires another look.'

Jesse gawped at him, his voice rising.

'*Another look?* He didn't fucking do it. It's that simple. And he's scared he's going to get blamed for this one as well. You look on your systems and say to yourselves, Amos Church likes killing people in Southampton Old Cemetery, it must be him. Page one of the idiot's guide to policing says a leopard doesn't change its spots. I thought you lot were supposed to believe in rehabilitation.'

They both knew they were hearing Amos' own words coming out of Jesse's mouth, some of Amos' paranoia and hysteria with it. They guessed it had been hard on Jesse living with it, knowing it was waiting for him when he got home from work every day. They allowed him his outburst, before Angel reined it in.

'I understand why he feels that way. He sees the murder in the paper, thinks, *shit, the bastards are going to blame me. Again.* He panics and comes to you for help. But then when he's sitting in your place all day long, he'll calm down and think about it rationally. And if he still thinks he's going to get blamed, it must be because he knows there's something else. We know Lois Sheppard called him two days before she was killed. We know she called him on the night she was killed. She wanted to talk to him about the Eric Impey murder. But we don't know what the purpose of the call on the night she died was. Did he meet her that night?'

After the litany of things everybody in the car did know, the question hung unanswered in the silent leathery ambience of the Bentley.

'I don't think so,' Jesse said. 'He told me he didn't answer it.'

With those last seven words, Jesse expressed his inner turmoil more eloquently than he had so far. The rot had set in. He didn't know if he believed his friend. And that doubt crucified him, that he wasn't worthy of the trust Amos had placed in him.

It was time to return to what Angel felt was about to lead into a big step backwards.

'A minute ago, you said Amos *wouldn't* listen. Not that he *won't* listen. The past tense. I don't think that was a slip of the tongue. He's not staying with you anymore, is he?'

Jesse placed both hands on the top of the steering wheel, gripped it like it was a lifeline to his continued sanity, blue-veined forearms as taut as his jaw.

'No. I accepted that he wasn't going to talk to you. So I persuaded him to at least talk to the people he works for. If he goes AWOL, they'll think he's back on the booze. He might lose his job. Then, when this all blows over, if it blows over, he'll be out of work. And that might make him go back on the booze . . .'

'A vicious circle.'

'Yeah.' Jesse's forearms tensed tighter, as if scared that if he didn't keep hold of the wheel, he'd use his fists to batter his own face. 'But I wouldn't let him just call them. Oh, no. I'm never satisfied, me. I told him he had to go into the office so that they could smell his breath, see for themselves that he hadn't turned back into the drunken bum he used to be. I kept on and on at him until he agreed.' Finally, Jesse stopped staring straight ahead, turned to look Angel in the eye so that Angel might see his pain. 'I haven't seen him since. I don't know if he got sick of me nagging him and found somewhere else to crash, or whether something's happened to him.'

They all heard it the same way as Jesse heard it in his heart.

Whether I sent him to his death.

29

The probation service had provided them with details of the company Amos Church had worked for ever since his release from HMP Isle of Wight. Walking With Heroes was a charity that worked with ex-servicemen, helping them adjust to life outside the military and introducing them to potential employers. It made sense that Amos chose to work for them. It was just a pity they hadn't been in existence when he left the Army himself.

Angel was at his desk when Kincade called them and asked to speak to somebody about Amos. Neither of them was expecting any problems, no reluctance to speak to them.

Which is why Angel was surprised to see Kincade sit up in her chair as if she'd been told to fuck off.

'I'm sorry, but would you repeat that name, please. I think I might have mis-heard.'

Angel watched her as the person on the other end did so, Kincade looking as if they'd switched to Swedish mid-call.

'No, that's alright. I know how to spell it.'

Angel was intrigued now. It was a strange thing to say. As if the other party had offered to spell *Smith* or *Brown*. Most

English names are easy enough to spell, and if it was foreign, Polish, say, with all the letters not often used in English names—z's and x's and y's in unexpected combinations—you'd ask for it to be spelled for you.

'You are not going to believe this,' she said, after she'd made an appointment and ended the call.

'Your face tells me you're right. What won't I believe?'

She wagged her finger at him, made him work for it.

'I asked to speak to whoever is the best person to talk to about Amos. Guess what name they gave me.'

Angel thought about it. Her reaction suggested it was the last name they would expect. Saying that she knew how to spell it implied it was also a name they had already come across. That narrowed it down to two people sharing the same surname as far as he was concerned.

'Either Ingrid or Conrad Fischer.' Feeling very pleased with himself.

She made a swiping gesture with her arm as if striking a gong, her voice resonating.

'*Wrong!*'

He was mid-nod congratulating himself when her reply registered.

'Wrong?'

'Yep. As in, not right. Want to guess again?'

He didn't give it a moment's thought. Threw out the most ridiculous suggestion he could imagine.

'My father. He's worked for them secretly all these years.'

'Think even more outrageous.'

He waved his hand at her, bored with the game now.

'I give up.'

'Lloyd...'

'That's not a name that's cropped up.'

'Impey.' She put her finger behind her ear as he flapped his mouth soundlessly at her. 'Cat got your tongue, sir?'

'You're right. I don't believe it.'

'That's up to you. But it doesn't change the fact that Eric Impey's son, Lloyd, has employed Amos Church ever since he got out of prison for killing his father.'

'For being *convicted* of killing his father. Two very different things.'

'True. It might suggest he's got his own doubts about that conviction, and is trying to make amends. We can ask him when we see him. Lloyd Impey has fitted us into his busy schedule at four o'clock this afternoon.'

'Let's hope it's his last appointment of the day. Something tells me we're going to have a lot to talk about.'

'THIS IS THE FIRST PLACE I'VE BEEN TO THAT ISN'T A HUNDRED times nicer than our office,' Kincade said, approaching what had once been a substantial family home now converted into slightly tired-looking offices that housed Walking With Heroes' operations.

Angel couldn't disagree, nor was he surprised.

'Same principles apply. The taxpayer wants to see every penny spent fighting crime. And if you're in the business of asking people to part with their hard-earned cash, you don't want them thinking your idea of a good cause is plush offices and a fancy car for yourself.'

She nodded like it made sense. Except the butter-wouldn't-melt look on her face told him something cynical was on its way.

'What about the church, sir? Isn't the principle the same? Or did all those peasants want a cathedral that cost enough to feed their families for a thousand years?'

He shook his head, pointed at the floor.

'That's insurance. Paying to not be sent downstairs. And before you ask, even if you make it to Chief Constable, you won't earn enough to put in the collection plate to stop you from going there.'

'See you down there,' she muttered under her breath, following him into Walking With Heroes' utilitarian office suite.

The same self-effacing theme continued in Lloyd Impey's modest office, the furniture looking as if it would be equally at home in a back-bedroom home office.

It also promised to be on the cramped side with the four of them crammed in, Lloyd Impey having invited a blonde-haired woman to join them.

'This is my sister, Helen. We run the charity together.'

It was only a fleeting impression, but it seemed to Angel that a scowl passed across Helen's face as her brother introduced her. As if irritated that the fact of her being his sister was always mentioned before her own name, making her subservient to him.

Except she didn't look to him like the sort of woman who was subservient to anyone.

There was only ever going to be one way to start the interview once they were all settled on a pair of slightly-too-small blue fabric sofas arranged in an *L* shape.

'It's a very unusual setup you've got here,' Angel said, looking from one to the other of them. 'The fact that you employ the man who killed your father.'

He was very careful to not so much as hint at what they'd discussed earlier. That Lloyd Impey—and presumably his sister, too—suspected that Amos Church had not been responsible for killing their father, and they wished to make amends. To see if either of them volunteered that information.

They didn't.

Instead, Lloyd launched into a long sales spiel about all the good work they did, as if he thought they might get their cheque books out.

'There are a lot of good causes competing for people's goodwill, Inspector. It's necessary to find a way to stand out. I'm not ashamed that we use . . .' He paused, searching for a term he was happy with. '*Sensationalist* tactics to get people's attention. We put our money where our mouth is when it comes to helping ex-servicemen, even going so far as to employ the man who killed our father. We're confident that once we've got people's attention, our good work speaks for itself.'

'The end justifies the means,' Angel said, more to stop Impey from saying it all over again than anything else.

'Exactly.'

The size of the room and the positioning of the sofas meant the two people in the corner of the *L*—Angel and Helen—were rubbing knees. Helen stood up and went to park her butt on the edge of her brother's desk, giving everybody a bit more room.

'Don't get us wrong,' she said. 'We hated Amos at first. We would've killed him if we'd been given the chance. But you lose a parent like that, you grow up fast. We looked into the circumstances, saw that Amos had suffered from PTSD. And the more we read about it, the more we understood the factors that led to our father's death, how Amos wasn't completely in control of his actions.'

Angel wasn't sure how much more of Saint Helen and Saint Lloyd he could stomach before he needed to get out. He was wishing he'd brought his cheque book, anything to get away quickly.

'He was a victim, too, in his own way,' he said, in an attempt to cut it short.

'That's right,' Lloyd said, taking over from Helen in what looked like a very slick double act. 'The thing is, I'd always wanted to go into the Army myself, even before Amos entered our lives.'

'Why didn't you?' Kincade said.

Lloyd touched his left shoulder.

'I dislocated—'

'*No*,' Helen interrupted, pointing at a blue asthma inhaler on her brother's desk. 'It was your asthma.'

Lloyd looked as if he was about to argue, decided against it.

'Whatever. I wouldn't have passed the medical. The upshot is, I already had an interest in the military when we were looking into PTSD and the other problems facing ex-servicemen. It suddenly occurred to me to start a charity in Dad's memory.'

'Fate,' Angel said.

'Karma,' Kincade added.

'Exactly,' both Impeys echoed, sounding like they were about to break into a rousing chorus of *Hallelujah*.

The double act was now so firmly in place, Angel and Kincade automatically looked at Helen to continue.

'Amos was still in prison when we started the charity,' she said. 'We were muddling along and it was obvious we needed something to give us a boost. We went to a marketing agency. The situation with Amos came up when we were telling them how we got started. And they said, give him a job when he gets out. We looked at each other. *Why didn't we think of that?*'

Angel felt like clapping as Lloyd and Helen smiled at each other. He knew Kincade was feeling the same way. Neither of them did, of course, although he doubted the Impey siblings would've minded.

'I'm guessing Amos was surprised when you offered him the job,' he said, momentarily forgetting which Impey was on next.

'It was done through a third party,' Lloyd said. 'They put it to Amos that he'd been offered a job by a charity helping ex-servicemen like him. Stressed all the good work being done to get him interested—'

'Then sucker punched him with who was behind it.' This from Kincade.

'If that's how you want to describe it, yes,' Helen said, out of turn. 'Personally, I like to concentrate on the fact that he's been with us ever since.'

'And have you discussed it with him in all that time?'

'No. You might find that hard to believe. I don't know.' Her expression said she cared even less. 'We were determined to act as if he was like any other employee. We didn't want him to feel we were patronising him or acting out of pity. I assume he was wary of bringing it up. Worried that if the discussion got out of hand, we might sack him. To be brutally honest, I got the impression he was using us at first. He was in a very difficult position. Employers weren't exactly lining up to offer him work. He therefore jumped at the offer of a job to get something worthwhile on his CV, planning to move on. Except he discovered that he liked the work and stayed. Be as cynical as you like. Tell me we're all justifying avoiding the issue after the event. That's your problem, but here we still are.'

Angel studied Helen as she lectured Kincade. Everything she said made sense and was plausible. She'd put a lot of thought into it. Perhaps because potential donors also found the Impey siblings too good to be true and she needed to win them over before they put their hands in their pockets.

He smiled to himself to think that the slickness with which she answered questions she was expecting were like control questions in a polygraph test against which her answers to the unexpected questions would be compared.

He put it to the test now.

'Were you aware of your father acting as a social uncle at the Jerusalem House children's home?'

He'd addressed the question to Helen, but Lloyd answered.

'We knew he volunteered there, yes. I'm not sure I've heard the phrase *social uncle* before.' His face hardened, his tone of voice with it. 'I hope you're not suggesting anything untoward went on, Inspector. This is our father you're talking about.'

Angel shook his head as if it had never crossed his mind.

'I'm not suggesting anything at all, Mr Impey. Your father volunteering and giving up his time is admirable. It's a sad reflection on the state of the world today that your own first response is to assume I was implying his behaviour was anything other than exemplary.'

He's an ex-priest, he knows what it's like to be guilty until proven innocent, Kincade thought, as Lloyd shrivelled under Angel's impassive gaze.

'Part of the role was taking the children on outings,' she said, in an attempt to get over the uncomfortable atmosphere that had descended on the room. 'Did either of you ever meet any of the children?'

Lloyd immediately looked at his sister.

She looked at her feet.

Angel and Kincade looked at each other.

Here we go . . .

Then Helen cleared her throat.

'Our father suggested it. I seem to remember my immediate reaction was to say, *why on earth would we want to spend time with them?* I'm sure I made *them* sound like something sub-human. I could be a precocious little madam at times. In my defence, I was only thirteen.' She looked directly at Kincade. 'You were a thirteen-year-old girl once. Maybe you can understand.'

Kincade didn't allow herself to be drawn in. But she didn't miss how Helen hadn't actually answered the question.

A natural break had been reached. They'd covered the ancient history. It was time to talk about the present. Everyone felt the change. Lloyd suddenly remembered his manners, clapped his hands together.

'Anyone want something to drink? Tea, coffee, water? Something stronger?'

Angel and Kincade both wanted something stronger, said they'd have water.

'I'll get it,' Helen said.

So that you can spit in it, Kincade thought and smiled at her.

'Same for me,' Lloyd said, as Helen headed for the door.

'Feel free to have something stronger,' Angel said, catching the disappointment in Lloyd's voice. 'It's not as if you're being interviewed under caution.'

Lloyd hesitated, then shook his head at his sister.

'You didn't come here to talk about the past,' he said, after Helen had left and closed the door behind her.

'No, we didn't,' Angel agreed, even though it had been illuminating.

'It's about the woman who was murdered in the cemetery, isn't it?'

'It is, but let's wait until Helen gets back.' He paused, long enough for Lloyd to pull out his phone. 'Actually, it won't hurt if you tell us where you were on that evening. It's just a routine question. Last Wednesday?'

Lloyd didn't even need to check.

'I was here. I work late most nights, but last week was worse than usual.' He tried an oily smile. 'No rest for the wicked, eh? I'm sure you know what it's like.'

'We do indeed, sir. What time did you leave to go home?'

'I didn't. Not on Tuesday or Wednesday.' He pointed at the sofa Angel was sitting on. 'You're sitting on my bed. And before you say it, yes, it's bloody uncomfortable.' He rolled his head in a figure of eight motion. 'My neck's still stiff.'

'Your wife must be very understanding.'

The remark knocked a lot of the bonhomie out of Lloyd's voice.

'If she'd been more understanding, she might still be around. I'm sure you and your colleagues know all about that, too.'

Angel ignored the attempt to draw him into the conversation again, changed tack.

'What about your sister? Where was she that night?'

Again, Lloyd didn't hesitate.

'In bed with a stomach bug. I remember because she was supposed to be going out that night. She was really upset about it.'

Angel shrugged, *these things happen*. A minute later, Helen came back carrying a tray containing four glasses filled with water.

'Did I miss anything important?'

'No, just getting onto the good stuff now,' Angel said, taking a glass. 'As you know, a woman was recently murdered in the same cemetery as your father. We need to speak to Amos about that.'

'Is he a suspect?' Helen said.

'Not at present. But we need to speak to him.'

'Why can't you leave the poor man alone?'

'Because we believe he might have information that is pertinent to our investigation. It's regrettable if it causes him distress, but solving this current murder is our priority. I'm sure you wouldn't have been happy if the detectives investigating your father's murder hadn't interviewed a person of interest because they didn't want to hurt his feelings.'

'I suppose not.' Her voice grudging.

'We've spoken to a friend of his who told us he's been lying low, but he came here to explain why he hasn't been at work.'

'That's right,' Lloyd said. 'It was the day before yesterday. He came in about six o'clock, after everybody had left for the day. He would've known I stay late most days. I assume he didn't want all of his colleagues quizzing him. Everybody's aware of his history.'

'I wasn't here at the time,' Helen chipped in, which added nothing other than to save them from having to ask.

Lloyd's expression changed, and his voice with it, made Kincade imagine Angel in his role as a priest. Giving the impression he understood men's weaknesses, how the devil leads them astray, despite rising above temptation himself.

'It was obvious why he wanted to come in, rather than call. To prove he was sober. Hadn't fallen off the wagon. I'd be lying if I said the suspicion hadn't crossed my mind. I was relieved to see that he hadn't.' He smiled, the sort he might use as he listened to a child make up a tall story. 'I should be indignant that he insulted my intelligence. Made up some excuse about a family emergency when it was obvious it was related to the murder that was all over the newspaper.'

'Lloyd told him to take as long as he needed,' Helen added. 'After the length of time he's worked for us, he deserves a sabbatical. A paid one, of course.' She smiled at Kincade, the sub-text clear.

He'll be happy we sucker punched him all those years ago.

Kincade smiled back.

'Do you know where he went afterwards?'

'Back to wherever he's staying, I presume,' Helen said. 'We know he's not at home. Lloyd called round. There was no answer.'

'We talked to the person he was staying with earlier today. He hasn't seen Amos since he set off to come here.'

Helen shrugged like it wasn't her job to find him, the dismissiveness immediately falling away as she jumped on the opportunity to criticise the police. Kincade bore the brunt of her attack.

'Perhaps he's so traumatised and scared of being wrongly accused for a second time that he left the country. We'd just given him an indefinite paid holiday, after all. That's what I'd do.'

Angel didn't look at Kincade, but he knew what went through her mind, mimicking Helen.

St Tropez is sublime at this time of year, Dahling.

It was time to change tack. The discussion had focussed for too long on how understandable it was for Amos to put himself out of their reach.

'Do you know the name Richard Terrell?' Angel asked.

Lloyd and Helen looked at each other. It gave them a useful second or two when they weren't meeting Angel's eyes before Lloyd answered for them.

'I don't think so.'

'Is that who Amos has been staying with?' Helen said.

Clever answer, Angel thought, weighing up whether to really shake the tree.

No, he's the witness who alleged that your father tried to abuse him.

'What about Patrick Quinn?' Kincade said, feeling Angel back down from the confrontation she'd also been contemplating.

'The name sounds familiar, but I can't think why,' Lloyd said, raising an eyebrow at Helen as if looking for help in placing the name.

'I know what you mean,' she said, shaking her head.

Good answer number two, Angel thought, getting to his feet. It was time to wrap things up.

Lloyd handed him a business card, told him to feel free to call at any time.

'I'll take one of yours, too, if I may,' Angel said to Helen.

She smiled apologetically, as if he'd been the third person to ask that day.

'I don't have any on me, I'm afraid. Lloyd's the front man, never leaves home without them. Sometimes I think he eats them, he goes through them so fast. I'm still working through box one.'

Lloyd came with them as far as the door to Walking With Heroes' office suite, left them to make their own way downstairs and out. A grey-haired woman in her late sixties was striding purposefully towards the front door when Angel opened it. He stepped smartly to the side, as did Kincade. The old biddy breezed past them, nose in the air and without acknowledging their existence, as if they were the paid help who didn't warrant a *thank you*.

'Bit snooty for the cleaning lady,' Kincade said, raising her middle finger at the woman's back.

Except Angel had other ideas about who it was heading up the stairs they'd just come down.

'I'M GOING TO HAVE A WORD WITH THE COLLEGE OF POLICING,' Kincade announced, once they were outside. 'Get them to update the authorised professional practice guidance for a new identification category. *VT1*. A person who wears Velcro trousers to stop them from sliding off anything they're sitting on.'

He smiled with her, the remark echoing what he'd felt himself.

'They were both too good to be true, weren't they? Saint Lloyd the Forgiving and Saint Helen, the patron saint of second chances.'

'In a slick, slimy way, yeah. It won't do their marketing any good if it turns out they gave the wrong man a job. *We've got all the best intentions, but we've got a bit of an issue with the details.* It might make donors wonder if they've got an issue identifying where the money should go.'

'Have you ever thought about entering a cynicism competition?'

She waved the facetious question away, as if it wasn't worth entering something you were always going to win hands-down.

'Lloyd got a bit touchy about the suggestion of abuse, didn't he?'

Angel was forced to correct her.

'He got *very* touchy, given it was only an unspoken implication about the possibility of abuse, not a suggestion.'

'But apparently they've never heard of Richard Terrell.'

He pointed at her, his earlier remark validated.

'See, more cynicism.'

'I noticed how you backed down from challenging them.'

He was thoughtful a moment as he made a quick reassessment about whether it had been the right call.

'I want to look into them a bit more first.'

'Same reason you didn't ask them if they know the Fischers?'

'This is spooky. You think it's because you're living with my father—'

'I'm his *lodger*.'

'—that we're starting to think alike?'

'If it is, Grace will definitely get her way. I'll be out of there, asap.'

30

'Thought so,' Kincade said, after they'd been driving for a couple of minutes.

Angel glanced across, saw her inspecting her tongue in the mirror on the back of the sun visor.

'What are you doing?'

'Checking how dry my tongue is.'

His pulse picked up as his mind did the translation, what it implied.

Let's go for a drink.

'I'll stop at a petrol station so you can get a bottle of water.'

He had no idea why he said it. Making what he knew was coming harder for her. It wasn't deliberately spiteful or awkward, more his subconscious slowing things down after she blindsided him.

'Some of the slime from the Impeys must have rubbed off on me,' she said. 'I've forgotten how to speak plainly and say what I mean. Do you want to go for a beer, Padre?'

He couldn't stop himself from looking at her again.

'You never call me *Padre*.'

We've never had a conversation of the sort I've got in mind, hung in the air between them, modified when she put it into words.

'There's a first time for everything.'

'I told you before, that's not something I want to hear coming from the person living in my father's house.'

'*Almost* everything,' she conceded.

'Where do you want to go?'

'You choose.'

What he heard: *My brain's scrambled.*

He made a quick decision based on the way he guessed the conversation would go. The fact that she wouldn't want, or be in any fit state, to drive back to Salisbury afterwards.

'We'll go to the Jolly Sailor at Bursledon. You can crash at my place. And don't worry about having to meet my mother. She's staying with Grace for a couple of days.'

The way she didn't complain about the unplanned overnight stay, the lack of fresh clothes for the next day, told him it was the right call.

The rest of the journey passed in silence. Had it not been such a difficult prospect hanging over her, he'd have hummed Chopin's *Marche Funèbre* to ease the awkwardness.

Fate proved that it never likes to miss a party when they'd got to the pub and carried their drinks outside. He groaned to himself when he saw the only available table.

'This is where I was sitting when Virgil Balan called me,' he said, as they sat down overlooking the river.

He immediately regretted the remark, reminding her as it did about the potential problems ahead if her predecessor ever decided he wanted his old job back. She took it in her stride, responding as if grateful for anything to put off what she had to tell him, if only for a minute or two.

'Either you haven't called Stuart Beckford, or you haven't told me.'

'I haven't got around to it, yet. But I will. Some things take a little time to build up to, even after you've made the decision.' Then, because it was so obvious why they were here, that his last remark referred to her more than him, 'I wish I kept a wire mesh screen in the back of the car. I could construct a pop-up confessional.' Marking a line down the table between them with the edge of his palm as he said it.

'That makes two of us. It's spooky that I called you *Padre* for the first time tonight.'

Fate up to its tricks, he thought, as a brief lull followed while they both took a long swallow of beer.

'Think I should get the next two rounds in now?'

'I almost suggested it when you ordered this one.'

He got up without another word and went inside, feeling almost as much relief as she did. What she was about to say would all be difficult, but the initial first step was almost the hardest—*I lied about my past*—because it was between them. The rest of it was history. Before they knew each other. It might have serious consequences for the future of their relationship, and that didn't make those first words any easier.

He took it upon himself to get them over it after he carried four pints out and lined them up on the table, easing things further by blaming his sister.

'I know you worked out Grace has been digging into your past, and that's why she called me. I'm guessing you told my dad about it a few days ago, and he said, *so bloody what?*'

She smiled softly, the last one for a while to come.

'He did. He also said you might not be so understanding. *I'm not sure he ever believed all that forgiveness crap he used to peddle.*'

'Peddle? Like I was a door-to-door salesmen selling cheap cleaning products?'

'His word. Anyway, you're right, I told him. It's only fair I tell you. Have you heard of ONA? The Order of Nine Angles? That's *angles*, by the way, not *angels*.'

'Vaguely. I couldn't tell you much about them.'

'I wish I could say the same. Basically, they're a Satanic Nazi cult...'

She explained that ONA, or O9A, is a militant Satanic terrorist network founded in the late 1960s. It elevates itself above the usual crackpot right-wing crazies by combining neo-Nazi ideology with what they call *Traditional* Satanism, their behaviour characterised by a commitment to breaking taboos and rejecting social norms.

In the pursuit of a militaristic new world order called the *Imperium*, ONA's writings condone and encourage human sacrifice and incite its members to commit rape—a requirement for *ascension of the Ubermensch*—as well as paedophilia and lynching, alongside more mainstream terrorist attacks to further their aims.

She took a sip of beer, as if that had any chance of washing away the bad taste in her mouth.

'It's a magnet for crazy sick freaks. You name it, members are in prison for it. Rape. Cannibalism. Torture of children. Necrophilia. Child pornography. One sick bastard streamed the mutilation of children live. You've got to share a video of child sexual abuse or a murder you've committed if you want to join one of their cells...'

She went on to explain how the group's structure was its strength—a network of autonomous clandestine cells known as *nexions,* rather than one central body for law enforcement to concentrate its efforts against. From its beginnings in the Welsh Marches of England, its influence had become far reaching and insidious, inspiring neo-Nazi extremist groups across the globe, including the US-based Atomwaffen Division and the UK's own Sonnenkrieg Division—a banned terrorist organisation known for the glorification of sexual violence and the use of sexual crimes as a means of undermining society.

'As far as they're concerned, the sicker, the better,' she finished. 'Gotta go to the loo.'

It made it a bit pointless him buying an additional two rounds to minimise interruptions, but he could hardly object. He spent the time mulling over what she'd said so far. The direction it was going corresponded with the way his suspicions about her had developed in the past months.

'I'm guessing Uncle James enters the story now,' he said, when she slid back onto the bench beside him, their backs against the residual warmth of the weathered red-brick wall.

Her uncle, Superintendent James Milne, was a big noise in SO15, the Metropolitan Police's Counter-Terrorism Command Unit. In the sanitised version of her fall from grace, his intervention prevented her from being kicked out altogether. Angel guessed his role was about to get bigger.

'He does. You might not know it, but the split between Islamic and extreme right-wing terrorism over here is now about sixty-forty. It's changed in recent years. The right-wing crazies are a growing problem. The result is tit-for-tat atrocities. You remember the Manchester Arena bombing?'

Angel did indeed. On the evening of 22 May 2017, Islamic extremist Salman Abedi detonated a nail bomb inside the Manchester Arena following a concert by American pop singer Ariana Grande. Twenty-two people were killed, a further one thousand and seventeen injured.

'Then there were the Christchurch mosque shootings in twenty-nineteen,' he said, the details easily coming to mind.

On 15 March of that year, right-wing extremist Brenton Tarrant killed fifty-one Muslims at two separate mosques in Christchurch, New Zealand. He streamed the first shootings live on Facebook. It was the first-ever live-streamed far-right terror attack, an achievement Tarrant no doubt bragged about to fellow inmates as he served his life sentence without the possibility of parole—the first time such a sentence had been handed down in New Zealand.

'Exactly,' she agreed. 'The list goes on. Anyway, intel was coming in about a sicko from the Order of Nine Angles called Morgan Brice who'd started a breakaway cell. He'd been radicalised after his cousin was injured at the Manchester Arena and lost half his face and one eye. He saw the Brenton Tarrant shootings and the spate of copy-cat attacks it inspired, thought to himself, *let's have some of that over here*.' She took a slurp of beer, banged the empty glass down on the table and moved the next one into place. 'Time for some family history. I need to warn you, it's going to strike an unwelcome chord with you. Uncle James has got a son. Duncan. Guess what he wanted Duncan to do with his life.'

Angel put his index finger against his lips, pretended to think.

'Become a police officer?'

'I thought you'd get that right.'

She was well aware of his own family history. The way he'd disappointed his father by becoming a priest rather than follow him into the Army. That failure on his part increased the pressure on his younger brother, Cormac, to enter the military, a decision which ultimately led to his suicide.

'And did Duncan toe the line, do what was expected of him?' she said.

'Absolutely not.'

'Correct.' She narrowed her eyes at him. 'Have you been cheating and looking at the answers?'

He held up his right hand, thumb holding the little finger down.

'Scout's honour.'

'Okay. Anyway, Duncan became a hairdresser.'

'I can see how Uncle James might have been a tad disappointed.'

'And he lives in Brighton.'

'Nice enough town.'

'With his husband, Ashley.'

Angel gave a long slow nod, *okaaay*.

'So Uncle James took a keen interest in your own career within the police.'

'He did. Not necessarily a bad thing...'

'Unless it's too blatant and your peers find out.'

'Correct. Uncle James is also a firm believer that the best way to live your life is to model yourself as closely as possible on Uncle James. He'd spent time working undercover, and floated it past me. I said I'd think about it, didn't really take it seriously.'

'You had a young family, after all. Doesn't exactly go hand-in-hand with the undercover life.'

She smiled, a sour grimace without humour.

'Seems Uncle James didn't get the memo about marital bliss. The next thing I knew, it was a done deal. Elliot hit the roof, understandably. I hadn't mentioned it, seeing as I hadn't taken the suggestion seriously. So, out of the blue, I had to break it to him.'

'Difficult.'

'We'll leave it there. Anyway, I'd been on the job for six months when the Morgan Brice situation reared its head.'

'Uncle James put your name forward?'

She raised her glass in a toast.

'Thanks a lot, Uncle James. Brice was planning a Brenton Tarrant-style attack. His contacts through ONA and other right-wing nutters were supplying the automatic weapons. He was planning it for Eid al-Adha. Do you know anything about Islamic festivals?'

'I'm aware of Ramadan, but that's about it.'

'Eid al-Adha is the feast of sacrifice. It celebrates the prophet Ibrahim's willingness to sacrifice his son Ismail when God ordered him to. It's the same story as Abraham and Isaac in the bible. Brice thought it was perfect. *You want sacrifice, I'll give you sacrifice.* What he really wanted to do was attack the Baitul Futuh mosque in Morden in south London. It's one of the largest mosques in Western Europe. He might have been a sicko and a nutter, but he knew it would also have the best security, so he lowered his sights. So long as he beat Brenton Tarrant's score of fifty-one dead, he'd be a happy sick fuck.'

'You were tasked with infiltrating the cell.'

'Yeah. Eid al-Adha lasts for three to four days, and we didn't know exactly when he was planning the attack, or which of two mosques he'd identified he was going to hit first.'

'What was your cover story?'

She glanced at him quickly, caught the smile on his face before he covered it with his beer glass.

'I don't know what's so funny.'

'Apart from the fact that you look like a cop and project confidence, you mean?'

She rocked her hand in acknowledgement.

'We settled on the Fire Brigade. It explained my stature and fitness—'

'And anybody who's prepared to run into a burning building is either confident or stupid.'

'True. And it's attractive experience to a terrorist who might want to burn things to the ground. The story was that I'd just lost my job when I met Brice. I'd been sacked when I told a racist joke and a Muslim administrator reported me. That gave lots of scope for me to be bitter. As you say, running into burning buildings, saving lives, and then being kicked out for something that nobody would've given a damn about ten years earlier. We laid it on even heavier. I was in a relationship with the Station Commander who had to sack me. He ended the relationship so as not to be tainted by association. And if all that wasn't enough, we invented a brother who'd been at the Manchester Arena and was injured, just like Brice's cousin. I was supposed to go with him but had to cancel at the last minute. It was fate sparing me so that I could fight another day, and so on.'

'Sounds like that should do it.'

'It did. And I was getting close, but not close enough. The clock's ticking. Eid al-Adha is approaching fast. The thing is, it was obvious Brice had the hots for me—'

'He's only human, after all.'

She dipped her head at him, even if it wasn't quite clear if it was a compliment or not.

'We first met in a shitty bar he frequented. I was flirting, but keeping him at arm's length. Stringing him along each time I accidentally bumped into him. I let the cover story slip out little by little until he was hooked.'

'Now he wanted to recruit you as well as get you in the sack.'

A spasm passed across her face as if she had a mouthful of sour milk and nowhere to spit it.

'Yeah. The thing is, they had two properties they were renting for all the crazies to live like animals in. I let it slip that the latest disaster in my life was that my landlord, Mr Singh, was kicking me out to make room for a family of refugees the government was going to pay him twice as much to house. Brice offered me a room in one of the properties. Luckily, not the one he lived in himself.'

'I'm guessing Elliot wasn't happy?'

The scowl made another quick dash across her face.

'I didn't realise you'd met him. No, as far as Elliot was concerned, I was already fucking Brice's brains out. The move into the property was so that I could service all of his sidekicks as well. I did actually waver at one point—'

'But Uncle James had a quiet word about doing your duty?'

'I didn't know you'd met him, too. Anyway, I moved in.'

He sensed a change come over her. So far, everything she'd talked about had been moving forwards, progress, despite the increased sacrifice she'd been forced to make by moving into Brice's property.

Things were now about to go south.

A brief smile more like a nervous twitch came and went in the blink of an eye, an acknowledgement of fate up to its tricks again.

'You know how they say the best lies contain the most truth? The story that was put out about my demotion was based on a real incident.'

'It just wasn't you.'

'No. But I was there. And when one of the protestors videoed it, my face was visible in the background. I looked very different to what I looked like in my undercover role, but if you looked hard enough . . .' She shrugged, *it is what it is*. 'People were coming and going in Brice's property all the time. Not all of them complete nutters, but all of them involved in demonstrations and civil unrest in some way or other. One of them must have seen the video and recognised me. Or, if not actually recognised me, it made them suspicious enough to put a tracker on my car.'

She lapsed into silence as she prepared to bare her soul, admit to her culpability that he'd felt like a black cloud gathering over them.

Out of the corner of his eye he saw a man come out of the pub interior, a pint in one hand, a newspaper in the other. They were sitting at a table big enough for four, both on the same side, the chairs opposite empty. It would be perfectly acceptable for the man to ask to share their table and quietly read his paper. Their conversation would be cut short just as she was approaching its climax. He stood up swiftly, moved to the other side of the table, effectively claiming it all for them exclusively. The man scowled at him, knowing what he'd done. He wandered back inside with a grumbled, *selfish bastard*.

The privacy came with a price. They were now sitting facing each other. There would be no looking out over the river, not making eye contact, as she finished her tale.

Like the disgruntled customer, Kincade knew what Angel had done. She flicked her head in the direction of the doorway the man had disappeared through.

'He wouldn't have stayed long if he'd eavesdropped.'

'Maybe not. But this isn't your local. I don't want to get banned.'

'Fair enough. Things were really bad with Elliot by now. He'd always had a problem with me being in the police, especially since I didn't need to work at all. Then I went undercover. And now I've moved in with the crazies, which allows me to kill two birds with one stone in his mind. Easier for the sex orgies, as well as keeping Uncle James happy, who I care more about than I ever have Elliot, yadda, yadda, yadda. Then he starts talking in terms of me abandoning the girls, who are of course driving him berserk. I agreed to meet him and them.'

'You were followed?'

'And photographed. But I didn't know about it at the time. I'm now being kept out of the loop by Brice, obviously. Both of his properties are under surveillance. I get a message from the team watching the other property telling me Brice is on the move, what the fuck's going on? Is this it, or is it a dry run? At the same time, I get a text from Brice—'

'A picture of your girls.'

'Yep. And a message. *If you say anything, they'll disappear and Christmas will come early for a paedophile.* It was Brice being clever again. The attack was planned for the Muslim feast of sacrifice, and he's saying to me, *are you going to sacrifice your girls in the name of the greater good?* I panic and freeze. This is not what I signed up for. All I can see is one particular sicko in the house running his dirty hands all over the girls as they're screaming and Elliot's screaming even louder at me, *I told you so, you selfish bitch!* And I'm getting more messages from control. *What the fuck is going on?* In the end they gave up on getting an answer from me, not that I knew what was going on anyway, made a decision to intercept. Brice was shot dead—'

'And there were no weapons in the vehicle. It was a dry run, after all.'

She coughed out a bitter laugh.

'Sounds like you know how these things work.'

'If *these things* is another way of saying life, yeah.'

They sat in silence for a while. He moved back to his original seat, making her smile as he did so.

'View better looking this way?'

He shrugged.

'It's not a bad looking brick wall.'

They sat for a while longer, enjoying the sense of calm that had settled. The inevitability of it all had sucked the venom out of her story. Left nothing but a hollow feeling of everything fucked up for all the best reasons and no good result, just pick yourself up and get on with the job.

Which segued easily into what they talked about now.

'I'm surprised you were only demoted down to sergeant.'

She scrunched her face, *it's not that straightforward.*

'I'd been given the nod that I was about to have DCI confirmed, subject to the successful conclusion to Operation Cock-Up. Meaning it was effectively two ranks demotion. It would've been all the way down to DC if Uncle James hadn't stepped in.'

'I'm guessing he was feeling on the guilty side.'

'For screwing my life and career up? Not sure. But he wasn't happy about the egg on his own face. He got over it, pointed out that my rapid rise through the ranks demonstrated my ability. It would be a loss to the force to lose my management skills and all that guff. On the face of it, a rare demonstration of pragmatism. The reality was a little different. Uncle James rose to his position because he's good at both the job itself and the politics that go with it.'

'Which is why I'll stay at DI until they pension me off.'

She took a break from her narrative to study him as he looked straight ahead across the mud flats and water.

'That's not necessarily a bad thing. Integrity counts for something.'

'I feel like I've come out for a beer with my dad.'

'You ought to take him for one more often.'

The sudden seriousness of the remark was like a flying anchor hitting the table. They looked at each other until he pointed at her.

'We're still talking about you.'

She grinned suddenly, what she said next bridging the divide between his situation and hers.

'It's all about fathers and sons. The chair of my misconduct board has got a son in the Met. He's desperate to get into SO15.'

'Uncle James' domain.'

'You got it. When Uncle James spoke to him, he only ever mentioned my name. But the chair of the board came away with the distinct impression they'd been discussing his son's prospects of getting into SO15. He decided busting me all the way down to DC was a bit harsh, after all.'

'And you manged to swallow your pride and accept his decision.'

'I did. Humble pie all the way. *Yum, yum.*'

Angel wasn't surprised by what she'd told him. He could've written it himself. But a couple of anomalies still bothered him. On a recent investigation, they'd met with DS Ian Wright, an ex-colleague of Kincade's from her undercover days. One particular line Wright had used during an acrimonious argument with Angel still stuck in Angel's mind.

You want to talk about morals and innocent lives lost, talk to your sergeant.

In the story Kincade had just told, the only life lost had been Morgan Brice's. And nobody would've described him as innocent.

Angel challenged her on it now.

She shook her head as if he was getting things out of proportion.

'He was exaggerating.' She paused, assessing whether to say more. In the end, she decided it could hardly be any worse than what had come before. 'Wright has got a big problem with me. He'll bad mouth me at every opportunity.'

Angel understood that. There would've been a lot of negative fallout after the operation went belly up. Except it had seemed personal with Wright. He said exactly that.

This time, she didn't shake her head at him. She gave him a big shit-eating grin, drove her fist into her open palm with a loud smack.

'I decked him. Now his pride's bent out of shape. And we all know the problems it causes when a man's pride is hurt.'

'Any particular reason? Or you just fancied hitting someone?'

'Both. He made a snide remark that the whole operation had been a cock-up and the only reason I'd got any information at all had been because of a cock-up of a different sort while I was on my back.'

'And suddenly he was on his back.'

'He was. He wouldn't have had a cock to put up anywhere if I hadn't been dragged off him.' She twisted to face him, her face much as he guessed it had been when Wright insulted her. 'For the record—'

'You don't have to say it.'

'*For the record*, I did not sleep with Morgan Brice. Even if I had, it's a much more complex issue than sanctimonious pricks like Wright make out.'

'I realise that.' Then, before she could tell him she wasn't sure he did, 'If you're deep undercover, and sleeping with someone allows you to gain information that makes the difference between success and failure, do you do it?'

'Exactly. If by sleeping with Osama bin-Laden, you could've stopped nine-eleven, I think you'd have three thousand grieving families lining up to pay for the condoms and a hotel room.'

It was a different way of putting it, but he couldn't disagree. All that was left was Wright's parting insult to him.

If she ever tells you the truth, you'll realise you and your sergeant are made for each other.

His mouth was halfway open when it struck him there was nothing to ask her about. It was true. They'd both done things they weren't proud of. They both accepted and lived with the consequences.

Besides, what was the point of asking her what Wright had meant? In order to answer, she would need to know his own past as well as he now knew hers.

And her knowledge was still far from complete.

. . .

'WHAT'S THAT?' LLOYD IMPEY SAID, LOOKING AT THE SCRAP OF paper his sister had placed on his desk like it was a winning lottery ticket.

'What does it look like, Lloyd?'

He sighed wearily. The interview with the two detectives had drained him, left him without the energy to verbally spar with her. Okay, it had been a stupid question, but they needed to focus, not fight.

'I can see that it's an address, Helen.'

She'd folded her arms across her chest after placing the scrap of paper on his desk. All the better to patronise him as she stood over him seated behind it. Now, she unfolded her right arm, pointed directly at him. She reminded him of their mother, her tone of voice, too.

'That's another thing. You know how much I hate it when you call me Helen.'

He shrugged, secretly enjoying her irritation, knowing the dismissive gesture would annoy her even more. He waved the scrap of paper at her.

'Are you going to tell me whose address this is, or not?'

'Who do you think?'

He was about to ask her if he looked like someone who gave a flying shit, when he finally caught on. The realisation kicked any weariness into touch, apprehension replacing it, along with a growing sense of not being completely in control of his own destiny.

'Amos?'

'Uh-huh.'

'You followed him when he left here the other night?'

'Somebody had to.'

A spike of irritation flared inside him, an accusation on his lips.

'Why didn't you tell me?'

She closed her eyes briefly, the gesture one that he recognised.

God give me strength.

'Because,' she said patiently, 'I knew the police would turn up eventually. I didn't want you getting a crick in the neck from looking at me so fast'—twisting her head sideways as she said it—'when they asked if we knew where he'd gone after leaving here.'

He didn't like it, but he couldn't disagree. What he didn't like even more was what he sensed coming over the horizon. It put a suspicious undertone into his voice.

'Why are you giving it to me now?'

'Because you need to go and talk to him.'

'I already talked to him when he came here.'

Her arms were firmly folded over her chest again, turning into their mother before his eyes.

'You might not have noticed, Lloyd, but things have changed.'

He shook his head, not a refusal, but in frustration.

Why didn't somebody put a pillow over Patrick Quinn's face?

If it hadn't already been too late, the damage already done, he wouldn't have put it past her to go out and do it herself.

31

Angel was aware of Kincade surreptitiously watching him. Checking to see if he was watching her. As if expecting things to be different after the revelation of the previous night.

Some things hadn't changed one iota, of course.

She'd given him a hard time over Durand after they'd got back to his place from The Jolly Sailor the previous evening. After having a good nose around, she volunteered unasked-for advice that his chances with the pathologist would be vastly improved if he bought a big box of candles, painted the walls black and a blood-red pentangle on the floor.

After she'd gone to bed, he spent an hour browsing the internet. It wasn't that he didn't believe what she'd told him about the Order of Nine Angles—a name he kept reading as *angels*. More a case of wanting to get a better feel for the undercover world she'd infiltrated, the toxic environment that had been her downfall.

When he'd had a bellyful of reading about psychotic misfits who should've been drowned at birth, he went onto YouTube and watched Florence Welch and The Rolling Stones perform *Wild Horses* live in London in 2018. The on-stage chemistry between Florence and the then seventy-five-year-young Jagger touched something inside him, restored a little of his faith in the human race. There was still some hope. After watching it three times back to back, he went and sat in the gazebo at the bottom of the garden. With Leonard settled comfortably on his lap, he tried to get his thoughts into some kind of order, decide whether Kincade's revelations would affect their relationship.

The not-clandestine-enough meeting with her girls was, on balance, an error of judgement, but an understandable one. Having never worked undercover and experienced the unique and unnatural strains it puts on a person's body and soul, he could only say how he hoped he would cope.

A voice inside him said, *don't bet on it.*

When the shit hit the fan, the operational disaster also served to highlight her humanity. And he'd choose a real person he could relate to, accepting their failings and weaknesses, over a ruthlessly-efficient professional with the empathy of a scorpion every time.

As for putting the obnoxious DS Wright on his arse, he was behind her all the way...

Her door was ajar when he went up to bed himself. She was out cold, more at peace than he'd ever seen her. Admittedly, he'd never watched her as she slept before. He stood in the doorway feeling slightly sleazy as if spying on her through the crack, until Leonard slipped past his legs and jumped onto the bed, causing her to stir and turn away from him.

The drive to work that morning had been mercifully short. Unnaturally bright and breezy snatches of conversation had been interspersed with periods of silence wondering what the hell to say next.

Now, in their small shared office, he couldn't deny he'd glanced her way a couple of times. A much-needed break from wading through Walking With Heroes' annual report and accounts he'd downloaded from the Companies House website in the aftermath of the interview with the Impey siblings.

Dull, dull, dull.

Until it wasn't.

After slogging through the main financial statements, he moved onto the detailed notes that followed. As with all charities, their funds were split into two main categories. Unrestricted and restricted. The former comprised monies donated to be used for any purpose the charity saw fit within their mandate—what cynics like Kincade would say paid for the plush offices and luxury cars for the people milking it at the top. The restricted funds had been donated for specific purposes, and were listed individually by donor in alphabetical order. He might have been stifling a yawn before, but he came wide awake when he got down the list as far as the letter C.

He called Kincade over, pointed to the name that had stopped him dead.

'The Congrid Fund,' she said, meeting his eye fully for the first time that day. 'And we don't believe in coincidence, do we?'

'No, we don't. It's got to be Conrad and Ingrid Fischer's company.'

She looked again, gave a low whistle.

'That's a lot of money. I think I'm going to start a charity. Your dad can be the figurehead.'

He shook his head, shattering her dreams.

'You've missed the boat. Walking With Heroes have already done that. Employing an ex-Para who's been in prison for murder. Besides, my dad didn't kill one of your parents.'

'No, but I'm working on him killing Elliot. He's quite amenable to the idea after three pints.'

He did her the favour of pretending he hadn't heard, went back to his computer and searched for the *Giving is Great* website. He entered *Walking With Heroes* into the site's search box. The page that came back was filled with colourful graphs and charts and tables of figures analysing the charity's activities and performance.

Kincade stopped him from scrolling too fast, jabbed her finger at a small sidebar in the funding section.

'There!'

The sidebar listed the top contributors for the past five years. Congrid Developments was ahead of the pack by a large margin. He continued scrolling until he got to the list of trustees. The name at the top surprised them.

Ruth Impey.

'Eric Impey's widow,' Kincade said, stating the obvious. 'Saint Lloyd and Saint Helen's mother. Funny how they never mentioned her.'

'Not really. What's Lloyd going to say? *My mum started it and now I work for her.*'

'Never underestimate male pride, eh?' She pointed at Ruth Impey's name on the screen. 'I bet she was the old cow we bumped into on the way out. The one who looked at us like we were shit on the bottom of her shoe.'

Angel was convinced of it. As he'd been at the time.

The second name on the list of trustees was no surprise at all. *Lloyd Impey.* The third was revealing, more than surprising.

Helen Evelyn Crane.

'That's his sister,' Kincade said. 'Crane must be her married name. Although I don't remember seeing a ring.'

'Do you always look?'

'I do when I meet someone like her. To see if any man would be stupid enough to put up with her.'

If he'd wanted to be cruel, he might have asked if she caught people looking at her own ring finger. He didn't, of course. She moved away from his desk, pacing the room as something about the name hovered on the periphery of her memory.

He was the same. A vague recollection just out of reach, the name lost in the accumulated mental junk of past and present cases that filled his head to overflowing.

He had a picture of Lisa Jardine in his mind, a typical Jardine-style remark on her lips.

Sounds like a useful person to know if you're in the construction business.

'That's it! She's the woman Conrad Fischer usually takes to charity events. Evelyn Crane. She must go by her middle name.'

'And only her brother uses her first name. I remember she scowled when he introduced her. I thought it was us.'

He was typing as they talked, entering *Conrad Fischer charity dinner* into Google, clicking on the images tab when the results came back.

Kincade was at his shoulder again by the time the page loaded, a screen filled with women in long black dresses on the arms of men in dinner suits and dickie bows, lots of big smiles and trays weighed down with glasses of fizz and exotic canapés.

He clicked the first one, the enlarged image confirming what they'd already seen.

'It's her. I thought it was strange when she said she didn't have any business cards.'

'She didn't want us to put her and Conrad Fischer together.' A spark of spiteful malice lit up her eyes, fuelled by the memory of the antagonistic exchanges between her and Helen, aka Evelyn. 'He pays a ton of money into her charity's coffers, and she provides something pretty to hang on his arm and show off to all the other rich businessmen. What does that make her? Something beginning with *W*? Rhymes with *more*.'

'It's okay, I think I've worked it out.'

Except they both knew it made her a lot more than that.

The connections were now impossible to ignore.

Amos Church had been convicted of Eric Impey's murder.

Impey's own children employed Amos in their charity after his release.

Impey's daughter, Helen aka Evelyn, was in a relationship with Conrad Fischer.

Fischer and his sister, Ingrid, were the closest thing Patrick Quinn had to family, a lifelong bond.

And, in his delirium, Quinn admitted to the murder of a man who could only be Eric Impey, begging for Amos' forgiveness.

It had a very circular feel to it. A spiral all the way down to hell. Perhaps with a stop-off at the Jerusalem House children's home on the way down.

'I don't suppose they'll use it,' he said, 'but I've got a great slogan for Walking With Heroes that explains why they employ Amos Church.'

He gave her a minute as she tried to read his mind, finally shaking her head in defeat.

'Keep your friends close, but your enemies closer.'

32

Jesse Hamilton was seriously worried. Four days since he'd given Amos a hard time. Nagging him like an old woman until Amos agreed to go to see his boss to explain his absence from work.

It seemed to Jesse that every thought to enter his head started with *if only*.

If only I'd let him call.

If only I'd gone with him.

If only I'd minded my own bloody business.

What was that old saying? *No good deed goes unpunished*. He was going to have it tattooed on his forehead if anything happened to Amos.

It was affecting his work, too. His own boss had commented on the change in Jesse's mood. Where *comment* was synonymous with *complain*, of course. Jesse wanted to punch him at times. Tell him to shove his job up his very important arse. The arrogant prick's idea of a personal problem was seeing somebody else with the same colour car. Or, horror of horrors, a lower-digit personalised number plate. If Jesse ever won the lottery, he'd buy the wanker a new plate as his parting gift when he resigned.

DICKHEAD 1

How's that for a low-digit plate perfectly suited to its owner?

Such were his thoughts as he sat in the Bentley's driving seat while the self-important prick finalised some deal to line his and his cronies' pockets at the expense of the poor or the planet.

Movement registered in the periphery of Jesse's vision, a sudden irrational thought hijacking his mind.

It was Amos. He'd recognised the ostentatious car and was coming to let him know he was okay, lying low where he wasn't a burden on his friends.

Except it wasn't, of course.

It was only one of his boss' sycophantic lackeys coming out of the building ahead of the main cabal of international financiers, as they liked to think of themselves.

Jesse flipped the sun visor down, took a quick look in the vanity mirror.

He couldn't disagree with his boss. He had a face like a smacked arse, had done for days.

He worked a smile onto his lips. It didn't sit right, so he let it slide off again.

His phone pinged as he was flipping the visor up again, his heart suddenly in his mouth. He wrenched the phone out of his pocket, almost ripped the lining.

If he hadn't been a big tough ex-Para protecting a very important knobhead, he might have cried with happiness when he saw Amos' name on the screen.

He tapped the message to open it, his mind racing ahead, anticipating what it might say.

I'm staying with Bob or Dave or Eddy.

I'm on the beach in Spain and bollocks to the cops.

Or even, *I'm in the pub drunk, come and get me.*

That would've been bad enough.

But the words on the screen made Jesse's blood run cold.

You've been a good friend, Jesse. Please don't blame yourself.

Jesse froze, his mind spinning away out of control.

Again, he was aware of movement off to the side.

He looked, saw his boss only yards away, a dirty look on his money-grabbing face that Jesse wasn't already out of the car, holding the door open like a well-trained ape.

Jesse didn't hesitate.

He hit the *start* button with the heel of his hand like he was trying to push it through the centre console. Stamped on the accelerator hard enough to kick it into the engine compartment, wheels spinning, the big car surging forward like a giant lilac-coloured missile, the very important prick left standing open-mouthed in a cloud of dust as Jesse took off.

He knew Amos, knew how his friend's mind worked. He'd kept a bottle of Johnny Walker Red Label in the house as a reminder of what he'd lost, of what had been taken from him, ever since he got out of jail. Jesse knew that if and when the day came when his friend couldn't face life any longer, he'd down the bottle of Scotch first, a final middle finger raised to fate.

Amos had gone home.

And Jesse knew it was the last place on either side of the grave he wanted to go.

The house looked as dead as what Jesse feared he would find inside when the Bentley skidded to a stop outside it. Jesse was out and running, the engine still purring behind him, as he charged up the front path. The door was locked. He went around the side, vaulted the low fence, his hand on the back door handle a heartbeat later. Also locked. He didn't waste time breaking the glass. Who leaves the key in the lock anyway? He stood back, drove a size eleven with thirteen stone of angry muscle and bone behind it through the door itself, the lock splintering the frame as the door exploded inwards.

He didn't bother with the downstairs rooms. Nobody kills themselves in the kitchen or the living room. The intimacy of the upstairs rooms was Jesse's destination, bounding up the stairs two at a time, heart racing in his chest.

He stood a moment on the landing, head snapping back and forth. Except he knew without knowing how that the bathroom was where his friend awaited him with unseeing eyes.

He would've given his right arm and both legs to be back in Iraq, walking unarmed into a room filled with jihadi insurgents rather than make the endless trek across Amos' landing carpet.

He pushed the bathroom door open with his foot, God knows why. It wasn't a crime scene, after all.

A crime against everything that's right and good and decent in the world, perhaps, but the police aren't in the business of investigating those.

He hung his head after the door swung slowly open, the urge to kick and punch and bite every living or dead thing consuming him, find some release, blessed or otherwise, from the pain burning inside him, an irrelevance, a mere bagatelle, compared to the pain that had driven his friend to take his own life.

Jesse dropped to his knees, rested his brow on the cold hard edge of the bath. Two words filled his tortured mind, the same two that would haunt and accuse him for the rest of his days. The easiest to say with hindsight, the hardest to listen to in the moment.

If only . . .

33

Kincade let out a weary sigh as she finished going through Conrad and Ingrid Fischer's joint alibi for what felt like the hundredth time.

'It's not going to change by you looking at it another thousand times,' Angel said, as she paused the CCTV footage supplied by the venue that had hosted the charity cocktail party the Fischer siblings were attending while Lois Sheppard was being strangled in Southampton Old Cemetery.

The footage from the front lobby clearly showed the Fischers arriving together at 8:15 p.m., and leaving again at 10:45 p.m., by which time Lois Sheppard was good and dead. CCTV cameras at the rear of the building covered the fire escape door. It had remained closed at all times, apart from when a cocktail waitress or a kitchen worker came out for a cigarette break. The Fischers had not snuck out and then returned after killing Lois Sheppard. End of.

Kincade knew he was right. That didn't mean she had to like it.

'There aren't even any suspicious breaks in the footage.'

'There rarely are in real life. Unless you think footage from another event has been spliced—'

'I don't think you can splice a cloud-based hard drive, sir. Even your dad has got a better grip on technology than you have.'

He might have justified himself, said he'd only been joking, had something not caught his eye. He'd been flicking through the Eric Impey file again, giving it half his attention as he listened to Kincade complain.

'What is it?' she said, when he failed to respond to her crack about his father.

'Somebody put a question mark next to Ruth Impey's alibi for the night her husband was murdered. That she was in Portsmouth visiting her sick mother.'

'Nothing else?'

'Nope. A single question mark. I don't know if I'm surprised or not.'

She knew what he meant. Richard Terrell's statement had been ignored, consigned to the growing *should've taken a closer look* pile. Why shouldn't a query about Ruth Impey's alibi have shared a similar fate? It was impossible to know whether it had been followed up and dealt with, or simply ignored. Either way, nothing could be done about it now.

Not quite nothing.

He typed a search string into Google—*Ruth Impey Walking With Heroes chairman*—and hit *return* after a moment considering whether to backspace and change *chairman* to *chairperson,* irritated at himself that it had even crossed his mind.

Five minutes later, he knew he had something, even if he wasn't sure exactly what.

'Guess what Ruth Impey's maiden name was,' he said, interrupting Kincade.

He knew she'd got it wrong the moment he saw the smug

smile—*this is too easy*—appear on her lips after only a few seconds' thought.

'Fischer?'

'Uh-uh. Crane.'

It took a moment for the unexpected name to register. Kincade's voice reflected the confusion when it did.

'Ruth Impey's maiden name was the same as her daughter's married name?'

He assumed *Kincade position #1* himself, swivelling gently back and forth in his chair as he said something that at first didn't appear to make sense.

'I don't think so.'

'It's the same name.'

'Yes, but I don't think the girl who was born Helen Impey ever married someone called Crane. At some point, she started using her middle name, Evelyn...'

'And decided to change her surname at the same time. Thought to herself, *I know, I'll use mum's maiden name.*'

'Exactly.'

'But why?'

'Good question, Sergeant. I think I'm going to pull rank and leave that with you.'

Kincade didn't get a chance to throw it back at him—*it's your theory, you work it out*—before Craig Gulliver entered the room. He looked as if he'd come to confess to Lois Sheppard's murder himself.

'Amos Church has been found dead. His friend Jesse Hamilton has just phoned it in.'

The abrupt way the news dragged Angel and Kincade back from the past into the present took a moment to adjust to. Kincade recovered first.

'How?'

Had it not been such a major setback, so depressingly sad and inevitable, Gulliver might have grinned at her.

He used his mobile phone, Sarge.

'Suicide.'

'Genuine, or assisted?' This from Angel.

'All the indicators point to genuine, sir. He slit his wrists in the bath.'

Angel pushed himself to his feet, pulled on his jacket feeling as if his own will to live had flowed from Amos Church's veins, leaving him empty, drained. Kincade was already out from behind her desk, making for the door.

Trailing behind her and Gulliver, Angel had no idea what fate had in store for him, how personal things were about to become.

Kincade pointed at the pathologist's Saab parked at the kerb outside Amos Church's house as they walked the last fifty yards from where they'd found a parking space.

'Doctor Death's already here.' She leaned in, lowered her voice. 'Don't worry, I won't say anything about me staying at your place last night. I don't want to upset her.'

The remark stopped him dead in his tracks, his voice incredulous.

'That's the most ridiculous thing I've ever heard. You do everything in your power to upset her.'

'She does the same.'

He started walking again, chiding himself for his stupid mistake.

'I was forgetting. Two wrongs make a right.'

'Sorry, I should've phrased it better. I don't mind upsetting her professionally, but I don't want to break her heart.' She clamped her hand over her mouth as if she'd said something inappropriate. '*Oops!* Silly me. She hasn't got one. Or if she has, it's got a sharpened stake through it.'

He didn't dignify the remark with a response, extended his hand for her to precede him up the path to Amos Church's front door.

The house was relatively empty of people. Unless they or the pathologist decided something was off, that the possibility of a crime looked to be more of a probability, the SOCOs wouldn't be needed.

He glanced into the front room as he passed the door. Jesse Hamilton was sitting on a sofa staring straight ahead. Angel didn't need to see his eyes to know their focus was elsewhere. Jesse didn't stir as Angel and Kincade went past the doorway and ascended the stairs. They could've driven past in a Challenger 2 battle tank and he wouldn't have noticed.

The bathroom door was open, Durand standing looking down at Amos Church as she spoke quietly into a hand-held recorder. She paused it when she heard them behind her.

'Your irreverent antics might be appropriate for once, Padre.'

In the past, he'd been known to play *The Last Post* on his harmonica when faced with the death of an ex-serviceman. Not today.

'I'll save it for the funeral, Isabel.'

Durand stepped to the side to allow them to see Amos Church in all his final indignity. Naked in a bath of pinkish-red water, he lay stretched out with his feet at the tap end, his head thrown back, eyes staring sightlessly at the ceiling from a face drained of blood. Both forearms lay on his thighs, facing upwards so that his wrists were visible. He'd slit them both lengthways, the mark of a man who means to do the job properly, not a cry for attention that a crossways cut often implies.

'I haven't found the blade yet,' Durand said. 'I would think it's still in the water.'

Angel knew that at other times Kincade would've been smiling to herself. Thinking, *don't drink it all at once, Doctor.* Today, the overwhelming sense of loss and pointless waste kept her face as rigidly impassive as his own.

Durand stepped closer to Angel, placed her hand on his arm.

'It's not going to be a good one, Padre.'

She moved out of the way so that he could see what she meant. Her body had been obscuring a wooden chair from view. An empty Johnny Walker Red Label bottle sat on it. A red Parachute Regiment beret hung from the neck. A mobile phone was propped against the bottle, and, against that, a folded sheet of paper.

Angel bit down and swallowed hard. Leaned forward hoping he'd misread what was written in capitals on the paper.

He hadn't.

Inspector Max Angel.

'*Jesus Christ,*' Kincade whispered, loud enough for them all to hear. 'He left you a personal suicide note.'

An uneasy silence descended on the room, interrupted only by the sound of a disrespectful drip coming from the old-fashioned bath taps.

Angel cleared his throat, headed for the door, his parting words for Kincade or Durand or anyone else who dared touch Amos Church's poignant valedictory display.

'Bag it all. I'll read the note later.'

Everybody finished the sentence in their own heads.

When I don't have the man who penned it lying dead in front of me.

Durand went to speak, to tell him she'd let him have details of the time of death and all the rest of the minutiae of Amos

Church's sad death later. She simplified it as she talked at his disappearing back.

'It looks like suicide, Padre, pure and simple.'

Kincade waited until she heard him get all the way to the bottom of the stairs before picking up the note with a blue-gloved hand.

It didn't take long to read, her reaction short and to the point.

'*Fuck.*'

She offered it to Durand, put it back against the mobile phone when the pathologist shook her head.

Downstairs in the front room, Jesse had his phone in his hand when Angel walked in. Looking through it, rather than at it.

'He left you a note,' he said, as if the pathologist, two detectives and whoever else had been in the bathroom had missed it.

Angel took a seat, mirroring Amos' pose upstairs. Legs stretched out, head thrown back against the seat cushion.

'I saw it. I haven't read it yet.'

'I didn't touch it.'

Angel waved the comment away.

'Wouldn't matter if you did.'

Jesse held his phone out towards Angel.

'He sent me a text. That's how I knew to come.'

Angel sat up and took the phone so as not to look uninterested, read it aloud under his breath.

'You've been a good friend, Jesse. Please don't blame yourself.'

He half-laughed, half-snorted, kept his thoughts to himself as he passed the phone back.

Hope it helps.

Then he invited Jesse to lay into him, unleash some of the guilt and anger consuming him.

'Any idea why he did it?'

He sat in silence as Jesse played his part, repeating what he'd said when they interviewed him in his probably-now-ex employer's Bentley. How it was their fault for not believing Amos the last time. How Amos was justifiably scared they'd treat him the same way this time. He said nothing he hadn't said before. But he spat the words at Angel with a lot more venom and loathing.

Angel took it all on the chin, tried again.

'Is there anything that acted as a catalyst? It's over a week since Lois Sheppard was killed. Why now?'

Jesse waved his phone in Angel's face, looking as if he'd do something more intimate with it if Angel was standing up.

'This is the first I've heard from him since he left my place to talk to his employer. Must've been something they said.'

Angel looked past the sarcasm, wondering if it was true.

'They told us they gave Amos indefinite paid leave.'

Jesse shrugged, shook his head, his thoughts directed inwards, not at what the Impeys might or might not have said to his friend.

'I should never have given him such a hard time.'

Angel got up, rested his hand briefly on Jesse's shoulder before leaving the room.

No, and now you've only got yourself to give the hardest time of all.

34

'Where are we going?' Kincade asked, when it became obvious they weren't heading back to the station.

'We've just seen a man driven to the edge of his sanity who took the only way out he could see. I thought we'd follow that unedifying experience with a visit to the man who started him on that road.' He flicked his head upwards. 'A man who has been punished with terminal cancer by somebody I used to believe in.'

Jesus, and you haven't even read the note, she thought. *Lucky the blade Amos used is still in the bottom of the bathwater.*

'Patrick Quinn?'

'Yep.'

'What for? You think he'll be lucid enough to talk to us?'

'I doubt it. I thought I might finish him off with a pillow on Amos' behalf.'

She wasn't sure she even wanted to look at him, let alone try to analyse what he'd said. She looked out the side window instead, said nothing, a picture of Amos Church lying dead in the bath in her mind.

She couldn't help wondering if his remark went beyond the current circumstances. Whether he wanted to avenge all men pushed too far by circumstances beyond their control. His brother, Cormac, for one. She had a feeling that if and when he ever told her why he'd turned his back on the priesthood, it would reveal a taste for Old Testament-style vengeance more than the forgiveness his father said he used to peddle.

She almost laughed out loud when they turned into Patrick Quinn's road, pointed a finger at the sky instead.

'Want to revise that comment about not believing in him upstairs anymore, sir?'

Ahead of them, Ingrid Fischer's white Mercedes was parked in front of Quinn's house. He shook his head, pointed downwards.

'No. That's him down there.'

'So, you believe in him?'

'Oh, yes. In our job it's hard not to.'

A single thought filled her mind as he parked behind the Mercedes.

I do not want to be in the room when you read Amos' suicide note.

Ingrid Fischer opened the door after Angel hammered on it for an inappropriately long time. Surprise pushed aside the irritation when she saw who it was being so disrespectful. Although Gulliver and Jardine had interviewed her previously, nobody ever opened the door to them and thought they were anything other than what they were. He introduced them, anyway.

'DI Max Angel, Ms Fischer. And this is DS Kincade.'

'You're too late, Inspector, if you were hoping to speak to Patrick. He died last night.'

Angel nodded. A short, sharp dip of the head to acknowledge receipt of the information. Kincade noticed how he didn't offer his condolences.

'I don't know whether his plea for forgiveness ever got as far as Amos Church, Ms Fischer, but he'll be able to ask for it himself now. Amos Church took his own life earlier today.'

When they discussed it later, neither of them would be able to say which of the emotions chasing each other across Ingrid's face was the dominant one. Surprise, relief, guilt, they were all there.

'I'm sorry to hear that,' Ingrid said, her words lacking sincerity, but highlighting Angel's failure to say something similar about Quinn.

'So are we,' he said, with more than enough feeling for all of them.

Kincade didn't know if Ingrid heard the sub-text, but it almost deafened her.

But not as sorry as you're going to be now that we've caught you here.

He started the process with a cold smile.

'We've got a lot to talk about, Ms Fischer. Shall we do it here on the doorstep, or are you going to invite us in?'

Ingrid stood back as they went past her and into the same cheerless sitting room where they'd interviewed the nurse, Sheila Doherty. Thankfully it wasn't so warm, the central heating turned off now that Patrick Quinn was beyond warming.

'What do you want to ask first, Sergeant?' Angel said to Kincade, when they were all seated uncomfortably—the atmosphere, not the furniture.

Kincade gave Ingrid a smile that would look good on a shark.

'Why did you accompany your brother to the cocktail party on the night of Lois Sheppard's murder, instead of his usual . . .' She paused as if searching for the right word, but in fact allowing Ingrid to read any derogatory term she chose—bimbo, floozy, tramp—into it. 'His usual companion. Helen or Evelyn

Crane née Impey, the daughter of the man Amos Church was convicted of murdering.'

The size of the information payload stole the words out of Ingrid's mouth, as it was supposed to. Kincade could have used a drip-feed approach, gradually letting Ingrid know how much they knew. Instead, she'd gone for the nuclear option. She held up her hand before Ingrid got her vocal chords moving.

'We'll come back to the staggering . . .' She glanced at Angel, a question on her face.

He nodded approvingly.

'Staggering, mind-boggling. Either one's good.'

'The staggering complexity of the interrelationships between you and your brother and the Impeys, but for now, tell us why you accompanied him on that particular occasion.'

Ingrid gave her an equally shark-like smile back. Angel thought it was better than Kincade's, and that was saying something.

'There's nothing sinister about it, as you seem to be implying, Sergeant. Evelyn had a stomach bug. One of those twenty-four-hour things.'

You mean one of those convenient twenty-four-hour things, Angel mentally corrected.

'It was a last-minute change of plan?' Kincade said.

'That's right. I wouldn't have made the arrangement with Lois Sheppard for that evening if I already had a prior engagement, would I?'

Her tone of voice said, *you might not get many social invites, but I have to manage my diary.*

'That takes care of my next question,' Kincade said. 'I was going to ask if you knew what Helen or Evelyn was doing when she wasn't on your brother's arm.'

Angel held his breath. Prayed Kincade didn't bulge her

cheeks to mimic vomiting or, worse, hunch down as if straining on the toilet. But he liked the way she kept saying *Helen or Evelyn*, a reminder of the convoluted relationships Ingrid would soon have to explain. She also had a way of making *on your brother's arm* sound like *under a lamp post on a street corner*.

'Do you know if she went to the doctor?' Kincade asked.

Everybody heard something else.

We don't believe you.

'I have no idea,' Ingrid replied, completely unflustered. 'Evelyn and I know each other, but we don't live in each other's pockets.'

Is that you starting to distance yourself? Angel thought, as Kincade gawked at Ingrid.

'Then you're the only ones who don't. I keep expecting to see people with six fingers, you're all so close. You don't happen to be in a relationship with Lloyd Impey, do you?' Then, when Ingrid didn't answer, 'That's a serious question, Ms Fischer.'

'The answer is no. I am not, nor have I ever been in a relationship with Lloyd.'

Angel couldn't put his finger on it, but something in Ingrid's tone of voice made it sound as if she wasn't only answering the question about Lloyd Impey. More a case of describing her attitude to the male population as a whole. As if Kincade had accused a vegan of eating bacon. He made a mental note, concentrated on what Kincade was saying.

'Yet you and your brother pay more money into his and his sister's charity than anyone else. You've been top of the league for the past five years. Or do you not have any say in how Congrid Developments spends its money? Your name forms part of the company name, but that's it. He did it to keep you happy. So that you can tell people, *I put the Ingrid in Congrid*.'

Angel looked at his feet to hide his smile. But if Kincade was hoping to rattle Ingrid with her mocking and insulting remarks, she was disappointed. Angel guessed Ingrid was used to it, and accepted it. Her brother was the driving force. End of. Kincade had phrased it differently, more offensively, that's all.

'You're right,' Ingrid said, the simple admission defusing Kincade's attack. 'Conrad makes most of the decisions.' She made a point of looking back and forth between Angel and Kincade. 'Men usually do.' She shrugged, looking straight at Kincade now.

I've accepted it, why can't you?

'Okay,' Kincade said, after they'd locked eyes for a length of time that made Angel feel uncomfortable. 'What do you think of the fact that the charity Conrad chooses to support so generously employed Amos Church, the man convicted of killing the Impeys' father.'

'It's admirable.'

'Too good to be true?'

'I think your job has soured your view of people, Constable.'

Angel felt as if he was watching a world-class chess match. Would Kincade correct Ingrid's deliberate mistake over her rank?

'If you ask my mother, the job chose me,' Kincade countered, earning a mental *Attagirl* from Angel. 'I was like it as a child. Getting back on track, give me your take on the fact that Patrick Quinn, a man you've known your whole life, confessed to Lois Sheppard that he'd killed a man, and was then begging for Amos Church's forgiveness, which implies that man was Eric Impey. Amos always claimed he saw three people leaving the cemetery before he found Impey's body, one of whom he thought was a woman.' She tapped her breastbone. 'Somebody like me, someone whose view of people has been so badly soured, might think those three people were Patrick Quinn, your brother and yourself. And you've donated huge sums of money to the Impeys' charity to ease your guilt over killing their father. You then abused your position as the biggest donor, applying pressure and forcing them to employ the man who paid the price for your crime. That eased your guilt even more as well as making them look like modern-day saints. Rich people always think money makes everything okay, that everything can be bought and paid for. I know, I used to be married to one.'

Kincade paused for breath, made Angel take a deep one himself. Ingrid jumped right in.

'Maybe that's why you're so bitter, Sergeant. That's by the by. If you're going to continue in this vein, throwing out wild accusations, I will be forced to insist on my solicitor being present.'

She looked directly at Angel, an unsubtle reminder that he would be the one to decide the way things progressed.

'There's something you're not saying, Ms Fischer,' he said. 'If DS Kincade's hypothesis were true, we would need to identify why you would have wanted to kill Eric Impey. We'll leave you now while we look into that. We *will* find the connection despite the setbacks caused by Amos Church and Patrick Quinn's deaths. I advise you to volunteer that information before we do. Please pass that advice on to your brother for us. I'm guessing it'll be a decision you'll make together for once.'

'GOOD JOB YOU'RE DRIVING, SIR,' KINCADE SAID, ONCE THEY WERE back in his car and about to drive off.

He looked at Ingrid's Mercedes directly in front of them, thought he knew what she meant.

'Why? Because you'd shunt her car?'

She shook her head, *you know nothing*.

'Uh-uh. It's always your fault if you drive into the back of someone. I'd drive around in front of her and reverse into her.'

'How does your mind even work like that?'

She showed him her eye teeth, a glint he didn't want to think about in her eye.

'You men have no idea.'

After the last fifteen minutes, he thought maybe he did.

35

Gulliver and Jardine had given Richard Terrell twenty-four hours since the somewhat surreal discussion with his wife the previous day. He still hadn't contacted them. He wasn't on holiday, and they'd left his wife in no doubt about how important it was for them to speak to him.

He was avoiding them.

Which is why they were sitting in Gulliver's car three houses down from the Terrells', waiting for him to get home. They'd knocked as soon as they arrived and found nobody in. After that, they'd canvassed the houses on either side and on the opposite side of the road, but nobody had seen a person acting suspiciously, as if about to throw a poisoned steak into the Terrells' garden.

The only relief from the tedious litany of negative responses had been when they'd talked to the neighbour who'd had the audacity to park in Richard Terrell's space. The man whose car Terrell subsequently vandalised, and who Mrs Terrell believed had poisoned their dog in a cruel and heartless act of revenge.

Two statements from that conversation stuck in their minds.

He's a wanker who thinks he owns the whole bloody road.

If I was going to poison anyone, it'd be him, not the dog.

Memorable they might be, but neither of those statements would make it into the official account of how they'd spent their day, nor did they provide any useful pointers regarding the way forward.

As an aside, Jardine had asked the neighbour to describe Terrell. *He's an ugly fat fucker* was unlikely to be appended to Terrell's entry in the PNC, but provided a useful way to pass the time, prompting calls of *not fat enough* or *not ugly enough* every time a man walked or drove past.

Terrell was something of a disappointment when he did turn up, parking in front of his house and climbing out of his car. Especially to Jardine.

'I was expecting him to look like Lurch with a beer belly.'

'Like everyone from the North East, you mean?'

She ran her eyes up and down Gulliver's body. Looked again at Terrell heading up his front path.

'He's not any fatter than you are.'

Gulliver didn't waste time trying to decide how much of an insult the remark contained, already getting out of the car to go after Terrell.

They caught him before he disappeared inside the house, his face falling even before they introduced themselves.

'How's the dog?' Gulliver asked, hearing Jardine's voice in his head.

You mean Jake or Mrs Terrell?

'Recovering,' Terrell said with a scowl his next words explained. 'Unlike our bank balance. You ask me, you lot should be arresting criminals like vets. Daylight bloody robbery. Taking advantage of people's emotions. I bet they've got a hidden camera that scans your eyes as you go in to see how red and sore-looking they are. Then they calculate how much you're prepared to pay.'

It was a fuller answer than Gulliver had been expecting, but it gave them a measure of the man.

'Glad to hear it, sir. I'm sure you would've remembered to call us, now that you're not so worried about him.' He extended his hand towards the front door. 'Shall we?'

The scowl hadn't moved off Terrell's face. Now it said something different.

If we must.

After opening the door, Terrell went all the way through the house to the kitchen, leaving them to close the door and trail after him. In the kitchen, he filled the kettle with what anybody could see was only sufficient water for one cup of tea, confirming it when he lifted a single mug down from a wall cabinet at the side of the cooker extractor.

We weren't thirsty anyway, Gulliver thought, not caring if Jardine came out and demanded some refreshments. He dived in when she didn't.

'We want to talk to you about a statement you made to the police in nineteen ninety—'

'I made it up.'

The surprise interruption and unexpected admission left Gulliver speechless momentarily.

'What do you mean, you made it up?'

'Exactly what it sounds like. It wasn't true. I made it up.'

Gulliver crossed his arms over his chest, an aggressive pose more than defensive. Terrell turned his back on him. Concentrated on spooning sugar into the mug after he dropped a teabag in.

Jardine had been standing at the back door, looking out at the rear garden where the Terrell's dog had been poisoned. Specifically, the alley at the bottom of it. She turned away from it to look at the two men, then barked an order at Gulliver.

'Caution him, Craig. We'll do this in the comfort of an interview room. Then we'll get a cup of tea, as well.'

Gulliver uncrossed his arms, stood up straight. Cleared his throat.

'You can't arrest me,' Terrell said. 'I haven't done anything.'

'You just admitted to perverting the course of justice,' Jardine replied. 'Get a move on, Craig. We haven't got all day.'

Gulliver cleared his throat again.

'This is bollocks,' Terrell said, his voice rising. 'Anyway, I was just a kid. And it was thirty-four years ago.'

Jardine stared hard at him, as if he was the man accused of abuse, not the accuser.

'We know you've been threatened, Mr Terrell. Your dog was poisoned. Your wife thinks it's the man across the street. You know better. So do we. I'm guessing she'd agree with us if she knew about the statement you made back then. But she doesn't, does she? I'm not blaming you. We've all got things in our past we'd rather stayed there. But things have changed. And if you think denying it now will make it all go away, you are very much mistaken. By the way, the tea in the station is shite. So's the coffee.' She glanced at her watch. 'What time does your wife get home?'

Terrell didn't need to look at his own watch.

'About half an hour.'

'Then I'd talk quickly, if I was you. Or . . . we . . . can . . . stretch . . . this . . .'

'Okay, okay.'

Jardine beamed at him.

'See. You can do it. Can you also multi-task?'

'*What?*'

Gulliver almost felt sorry for Terrell. He'd worked with Jardine long enough to know what she meant.

'She means, make us all a cup of tea while you're talking.'

'Exactly. And after that you can show us the email threat I'm guessing you got when you went on your computer after your wife went to bed. The one that told you to keep your mouth shut. Like Rover should've done.'

'I think the dog's name is Jake,' Gulliver pointed out.

She nodded her thanks.

'How long before Mrs Terrell gets home, Craig?'

'Twenty-seven minutes.' He paused. 'And counting.'

They both looked at Terrell.

'You'll need more water in the kettle,' Jardine said, pointing at the tap. She went to the sink and filled the kettle herself when Terrell didn't move or say anything. 'There. I've started it for you.'

'Twenty-five minutes,' Gulliver intoned, sounding like he'd got a new job as the talking clock.

Terrell finally galvanised himself into action, taking another two mugs down from the wall cabinet, placing them beside his own.

'What I said earlier was true. I wasn't abused myself. I was too big for that pervert Impey to try it on. He knew what he'd get. I'm not even sure he was interested in boys. But I knew something bad was going on. I thought if I only said I suspected him, nobody would believe me. I thought you'd take more notice if I said it had happened to me.' He shrugged. *Seems I was wrong.* 'I thought it would make you start investigating. Ask the other kids who were too scared to come forward. There's a big difference between volunteering and answering a direct question.'

Gulliver was impressed by the maturity of Terrell's teenage thinking, even if his method of putting it into practice was suspect.

'Do you know the names of anybody who was actually abused?'

Terrell glanced at the kettle which had just finished boiling. He filled all three mugs, his back to them as he did so. They exchanged a look, an unspoken, *is this it?* as he built up to something before facing them again.

'I don't know if it was related, but one kid tried to kill himself.' He twirled his finger at his temple. 'He was a bit odd. It might have been that. He has psychological problems.' He grinned suddenly, suppressed it even faster. 'You know what kids are like. We just thought he was nuts.'

'What was his name?' Gulliver asked, feeling like he had to squeeze the words out through the tightness in his chest.

'Quinn. Patrick Quinn.'

Gulliver and Jardine didn't need to look at one another. They both remembered Jardine asking Ingrid Fischer how she knew Quinn. Ingrid replied that their parents were friends. She'd also added that they were now all dead. It was possible Quinn's parents died when he was a teenager and he'd been taken into care, but remained in contact with Ingrid and her brother. Another possibility existed, of course.

Gulliver gave Jardine a subtle nod—*you ask him*—when Terrell made the question redundant, still reminiscing about his time in the home.

'Quinn was nuts, but nobody took the piss out of him. Everybody knew, if you upset Quinn, Conrad Fischer's gonna punch your lights out.' He hooked his two middle fingers together like links in a chain. 'It was one of those strange friendships you can't explain. Conrad looked out for Quinn like he was his little brother.'

Gulliver and Jardine's heads were going up and down like a pair of nodding dogs in a car rear window.

Of course we knew Conrad was in the children's home.

'Some of the kids read more to it,' Terrell continued, taking on a conspiratorial air. 'There was a rumour Conrad was gay, although we called it *queer* back then. He fancied Quinn, and that's why he was so protective. Except Quinn wasn't interested. He had the hots for Conrad's sister, Ingrid.'

Gulliver and Jardine's heads were going to fall off soon.

Of course we knew that as well.

'Quinn and Ingrid were together for a while. Then she dumped him. When he tried to kill himself, we didn't know if it was because of that, or because Impey was giving him what he wasn't getting from Ingrid anymore. He was a pretty fucked-up kid. It might just have been because he had a screw loose, who knows?'

Terrell had forgotten all about the tea as he talked. He remembered it now, fishing the tea bags out of the mugs with a spoon and dropping them in the sink. He smiled apologetically as he handed them both a mug of the stewed brew after adding too much milk in an attempt to compensate.

'Probably as bad as in the station, eh?'

'Not quite that bad,' Gulliver lied.

'Worse,' Jardine said.

They all took a slurp and grimaced. Gulliver asked the obvious question.

'Do you think Quinn was involved in Impey's murder?'

Terrell's face compacted as if the tea was worse than he'd realised.

'I don't know. He was in hospital for a few days recovering after he tried to top himself. I can't remember if he was still there when Impey was killed.'

'What about the kid who looked out for Quinn? Conrad Fischer.'

Terrell shrugged, *you tell me.*

'Is that who threatened you?' Jardine said, when Terrell took too much of an interest in his stewed and not-very-hot tea.

'Could be. But don't they say poisoning is a woman's way of

killing? Ingrid Fischer always had a nasty streak. Especially after she dumped Quinn.'

Jardine went to the sink and poured the remains of her tea down the drain.

'You're not doing such a bad job of poisoning yourself, Mr Terrell. What you said about it being a woman's thing? Is that something you read on the internet? Or is there something specific you want to tell us?' *Or are you trying to cause her trouble because you tried your luck and she rejected you, too?*

Terrell shook his head as if wishing he'd never opened his mouth. He poured his own tea down the sink, rinsed the mug with cold water.

Bet you wish you could wash your hands of the past as easily, Jardine thought, as they saw themselves out.

36

'Put that bloody thing away,' Olivia Finch snapped, 'before I shove it somewhere that's a little too close for comfort, given the potential implications in the Eric Impey debacle.'

Angel made an easy guess.

'My arse, ma'am?'

'Yes, Padre, your arse. Even if it is too old to be of interest to a pervert like Impey.'

He looked at the harmonica in his hand, her irritation confusing him.

'Don't you like *The Last Post*, ma'am?'

'I like Californian Pinot Noir, Padre, but I don't drink it in the office.' She waved Amos Church's suicide note at him. 'For one, it's not nearly strong enough. I feel like I should have a glass of whisky to wash this down.'

'That makes two of us. And it hasn't even got your name on the front.'

'I still fail to see how playing that bloody mouth organ helps.' She gave him a knowing smile. 'Unless it's your way of spreading the pain around.'

He slipped the offending instrument into his pocket, went to gaze out of the window, seeing nothing but his reflection in the glass—a man who looked as if he knew how Amos Church had felt as he cut into his veins with the razor blade found in the bottom of the bath after it was emptied.

Behind him, she read through the note a second time.

I've been told you're Carl Angel's son. That means you're a good man. If you've inherited your father's genes, you're probably bloody-minded and determined, too. After last time, I don't have the strength to fight you and the evidence that points at me. The bottle of Johnny Walker was a reminder of everything I lost. I knew that if I ever put it to my lips, I would meet my maker soon after. He knows the truth, and I will be judged accordingly. I can't risk you not finding it, too, and a jury of my so-called peers getting it wrong a second time. I hope you catch the bastard who killed Lois Sheppard.

Angel waited until he judged from the depth of silence that she'd finished.

'Go ahead and say it.'

'Say what?'

He turned away from the window, gave her a look that spoke of the years they'd known each other.

A hint of a smile curled her lips, despite the circumstances. *You got me.*

'I didn't know you'd met him, Padre. That bit about being bloody-minded is spot on.'

'I prefer to concentrate on the *determined* part. Have you watched the video I emailed you, yet?'

Before taking his own life, Amos Church had recorded a video on his phone, along with a voice recording they would listen to shortly.

Angel came to stand at her shoulder while she found the email.

'It's like watching my holiday video at Christmas,' he said when she opened the first attachment. 'About as exciting, but without the mince pies and silly hats.'

She hit *play*, and together they watched a 360-degree video tour of Amos Church's bathroom. The bath filled with hot water was clearly visible, the condensation on the mirror above the basin testament to how hot it was. The wooden chair was in place, and on it, the bottle of Johnny Walker Red Label and Amos' red Parachute Regiment beret.

'And there's the suicide note,' he said sourly, in case she'd lost the use of her eyes.

The video ended after a full 360-degree sweep of the empty bathroom. A caption had been added to it. Finch read it aloud.

'I don't want anybody to get the blame for my death, not even those who deserve it. Here's a nice easy one to solve on me.' A smile curled her lips at Amos' gallows humour. 'He likes to involve us, doesn't he?'

'Doesn't he just. Wait until you hear the video recording.'

'I can't wait.'

She opened the second attachment, clicked *play*. Immediately paused it.

'That sounds like a toilet flushing.'

He let the smile that would soon be a distant memory creep across his face.

'I don't ever want to hear anyone say you didn't rise to your current position on the basis of merit, ma'am.'

'Up yours, Padre. Why do you think he starts the video with a toilet flush?'

'I'm guessing somebody turned up at the house unexpectedly. Someone he decided he wanted to record. He made an excuse about going to the loo, started the recording and flushed the toilet for authenticity.'

'Makes sense. I notice how you don't hear the seat being put down.'

'You hit *pause* too early.'

The look on her face told him what she thought of that. She clicked *play* again, put her finger behind her ear when the sound of a toilet seat being lowered was not heard.

'Soft close,' he said under his breath as the recording resumed.

How did you know where I was?

'That's Amos Church,' Angel said.

'I'd worked that out for myself. I am a DCI, remember.'

Evelyn followed you here after you came to see me.

'And that's Lloyd Impey.'

Why?

Because we're concerned about you, Amos. We didn't want the police to turn up in a month's time saying you'd been found dead after a neighbour complained about the smell.

'He tells it how it is,' Finch said, falling silent as Amos responded.

I'm touched, but you don't need to be.

I'm afraid the police have already interviewed us. Two detectives. The woman was very aggressive.

Angel gave Finch's shoulder a prod, *see, it wasn't me*. It suddenly occurred to him that he didn't need to stand at her shoulder to listen to the recording. He moved away, helped himself to a cup of coffee from her private machine.

Lloyd Impey was still talking as Angel leaned against the wall and sipped.

They know Lois Sheppard called you immediately before she was murdered, Amos. They want to know why. To be honest, I want to know why.

'He's probably jabbing his chest,' Angel said, jabbing his own.

'Shush now.'

Lloyd was still talking.

They know Lois Sheppard was looking into your conviction.

'Notice how he avoids saying *for killing my father*,' Angel said.

'I said shush.'

They're talking about you killing her because you're worried that raking it all up will make you go off the rails. That you'll start drinking again and throw away what you've achieved since getting out of prison.

'Pause it,' Angel said, at exactly the moment Finch did so. 'We didn't say any of that. We said we thought he might have information. That's all. We didn't say anything about the phone calls or Lois looking into Amos' conviction or why Amos wouldn't be happy about her doing that. There are only two ways Lloyd Impey could even know about the phone calls. There's a chance the company provided Amos with his phone, and they get the itemised bills. The other possibility—'

'Is that they've got Lois' phone.'

'Yep. And they could only know what Lois was doing if Ingrid Fischer found out and told them. They're thick as thieves, so it's highly likely.'

Finch digested the information, as he had when he'd first listened to the recording. With Amos Church less than twenty-four hours dead by his own hand, it didn't take a rocket scientist to work out what Finch now put into words.

'Ignoring for now how he got the information, Impey is deliberately stressing the worst possible way of interpreting the circumstances.'

'Exactly. It might be to justify what he says next.' He shrugged. *You can be the judge of that.*

'Pour me a cup of my own coffee first, will you?'

He did so, carried it over. She waited until she'd taken a mouthful before resuming the recording.

As before, Lloyd Impey was doing all the talking, after clearing his throat nervously.

I'm afraid we're going to have to let you go, Amos. One murder when you were a drunk with PTSD was an act of charity on our part—

I've repaid that charity a thousand times over.

We know you have, Amos.

You've never had a more loyal member of staff.

I'm not disputing that.

You've benefitted from how good it makes you look.

Yes, we have. It's been win-win all round. For us, for you, and for all the ex-servicemen we help. And if it wasn't for Lois Sheppard, everybody would be saying, Amos paid for his crime, he learned his lesson. Now people are asking, did he learn his lesson? Did he only learn it until it was in his interests to unlearn it? The media are making a big fuss of her being a palliative care nurse. They're talking about you being a monster, a serial killer in the making.

Angel closed his eyes as he listened to Lloyd Impey twist the knife. He tried to imagine how it must have made Amos feel. Was he already running the bath in his mind? Placing the chair and arranging the rest of the poignant scene? Desperately wanting Lloyd to go so that he could just get on with it and make the pain stop?

Angel could sympathise. Impey's voice was grating on his own nerves, his fists clenching and unclenching as he listened.

If we don't let you go, Amos, Walking With Heroes will suffer. I know it's hard on you, but it's hard on a lot more people coming out of the forces if people lose faith in us. We don't look charitable anymore. We look like idiots who've been cynically manipulated by a murderer. Who's going to trust us with their money?

Angel and Finch said nothing as a long silence stretched out. Angel knew what was coming, his jaw clenching in anticipation as the anger rose up inside him. He held Finch's gaze as Lloyd delivered the killing blow.

I'm sorry, Amos, I truly am. Please don't do anything stupid.

'You think Impey went upstairs and ran the bath for him?' Angel said, when the words finally got through the anger. 'Carried the chair upstairs while Amos got undressed?'

Finch was quiet for a long time, sipping thoughtfully at her coffee, then peering into the cup as if surprised at where it had gone. When she spoke, it was more a reflection of what she knew about him than Lloyd Impey or Amos Church.

The death of a soldier—serving or former made no difference—pushed to the limit and then beyond by circumstance, to the point where a one-way ticket to oblivion was the only way out, was beyond the pale for Angel. Listening to Lloyd Impey emphasise the seriousness of Amos' predicament while hiding behind a supposed interest in the greater good—akin to a verbal cattle prod herding Amos down the road to self-destruction—put a strain like no other on Angel's ability to remain detached and professional.

'You are not to approach Impey on your own.'

He smiled at her as he imagined Impey's neck in his hands. Adam's apple under his crushing thumbs, eyes bloodshot and bulging, pulse thumping at first urgently and then slower, weaker as he squeezed.

'I wouldn't dream of it, ma'am. I'll take Kincade with me.'

Finch looked as if she was counting to ten, her voice not betraying what he knew was going on inside.

'You and Kincade are not to approach him on your own.'

He pushed aside the mental image of his hand on Kincade's face, fingers splayed, as he held her at arm's length while continuing to crush the life out of Impey with his other hand, guttural animal sounds coming from Kincade's mouth, the feel of her bared teeth underneath his palm.

'No problem. We'll take someone with us who's got a good handle on what is fair and just in life compared to what needs to be eradicated from the face of the earth.'

Finch gave a decisive nod as befits the ranking officer in the room.

'You know what? I'll go myself.'

37

Angel knew as well as Finch did that they were on sticky ground in terms of what Lloyd Impey had done. Taking his words at face value, he'd expressed his concern for Amos' welfare, performed an unpleasant and difficult job in terminating his employment for very understandable reasons, and urged him not to do anything rash as a result.

That's how an alien with a phrase book would interpret it. Anyone who used the English language on a daily basis would hear a litany of damning circumstantial evidence shoved down Amos' already-scared throat, culminating in a subconscious prompt about what Amos could do about it.

Section 2 of the Suicide Act 1961 states that a person commits a crime if they encourage or assist a suicide or attempted suicide with the intention of doing so. The consent of the Director of Public Prosecutions is required before an individual can be prosecuted.

Or, to put it another way, *good luck with that, we're not holding our breath.*

The question of how Impey came by the information he used to scare Amos literally to death had also become less damning as Angel thought about it when returning from Finch's office to his own. Another explanation had presented itself. It had always seemed unlikely that Ingrid Fischer had not discussed Patrick Quinn and his ramblings about Amos with Lois when they went to The Cowherds together, as Ingrid claimed. Angel now took that as fact. It was possible that in the course of that discussion, Lois told Ingrid she was looking into Amos' case, and had been in touch with him. Ingrid passed that information on to the Impeys. Lloyd Impey then gave it his own spin, attributing the information to them when he used it against Amos.

They could bring him in and start shaking the tree. Except Angel had a feeling that Lloyd Impey, a man so slick he made a diesel spill appear grippy by comparison, would find a way to twist and reinterpret everything they threw at him. They could play him the voice recording. Except he'd say the fact of Amos recording it in the first place was proof of his paranoia and dangerous instability even before Lloyd opened his mouth. Angel wanted more before he went up against Impey and his sister.

As if that wasn't enough, the threatening email Richard Terrell had provided them with promised to be equally as difficult to pin down.

It had been sent from a Gmail account: *Jerusalem_House-1990@gmail.com*. Google Ireland, responsible for user accounts across Europe, was happy to respond to official enquiries, both law enforcement and other government agencies. It required a warrant, which wasn't a problem. Google's sense of its own importance could be. They would review the request and then release limited information as they saw fit. Even if Google did the right thing, all they could provide was the information supplied to them. That would no doubt include the number of a burner phone and an address at the North Pole, care of Mr F. Christmas.

Everything had the feel of two steps forward, one step back. Except, after listening again to Lloyd Impey goading Amos Church into an early self-dug grave, Angel felt as if he had that the wrong way around.

'I can still hear Impey's voice in my head,' he complained to Kincade, dropping heavily into his chair.

'I know what you mean.'

'By the way, you're not allowed near him on your own. Finch's orders.'

'Is that so? You're not mistaking my face for a mirror, are you?'

They stared at each other for a long moment before he relented.

'Okay. *We're* not allowed near him without a chaperone. So, anything new?'

'As it happens, yes. I've been researching Conrad Fischer...'

She explained that she'd found an old interview with Fischer from his early days when he was still on his way up and an advocate of the maxim that there's no such thing as bad publicity.

'He's a typical rags-to-riches success story. I don't know about nowadays, but back then he didn't have a problem admitting that he'd grown up in care. How it made him twice as determined to succeed—'

'And taught him the valuable lesson that people do bad things every day of the week and get away with it?'

She scrunched her face, rocked her head from side to side.

'I must have skimmed over that part. Anyway, when I got bored singing the Conrad Fischer rah-rah-rah song, I did a search for the Jerusalem House children's home. Seems not everyone agreed with Conrad that it had been the making of him. Someone burned it to the ground in two thousand and five. Suspected arson, but the investigation didn't go anywhere.'

'Was this while it was still active?'

'Uh-uh. It had closed its doors the year before, after a less-than-glowing report from the Commission for Social Care Inspection. They were responsible for monitoring children's homes before Ofsted took over.' She glanced briefly at her computer screen. He got the impression it was so that he didn't see the smile forming on her face. 'I thought you might like to have a word with the SIO on the arson investigation, sir. See if he can tell you about what might not have made it into the file.'

She was having a difficult job suppressing the smile now. He had a good idea why.

'I get the feeling this would be a good time to pull rank, Sergeant. Why don't you tell me the officer's name? Then I'll decide.'

She let the grin come now, flicking her eyes at the ceiling.

'It was an ambitious DI called Horwood.'

He joined her in looking at the ceiling as if Superintendent Horwood could hear them through it, scowling down at them.

'Much as it pains me to do it, Sergeant, I *am* going to pull rank this time.' He made shooing motions with his hands. 'Off you go. Try not to make it sound as if the Super missed something blindingly obvious.'

She shook her head, not so much insubordination as a problem he hadn't seen.

'If my career hadn't hit a speed bump and I'd made it to DCI, I'd agree with you, sir. But I don't think a lowly DS should interrogate—'

'Is that what it'll be?'

'The mood you're in, I don't see how it can be anything else. Anyway, it's inappropriate for a DS to question a Superintendent about what he missed in his haste to climb the greasy pole.'

'You know, I think maybe it's best you don't talk to him, after all.'

She gave him a smug *told you so* smile as he pushed himself to his feet.

'And sir . . .' She waited until he'd given her permission to go ahead with a weary roll of his eyes. 'Go easy on him.'

HORWOOD WAS STANDING AT THE WINDOW WHEN ANGEL WAS shown in. Gazing out across the freight yards towards the Horizon cruise terminal where a floating city filled with holidaymakers preparing to overeat their way around the globe was berthed. He glanced briefly at Angel as he entered. When he looked back at the view, it was in a more easterly direction.

'I heard a rumour Kincade is living in Ocean Village Marina.'

Angel was surprised such things filtered up as far as the top floor, even if the Super was a little behind the curve, hopefully to remain that way.

'It belongs to a friend of her estranged banker husband, sir,' he said, congratulating himself on a perfectly disingenuous answer.

'Not what you know, but who you know, eh?' Horwood mused, living up to his reputation as a man who liked a cliché.

'Exactly sir.' He pointed at the stacked shipping containers in the freight yard on the other side of West Quay Road. 'I'd be living in one of those if I asked one of my friends.'

Horwood smiled briefly, the lower-rank-bonding session now officially over.

'What can I do for you, Max?'

'The Jerusalem House children's home, sir. You were the SIO when it was burned to the ground in two thousand and five.'

Horwood drifted away from the window, took his seat

behind his vast desk. He waved his hand vaguely at the visitors' chairs as his mind went to work.

'Am I to assume it links in some way to the murder of Lois Sheppard?'

'The home certainly does. So when it burns down in suspicious circumstances...'

Horwood interlaced his fingers over a stomach that had grown substantially since his days as an up-and-coming young DI. It made Angel wonder at what point in life a man changes from interlacing the fingers behind the head to over the stomach.

'It was arson,' Horwood said, no room for doubt in his voice. 'Fire Brigade investigators found evidence of an accelerant. I can't remember what exactly. I seem to think suspicion rested pretty firmly on a former resident of the home. Apparently, he'd threatened to do it before. A very troubled young man...'

Angel allowed Horwood a moment to remember before supplying the name that was bouncing off the walls.

'Patrick Quinn?'

'That's it.' The hands came off his stomach as Horwood leaned forward, rested his elbows on his desk. Angel imagined him already writing the press release: *Superintendent Marcus Horwood supplies vital evidence in solving the brutal murder of palliative care nurse, Lois Sheppard*. His next words proved it. 'Is he involved in the Sheppard murder?'

'Indirectly, yes. Unfortunately, he died of cancer a couple of nights ago...'

Horwood leaned back in his seat, his hands over his paunch once again, as Angel gave him the edited highlights of the investigation's progress so far. Although he gave the impression of a man dozing off after a good lunch, Angel wasn't fooled for a minute. He didn't miss the way the names Ingrid and Conrad Fischer registered in Horwood's eyes, nodding imperceptibly to himself as if Angel was supplying names he'd been waiting to hear.

Horwood took them back to the arson investigation when Angel had finished, the reason for his reactions becoming clear.

'Quinn was the main suspect, but he had an alibi . . .' He opened his pen-pushing hand towards Angel.

'Ingrid or Conrad Fischer?'

Horwood nodded like he knew he'd made the right decision letting a failed priest join the force.

'It was Ingrid. No doubt they thought it would be too suspicious if it was Conrad, since he owned the building. He bought it after the children's home shut down. Obviously, the suspicion at the time was that it was an insurance job. What you've just told me suggests it might have had nothing to do with that. Fischer was rich enough by then to not worry about the money, anyway.'

Angel immediately knocked down one obvious alternative.

'He used to make a big fuss about his rags-to-riches success story. It doesn't seem likely he burned it down as an act of revenge against a place that had blighted his young life.'

'No, but there was a big hoo-ha when he bought it. He boarded it up and padlocked it before they had a chance to clear all the records out. Wouldn't let anybody back in. The fire was started in the admin office, not the bedrooms, which you might expect if he'd been abused. It didn't cross our minds at the time that it might have been the records he wanted to destroy.'

It wasn't necessary to spell it out as they held each other's gaze. Those records would have detailed Eric Impey's involvement, the children in the home he came into contact with. Without those records, all that was left was the memory of former residents such as Richard Terrell.

'You could try speaking to Rex somebody,' Horwood went on. 'I can't remember his last name.'

'I'm surprised you remember his first name.'

A fond smile softened Horwood's face.

'I had a springer spaniel called Rex at the time. Lovely dog. Anyway, Rex somebody was the second-in-command at the home. Decent chap. Had a lot more contact with the kids than his boss ever did. In a good way. Nothing sinister about him.' Tapping his middle finger on the desk a couple of times to underline his point. He glanced at his watch as if it told the time in years, not hours and minutes. 'He'd spent his whole career there. He was only about forty when it closed down. He'll still be around. His details will be in the file.'

Angel stood up at the same time Horwood did, the meeting at a natural end. Except Angel knew it wasn't completely over as Horwood came around from behind his desk and led him towards the door.

'Damn shame about Amos Church. Don't take it too hard, Max. It wasn't your fault. I just wish I could get my hands on Malcolm Bent-Arrow. I know you young bloods think we all made it to the top on a tide of incompetence and worse, but old Bent-Arrow knew how to cut a corner. He's the one to blame, not you.'

And you think that makes it any easier? Angel thought, as the Super's hand steered him through the open door.

38

'Are you okay with this?' Gulliver said, immediately regretting it when Jardine twisted in her seat to look at him better as she jumped down his throat.

'Are you okay with a poke in the eye?'

'Just asking.'

'What? You think I'm going to burst into tears mid-interview?'

Gulliver didn't actually know what to think—apart from the fact that he'd like to poke Angel in the eye for sending them to interview Rex Marshall. That was unfair. Angel wasn't aware of Jardine's family problems back in the frozen wastes of the North East. How they were a little too close for comfort to what had gone on at the Jerusalem House children's home.

That made it his own fault. In his defence, he couldn't go telling tales out of school about his partner to their boss.

It was actually Jardine's brother, Frankie's, fault for being the sort of person who attracted trouble and went looking for it if it was slow finding him.

Except it would be a cold day in hell before those words came out of Gulliver's mouth.

A while back, Frankie had been arrested and charged with assaulting Ryan Cox—his girlfriend Josie's ex-partner—in a pub in Newcastle, after Cox was abusive towards them. Cox subsequently dropped the charges. Two weeks later, Cox accused Frankie of interfering with his and Josie's four-year-old daughter, Rowan, who lived with her mother, as did Frankie.

Frankie was arrested again and released on pre-charge bail. After twenty-eight days, he surrendered to custody and was released without charge.

That happy result came about after Jardine risked her career by accessing the PNC for personal reasons, looking into Cox's new girlfriend, Stacey Reynolds', background. Jardine discovered that Reynolds had a history of falsely accusing her partners, first of assault and then rape. Jardine had a quiet word with a friend in the Northumbria Police, suggesting that as a serial accuser, Reynolds had been behind Ryan Cox coaching his daughter into making the false accusation against Frankie.

So far so good, as far as Gulliver could see.

Things then changed for the worse. Jardine became increasingly bad tempered, the legendary sharpness of her tongue taking on a new, keener edge. Gulliver had been afraid to ask, eventually plucking up the courage and doing so the previous day.

Jardine had let out a long-suffering sigh when he refused to be fobbed off.

'I wouldn't have said anything to Frankie, but he's not stupid. He was released without charge and all they told him was that the focus of the investigation had changed.'

'He saw his big sister's hand at work.'

'Yeah. So he asked me outright. I know what he's like. He wouldn't ever have let it drop until I told him the truth. So I did. And I told him not to say a word to anyone, or else I could end up in deep shit.'

Gulliver shook his head at his partner's naivety.

'Problem on the phone line between the North East and civilisation?'

'Yeah. He heard the warning as, don't tell anyone *apart from Josie*.'

He held up a hand to stop her.

'I've never been to Newcastle—'

'They don't let posh Southern twats in.'

'—but I can guess the rest of it. Josie went around to Cox's house and assaulted Stacey Reynolds?'

'Yep.' She made a rolling gesture with her hand, *keep it coming*.

'Cox ended up hitting Josie, either accidentally or deliberately?'

'You're doing great. You're almost an honorary Northerner.'

'So Frankie went around there and beat the everloving shit out of Cox again.'

Jardine punched him on the shoulder, harder than she meant to.

'I would say congratulations, except the whole situation makes me wish I was a bloody Southerner, myself. Anyway, Frankie was arrested yet again. He's probably got his own cell in the local nick.'

'What's he been charged with?'

'Being himself. Stupidity. Take your pick. And that's not all.'

It never is, Gulliver thought, a nasty premonition taking shape in his gut.

'Stacey Reynolds is a bitch,' Jardine went on, putting a lot of heartfelt emotion into the word, 'but she's not a stupid bitch. She's stirring up the shit. How did the cops know to start looking into her past? Isn't Frankie's sister a cop? She's got some scumbag solicitor on board milking it. It's only a matter of time before it all comes out.'

'At least Frankie isn't going to jail for molesting a four-year-old little girl. That's the most important thing.'

She'd given him a watered-down smile at his laudable attempt to look on the bright side, come what may.

'Yeah. And you might get someone who doesn't give you such a hard time as a new partner when they kick me out.'

That had been yesterday.

And today, he'd made the mistake of asking if she was okay.

It was a pretty stupid thing to say, now that he thought about it.

Rex Marshall hadn't been difficult to trace. As Superintendent Horwood had said, his details were on file. They hadn't changed in the almost-twenty years since he'd been interviewed as part of Horwood's arson investigation. Same address, same mobile number.

His occupation was a different story. After his employment came to an end when the Jerusalem House children's home closed down, he took the opportunity to indulge a lifelong desire to become a landscape gardener. The reality had been a little different to the dream, his clients more interested in his weeding abilities than his design skills. Despite that, he'd stuck with it.

After twenty years of having his hands wrist-deep in dirt all day long, it was unfortunate to have to question him about filth of a different kind, but into each life some rain must fall.

Shaking hands with him was an experience akin to tripping over in the street and grazing your palm on the rough tarmac. After that ordeal was out of the way, he led them through the house and out into the garden, and from there to a massive shed at the bottom of it that stretched from one side of the garden to the other.

It was a first for both Gulliver and Jardine, but if it relaxed Marshall and encouraged him to speak freely, they were all in favour. Nor was it as spartan as a glimpse from the house might suggest. An old sofa and an easy chair were arranged around a coffee table that had started life as a packing crate, and a dirt-stained kettle was plugged into a decidedly unsafe-looking electrical socket.

Marshall put the kettle on without asking. Neither of them enquired if it had been filled directly from the water butt outside —what you don't know can't hurt you.

Tell that to the dysentery pathogens.

'We understand you worked at the Jerusalem House children's home at the time when one of the volunteers, Eric Impey, was murdered,' Gulliver started, feeling slightly ridiculous squeezed in next to Jardine on the small sofa while Marshall stood over them.

'That's right.' Very guarded. 'That was a long time ago.'

'It might have a bearing on a current case.'

'The nurse who was murdered in the same cemetery.' He said it without hesitation or doubt in his voice. It was hardly rocket science, after all. Seemed it had also been preying on his mind. He proceeded to volunteer his opinion, whether they wanted to hear it or not. 'I always thought the man who was convicted . . .' He paused until Gulliver offered the name, *Amos Church*. 'Was railroaded. I worked in the care system for almost twenty years. I saw a lot of damaged people. That man needed help, not punishing. Your presence here suggests you've come around to the same point of view.'

Gulliver interpreted the remark as an invitation to work a broomstick up his arse.

'Recent developments have forced us to re-evaluate the soundness of that conviction.'

Marshall showed him a mouthful of teeth that looked as if he used them to cut his clients' lawns.

'You'll go far, son. That's half the reason I got out. All that paperwork and bureaucracy and bullshit. I saw the way things were going. No time left to do the job.'

'Which explains why you used volunteer social uncles and aunts to help look after the kids.'

Marshall gave him an admiring nod.

'Neatly done. Got me off my hobby horse and back onto Eric Impey.'

'What did you think of him?'

Marshall had let the kettle boil and then switch itself off again. He glanced at it now, did nothing about it. With the question still open about where the water came from, neither Gulliver nor Jardine pushed him. He came and sat in the easy chair, took a small knife with a curved blade out of his pocket and started to clean under his fingernails with it.

'At the time I thought he was genuine. Two minutes of you being here, and I can't stop my mind from trying to reassess him with the benefit of hindsight.'

'And is that resulting in a different assessment?' This from Jardine.

'I'm not getting an *aha* moment, if that's what you mean. *Now everything makes sense*. He was a family man with a good job. He had an attractive wife who was a lot younger than him, and two children of his own.'

'Did he bring them with him?'

'Occasionally. Other times, they'd be in the car when he turned up to take the kids out for the day.'

'You're aware that one resident came forward and accused Impey of attempted abuse.'

Marshall gave a reluctant nod.

'I am. And it was disregarded by the police at the time.'

'What did you think about that?'

'That you'd done your job, what else? You'd investigated and found that it wasn't true. It was attention seeking or a petty act of spite. It's feeling like I was wrong to have put so much faith in you.'

Gulliver and Jardine had worked together for long enough to arrive at unspoken agreements. That's what happened now, something passing between their touching hips. Even if Marshall had harboured suspicions about Impey at the time, he wasn't about to admit to them now, lay himself open to criticism about why he said nothing. Continuing to push him would only alienate him.

Gulliver had glanced around the room as they talked. It was clear that the sofa and chair were second-hand and other items such as the coffee table had been re-purposed. But everything to do with Marshall's work was a different matter. A place for everything and everything in its place. Tools hung from hooks and were arranged logically—forks, shovels, rakes, and so on. The shelves lining the walls were neatly stacked with chemicals for encouraging some plants and killing others, the different fertilisers and herbicides and pesticides kept well apart. The gardening calendar on the wall by the door was covered with neat annotations in different coloured ink. It seemed safe to assume Rex Marshall would've been as orderly in his previous job, however much he complained about the bureaucracy stifling him. Gulliver didn't believe he would've simply walked away from it all when the home closed down, before Conrad Fischer put a padlock on the door.

'You're aware the home burned down—'

'*Someone* burned it down.'

'—a year after it closed. That remark suggests you've got your own views on what happened.'

'If it wasn't Patrick Quinn, I'm a monkey's uncle.'

'What makes you say that?'

'Because he was a very troubled young man who no doubt grew up into a troubled adult. Besides, he'd threatened to do it more times than I can remember. I told the police at the time. Inspector Horlicks, I think it was. But Quinn had an alibi. One of the Fischers. *Surprise, surprise.*'

It was nothing they hadn't heard from Angel when he briefed them after talking to Superintendent Horwood, but it was worth pursuing from a different perspective.

'I'm assuming the three of them were pretty close,' Gulliver said.

'Inseparable. Especially Quinn and Ingrid Fischer. I always thought they'd end up together, but then something happened and Ingrid wasn't interested anymore.' He shook his head as if bewildered by the strange things hormones do to teenagers. 'It wasn't as if she hooked up with anyone else, either.'

Gulliver and Jardine could believe it of the cold fish, Ingrid. Gulliver felt obliged to bring Marshall up to date.

'They remained lifelong friends, despite that. Mr Quinn died a couple of days ago from cancer.' He paused to allow Marshall time to say something meaningless and insincere, carried on when he didn't. 'Do you remember when he tried to commit suicide?'

A cloud passed over Marshall's face, his voice equally sombre.

'I do. I found him. He'd tried to hang himself with a sheet he'd cut into strips. I think he must've seen it on TV.'

'Did you ask him why he did it?'

Marshall laughed without humour at the memory.

'He said, *because life is shit*. He didn't explain in what way. It could've been because Ingrid dumped him around that time. He was really cut up about it.'

'Going back to when the home burned down,' Jardine said,

'we understand all the records were still there and went up in flames.'

'That's right. Apart from what I'd taken with me.' He saw the look on their faces, misinterpreted it as disapproval rather than stunned disbelief at what had fallen into their laps. 'I didn't take any of the official records, of course. Just photographs and other memorabilia. The sort of thing that would've been chucked in the bin.' He pointed at a dusty cardboard archive box sitting under a workbench. 'Reading about the murder in the cemetery made me think of Eric Impey and working at Jerusalem House. I'd forgotten about the stuff I took with me. I got it down from the loft the other day.'

Down from heaven, more like, Jardine thought, as she and Gulliver shared a look.

Marshall only needed to get halfway out of his chair to reach the box. He dragged it across the floor, moved the packing-crate coffee table to the side and set the box between them. It was stuffed full of photographs, a few of them framed, most of them loose.

'You can take the whole box away with you if you like.'

'We wouldn't know what we were looking at,' Jardine said, with a shake of her head. 'Can you find some of Quinn and the Fischers?'

Although Marshall had steadfastly refused to get caught up in any conversation about Eric Impey, he knew that was their focus.

'With Impey, you mean?'

'Not necessarily. Let's just see what you come up with.'

'It might take a while.'

'We're not in any rush.' She bounced up and down on the sofa a couple of times. 'It's comfy enough sitting here. Even if Craig has got most of the sofa.'

Gulliver pushed his hip further into her in response while

Marshall lifted most of the photographs out in one big pile and dumped them on the floor between his feet.

Jardine considered asking a provocative question as she watched Marshall flicking quickly through the photographs. He'd said that he thought Amos Church was innocent. He also maintained that Eric Impey's conduct was beyond reproach, giving no grounds for one of the children in his care to wish him harm. It seemed reasonable to ask who Marshall thought *did* kill him. Except it might put an end to his current helpfulness. She held her tongue, wishing there was some way to get credit for that out-of-character restraint.

They both came alert, sitting forward on the sofa, when Marshall stopped flicking through the photos and pulled one out. Except it was a false alarm. Marshall gave an apologetic smile.

'Sorry. It's one of me. I can't believe how young I look.' He offered it to Jardine who felt obliged to take it, show some interest.

'You weren't bad looking back then.'

Marshall took it back and put it to one side as Gulliver rolled his eyes at her. She'd give him hell if he said something similar to a female witness.

Not more than a minute later, Marshall stopped again, the look on his face telling them he'd found something. He handed a photograph of three smiling teenagers to Jardine.

'That's Quinn and both Fischers. Quinn's on the left.'

Jardine held it so that Gulliver could also study it. It was unremarkable, except for the fact that Ingrid Fischer, standing between the two boys, had her arm draped around Quinn's neck.

'Before it all went wrong between them,' Jardine said.

'So it seems,' Marshall agreed.

He'd accumulated a number of photographs to show them as they studied the first one. He passed the next one across now.

It showed Quinn and Conrad in British Army DPM camouflage jackets and trousers, berets on their heads.

'They were in the Army Cadets,' Marshall explained. 'I'm surprised Quinn lasted five minutes. He didn't take well to discipline of any kind. It must have been Conrad Fischer's influence.'

Gulliver kept quiet as he looked at the photograph. At university he'd joined the Officers' Training Corps, a military training program operated by the British Army that aimed to develop leadership abilities and give recruits the opportunity to get a taste of military life without any future commitment. Jardine would give him hell if she knew there were similar photographs floating around of him kitted out like a toy soldier in full camo gear and toting a rifle. He'd never live it down, Jardine barking at him like a sergeant major, even if he went up in Angel's estimation.

Their attention was drawn from the photograph by a thoughtful *hmm* from Marshall.

'I'd forgotten about that.' He passed another photograph across. This one showed three teenagers standing proudly in their Army Cadet uniforms. Marshall tapped the boy who hadn't been in the previous photograph. 'That's Eric Impey's son, Lloyd.'

Gulliver and Jardine felt as if the three Army Cadets had climbed out of the photograph and stabbed them in the arse with their bayonets. Helen aka Evelyn Crane, née Impey, had gone to great lengths to stress to Angel and Kincade that she and her brother had never spent time with any of the children from the home. It hadn't been a quick, dismissive lie, either. She'd made up a whole story about being such a little madam their father had decided it was best to keep them apart.

Marshall was lost in his past as they stared at the proof of that lie, his next remark as much to himself as them.

'Strange how things work out. Quinn lasted, despite his aversion to being told what to do. And Lloyd didn't last long at all. Dislocated his shoulder really badly. I seem to remember he wanted to join the regular army when he was old enough. It put paid to that.'

Marshall's words confirmed what Lloyd Impey had told Angel and Kincade. That his inability to join the Army himself prompted him to start a charity helping ex-servicemen. Except his sister had interrupted when he started to explain about his shoulder, claiming Lloyd's asthma was the problem.

'How did it happen?' Gulliver asked.

They didn't miss Marshall's discomfort at the question. He made a big show of thinking about it, the equivocation coming off him in waves while he formulated a reply.

Jardine didn't wait for him to concoct something.

'It's a straightforward question, Mr Marshall. If you don't know or can't remember, say so. Except I think you do know and you don't want to say. I shouldn't have to remind you that this is a murder investigation. Obstructing it is a very serious matter.'

Marshall sagged visibly in front of them, the remainder of the photographs held limply in his hands, forgotten.

'I don't recall what Lloyd said happened. But I do remember another child coming to me, telling me he'd overheard Quinn and Conrad Fischer talking. Lloyd told them it was his father's fault. It was very vague, and this particular child was a real little tell-tale.'

Jardine gave him an uncompromising stare.

'You did nothing about it.'

It sounded to Gulliver a lot like, *you weak-willed, pathetic man.*

Marshall looked as if that's what he felt like. He tried to justify himself, nonetheless.

'It didn't happen at the home, didn't involve one of our children. It might not even have been true—'

'No. But it potentially cast a volunteer in a very poor light. The sort of light that makes it easier to understand somebody having a grievance against him.' She flicked her finger at the photographs in Marshall's hands. 'Let's go back to those. See what other memory triggers might be in there.'

Marshall did as instructed, but in a very desultory way. As if he'd been asked to dig out his own death warrant. Despite that, he smiled to himself at a photograph he found a minute later. He passed it to Jardine. She immediately shook her head.

'Who is it?'

Gulliver took it from her when Marshall didn't answer, made an informed guess.

'Ingrid Fischer?'

Marshall nodded, *well done*, as he took it back.

'Yeah. She hacked all her hair off one day. God knows why. It made her look like a boy. She did it around the time she dumped Quinn.' He gave them a sour smile. 'These days I'd have to say something like she was exploring alternative versions of her sexuality, or some other bollocks invented by a self-appointed expert who won't get paid nearly as much if he says she's a normal teenager full of hormones running riot. Another reason I'm glad I got out.' He'd continued flicking through the photographs as he volunteered his opinions, pausing at another one now. 'Do you want to see a picture of Impey?' Making it sound as if he'd found a picture of a giant dog turd on the Jerusalem House front lawn.

Jardine stuck out her hand instead of answering. Marshall slapped the photograph down into it. Gulliver leaned over to take a look.

Impey looked like they'd expect an assistant manager in a High Street bank to look like. Unremarkable. A witness providing a description would describe half of the male population who hadn't gone bald. If people were colours, Impey was grey.

He was standing smiling broadly, his arms around the shoulders of two teenage girls standing one on either side of him. Both girls were aged around thirteen, their pasted-on smiles lacking the genuine pleasure obvious in his.

An adrenal spike went through Gulliver and Jardine as they looked past the girls at the wall behind them.

'Where was this taken?' Gulliver said.

Marshall took the photograph back, studied it.

'The prayer room in the home.' His earlier admission had knocked the stuffing out of him to the extent that he didn't even ask why.

'Was that picture always on the wall?'

Marshall took another look.

'As far as I remember.' The strange turn the questions had taken was now too much for him. 'Why?' He looked again when neither of them answered him. 'I think it's a Rembrandt, isn't it? Not an original, of course.'

Nobody laughed.

But they sure as hell wanted to. Maybe dance around the shed, too.

39

'I wouldn't put it on my wall,' Kincade said, 'but I suppose it's appropriate for a prayer room.'

Angel took the photograph back from her, studied it again.

'No tights around her wrists.'

She glanced at him to see if he was being serious.

'I don't think tights had been invented in Rembrandt's day, sir.'

'I suppose not. But is it just coincidence?'

The reproduction painting on the wall behind Eric Impey and the two teenage girls was of Rembrandt's *Old Woman Praying*. As Angel pointed out, there were no tights around the woman in the painting's wrists, but her hands were in the exact same position as Lois Sheppard's had been posed—held together in prayer in front of her chest.

Was the pose inspired by a subconscious memory in the killer's mind when trying to think of a way to muddy the waters? Make it look as if a roving evangelical lunatic had murdered her for her sinful ways?

Or were they clutching at straws?

'The Impeys lied about mixing with kids from the home,'

Kincade pointed out. 'If they were squeaky clean with nothing to hide, they'd be making a big fuss about it. Not only did they employ Amos Church, they even spent their childhood playing with underprivileged children. They'd be off the scale of the saintliness meter, if there is such a thing.'

'If there is, you wouldn't move the needle off zero. Nor would the Impeys if what you're suggesting is true. That they were involved in their own father's murder.'

'According to Rex Marshall, Eric Impey dislocated his son's shoulder badly enough to destroy his dreams of joining the Army. And if you remember, Lloyd Impey's sister was very quick to say it was because of his asthma, get us off the subject of his shoulder.'

Angel did remember. What he remembered more was the slickness of the Impey siblings' performance, the polished story they'd rolled out to explain their altruistic behaviour.

'They've got a good reason to want the past to stay buried. They're billing themselves as the people who employed the man who killed their own innocent father. A pitiful wretch with PTSD, the sort of man they now devote their lives to helping. Even if they weren't directly involved in their father's murder, it doesn't look so great if they knowingly allowed that same PTSD-suffering veteran to carry the can for the murder of their paedophile father by children he abused. Children who might have grown up into the people making the biggest contribution to their charity in the hope of easing their own consciences, as well as paying for their silence.'

She pulled her head back as if she'd been standing too close to the oven when she opened the door, decided against asking him to repeat it more slowly.

'You're right. I wouldn't give my money to people like that.'

Trouble was, it didn't matter how much they were in agreement, they didn't have anything directly linking the Impeys or the Fischers or a combination of both to the murder of Lois Sheppard.

With the best will in the world, it was difficult to avoid the trap of viewing everything in the light of what appears to be the most promising avenue of investigation, trying to make new discoveries fit old theories. It's basic human nature to pursue something that feels achievable, not waste time pissing into the wind.

Ask DI Malcolm Bent-Arrow.

'GET YOURSELF OUTSIDE OF THAT,' SIOBHAN ANGEL SAID, PUTTING a fried breakfast Craig Gulliver would give his right arm for—and which was big enough for both of them—in front of Angel.

He tipped his head sideways to look at where the food appeared to meet the table.

'Is there a plate under there, or is it held together by—'

'Motherly love? Is that what you were going to say, Max?'

Angel didn't reply and got stuck in. He didn't want to think about what it was going to do to his digestion, eating eggs, bacon, sausage, mushrooms, tomatoes and fried potato bread—brought from Ireland by his mother—a couple of hours before going to bed.

She put a bucket of strong tea down beside his plate, took a seat opposite him at the table to watch him eat.

'I don't know what you lived on before I arrived. Your nerves, by the look of you. I hope your detective sergeant is feeding Carl properly.'

Angel nearly choked on a piece of sausage trying to imagine Kincade putting a similarly stacked plate of greasy food down in front of his father, the simple pleasure of watching him eat all she needed to sustain her.

'You're even quieter than normal, tonight,' Siobhan said, when he didn't reply.

Angel mumbled something through the food in his mouth. He tried again after he'd swallowed it, tapping his plate with his knife.

'I'm on a deadline. I can either eat or talk, but not both, if I want to be in bed before midnight. And I remember what happened the last time I didn't finish every last scrap of food on my plate. *Whack!*'

She gave him a knowing smile.

'I don't know what it is about children makes them think their parents don't know them inside-out. Make as many excuses as you like, Max, but I know when something's weighing on your mind.'

Leonard came through the cat flap at that point, something small and not long for this world in his mouth.

'Looks like Leonard's caught something,' Angel said. 'Could you fry it in the bacon fat for him? That's what I normally do.'

She gave him the same smile, impervious to his attempts to get her to leave the room in disgust.

'He's let it go,' Angel carried on, pointing into the corner where the terrified shrew or mouse had run thinking it had a chance to escape. 'He'll play with it until he gets bored. I catch them if I can, let them go. Except if he gets to it first, he kills it straight away.'

She folded her arms over her chest, settled back into the wooden chair that was a little too similar to the one in Amos Church's bathroom for Angel's liking.

'Prattle on as much as you like, Max. But we're going to talk about what's on your mind whether you like it or not.'

It was pointless resisting, and he knew it.

He put down his knife, fished in his pocket for his phone with one hand, using the other to chase egg yolk around the plate with a chunk of potato bread—proof that men can multi-task as well as any woman. He found the photograph he'd taken of Amos Church's suicide note, slid the phone across the table.

'That was addressed to me personally by a man who then slit his wrists in the bath.'

Siobhan squinted at the screen, gave up trying to read it and went in search of her glasses. It gave him a moment's breathing space. Leonard took advantage of his new enemy's temporary absence and sidled up to the table, his prey temporarily forgotten. Angel dropped a chunk of sausage and half a rasher of bacon onto the floor. Leonard turned his head to the side and started eating.

Siobhan came back into the room and tut-tutted, the mildness of the rebuke proof that she'd recognised the suicide note as the cause of her son's distress.

'Don't read it aloud,' he said, trying to make light of it. 'I don't think I can stand to listen to it in your accent.'

He watched her as she read through it, not sure whether she was reading slowly or reading it twice. She put it carefully on the table when she'd finished as if it were a priceless religious relic.

He knew what she'd do next, even before she said anything. He picked up his plate, half-eaten food still on it, and stood up just as she stretched her hand out across the table to rest it on his. He felt no guilt at rejecting her offer of comfort. As she'd said, she knew her son.

He mouthed, *don't give the leftovers to the bloody cat* along with her as he scraped them off the plate into Leonard's bowl. After putting the dirty dishes in the sink, he rested his rump against the kitchen counter and waited for her to begin.

'You need to get a house with a bigger kitchen, Max, if you want to get any further away from me.'

If he'd wanted to be cruel and take an easy way out of the

upcoming post-mortem, he might have said, *Belfast worked well for me.*

'Talk to me,' she said, surprising him with the simplicity of it, rather than trying to ease into the discussion with a joke about how Amos had the measure of Angel and his father, both.

'What's to say? Amos Church couldn't have known our family history. He couldn't have known the guilt I feel over Cormac taking his own life. You think that makes it any easier?'

Her voice was barely above a whisper when she answered, the softness of it in no way implying her pain was any less than his.

'No. I know it doesn't.'

'*Jesus Christ!* He almost sounds like Cormac. That sad, resigned way he's accepted that he can't fight the shit life's thrown at him any longer, but at least he can go out on his own terms. A final *up yours* to a world that doesn't care. Nobody can take that away from him.' He jabbed his chest angrily with a rigid middle finger. 'Not even me.'

Siobhan decided to say something stupid.

'You're not being logical.'

'*Logical?* What's logic got to do with anything?'

'He couldn't afford to take a chance on you. Even if you decided to take on the whole bloody criminal justice system on his behalf, he's the one who loses if you're not up to it. Would you gamble your freedom on that?'

'Maybe I asked myself that very question. And there's the problem. To realise that I don't even trust myself to get it right.'

He saw the effort it took her to stay seated, not come to him, fold him into her body. She looked at him a long time before risking more words.

'Please don't talk like that, Max. Cormac stopped believing in himself. That's why he did what he did. I can't lose another son.' She wagged her finger at him before he could object. 'Don't try to tell me it's not in you, that you'd never do it. It's in us all, if we're pushed far enough. If and when we decide it's time, nobody can do a thing about it. You could've taken the first plane to Iraq and sat with Cormac for a month of Sundays and he'd still have killed himself the minute you were safely on the plane home again. And if you think you've got something about you that proves me wrong, you and me need to have a talk about the sin of pride.'

He didn't necessarily agree with her, but he couldn't blame her for trying to make him feel better. He filled the kettle to make a fresh—and not so strong—cup of tea, because everybody knows problems look a lot smaller when you've got a nice cup of tea in your hand.

Siobhan smiled approvingly. She'd taught her boy well. Then she proved her earlier remark right, that she knew her son better than he wanted to believe.

'You think I don't know what the real problem is, don't you, Max?' She picked up his phone still sitting on the table, waved it at him. 'Something, some*body*, pushed this poor man over the edge. You won't rest until you find him.'

He bit his tongue, didn't tell her he already had. It didn't change the truth in her words.

'You're worried you won't be able to control yourself when you do. You're scared of history repeating itself, where you'll go next if it does.'

40

Angel was sitting at his desk trying not to think about the things he should be thinking about—Amos Church's suicide note, the conversation with Lloyd Impey that precipitated it—when his phone rang.

It was Jack Bevan on the front desk. Bevan's opening words were as cryptic as they always were, a trait Angel attributed to being Welsh.

'Fancy a jog on the common, Padre?'

Angel's pulse soared at the mention of the common, as if he'd already run a lap of it flat out.

'Not with you, Jack. I wouldn't be able to carry you back after you collapse. Although I seem to remember there's a lot of mountain goat in your family, so maybe you'd end up carrying me.'

Bevan chuckled good-naturedly.

'My running days are long gone, Padre. But a young lady walked in a minute ago who saw something interesting when she was out running on the common herself. I've put her in confessional ... sorry, interview room number one.'

. . .

Sienna Segal was slim and athletic-looking, dressed in tight-fitting floral leggings and a blue sweat top. With her long, dark hair tied in a ponytail, she looked exactly like the women Angel saw jogging on the common putting more effort into flicking their ponytail than moving forwards. The impression was reinforced by a plastic water bottle that would prove to be a vital factor in her statement sitting on the interview-room table in front of her.

'I jog on the common most days,' she explained, after the introductions had been made. 'I've got a couple of set routes, depending on how far I want to go, but I always try to stop at The Cowherds halfway round.'

Angel wasn't a runner, but he was tempted to ask whether that wasn't counter-productive. He kept it to himself.

'I do some stretching,' Sienna went on, sounding as if she was about to demonstrate the particular exercises against the interview-room wall. 'And I sneak into the ladies' toilets to refill my water bottle.' She held it up as if she was standing in front of a jury. 'The thing is, I don't read the newspaper, so I wasn't aware of the murder in the cemetery. Then I had lunch with a friend yesterday who knows I jog on the common, and she told me all about it.'

Sienna went on to tell them how she'd seen two women sitting at a table at the front of the pub. Kincade pushed photographs of Lois Sheppard and Ingrid Fischer across the table.

'That's them,' Sienna confirmed. She pointed at Ingrid Fischer. 'She was driving a white convertible Mercedes with a red roof. I remember because I was really tired that day. I felt like asking her for a lift home, although she wouldn't have wanted me sweating all over her expensive leather seats.'

Angel and Kincade smiled politely with her. Then Angel asked if she'd seen Ingrid Fischer leave.

'Yeah. I'd just snuck in to fill my water bottle and was coming out again. The woman with the Merc was standing by her car on her own. The other one was still at the table.' She touched her hair where it was tied in a ponytail. 'The Merc driver was a real poseur. She was standing by her car tying her hair back. At first, I thought it was because she was going to put the roof down and she didn't want it blowing in her face. But then she got in and drove off with the roof still up. I thought, yeah, you were just making a fuss until you were sure everybody had seen you getting into your fancy car. It didn't surprise me when I thought about it. She looked like that sort of woman. Do you know the pub at all?'

Momentarily, Angel thought Sienna was attempting to draw them into the conversation. *Have you been to the pub and seen the sort of poseurs in their fancy cars I'm talking about?* Except the way Sienna sat forward in her chair suggested it wasn't that at all.

'We're familiar with it,' Angel confirmed, feeling as if they were approaching what had prompted Sienna to come forward.

'Then you'll know you've got the pub itself, then some tables, then a few parking spaces.' Making short hops across the table with her hand to demonstrate each step. 'In front of that is the access road, and then there's some grass and trees before you get to the main road. That's where I saw the other woman. Half hidden behind one of the trees like she'd been watching the other two.'

Angel was aware of Kincade beside him, equally still, the word *breakthrough* passing between them on a subconscious level.

Sienna took a sip of water from her bottle, scrunched her face, doubt edging into her voice.

'I now know the woman at the table was murdered. It's so hard not to let that distort my memory. But it was definitely like she was hiding. Nobody stands behind a tree for no good reason.

Anyway, she approached the woman at the table. I got the feeling she waited until the woman in the Merc had driven off.'

She looked at them both, desperate for them to accept the impressions she couldn't properly explain. Angel reassured her.

'There's a good chance that's exactly what she was doing. Can you describe this woman?'

'Also blond. Also about forty-five to fifty. Medium height. Average build.'

It was a very generic description. Despite that, it fitted a woman who was supposedly suffering from a twenty-four-hour stomach bug to a T.

They would show Sienna further photographs shortly, but for now, Angel asked her to explain what happened next.

'It was obvious the woman at the table—'

'Lois,' Angel prompted.

Sienna smiled to acknowledge the correction, tried again.

'It was obvious Lois didn't know her. She was very wary. Like you would be if a stranger walks up to you and starts talking to you.'

'Could you hear what was being said?'

'No. Too much music coming from the pub, as well as traffic noise. And I didn't want to get too close. Anyway, Lois suddenly looked like she was really interested. You can tell from the body language.'

She looked at them again for confirmation. Angel nodded, *yes you can.*

'The woman was pointing at the seat where the woman in the Merc had been sitting. Then she pointed at where the car had been parked. She was obviously talking about her.'

Angel dipped his head again, *yes, we'd worked that out.*

'Then the woman started crying. Just like that. Lois said something and the woman shook her head. Then she walked off down the path through the trees that leads onto the common.'

Angel half expected her to point out that from there it was a short walk to Southampton Old Cemetery.

'What happened next?' he said, to head the possibility off.

'Lois got out her phone and made a call. It looked like it went to voicemail. She was really pissed off when it wasn't answered. She was staring down the path where the woman had gone. It was like she couldn't decide what to do. Then she jumped up and went after her.'

'Did you follow them?' Kincade said.

'No. It was getting dark. I don't like being on the common at night.' She smiled sheepishly. 'Looks like I was right to be careful. I might be dead, too.' Her face fell as the other way of looking at it hit her hard. 'Or Lois might still be alive.'

Only temporarily, Angel thought, but was unable to say, thereby guaranteeing Sienna a change of route, down the road to guilt and self-recrimination.

Kincade took a photograph from the file, pushed it across the table.

'Is that the woman you saw?'

Sienna only needed a quick glance, no room for doubt in her voice. Only relief that even if she hadn't prevented Lois' death, she might at least help catch the killer.

'Definitely. Is that who killed her?'

'And would you be able to show us exactly where you saw her hiding behind a tree?' Angel replied, ignoring her question.

Sienna hesitated, as if assessing whether it was worth repeating her question, before accepting that it wasn't.

'Yeah. I'm going to see her hiding behind it every time I run past.'

. . .

'I'M ALMOST AFRAID TO ASK YOU THIS,' ANGEL SAID, ONCE HE AND Kincade were back in their office, 'but is Ingrid Fischer a poseur—'

'Definitely.'

'—fixing her hair until everybody's noticed her, or was it a sign to Evelyn Crane hiding behind the tree?'

'No reason why it can't be both. She's a snooty, stuck-up cow every day of her life. And it was a signal on this particular occasion. Hair in a ponytail—*Lois knows too much.*'

'Assuming that's the case, what did Evelyn say when she approached Lois? What was it that made Lois go after her?'

Kincade assumed *position #1* and thought about what Sienna Segal had told them.

'Something about Ingrid Fischer...'

'Obviously.'

'Something that upset her...'

'Like?'

'That bitch and her friends murdered my father and they've got away with it for all these years?'

He picked up the theme, ran with it.

'Lois is thinking, hang on, that fits with what Patrick Quinn is saying about killing someone. Tell me more.'

'And Evelyn says, I can't, it's too upsetting. But I couldn't live with myself if I didn't warn you to be careful. Then she runs off in tears.'

'As women do.'

'*Some* women do,' Kincade corrected, a statement he had no problem agreeing with when applied to her.

'Lois tries to call Amos,' he carried on. 'She's so excited, she can't wait until their meeting the next day, not while she's got Evelyn in sight.'

'It goes to voicemail. She's got to make a decision...'

'Evelyn's disappearing into the night...'

'It might be the only chance she gets. She jumps up and goes after her. She's hooked now. It wouldn't have been difficult for Evelyn to lead her on. *Let me show you where that murdering bitch killed my poor father*. *If I can find the way through my tears. Sniff, sniff.*'

He couldn't help laughing as she got into the part, even if she overplayed it.

'She might have needed to tone it down a bit, but you're right. The more reluctant Evelyn seemed as they headed deeper into the common, the harder she pretended to try to get away from this nosy, interfering woman, the more Lois begged her to lead her to her death.'

41

With Sienna Segal's eye-witness testimony, Angel was almost at the point of arresting Evelyn Crane and charging her with being an accessory to the murder of Lois Sheppard.

Almost.

He'd been thinking about Richard Terrell. Although disregarded at the time, the statement he'd made in 1990 had started them looking into the sordid underbelly of Eric Impey's life. It had also concentrated their thinking in terms of Impey abusing young boys. Subsequently, Terrell made a throwaway remark to Gulliver and Jardine that he wasn't even sure boys were the focus of Impey's unnatural attentions. After seeing the picture Rex Marshall found of Impey with two unhappy-looking teenage girls, Angel was convinced of it.

All of which meant he wanted to take a run at Ingrid Fischer first.

Despite her detached and icy calm, he believed she was also the weakest link. Catching her at an emotional low ebb after the death of Patrick Quinn was an added bonus. It was an approach that was unlikely to fast track him into heaven, but it was the way to go, nonetheless.

When invited in to be questioned under caution, her solicitor rightly advised her that she was within her rights to refuse, but any such refusal might well result in her being arrested. She acquiesced, and was interviewed by Angel and Kincade, Mr Clive Babington in attendance.

Angel kicked off by removing a photograph from the file. Both Ingrid and Babington sat forward slightly, expecting the photograph to be pushed across the desk towards them.

Instead, Angel showed it to Kincade, tapping one of the three people in it.

'What do you think of him?'

Kincade took it, her mouth twisting into a scowl.

'I'll be worried in a few years' time if one of my girls brings a boy like him home.'

Angel took it back, pushed it across the desk. It was the first photograph Rex Marshall had shown Gulliver and Jardine. The one of Ingrid and Conrad Fischer with Patrick Quinn, Ingrid with her arm draped lovingly around Quinn's neck.

'Patrick Quinn,' Angel said, sounding as if he was about to toast a sadly-missed mutual friend. 'By the way, sorry about the other day. I'd just got back from seeing Amos Church lying in a bath of his own blood after he slit his wrists.' He held his left wrist towards Ingrid, ran his fingernail lengthways down it. 'The way you do it if you mean it.'

He held her gaze, the unspoken words loud and clear.

We'll be getting onto Quinn's suicide attempt in a minute.

'Anyway, I'd just got back, and I forgot my manners. I'm sorry for your loss.'

'Thank you, Inspector. Forgive me if I don't say how much that means to me.'

He ignored the sarcasm, tapped the photograph.

'I can see what a loss it was. I know he had his problems, but I bet that made him a real live wire. Didn't like rules or being told what to do. The sort of bad boy who gives a teenage girl a warm rush in her . . .'

He glanced at Kincade.

'Stomach, sir.'

'Thank you, Sergeant. In her stomach.'

He gazed at the photograph a while longer, as if wishing he were a teenage girl himself. Then the wistfulness was gone, a bright up-beat enthusiasm in its place as he addressed Ingrid.

'I bet you couldn't believe your luck. I don't want to pry into how you ended up in the home, but I'm guessing it felt like a kick in the teeth from life itself.' He paused, got nothing back. 'But then you met a boy who made you realise your life wasn't over before it started. A boy who made you look forward to every new day, each one better than the last . . .'

Kincade gave him a sideways glance.

'You sound like you're reading one of the soppy romances my mother reads, sir. But I have to agree, it's pretty perfect. What happened?'

He allowed his face to harden as he opened the file, removed the photograph of Eric Impey standing smiling between two teenage girls. He placed it on top of the one of Quinn. Not side by side, but on top, eclipsing it physically and symbolically. His voice had a steely edge to it now.

'That's what happened, Sergeant. Eric Impey happened.'

Kincade knew how much he hated what he was about to do. To trample on Ingrid's emotions. Do everything in his power to make her scream, *enough, I'll tell you what you want to know, you heartless bastard*. She glanced down at the table as he began to lay into Ingrid.

'He touched you, didn't he, Ingrid? Touched you in all those secret places you dreamed of Patrick touching you. And afterwards you went into the toilet and you were sick until nothing was left but dry heaving. You felt so dirty you tried and tried to scrub yourself clean, but you couldn't get clean, could you, no matter how hard you scrubbed, how red-raw your skin was when the hot water finally ran out and you were left shivering in the corner?' He tapped his temple with his middle finger, his voice filled with the understanding of the way people's own minds torture them. 'It's not only physical, is it? It screws with your mind. Makes you doubt yourself, question the sort of person you think you are. *Am I to blame? Did I encourage him? Did I want him to do it?* Until your mind's a crazy, screaming mess of jumbled thoughts and all you want is for it to stop.'

He fell silent. Allowed Ingrid the chance to say, *yes, I was that person*. He continued when she didn't.

'You were confused and angry and helpless with nobody to turn to. But there was one thing you *did* know, wasn't there? You didn't want any man touching you again. Not ever. You hacked off your hair, made yourself unattractive so they wouldn't want you anyway. *Not even Patrick.*'

He rearranged the photographs so that the one of Quinn was back on top. Ingrid looked through it, her eyes unfocussed as he continued with his relentless assault.

'Patrick loved you as much as you loved him. Maybe more. Except he wasn't as strong as you were, was he, Ingrid? Forget his issues, he just wasn't as strong emotionally. You rejecting him tore him apart.' He held up both hands, drew the right one down vertically in long tearing motions. 'Like he tore a sheet apart and tried to hang himself with it. Did he see that in a film when he came up for breath after snogging in the back row with you?'

Babington cleared his throat.

'Could you get to the point, Inspector? And less of the amateur dramatics.'

Angel glared at him, took advantage of what the lawyer had unwittingly said.

'You obviously haven't familiarised yourself with the Eric Impey murder, Mr Babington. He was interested in amateur dramatics himself.' He turned to Ingrid, Babington already dismissed. 'Is that how it started? An innocent-sounding request. Would you like to come and watch me in a play, Ingrid? Actually, it's just me and you in it. By the way, it's a bedroom scene.'

'And it's got a far from happy ending,' Kincade added, sounding as if she'd co-authored Angel's little production.

He shook his head solemnly, echoed the sentiment.

'About as far from happy as an ending can get. One that blighted so many lives. Yours, Ingrid. Patrick Quinn's. Your ex-husband's and however many other failed relationships came before and after that. What were you at the time? Fourteen? You could've had thirty good years with Patrick if that man'—he jabbed the photo with an angry finger—'hadn't abused you.'

He sat back, crossed his arms over his chest.

Ingrid was staring at him with undisguised hatred. As if he'd turned into Eric Impey before her eyes, his hands already crawling over her body. Whatever vitriol-filled words she wanted to spit at him refused to come.

He cocked his head at her, worked some confusion into his voice.

'You're looking at me as if I've got that wrong, Ms Fischer. Do you want to put me straight?'

She wants to put you in the ground, Kincade thought, as he carried on.

'Explain to me why you dumped him if it wasn't because Eric Impey molested you. Because you couldn't stand any man touching you afterwards. Tell me why Patrick tried to kill himself if it wasn't as a result of that rejection.'

'Your questions are ridiculous,' Babington objected. 'How is my client supposed to know what was going on inside the head of a young man with mental health issues more than thirty years ago?'

Angel gave him a look—*who said you could speak?*—then leaned forward, twisting his head sideways and up to look into Ingrid's eyes as she stared at the table top.

'I'm waiting, Ms Fischer. Prove me wrong. Give me an alternative explanation.'

'That's long enough, sir,' Kincade said, after a minute's silence had stretched out. 'There is no alternative explanation. Eric Impey abused her. She gave Patrick the heave-ho. Patrick's already a basket case. He tries to top himself.'

He nodded along as she spoke, made a rolling gesture with his hand, *keep it coming*.

'So they decided to kill Impey. Ingrid here doesn't want Patrick touching her, but she's got a different sort of warmth in her belly at the thought of watching him cave Impey's head in with a hammer.' She looked directly at Ingrid. 'Isn't that right, Ingrid? Put that craziness inside him to good use. Like you did when you got him to burn the home down after your brother bought it. It's good to have a crazy friend at times.'

The cool detachment with which Ingrid had viewed them, as if listening good-naturedly to a couple of children making up wild stories, slipped for the first time at the mention of the fire.

'Yes, we know all about that,' Angel said. 'Patrick's your man when you want something doing that you can't or don't want to do yourself. Except you wanted to be there, didn't you?' He slapped the back of his right hand into his open left palm. 'You wanted to hear the wet smack as Patrick drove the hammer into the back of Impey's head, feel it reverberate in your belly. But who else was there? Amos Church saw three young people leaving the cemetery in a hurry.'

'Another ludicrous question,' Babington said. 'How can my client know if she wasn't there herself?'

Angel ignored him completely this time, didn't even dignify the remark with a dismissive glance Babington's way.

'It was your brother, Conrad, wasn't it? We know he always looked out for Patrick. Wouldn't let any of the other kids take the piss out of him. What's he going to feel about a pervert who's the cause of him trying to kill himself? They were in the Army Cadets together. Saw themselves as Rambo and Jean-Claude Van Damme. Their latest mission, should they choose to accept it, *kill Eric Impey.*'

Ingrid showed no reaction at the mention of her brother's name, as if Angel had blamed a perfect stranger. He glanced at Babington who adjusted his shirt cuff to hide the fact that he'd been surreptitiously looking at his watch. Babington gave him a smug smile.

'Do you have a single thing to back up these outrageous accusations, Inspector?'

Good point, Angel thought, knowing the question would come eventually. He was saved from having to think up a reply by a knock at the door. Gulliver stuck his head in a moment later.

'A quick word, sir . . .'

42

'I'm guessing this isn't to ask me if I want a sandwich from the cafeteria,' Angel said, seeing DCI Finch in the corridor along with Gulliver when he and Kincade stepped outside.

'Mrs Ruth Impey just walked in,' Finch said, before Gulliver could reply. 'She wants to make a statement in connection with the murder of her husband.'

A lot of things came together for Angel in that moment. The unexplained question mark in the Eric Impey file next to his wife's alibi. Her daughter changing her name, taking her mother's maiden name. Her son suffering an injury in suspicious circumstances, rumoured to have been inflicted by his father. But more than anything, he heard his own mother's voice. Standing in his kitchen after she'd placed a mountain of food in front of him. He'd joked that he couldn't see the plate under it all, questioned how it was held together. He could hear her voice in his head, feel the depth of emotion behind it.

Motherly love.

'She wants to confess to it?'

Finch rocked her head from side to side.

'She's got the look of someone who's made a big decision. How's it going in there?' Pointing at the interview room door.

'A statement from the murdered man's widow is exactly what we could do with.'

Finch raised her eyes towards the ceiling.

'Don't ever tell me he doesn't still love you.'

Angel noticed how vigorously Kincade and Gulliver nodded in agreement. And it wasn't only sucking up to Finch.

SITTING AT THE INTERVIEW ROOM TABLE, HER HEAD HELD HIGH, Ruth Impey made Angel think of a French aristocrat dragged from her chateau by a baying mob of bloodthirsty peasants. She would submit with dignity to their simple-minded idea of justice, accept the consequences of their flawed judgement in the knowledge that God and righteousness were on her side.

She had refused the offer of legal representation, rejecting Clive Babington's offer to represent her after the interview with Ingrid Fischer was cut short.

She was there to sacrifice herself and nobody was going to get in her way.

Nor did she waste any time getting down to brass tacks.

'My husband was a paedophile. He liked young girls. He was ten years older than me when we married. I was only eighteen at the time, barely more than a girl myself. It soon became clear he liked them even younger. He lost interest in me after I'd had the children. I'd filled out, become more womanly.'

It was a good, confident start, sounding as if she was reading bullet points from a prepared statement. She flagged now, the effort of saying it out loud more difficult than the practiced eloquence of what she'd prepared in her head. She took a sip of tea in preparation for the next, bigger step into her shame and guilt.

'I blame myself for not seeing the signs earlier. For *refusing* to see the signs.' She waved her hand as if swatting at a persistent, irritating fly. Except it was herself she was annoyed at as she caught herself about to try to justify her weakness. 'You don't need to hear me making excuses, or how it got to the stage it did. What matters is that it did, and it came to a head when Evelyn, as she likes to be called now, was thirteen.' She drew a deep breath in through her nose, her chest swelling with it in front of them, as if more difficult admissions required more oxygen to fuel them. 'She became sullen and withdrawn, prone to tears. I tried to tell myself she was a typical teenage girl starting a difficult time of change in her life.' She looked directly at them, made sure she met their eyes in turn. 'Except I knew it was more than that.'

Angel was aware of Kincade holding her breath beside him. Praying Ruth didn't draw her into the narrative with a personal question, try to create a bond to ease what was coming.

'What made you accept it?' he said, feeling Kincade relax.

'My son. He'd dislocated his shoulder. They were talking about torn ligaments and nerve damage and long-term lack of mobility. I knew it hadn't happened as a result of him falling off his bike, as he claimed. For one, he didn't have any other cuts and bruises. My mother was very ill at the time. I'd been visiting her in Portsmouth when it happened. I felt the atmosphere in the house as soon as I got back.' She closed her eyes, even though Angel knew it wasn't necessary to do so in order to take herself back in time, that the memories would hijack her at any time of the day or night, as his did him. 'I badgered Lloyd until he told me what really happened.'

Angel said it for her as she struggled to get the words out.

'Your husband injured him when he was trying to protect his sister.'

Ruth nodded, a wet sheen in her eyes now. Angel guessed

they would be dry again if and when she admitted to killing her husband.

'Lloyd caught him sneaking into Evelyn's bedroom. He tried to stop him. My husband twisted his arm up behind his back and held him at the top of the stairs. Threatened to throw him down them if he ever said anything. Then he frog-marched him back into his own room, dislocating his shoulder as he pushed him in. I don't suppose he meant to do it.' A look of remembered hatred twisted Ruth's face. 'I don't mean because he wouldn't hurt his own son. I mean because he knew it was something that had to be explained when I got back.'

Ruth paused and drained the plastic cup of tea in front of her. They'd reached a watershed. The background story was over. Now she would tell them what she'd done about it. It wouldn't be a happy story. Angel had a premonition it would be a clever one, melding truth and fiction while involving participants who were no longer alive to contradict her. Although he expected Ruth Impey to sacrifice herself in the next few minutes, he also expected her to do everything in her power to mitigate the circumstances.

'I pretended I had to visit my mother again,' Ruth started. 'I was convinced something would happen again.' A flash of horror went across her face, looking from Angel to Kincade and back again. 'I don't mean to Lloyd. I would never have done that.'

They both smiled, *yes, we understand that.*

'I actually drove to Portsmouth and back again,' Ruth admitted. 'To fill the day.'

And perhaps to ask your mother face-to-face to corroborate your story, Angel thought.

'I waited around the corner until I knew my husband would be home from work. Then I sat in my car down the street from the house.'

'What did you plan to do?' Kincade interrupted. 'How would you know what was going on in the house?'

Ruth shook her head at her, *don't interrupt*.

'I don't know. And I didn't have to find out. I saw Evelyn and my husband coming out of the house together. It wasn't as if she was running away and he was chasing her. They were both smiling, as if they were looking forward to going somewhere. I followed them.'

Angel allowed Kincade to state the obvious.

'To Southampton Old Cemetery.'

'That's right. I was getting a really bad feeling by this time. I thought about calling the police, but what would I have said? My husband and daughter are taking an evening stroll together? Would you have cared?'

She looked back and forth between them until Angel admitted that they might not have.

'I followed them into the graveyard. I was fifty yards behind trying to keep hidden when suddenly two other figures appeared from off to the side. They cut in front of me, directly behind my husband. They didn't see me.'

Again, Angel allowed Kincade to take the lead.

'Did you recognise them?'

'Only one of them. The other one had his hood up.'

When they discussed it later, both Angel and Kincade would admit that it took a superhuman effort to not look at one another, *here we go* . . .

'It was Lloyd's friend from the Army Cadets. Patrick Quinn.'

'And you didn't see the other one's face?' Kincade said, feeling as if she was going through the motions.

'No.'

'Or get an impression of who it might be?'

'No.'

Kincade hesitated briefly, decided against wasting any more breath.

'What happened next?'

'Quinn suddenly rushed forward. He raised his arm and hit my husband over the back of the head with a hammer. My husband fell and was lying on the ground moaning. The three of them were standing over him. Quinn offered the hammer to Evelyn. She shook her head. Then he offered it to the other boy—'

'Are you sure it was a boy?'

Kincade's question crystallised Angel's thinking. He'd been trying to reconcile Ruth's account with his own suspicions when interviewing Ingrid. He'd been convinced Quinn and Ingrid had been two of the three young people Amos saw. He'd thrown Conrad's name into the mix to see how Ingrid would react. She hadn't.

Now, Ruth was also talking in terms of three people. Evelyn, Quinn and another boy with his hood up. No mention of Ingrid. But if he dropped the assumption that Ruth's third person was a boy, it made perfect sense that it was Ingrid, her hair hacked off, underneath the hood.

The three people Amos Church saw were the two girls who'd been abused—Ingrid and Evelyn—and the boy who took it the hardest, Quinn.

Angel was brought back to the here and now by the sharpness of Ruth's tone as she responded to Kincade's question, a spasm of irritation passing over her face.

'I'm assuming it was a boy. I don't know for sure. Anyway, he or she also refused the hammer. Quinn was getting very agitated. He wasn't happy being the only one to hit my husband, but the others had started to move away. Then Quinn dropped the hammer and the three of them hurried away in the opposite direction.

'I approached my husband. He was still on the ground, moaning. Something snapped inside me. He was stretching out his hand like he wanted my help. And all I could see was him putting it on our daughter and her crying, begging him to stop. I couldn't stand it. He was begging me, *please*. I was thinking, did that make you stop when Evelyn begged you, please? I picked up the hammer and hit him over and over until at last he stopped moving and whimpering. I knew he was dead. All I could think was, *good riddance, you filthy, disgusting pervert.*'

She rested her elbows on the table, head gripped by the hair in her hands, a vitriolic mantra on her lips.

Filthy, filthy, pervert. I hate you, hate you, hate you.

Angel called a break, as much for himself as Ruth, went outside with Kincade. She jumped down his throat before he opened his mouth.

'*Yes!* If that's what you were going to ask. Yes, I could do it to Elliot if I found out he'd abused the girls.'

The forcefulness of the outburst rocked him back on his heels, put an end to any thoughts about discussing what they'd just heard.

'I'll get some tea,' he said instead, left her standing there, back against the wall, looking up at the ceiling. He could've told her she was wasting her time.

No easy answers up there, I'm afraid.

RUTH IMPEY LOOKED AT THE PLASTIC CUP OF TEA ANGEL PLACED IN front of her as if he'd brought her a beaker of poison so that she could do the honourable thing. She pushed it aside before continuing.

'I was standing in a daze when I heard somebody coming. I know now, of course, that it was Amos Church. I crept away, taking the hammer with me. I didn't know what would happen, that he would rob the body and get blamed.'

Angel tapped the side of Kincade's foot with his own. *Don't say anything.* It would have been very easy to accuse Ruth. *You let him take the blame even when you did know.* It would only alienate her. He was also hoping she would justify herself voluntarily.

On cue, she hung her head. This time, it felt more like an act, lacking the depth of emotion she'd displayed earlier.

'I felt guilty letting him take the blame. But I asked myself, *what happens to my children if I'm in jail?* They'll be put into care. They'd grow up as the children whose parents were a paedophile and a murderer. What kind of a start in life is that?'

'Much better to live a lie as victims,' Kincade said, stressing the last word. 'The children whose father was so cruelly taken from them by an ex-soldier with a drink problem.'

Ruth looked at her, nose wrinkling as if a tramp like Amos Church had once been had joined them in the small, airless room.

'Ignoring your insolent tone, Sergeant, that's exactly what I thought. And that's why I started Walking With Heroes—'

'You started it?'

'Of course. Who do you think started it?' A smile curled her lips briefly as the answer came to her. 'I allow Lloyd to say that it was his idea. Better than him telling people he works for his mother. You have to be mindful of a man's pride if you want the best from him.'

'Was it also your idea to employ Amos Church?'

'It was.' She put her hand over her heart. 'I committed the crime he paid the price for. Whether you believe me or not, I still carry that guilt around with me. But it sounds so much better for Lloyd to claim he's so selfless, he can even employ the man who killed his innocent father.' She shook her head, regret colouring her voice. 'I hope it doesn't all have to come out.

Walking With Heroes does so much good work. It would be a bigger crime than what I did thirty-four years ago to see all the people we help lose out.'

'It would,' Angel agreed, 'which begs the question, why have you come forward now and risked that happening?'

'I was responsible for a gross miscarriage of justice back then. I refuse to be responsible for another one. You would've got to the bottom of Evelyn being abused by her father and Lloyd being injured trying to protect her. You've already got Patrick Quinn's deathbed confession. In your minds you would have the three people Amos Church always claimed he saw leaving the cemetery. I couldn't take the chance that you're the sort of lazy policeman who's happy to focus on the first easy answer, like your predecessor who never looked any further than Amos Church. I don't know if you would've had enough evidence to convict them after all these years, but I wasn't going to take that chance, either. I've lived with Amos Church paying for my crime, but not my children.'

NOT FOR THE FIRST TIME, OLIVIA FINCH PRAYED FOR GOD TO GIVE her the strength to deal with her own personal nemesis, a man who was never satisfied.

'I believe Ruth Impey's story up to when Quinn hit Impey with the hammer,' Angel said. 'But I'm not convinced about what happened afterwards.'

'There's nothing we can do about it, Padre, even if she's lying to protect her children.' She took hold of her little finger, started counting off the points. 'Number one. And this is a biggie. She admits it. And I'd put my pension on the fact that she'll never retract it. Two. Everything she said fits with what we already know or suspect, down to the question mark over her alibi in the original file.' She moved onto her ring finger, having forgotten to do so after point one. 'Three. It's extremely plausible. The best reason in the world. Ask any mother.' She looked around. 'Where's Kincade?'

'Hiding, ma'am. So that you don't ask her. She already said *yes*, anyway. Is there a four?'

Finch fixed him with her *don't be an arse all your life* glare.

'Yes, Padre, there is. *Four*. There's nobody left alive to contradict her. So, unless you've still got your hotline to the man upstairs, we're never going to be able to contradict her, either.' She saw his lips twitch, stuck a rigid digit an inch off the end of his nose. 'There will be serious consequences, including actual bodily harm, for anyone who tries to make a comparison with DI Bent-Arrow railroading Amos Church thirty-odd years ago.'

He showed her his palms.

'The thought never crossed my mind, ma'am. And I'd like to wish you a restful night's sleep tonight, comfortable in the knowledge that justice has been seen to be . . . sorry, I mean *has been* done.'

She gave him the *arse all your life* look one more time and turned on her heel, wondering why God hated her so.

43

The epiphany Angel experienced during the interview in putting Ingrid and Evelyn together convinced him more than ever that Ingrid had pumped Lois Sheppard for information, before signalling to Evelyn watching from her hiding place in the trees.

They'd asked Ingrid to wait whilst they interviewed Ruth Impey, believing that it would be a short interview—just long enough for Ruth to get a confession out. Ingrid's lawyer, Clive Babington, had advised his client that it would be better all round to agree. The sooner they got it over with, the sooner they could leave.

Angel and Kincade knew better.

He started with the good news as soon as the interview reconvened.

'You're off the hook for Eric Impey's murder.'

Ingrid gave an almost imperceptible nod. Coupled with the arrogance of her stare, it said she'd been unaware she'd been on it in the first place.

Babington said something meaningless along the lines of *I should think so, too.*

'Impey's widow, Mrs Ruth Impey, has made a full confession,' Angel went on. 'As a result of that confession, we now know that the three young people Amos Church saw leaving the cemetery were yourself, Patrick Quinn and Evelyn Crane, or Helen Impey as she was back then.'

Some of the arrogance slipped off Ingrid's face at the name Evelyn Crane. It was a very different reaction to when Angel floated her brother's name in the previous interview. *You've got it wrong* had just changed to *how much else do you know?*

She remained silent as Angel continued.

'You didn't know Ruth Impey was there, did you? That she'd killed her husband after the three of you attacked him and left him for dead. Is that why Patrick Quinn begged for Amos Church's forgiveness? Because he spent his life believing he'd killed Eric Impey?' He pointed directly at her. 'Have you spent your life living with that same guilt? Did you take your turn with the hammer? Because somebody did. Somebody who put their heart and soul into beating Impey's head to a bloody pulp. Thanks to Ruth Impey, we'll never know exactly what happened. Justice and truth are lying face down, bleeding into the dirt. Just like Eric Impey.'

Ingrid shook her head, some of the arrogance back.

'No. Justice is alive and kicking, stronger for the death of a degenerate like Impey.'

Angel allowed her a moment up on her moral high horse before pulling her off again.

'And is it stronger for Lois Sheppard's death? What was her crime on your personal scale of evil? Being nosy? Wanting to learn the truth? Seeing justice done?' He indicated Kincade and himself with a sweep of his hand. 'The sort of justice we believe in, that is.'

Ingrid shook her head again, her expression bordering on pity for him at the position he was in.

'No, the sort of justice you're to *uphold*. There's a difference. I can see in your eyes that you believe in the same sort as me.' She'd addressed them both, but now she concentrated on Kincade. 'You especially. You've got children, haven't you? You understand.'

Kincade stared her down rather than respond. Ingrid shrugged, muttered under her breath.

'You won't answer because you know I'm right.'

Ingrid had conveniently focussed on Eric Impey, a murder she felt comfortable justifying. Angel steered her back to Lois Sheppard.

'Is this what you talked to Lois about? Your kind of justice. Did you tell her the truth? Then ask her, *doesn't that sound like justice to you?* The death of a pervert who ruined so many lives. But did she side with us?' Tapping his chest as he said it. 'Ask you who the hell you thought you were to make those decisions? Did you know she wanted to be a police officer herself?'

After the litany of rhetorical questions, it took Ingrid a moment to realise he was waiting for an answer.

'I wasn't aware of that, no.'

'And I don't see how it's relevant,' Babington added, as if anybody cared.

Angel gave him a look that combined *you wouldn't* with *I wouldn't care if you did*, before going back to Ingrid.

'That means she had respect for the law, an interest in the truth, rather than your personal view of justice. Is that what sealed her fate? Made you tie your hair back in a ponytail as you stood by your car. The signal to Evelyn Crane hiding in the trees. *She won't play ball. Over to you.*'

They both saw the mention of tying her hair back register in Ingrid's eyes. Surprise, quickly giving way to fear.

Except it was different to the last time they'd surprised her with how much they knew, when they mentioned Quinn burning down the Jerusalem House children's home.

On that occasion, she was surprised they knew anything about it at all. This felt as if they were wrong about what they thought they knew.

And Angel wondered if they were.

Had Ingrid given a signal—*Lois is not a threat*—only to have it misinterpreted, or deliberately disregarded, by Evelyn? And Ingrid's fear was now that she would pay the price for something that wasn't her fault?

Sitting next to her, Babington was aware of the change that came over her, the unassailable confidence leaching out of her. He put his hand on her arm as he addressed them, digging deep into the well of pompous righteousness.

'My client is here voluntarily. She's had to listen to you make a lot of vile accusations and personal slurs. Either charge her, Inspector, or we'll end this interview right now.' Tapping his middle finger on the table as he said it.

Angel watched Babington's finger as the sanctimonious prick lectured him, promised himself he'd snap it at the knuckle if he did it again.

And he thought about Lois Sheppard, the wannabe detective. The amount of detail she could have unearthed about the murder of Eric Impey without the resources available to them. Her friend Moira Woodward told them she didn't even have Impey's name. Even if she did, the internet wasn't available to the public until 1993. The details of Impey's murder three years earlier wouldn't have been online for Lois to find. She worked long hours, didn't have the time—and probably not the inclination—to spend hours poring over newspaper archives in the library. All she had was a dying man's narcotic-induced ramblings and an appointment with Amos Church. An appointment everything they'd learned about him suggested he wouldn't attend, wanting nothing more than to be left in peace.

It didn't feel like much of a threat to Angel.

He held his index finger towards Babington, busy puffing himself up in preparation for earning his fee with more pompous indignation on his client's behalf.

'You didn't give the go ahead to kill Lois Sheppard, did you, Ingrid? Putting your hair in a ponytail meant the opposite. *She's not a threat.* But that didn't suit Evelyn Crane and Lloyd Impey, did it? They went ahead regardless.'

'They were never meant to kill her. Just scare her.'

Kincade snorted, pointed her finger at Ingrid.

'You keep telling yourself that. Maybe you'll end up believing it.'

'So why did they?' Angel said, more constructively. 'You've just given the signal. *She knows nothing.* Evelyn should've turned around and gone home. Why didn't she?'

Ingrid shook her head at him.

'Something to do with your brother?' Angel suggested, to be provocative as much as anything else. 'He's in a relationship with Evelyn—'

The look on Ingrid's face stopped him dead, told him he couldn't be more wrong.

'My brother is gay, Inspector. Evelyn accompanies him to social engagements, that's all.' She glanced at Kincade, a fast, dismissive flick of the eyes, her nose wrinkling at the same time. 'I believe your sergeant referred to her as *something to hang on his arm*, or something equally disrespectful. Evelyn likes the nice things in life, and Conrad feels happier accompanied by a woman at business and charity events. He's old-fashioned that way. Evelyn has always wanted it to be more, but Conrad was only ever interested in Patrick.' She smiled sadly at the games fate had played with their young lives. 'Evelyn wanted Conrad. Conrad wanted Patrick. Patrick wanted me. And thanks to Eric Impey, I didn't want anybody at all. I'd call that pretty fucked-up, wouldn't you, Inspector?'

He went to speak but she held up her index finger towards him, as he had towards Babington.

'Before you rush out and arrest Conrad, he was away on an Army Cadets training exercise on some godforsaken Welsh mountain when Impey was murdered. And as far as the Lois Sheppard situation is concerned, the first he knew of it was when I told him what Evelyn had done.' She looked directly at Kincade as if she personified every jealous person she'd ever looked down her nose at. 'For once, the evil, money-grabbing businessman is not to blame. How disappointing for you. It's the people who're jealous of what he's got that you need to look at.'

'You're talking about the Impeys?' Angel said.

She shrugged, *who else?*

'Conrad told them—'

It was as if Ingrid faded before his eyes, the last woman to sit across the table from him—Ruth Impey—taking her place, her callous words in his mind.

I allow Lloyd to say that it was his idea. Better than him telling people he works for his mother. You have to be mindful of a man's pride if you want the best from him.

'Told who, specifically?'

Ingrid gave him a patronising smile. *At last!*

'Well done, Inspector, you've worked it out. Who the driving force behind Walking With Heroes really is. Conrad told Ruth Impey we couldn't afford to keep making the same level of donations as we have in the past. We've kept them afloat almost single-handedly for the past five years. Who knows what withdrawing that support does to the mind of a person like her?'

Makes her tell her children to kill Lois Sheppard just to be on the safe side? Angel wondered, as he wrapped things up.

It would be for the Crown Prosecution Service to decide whether Ingrid Fischer was charged with conspiracy to murder Lois Sheppard, whether the *mens rea*—the intention or knowledge of wrongdoing that is an essential part of a crime—was present. As for her involvement in the murder of Eric Impey, that was even more nebulous after more than three decades.

'She's a piece of work,' Kincade said, once Babington had ushered Ingrid out on a tide of righteous vindication. She pinched her finger and thumb together. 'I was this close to accusing her of being a cold-hearted monster guzzling champagne and filling her snooty face with fancy canapés after giving the go-ahead for Lois Sheppard to be killed. Looks like she's just a common or garden stuck-up frigid bitch.'

'I'm not sure I'd put it quite like that.'

She gave him a look as if he'd said Ingrid was the nicest person he'd met in a long while.

'You sound like you believe her. And understand her.'

'Not sure. But I understand how Eric Impey abusing her turned her into what she is. I also think she blames Ruth Impey. She might be aloof and bitter, but she's not stupid. At some point in the last thirty years she worked out that Ruth must have known about her husband's unnatural interests. Ruth admitted as much to us. And Ingrid blames her for doing nothing about it. In her mind Ruth was almost worse than him. He was a pathetic creature following unnatural urges he couldn't control. She was a rational woman who chose to look the other way.'

'That's why Ingrid as good as gave us the Impeys.'

'That, and the fact that they screwed her when they went

ahead and killed Lois Sheppard anyway, just to be on the safe side.'

Kincade laughed suddenly, a sharp, incredulous bark.

'Who would think I'd ever agree with a bitch like Ingrid? But she was right. It's all about as fucked-up as you could get.'

44

Lloyd Impey and Evelyn Crane were arrested at the premises of Walking With Heroes two hours later. Non-intimate DNA cheek swabs were taken as part of the booking-in process, their mobile phones seized.

Angel elected to interview Evelyn first. He was relieved when Kincade didn't ask why. He wasn't sure himself. On a subconscious level, he was hoping that in the midst of the abuse and twisted interrelationships that led to Eric Impey and Lois Sheppard's murders, Evelyn might reveal some mitigating circumstances that made it less likely he punch Lloyd Impey the minute he set eyes on him.

Ingrid Fischer's lawyer, Clive Babington, also acted for both Lloyd Impey and Evelyn Crane. Angel gave him a cold smile—*you won't be as lucky this time*—when he and Kincade took their seats at the interview-room table. He placed a file on the table in front of him, a hand-held digital recorder on top of that, then began.

'Were you aware your mother came into the station earlier today to make a voluntary statement in relation to the murder of her husband, your father?'

Evelyn stared at him as if he was speaking a foreign language. He spelled it out more bluntly.

'She admitted to the murder and has been charged accordingly.'

'I don't understand.'

'What's not to understand?' Kincade cut in, as Evelyn tried to make sense of the bombshell Angel had dropped on her. 'She told us she killed him because he was sexually abusing you...'

Evelyn sat in stunned silence while Kincade ran through the details of her mother's confession, naming Quinn, Ingrid and Evelyn herself in the process.

'Your mother will take the full rap, even though we believe you and Ingrid Fischer took your turn with the hammer. Unless there's something you can tell us that proves she didn't do it...?'

Angel hit the *play* button on the digital recorder when Evelyn failed to answer. A deliberately abrupt change in direction designed to keep Evelyn off balance as she reeled from the revelation of her mother's confession. Lloyd Impey and Amos Church's voices immediately filled the room. The sub-text of everything Lloyd said rang out loud and clear, ending with the disingenuous self-fulfilling warning, *I'm sorry, Amos, I truly am. Please don't do anything stupid.*

'We believe you put your brother up to that,' Angel said, the anger rising up inside him. 'You told us you weren't present when Amos came into the office. That's because you were hiding outside, waiting to follow Amos back to where he was staying. You then sent your brother there to push Amos over the edge.'

He wasn't aware of whatever excuse or denial she made in response, too busy opening the file he'd brought with him. He pulled out a photograph. Studied it for a long while, his face hardening, before placing it face-down on the table. He pushed it towards her with one finger.

'Turn it over.'

'Do as he says, Evelyn,' Babington said, when it became clear Evelyn wasn't about to.

Angel gave him an approving nod. *That's the first sensible thing you've said all day.*

Evelyn reached for the photograph as if it was balanced in the jaws of a rabid dog. She flipped it over and closed her eyes, too slow to stop the image of Amos Church, naked and dead in a bath filled with his own watered-down blood, from burning itself into the backs of her eyes.

Angel had no problem working the disgust he felt into his voice.

'This is the man you all allowed to pay the price for your crime. The man you cynically exploited after he was released from prison, pretending to help him, but actually keeping an eye on him in case he became a risk.'

He pulled out his phone, found the edited recording he'd made of Lloyd Impey's last words to Amos Church. He tapped *play*, stared hard at Evelyn as her brother's voice filled the room once more.

I'm sorry, Amos, I truly am. Please don't do anything stupid.

'You want some good news, Ms Crane? We won't even be attempting to convict Lloyd for that. It's too grey an area.' He extended his hand towards her lawyer as if he were an ambulance chaser, contempt in his voice. 'Someone like Mr Babington here would supply the weasel words for him to wriggle out of it.'

Babington sat forward, the first blustering words of objection forming on his lips. Angel silenced him with a look, thrust his phone at Evelyn.

'Are you wondering why I'm making you listen to this? It's for when you try to tell me being abused gives you carte blanche for the rest of your life as you sit way up there on your moral high horse.' He waved the phone in her face. 'This will make sure I don't forget how your brother talked Amos Church into killing himself. And if that's not enough, Amos addressed his suicide note to me, personally.' He brandished the phone at her, not quite so much in her face this time. 'I've got it on here. You want to read it? No? He said he couldn't trust me to find the truth hidden under all the lies you and your brother tell.' He dipped his head, shaking it from side to side as his breath exited noisily through his nostrils like a pain-crazed *Toro Bravo* preparing to charge the matador. 'I can't tell you how angry that makes me.'

'He's going to crucify you,' Kincade said, when Angel fell silent. 'And I'm here to help him do it. I might even have understood your *God's on my side even if the law isn't* justification for killing your father, but you went too far when you killed Lois Sheppard. If you believe you're so right, you should've taken your chances, let a jury of your peers decide if they agree with you. Well, we're all going to find out when they try your mother. I feel sorry for you in a way. I can understand what your mother's doing because I've got two daughters. You can't. You've never had children. And I feel sorry for you because that wasn't your fault. That's down to your own father.'

Evelyn had shied away under the weight of the uncompromising truth in Kincade's words. Angel was forced to lean forwards to get in her face again.

'Sorry or not, we're still going to nail you to the wall.' Then, to Kincade, 'Tell her how, Sergeant.'

Kincade looked like an attack dog finally let off the leash, the thrill of the chase that only ever had one ending in her eyes and in her voice.

'We have a witness who saw you hiding in the trees watching Lois and Ingrid. She saw Ingrid tie her hair back as a signal. Ingrid told us that signal meant Lois was not a threat. Yet you went ahead with the plan as if she was. Do you want to tell us why?'

'I'm sure you're about to tell me.'

'Damn right, I am. Lois wasn't a threat to the Fischers. She had next to nothing apart from Patrick Quinn's incoherent deathbed ramblings. She didn't even know who he claimed to have killed. And the Fischers have got lots of money. They can afford expensive lawyers.' She glanced at Babington, the subtext clear—*good lawyers, unlike your own*. 'But it's different for you, isn't it? Conrad just pulled the plug. No more donations. He was your biggest contributor by a country mile. You might've survived, limping along. But not if there was a whiff of scandal and all the other donors followed suit.' She looked at Babington, as if it was necessary to address her next point to him as a legal professional. 'Here's the thing, Mr Babington. It didn't matter that Lois Sheppard had next to nothing. We're not talking about proof here. Evidence that would stand up in a court of law. All she needed to do was start digging, start making a fuss, for the rot to set in.' She went back to Evelyn. 'And suddenly people are asking questions. Are those too-good-to-be-true Impeys too good to be true, after all? Are they a bunch of cynical liars exploiting poor old Amos Church? Who cares about details or proof? Smells a bit fishy to me. *Move on*. Find another worthy cause to give your money to and feel good about yourself. And then where would you and your brother and your mother be, Ms Crane? On the street, that's where.'

The unspoken words were all the louder for remaining unsaid.

Like Amos Church used to be before your family ruined his life.

Angel watched Evelyn as Kincade laid it out in perfect logical detail, saw the confirmation in her eyes. As if re-living the difficult, desperate conversations around Walking With Heroes' boardroom table in the aftermath of Conrad Fischer— the boy from the Jerusalem House children's home made good —turning off the tap.

'That's the why,' Kincade said. 'Let's get back to the how. You approached Lois and spoke to her, pretended to get upset and walked off. It doesn't matter what you said, what story you made up. It was sufficient to make Lois follow you.'

Angel put an evidence bag containing a mobile phone on the table as Kincade spoke. He pushed it an inch towards Evelyn.

'Do you recognise that phone, Ms Crane?'

Evelyn glanced at Babington. He nodded, *there's no point denying it*.

'It looks like mine.'

'That's because it is,' Angel said. 'There's a text you sent to your brother on it. A single thumbs-up emoji sent at seven fifty-two p.m. on the night Lois Sheppard was brutally murdered. A minute after you'd walked away from her and she followed you. Why did you send that text, Ms Crane? What did the emoji mean?'

Kincade picked up the evidence bag before Evelyn had a chance to answer.

'We've reviewed all the messages on this. You're a product of your generation. You type everything out in full with proper punctuation. You don't use abbreviations. And you certainly don't use emojis.'

'I'm the same.' This from Angel.

'So what was the purpose of this single, out-of-character thumbs-up emoji at exactly the time Lois Sheppard started following you onto the common? And please don't insult my intelligence by saying it was a butt dial.'

Angel tapped *play* on his phone, talked over Lloyd Impey telling Amos not to do anything stupid.

'I'm going to play this every time you don't answer a question. It'll be irritating as hell—'

Kincade gave him a look, *you got that right.*

'—but it'll keep our focus laser sharp. So, are you going to answer my colleague's question? No? Okay, let me make a suggestion. *We're on.* Or *I'm on my way.*'

Kincade threw in a couple more.

'It's working. She's following me.'

They paused, gave Evelyn a chance to suggest some of her own. Angel continued when she didn't.

'We've seen it being received by your brother. What we don't have is the cell site data. *Yet.* When we do, that's going to show his location. Want to guess where we think it'll be?'

He tapped *play* again when she refused to answer, Lloyd's voice filling the room.

I'm sorry, Amos, I truly am. Please don't do anything stupid.

Kincade gave him a look.

'That's starting to get really irritating, sir.'

'I know.' Sounding very happy about it. He went back to Evelyn. 'We all know it'll be Southampton Old Cemetery where Lois Sheppard was murdered. You led Lois there. Lloyd stepped out from wherever he'd been hiding behind a tree and hit her over the back of the head.'

'A carbon copy of how your father was attacked,' Kincade chipped in.

Angel raised a finger, *not quite*.

'There was no dirt on her knees or hands. That means you caught her as she fell, held her ready for Lloyd while she was all woozy.' He stood up, went to stand behind Kincade. 'Then Lloyd strangled her with a pair of tights. Except it wasn't quite that simple, was it?'

He held his hands two feet apart as if gripping an imaginary pair of tights. Looped them over Kincade's head, crossing his wrists at the back of her neck and pulling them towards him. Straining as if putting everything he had into tightening them around her throat.

'It takes a lot of strength to strangle someone.' He pulled his crossed wrists tighter into his body. 'Even if they aren't struggling against you. It's impossible to do it at arm's length. You end up pulling your victim towards you as you do it. That's half the attraction for the real crazies. Up close and personal. But not for Lloyd. Because he's got asthma.'

Kincade interrupted, pointed at Evelyn.

'You alerted us to that. You were so desperate that we didn't find out about his dislocated shoulder, you interrupted him, told us it was his asthma that prevented him from getting into the Army.'

'We believe it's allergy-induced asthma,' Angel continued. 'He's allergic to cats. Lois' mother has got a house full of them. I came away with my trousers covered in cat hair after we went there to notify her about her daughter's murder. Lois' clothes were covered with cat hair. That's not all. Lloyd will have been getting stressed hanging around in the cemetery waiting to kill her. That's another well-known trigger for asthma. He'll have started wheezing as soon as he got close to Lois.' Angel pulled his hands tighter into his body. 'And when he'd got her really close, he sneezed or coughed. If he had any sense, he turned his head away. But it wasn't enough. Saliva still went all over the tights wrapped around his hands in front of his own chin as he was strangling her.'

Kincade wagged her finger at Evelyn, her voice filled with derision at Evelyn and her brother's final act of stupidity.

'Should've taken the tights away with you. Kept them as a trophy, instead of using them to pose her as if she was praying. Whose bright idea was that?'

Evelyn stared back at her as if she was asking herself the same thing.

'We haven't got the cheek swabs analysed yet,' Angel said, 'but when we do, Lloyd's DNA is going to match what we recovered from the tights used to strangle Lois Sheppard. And that, Ms Crane, is exactly how I'm going to nail you and your brother to the wall.'

Kincade gave him a pained look.

'How *we're* going to nail you,' he corrected.

Evelyn had remained silent throughout. It wasn't as if she could've interrupted—*no, it didn't happen like that*—without implicating herself.

In terms of a verifiable sequence of events, an unaccounted-for gap existed between Evelyn sending a text message confirming that Lois was following her onto the common and Lloyd's saliva ending up on the tights, but that didn't invalidate the steps supported by forensic and third-party evidence on either side.

'Have you got anything to say?' Angel said. 'Blame it all on your brother, maybe?' His face compacted as an immediate problem struck him. 'Except that's the last thing you want to do. This whole mess started when he stood up for you when your father tried to molest you. That's no way to repay him—'

He wouldn't fully understand until later why she suddenly burst into tears quite so explosively.

45

Angel took the seat directly opposite Lloyd Impey at the interview room table, the familiar anger rising up inside him. Like an old friend rousing itself, the periods of slumber between outings growing ever shorter. His hands ached with the desire to choke the life out of the man he blamed for Amos Church's death. He could feel Lloyd's Adam's apple under his thumbs, hear the sharp snap of the hyoid bone breaking. Taste his fear. See the pin-prick petechial haemorrhages appear in his eyes. *Ping! Ping! Ping!* Like popcorn exploding in a hot pan. He glanced at Kincade giving him a curious look back. *He'd be dead before even you could stop me.*

Lloyd dropped his eyes as Angel let the full weight of his contempt bear down on him again, the anger leaching out of him, leaving only disgust behind and a job to be done.

He started the interview in the same way as he had the previous one, tapping the table with his finger as he delivered the news.

'Your mother admitted to killing her husband at this very table just a few hours ago.'

Lloyd's reaction was very different to his sister's. She'd been surprised, confused. *I don't understand.* He took the information on board with nothing more than a knowing nod of acknowledgement. *I thought she'd do something like this.*

'I have my reservations about that confession,' Angel admitted. 'I believe you do, too.' He gave Lloyd the opportunity to agree or deny it, continued when he did neither. 'Your behaviour is not consistent. On the one hand, you intervened and ended up being injured when you tried to protect your sister. But we're supposed to believe you sat back and did nothing when she and another teenage girl, Ingrid Fischer, hatched a plan to kill the man abusing them? A plan involving Patrick Quinn, a boy with mental health problems who'd recently tried to kill himself. Those three couldn't have organised a piss-up in a brewery in the state they were in. You expect me to believe you weren't involved? You were in the Army Cadets. I went on their website earlier and watched the promotional video. It's full of words like leadership, tactics, independence, resourcefulness, pride. So I have to ask you, Mr Impey, did you come up with the plan to murder your father?'

Lloyd glanced at Babington, went back to Angel.

'No comment.'

Ordinarily, Angel would've been disappointed to start down the *no comment* route so soon. Except, today, it felt more like Lloyd buying himself time to think.

'Your mother told us she followed your sister and father to the cemetery,' Angel went on. 'That confused me. How did your sister persuade him to go? It's not a normal family thing to do.'

Kincade immediately agreed.

'My kids don't say to me, *can we go to the cemetery tonight, Mum?*'

Angel pointed directly at Lloyd, his voice accusing.

'This is where you come into it. Your father had just injured you. Threatened to do worse if you said anything. Your mother didn't mention seeing you leave the house. I think that's because you were already hiding in the cemetery. You told your sister to tell your father you'd run away from home and you planned to go to the police. What I can't get my head around is how your sister sold it to your father. He was abusing her, for Christ's sake. And suddenly she's telling him where you're hiding before you go to the police.' He stared long and hard at Lloyd. Not that Lloyd was aware of it, his gaze fixed on the table top as Angel pushed him deeper into the darkness of his past. 'You're not proud of this part, are you, Mr Impey? What did you tell your sister to do to persuade your father to go to the cemetery with her?'

Lloyd raised his head and Angel knew they were done with the *no comment* game.

The pain he saw in Lloyd's eyes spoke of the understanding Lloyd craved for what he'd done, even if he couldn't ever have approval.

'You're right. I'm not proud of myself. I told her she had to tell him she didn't want him to go to prison. That's why she was going to show him where I was hiding.' He swallowed thickly, his voice raw when he forced the next words out. 'To make him believe that, it was necessary for her to make him believe she enjoyed what he did to her. She never told me how she made him believe her. And I never asked. But he followed her there.'

An uneasy stillness settled on the room as each of them tried not to dwell on Lloyd's quietly-spoken words, lest thoughts they could never unthink tainted their minds, unwelcome mental images spawned by their own prurient imaginations shaming them, staying with them long after the interview was over.

Angel wanted to turn back the clock. Interview Evelyn Crane, the woman who used to be the girl Helen Impey before her life was ruined, all over again.

Not go at her quite so hard. Not play the recording quite so many times.

Sometimes he wondered how he'd ever been a priest. How anyone could've allowed him to guide others down the path to a better life.

He broke the deathly silence in the room before they all turned to stone.

'What happened in the cemetery?'

Lloyd told the same story his mother had. How Patrick Quinn rushed forwards and hit Eric Impey on the back of the head with a hammer as Evelyn led him through the graveyard. How they'd all stood over him as he lay on the ground at their feet. Except there'd been four of them, not three. Himself, Quinn, Evelyn and Ingrid. The other three were horrified by the stomach-churning reality of it all. By what had already been done. By what lay ahead, the things that sounded so simple, so righteous, when they planned it.

'I sent them away,' Lloyd said. 'Quinn was freaking out. Didn't want to be the only one who'd hit him. The girls looked like they were going to throw up, listening to the man who'd abused them moaning pathetically on the ground. I killed him after they'd gone. My own father.'

Angel wasn't sure why Lloyd said those last three words. *My own father.* Perhaps to prove to himself, as he had many times before, that they were only words. They meant nothing in themselves, beyond describing a biological fact. The man they were applied to was no father of his, nor his sister's, not in the real sense. He was a monster. And there's no shame in killing a monster, whatever the law says.

It still wasn't enough for Angel, Kincade's voice screaming to be heard above the bedlam in his head.

It never is.

He knew as well as anybody that people will do more to

protect a loved one than they do in their own defence. He didn't want to hear the salacious details of what Evelyn Crane had suffered as a girl. But he needed to hear what enabled her brother to beat their father to death with a hammer. Because Lloyd Impey still had a lot of catching up to do in Angel's book, proof of his deficit just the tap of a *play* button away on the digital recorder.

'There must have been a catalyst. He'd been abusing her for some time. And nobody kills a man over a dislocated shoulder.'

Lloyd shook his head, *if only that's all it was.*

'I crept back into Helen's . . . I suppose I should say Evelyn's room. I still can't get used to calling her that, after all these years. Anyway, after I heard our father go back into his own room, I went into my sister's bedroom. She had her back to me, sobbing quietly into the pillow. She flinched when I sat on the edge of the bed. Cried out when I put my hand on her shoulder. She was scared he'd come back for seconds. When she realised it was me, she turned onto her back and looked up at me.' He cleared his throat noisily a couple of times, looked up at the ceiling as he drew breath deep into his lungs, fighting to get the words out. 'She pulled the pillow out from under her head, thrust it at me. Begged me to put it over her face and smother her. *You'd do it if you loved me.* She meant it, too. Told me to fuck off when I refused. Turned her back on me.

'I lay down beside her. I was outside the covers, but it didn't stop her from grabbing my hand, trying to put it between her legs. She said, *he's been there, why not you?* I felt as dirty as my father, just for being male. And I knew that one day she would kill herself when she didn't have the strength to hold onto the bitterness and hatred and realised there was nothing there at all when it was gone. I knew I had to get rid of the problem at source, or spend the rest of my life blaming myself for her death.' He smiled at Angel, eye teeth on show and nothing behind his eyes except endless blackness. Flexed the fingers on his right hand as he wet his lips. 'My father made a mistake. He dislocated my left shoulder. You know what was running through my mind as I hit him with the hammer over and over and over?'

Angel did. He was sure Kincade did. Babington didn't have the faintest idea. Lloyd told them all anyway, a sing-song lilt in his voice as he chanted the murderous mantra.

'He's been there, why not you? He's been there, why not you? By the end of it, he wasn't ever going there again.'

With Lloyd's voice still playing in his head, Angel called a break. For himself and Kincade as much as Lloyd. He stood outside in the corridor with her, neither of them saying anything for a long while. Then he got out his phone, played the recording they'd both heard too many times.

I'm sorry, Amos, I truly am. Please don't do anything stupid.

Self-loathing filled his voice when he mimicked himself after it had finished.

'It's for when you try to tell me being abused gives you carte blanche for the rest of your life as you sit way up there on your moral high horse. Remember who said that?'

She pointed at him, *you did, sir.*

'Doesn't mean it's not true.'

'I know. I just wish I hadn't said it with quite so much venom.'

She pointed down the corridor in the vague direction of the lifts where the vending machines lived.

'See if you can get yourself a cup of hindsight. I'll have one, too.'

'I don't think there's a single thing in my life that would be the same if that was available. C'mon, let's get this over with.'

An awkward silence hit them when they entered the room. Angel guessed—or was that prayed? —that Lloyd had told

Babington he was going to admit to everything against Babington's advice.

They'd find out soon enough.

Lloyd immediately picked up from where he'd left off.

'My mother turned up and caught me red-handed. She looked at her husband lying dead on the ground. You know what she said to me?'

Angel thought back to interviewing Ruth Impey. How she'd tried to take the blame for her husband's murder. Her admission that she'd known in her heart what he was doing to her daughter.

'Thank God you've got the strength to do what I never could?'

'I'm impressed, Inspector—'

Don't be, Angel thought.

'—that's almost word for word. People talk about the special bond between mothers and daughters.' He flicked his fingers dismissively, his voice equally so. 'It doesn't come close to the bond we forged that night. We were crying and hugging each other when we heard Amos Church approaching. We didn't have time to get away so we hid behind one of the big gravestones. We watched him as he robbed the body. It didn't seem to us that he gave it much thought. That he had to fight his conscience before robbing a still-warm corpse. That's what made up our minds. He wasn't as guilty as I was, but he was far from innocent. We let him take the blame. Look down your nose at me all you like, but I knew what my mother would've done if your colleagues from back then hadn't been as happy as we were to blame Amos. I'm nearly fifty and she's still trying to protect me. Back then, she'd have taken the blame like a shot. When it came to a straight choice between her and some wino with PTSD, Amos Church was always going to jail.'

Angel experienced a second epiphany as he listened to Lloyd

wax lyrical about bonds forged in adversity and sacrifices made. Now he understood why Evelyn had burst into tears so explosively when he suggested she might want to put all the blame for Lois Sheppard's murder on her brother.

'The bond with your mother was still as strong as ever thirty-four years later, wasn't it?'

Lloyd couldn't have looked happier if Angel had told him he was free to go. The understanding he craved was finally his.

'Stronger. The plan was for Evelyn to lead Lois to where I was waiting at the grave with my mother. The three of us, the whole family, would tell Lois what happened. What each of us had suffered. Hope she would understand. And that once she had all the facts she wouldn't feel the need to keep on digging. Point out to her that all she had was Patrick's deathbed ramblings. All she would achieve would be to start rumours that might well be the end of Walking With Heroes and all the good work we do. Nothing would ever be proved against us after all these years. We wouldn't be punished, if that was her aim.'

Angel hadn't wanted to interrupt as Lloyd talked, risk him deciding he'd said too much already. Now, he jumped in as Lloyd paused at a natural break.

'Ingrid Fischer told us you wanted to scare her, not explain and appeal to her.'

A spasm of irritation contorted Lloyd's face at having his story questioned. His response was dismissive, towards both Ingrid and Angel.

'That's what we told her. Ingrid is the sort of person who understands threats and fear more than reasoning. She was the only one who knew Lois. We needed her. And she would never have agreed to be part of it if we'd told her what we were really planning to do.'

Angel didn't need to look at Kincade to read her thoughts.

That sounds like the bitch I've met.

'Fair enough. Going back to your plan, what was going to happen if Lois didn't play ball? Said she didn't care how much you'd suffered, you still didn't have the right to play God. Told you she was coming straight to us with what you'd just told her, and who gives a shit whether your precious charity goes down the toilet.'

The answer was bouncing off the walls. Angel put it into words when Lloyd just shook his head at him.

'Lois wasn't strangled with her own tights. They were a brand-new pair brought along for that specific purpose. Did you bring those tights with you, Mr Impey? Were they a pair your ex-wife left behind when she moved out? Did you buy them yourself? You ask me, it's more likely Evelyn or your mother brought them along. And I'm getting the feeling they might not have told you.'

Angel couldn't decide whether Lloyd was stupid or simply refusing to see what was staring Angel in the face. All the way through, Lloyd had used the word *we* as he talked about their plans, but even a glass eye in a duck's arse could see he was being manipulated himself as much as he believed he'd manipulated Ingrid.

The way he waved his hand half-heartedly, his voice equally weary, suggested he realised it now, when it was too late.

'In the end, it didn't matter what the plan was supposed to be, what contingency plans we did or didn't have. Everything changed when I received the text from Evelyn. Suddenly it was real. It was actually happening. My mother decided she didn't want Evelyn to have any part in it. She wasn't prepared to put her through the ordeal of baring her soul to an interfering perfect stranger. Re-living the events that made her beg me to smother her with a pillow. Then pleading with Lois for her approval, as if she was the final arbiter of right and wrong. She left me there, went to intercept Evelyn and Lois. I could've told her I didn't want any part of it. Except she would've gone ahead on her own. God knows what would've happened. I waited while she went to meet them. She sent Evelyn home, led Lois back to the grave herself.'

He held Angel's gaze, challenging him to state the second, unspoken change to the plan. Angel had no problem obliging.

'You didn't even try to reason with Lois, try to explain, did you?'

'No. My mother had made up her mind. She'd brought the tights with her. She wasn't going to risk anything happening to me, Evelyn or Walking With Heroes.' He looked directly at Kincade, as if his confession had been rewarded with an insight into other people's lives, their hearts. 'I don't need to tell you what happens to anyone who comes between a mother and her children.'

Kincade slowly shook her head at him, eyes not quite in focus. *No, you don't.*

Amen to that, Angel thought with a sideways glance at her. *It would take a braver man than me.*

46

Amos Church was buried in Southampton Old Cemetery on a bright, blustery day three weeks later, not far from the grave that figured so prominently and tragically in his life, after a special dispensation was granted on account of the unique circumstances.

There were only four mourners.

Jesse Hamilton and Carl Angel wore their immaculately-pressed brown Parachute Regiment No. 2 dress uniforms with belt and medals, red berets on their freshly-barbered heads. Angel sported a black suit and black silk tie and could easily have been mistaken for the undertaker. Kincade was elegant and virtually unrecognisable in a knee-length black dress under a charcoal grey coat, its dark red collar a perfect match for the ex-soldiers' berets. Angel couldn't help but wonder how she'd looked on her wedding day.

The service itself was short and simple. Angel hoped, as did the other three, that his own send-off would be as dignified. In the windy otherworldliness of the slightly unkempt cemetery with the late-summer leaves rustling irreverently overhead, it was possible to believe that humanity had suspended its grossness and excesses for this sad day, even if none of those present subscribed to the enduring myth of a better place awaiting.

Sorrow shook the small gathering like a sudden, stronger gust of wind as the priest recited the familiar prayer of ashes and dust and hope and eternal life. Then Jesse stepped forward, laid a single dark crimson rose across Amos' own, somewhat dog-eared, red beret sitting on top of the coffin. Head held high and back straight, he read W.H. Auden's *Funeral Blues*, the poignant words catching in more throats than his own.

Angel stepped up when Jesse stepped back as if they'd practiced it a thousand times. The others stood, heads bowed and hands clasped lightly in front of them, as a distinctive rising perfect fifth from C to G sounded, marking the beginning of *The Last Post*, that haunting fanfare normally played on the bugle that puts a lump in the throat like no other, brings a hot stinging to the back of the eyes.

Watching Angel as he stood, hands cupped around the harmonica at his lips and lost to the world in the evocative melody, Kincade tried not to think what bitter-sweet thoughts assailed him. How far from his mind could the memories of his dead wife be? No longer by his side on account of the self-same instrument he now used to bid Amos Church farewell, send him on his way down that same lonely road.

With the coffin in the ground and dirt thrown upon it in final recognition of Amos' return to the earth from whence he came, they made their way back towards their cars. It was a familiar route to Angel and Kincade, not marred on this occasion by busy, white-suited SOCOs, glaring arc lights and the noisy rumble of a mobile generator.

'You didn't wear your uniform,' Carl Angel said to his son, his tone a balanced mix of accusation and criticism.

Angel touched his throat lightly, an unwelcome reminder of

the last time he was here, Lois Sheppard strangled to death and sitting against a nearby gravestone.

'I couldn't decide between that or my dog collar.'

'I suppose a suit's better than that,' Carl grumbled. 'Most things are.'

Kincade took the old warhorse's place at Angel's side after Carl veered off to talk to Jesse, in his opinion the only other correctly dressed person in attendance.

'I'd like you to play that at my funeral,' she said, linking her arm through his. 'If I die before you, of course. I never thought I'd get choked up by a man with a mouth organ.'

'Ye of little faith,' he said, horrified to hear one of his mother's favourite phrases coming out of his own mouth.

She hesitated, unsure how to broach what she wanted to say next. It felt as if everything could be traced directly back to his wife's death. In the end, she just came out and said it.

'Did you get in touch with Stuart Beckford yet?'

'I did, yes. He said he never wants to see me again.'

She let go of his arm as if an electric shock had gone through it, stared open-mouthed at him.

'Are you serious?'

'Of course not.' He stuck his elbow out for her to link arms again.

She took it, determined not to laugh with him.

'*Idiot.*'

'It went to voicemail. I left a message. He hasn't got back to me yet.' He glanced at her on his arm, grinned. 'That surprised you, didn't it? You thought I'd never get around to it.'

She couldn't deny it. Nor could she control the faint sense of apprehension that went with it. He'd taken the first small step that might lead to DS Beckford wanting his old job back. She worked hard to fill her voice with enthusiasm she didn't feel, knowing she wasn't fooling anybody. Least of all him, the man with perfect insight and a back door into people's hearts.

'About bloody time, too.'

With her arm linked through his she was very aware of his body against hers. The warmth of it, the way he moved. She was distracted, looking to the left admiring a sad-faced winged angel with only one hand, when she felt him stiffen, his stride faltering momentarily.

She looked front, her own breath catching at the sight of a man waiting by the Non-Conformist Chapel where their cars were parked, his rump resting against a bright red, older-model Porsche Boxster that hadn't been there when they arrived. Long legs stretched out in front of him, his arms folded over his chest, he watched them approach like an angry parent waiting up past midnight for a rebellious child's return.

Even before Angel opened his mouth, the tightness in Kincade's chest told her his presence heralded far more than an ear-roasting for staying out past curfew.

'Speak of the devil and he shall appear,' Angel said quietly. 'That's Stuart there, waiting for us.'

ALSO BY THE AUTHOR

The Angel & Kincade Mysteries

THE REVENANT

After ex-drug dealer Roy Lynch is found hanged in his garage, a supposed routine suicide soon becomes more insidious. As the body count rises, DI Max Angel and DS Catalina Kincade are forced to look to the past, cutting through thirty years of deceit and betrayal and lies to reveal the family secrets buried below. The tragedy they unearth makes it horrifically clear that in a world filled with hatred and pain, nothing comes close to what families do to one another.

OLD EVIL

When private investigator Charlie Slater is found shot dead in his car on historic Lepe beach, DI Max Angel and his team find themselves torn between the present and the past. Did Slater's own chequered past lead to his death at the hands of the family he wronged? Or was it the forgotten secrets from a lifetime ago he unearthed, old evil spawned in Lager Sylt on Alderney, the only Nazi concentration camp ever to sit on British soil?

FORSAKEN

When DI Max Angel and DS Catalina Kincade are called to a hijacked lorry, what they find inside makes them think its destination was a slaughterhouse, not a warehouse. The discovery of a woman's hairs on a blanket makes it clear that cheap Romanian refrigerators weren't the only goods the murdered driver was transporting. After the human cargo is set free by the killers, Angel and Kincade find themselves caught up in a race to locate the girl before the people traffickers catch her and condemn her to a life of sexual slavery.

JUSTICE LIES BLEEDING

When Angel and Kincade are called to Southampton Old Cemetery, not all of the dead bodies they encounter are ancient relics buried six feet underground. In the untamed wilderness of the cemetery's darkest corner a woman sits propped against one of the old gravestones, her hands bound together as if in prayer. As Angel and his team piece together the final days of her life and it becomes apparent she went voluntarily to her death, two questions vex the team - who did she arrange to meet in a graveyard at night and why?

The Evan Buckley Thrillers

BAD TO THE BONES

When Evan Buckley's latest client ends up swinging on a rope, he's ready to call it a day. But he's an awkward cuss with a soft spot for a sad story and he takes on one last job—a child and husband who disappeared ten years ago. It's a long-dead investigation that everybody wants to stay that way, but he vows to uncover the truth—and in the process, kick into touch the demons who come to torment him every night.

KENTUCKY VICE

Maverick private investigator Evan Buckley is no stranger to self-induced mayhem—but even he's mystified by the jam college buddy Jesse Springer has got himself into. When Jesse shows up with a wad of explicit photographs that arrived in the mail, Evan finds himself caught up in the most bizarre case of blackmail he's ever encountered—Jesse swears blind he can't remember a thing about it.

SINS OF THE FATHER

Fifty years ago, Frank Hanna made a mistake. He's never forgiven himself. Nor has anybody else for that matter. Now the time has come to atone for his sins, and he hires maverick PI Evan Buckley to peel back fifty years of lies and deceit to uncover the tragic story hidden underneath. Trouble is, not everybody likes a happy ending and some very nasty people are out to make sure he doesn't succeed.

NO REST FOR THE WICKED

When an armed gang on the run from a botched robbery that left a man dead invade an exclusive luxury hotel buried in the mountains of upstate New York, maverick P.I. Evan Buckley has got his work cut out. He just won a trip for two and was hoping for a well-earned rest. But when the gang takes Evan's partner Gina hostage along with the other guests and their spirited seven-year-old daughter, he can forget any kind of rest.

RESURRECTION BLUES

After Levi Stone shows private-eye Evan Buckley a picture of his wife Lauren in the arms of another man, Evan quickly finds himself caught up in Lauren's shadowy past. The things he unearths force Levi to face the bitter truth—that he never knew his wife at all—or any of the dark secrets that surround her mother's death and the disappearance of her father, and soon Evan's caught in the middle of a lethal vendetta.

HUNTING DIXIE

Haunted by the unsolved disappearance of his wife Sarah, PI Evan Buckley loses himself in other people's problems. But when Sarah's scheming and treacherous friend Carly shows up promising new information, the past and present collide violently for Evan. He knows he can't trust her, but he hasn't got a choice when she confesses what she's done, leaving Sarah prey to a vicious gang with Old Testament ideas about crime and punishment.

THE ROAD TO DELIVERANCE

Evan Buckley's wife Sarah went to work one day and didn't come home. He's been looking for her ever since. As he digs deeper into the unsolved death of a man killed by the side of the road, the last known person to see Sarah alive, he's forced to re-trace the footsteps of her torturous journey, unearthing a dark secret from her past that drove her desperate attempts to make amends for the guilt she can never leave behind.

SACRIFICE

When PI Evan Buckley's mentor asks him to check up on an old friend, neither of them are prepared for the litany of death and destruction that he unearths down in the Florida Keys. Meanwhile Kate Guillory battles with her own demons in her search for salvation and sanity. As their paths converge, each of them must make an impossible choice that stretches conscience and tests courage, and in the end demands sacrifice—what would you give to get what you want?

ROUGH JUSTICE

After a woman last seen alive twenty years ago turns up dead, PI Evan Buckley heads off to a small town on the Maine coast where he unearths a series of brutal unsolved murders. The more he digs, lifting the lid on old grievances and buried injustices that have festered for half a lifetime, the more the evidence points to a far worse crime, leaving him facing an impossible dilemma – disclose the terrible secrets he's uncovered or assume the role of hanging judge and dispense a rough justice of his own.

TOUCHING DARKNESS

When PI Evan Buckley stops for a young girl huddled at the side of the road on a deserted stretch of highway, it's clear she's running away from someone or something—however vehemently she denies it. At times angry and hostile, at others scared and vulnerable, he's almost relieved when she runs out on him in the middle of the night. Except he has a nasty premonition that he hasn't heard the last of her. Nor does it take long before he's proved horribly right, the consequences dire for himself and Detective Kate Guillory.

A LONG TIME COMING

Five years ago, PI Evan Buckley's wife Sarah committed suicide in a mental asylum. Or so they told him. Now there's a different woman in her grave and he's got a stolen psychiatric report in his hand and a tormented scream running through his head. Someone is lying to him. With his own sanity at stake, he joins forces with a disgraced ex-CIA agent on a journey to confront the past that leads him to the jungles of Central America and the aftermath of a forgotten war, where memories are long and grievances still raw.

LEGACY OF LIES

Twenty years ago, Detective Kate Guillory's father committed suicide. Nobody has ever told her why. Now a man is stalking her. When PI Evan Buckley takes on the case, his search takes him to the coal mining mountains of West Virginia and the hostile aftermath of a malignant cult abandoned decades earlier. As he digs deeper into the unsolved crimes committed there and discovers the stalker's bitter grudge against Kate, one thing becomes horrifyingly clear – what started back then isn't over yet.

DIG TWO GRAVES

Boston heiress Arabella Carlson has been in hiding for thirty years. Now she's trying to make it back home. But after PI Evan Buckley saves her from being stabbed to death, she disappears again. Hired by her dying father to find her and bring her home safe before the killers hunting her get lucky, he finds there's more than money at stake as he opens up old wounds, peeling back a lifetime of lies and deceit. Someone's about to learn a painful lesson the hard way: Before you embark on a journey of revenge, dig two graves.

ATONEMENT

When PI Evan Buckley delves into an unsolved bank robbery from forty years ago that everyone wants to forget, he soon learns it's anything but what it seems to be. From the otherworldly beauty of Caddo Lake and the East Texas swamps to the bright lights and cheap thrills of Rehoboth Beach, he follows the trail of a nameless killer. Always one step behind, he discovers that there are no limits to the horrific crimes men's greed drives them to commit, not constrained by law or human decency.

THE JUDAS GATE

When a young boy's remains are found in a shallow grave on land belonging to PI Evan Buckley's avowed enemy, the monster Carl Hendricks, the police are desperate for Evan's help in solving a case that's been dead in the water for the past thirteen years. Hendricks is dying, and Evan is the only person he'll share his deathbed confession with. Except Evan knows Hendricks of old. Did he really kill the boy? And if so, why does he want to confess to Evan?

OLD SCORES

When upcoming country music star Taylor Harris hires a private investigator to catch her cheating husband, she gets a lot more than she bargained for. He's found a secret in her past that even she's not aware of - a curse on her life, a blood feud hanging over her for thirty years. But when he disappears, it's down to PI Evan Buckley to pick up the pieces. Was the threat real? And if so, did it disappear along with the crooked investigator? Or did it just get worse?

ONCE BITTEN

When PI Evan Buckley's mentor, Elwood Crow, asks a simple favor of him – to review a twenty-year-old autopsy report – there's only one thing Evan can be sure of: simple is the one thing it won't be. As he heads off to Cape Ann on the Massachusetts coast Evan soon finds himself on the trail of a female serial killer, and the more he digs, the more two questions align themselves. Why has the connection not been made before? And is Crow's interest in finding the truth or in saving his own skin?

NEVER GO BACK

When the heir to a billion-dollar business empire goes missing in the medieval city of Cambridge in England, PI Evan Buckley heads across the Atlantic on what promises to be a routine assignment. But as Evan tracks Barrett Bradlee from the narrow cobbled streets of the city to the windswept watery expanses of the East Anglian fens, it soon becomes clear that the secretive family who hired him to find the missing heir haven't told him the whole truth.

SEE NO EVIL

When Ava Hart's boyfriend, Daryl Pierce, is shot to death in his home on the same night he witnessed a man being abducted, the police are quick to write it off as a case of wrong place, wrong time. Ava disagrees. She's convinced they killed him. And she's hired PI Evan Buckley to unearth the truth. Trouble is, as Evan discovers all too soon, Ava wouldn't recognize the truth if it jumped up and bit her on the ass.

DO UNTO OTHERS

Five years ago, a light aircraft owned by Mexican drug baron and people trafficker Esteban Aguilar went down in the middle of the Louisiana swamps. The pilot and another man were found dead inside, both shot to death. The prisoner who'd been handcuffed in the back was nowhere to be found. And now it's down to PI Evan Buckley to find crime boss Stan Fraser's son Arlo who's gone missing trying to get to the bottom of what the hell happened.

Exclusive books for my Readers' Group
FALLEN ANGEL

When Jessica Henderson falls to her death from the window of her fifteenth-floor apartment, the police are quick to write it off as an open and shut case of suicide. The room was locked from the inside, after all. But Jessica's sister doesn't buy it and hires Evan Buckley to investigate. The deeper Evan digs, the more he discovers the dead girl had fallen in more ways than one.

A ROCK AND A HARD PLACE

Private-eye Evan Buckley's not used to getting something for nothing. So when an unexpected windfall lands in his lap, he's intrigued. Not least because he can't think what he's done to deserve it. Written off by the police as one more sad example of mindless street crime, Evan feels honor-bound to investigate, driven by his need to give satisfaction to a murdered woman he never knew.

Join my mailing list at www.jamesharperbooks.com and get your FREE copies of Fallen Angel and A Rock And A Hard Place.

In memory of Doreen Heaney

---

*May He support us
all the day long,
till the shades lengthen
and the evening comes,
and the busy world is hushed,
and the fever of life is over,
and our work is done.
Then, in His mercy,
may He give us a safe lodging
and a holy rest
and peace at the last.*

Printed in Dunstable, United Kingdom